Praise for *The Ventriloquist's Tale*

'Striking and brilliant ... a tale of sensual bliss and comedy.' *Daily Telegraph*

'Melville is a superb storyteller, capable of writing that is both earthy and expansive, sharp and lyrical.' *Observer*

'A beguiling first novel ... absorbing fiction that wears its complex ideas lightly – with compassion and mischief.' *Guardian*

'Beautiful cadences and luminous writing.' *TLS*

'A must.' Graham Swift, *Sunday Times*

'Brilliantly juxaposes South American and western attitudes to history in a dazzling story.' Caroline Gascoigne, *Sunday Times*, Books of the Year

'A sharply funny, richly fantastical story, in prose as rich and corrupt as her sensual characters and luxuriant settings ... An exhilarating novel that combines myths and modern life with a dazzling exuberance.' *Mail on Sunday*

'An exotic yet contemporary novel, rich in sensuous understanding., and threaded through with delightful intellectual games.' *Literary Review*

'A remarkable, enthralling first novel ...' *Scotland on Sunday*

Praise for *Shape-shifter*

'Pauline Melville is a find ...' *Guardian*

'Excellent, with immense verve and skill she shows how the English language has been taken over and transformed by those people whose ancestors were forced to speak it. A very impressive and enjoyable book.' *New Statesman*

'An exceptionally talented writer of prose fiction ... Melville's descriptive powers are especially acute.' *TLS*

Pauline Melville

EATING AIR

A Novel

TELEGRAM

This first edition published in 2009 by Telegram

ISBN: 978-1-84659-076-4

Copyright © Pauline Melville, 2009

A full CIP record for this book is available from the British Library.
A full CIP record for this book is available from the Library of Congress.

Printed and bound at Thomson Press (India) Ltd.

TELEGRAM
26 Westbourne Grove, London W2 5RH
2398 Doswell Avenue, Saint Paul, Minnesota, 55108
Tabet Building, Mneimneh Street, Hamra, Beirut
www.telegrambooks.com

I eat the air, promise-cramm'd ...
William Shakespeare

I rise with my red hair
And I eat men like air.
Sylvia Plath

For Angus

Note from the Narrator

I want to tell the story of these extraordinary events without drawing attention to myself or implicating myself in any way. I was involved only in the most tangential way, I can assure you – more by association than anything else. These days it is possible to be locked up for even hinting that terrorism can be glorious or for having the wrong friends and courts don't take into account the law of unintended consequences. So it's *sotto voce* for me. To be on the safe side I have to present truth as fiction.

I prefer to write in cafés. I move around. The Head in the Sand café in Camden Town is my current haunt. Every morning the proprietor brings me a glass of rum steeped in hot peppers, a black coffee, two dishes of grilled peanuts and my newspaper. I wear dark glasses with the right, coffin-shaped lens knocked out to make sure, in these lean times, that no-one steals my food. The place is a little down-at-heel but I like the sludge-olive décor and those trendily scuffed wooden floors, bentwood chairs and the menu chalked on a blackboard behind the counter. Who am I? I come from Surinam. My complexion is cinnamon. I am as slim as Barack Obama. My style is that of a graveyard dandy; black hat, black coat and a silver cane – it's possible to dress like this in London without attracting undue attention. Oh ... and I think highly of myself which is always good for one's health. I write in the daytime. At night I play piano in an upstairs bar at Mambo Racine's, a casino, dance hall and brothel in Brewer Street just behind Piccadilly Circus. I play bland intertwining melodies as background music. The manager makes sure that there is a glass of rum on the piano top and a small wooden box of Cuban cigarillos which I smoke at the back during breaks.

As for the rest of my biography, skip the details and take my word for it. I'm a marvellous person.

The Head in the Sand café is well placed for me. It's at a crossroads. From an early age I have been an observer of the human race. (Nothing is more likely to dry up the heart.) Daily I watch the tame mass of unresisting citizenry, forming itself into a self-regulated slinking creature, shopping with its eye, endlessly acquisitive, nosing through the streets. Recently the sight has made me restless and impatient. Whenever I come to a set of automatically opening doors I want to rush and throw myself through them before they have a chance to open. People need a little exhilaration, don't they? Some excitement outside the warmth of the family circle? Something to induce that endorphin spike; a few meteoric moments in the cause of an idea; some extremism to clear the pethidine from the veins? Some danger? Every narrator worth his salt likes a good war. It's the peaceful existence which is the cause of my terror. I ask myself the question that philosophers must always ask themselves: Will my bum ever forgive me for sitting around all day like this?

I am in two minds. Should I write a sprawling, nineteenth-century, bag-of-bones novel with all the energy of vulgarity or stick to the clear austere prose style that takes its key from the dead?

There's such a thing as too much good taste.

It is a photo of my fellow-countrywoman, Ella de Vries – taken before the catastrophe – that prompts me to write. There are few enough of us Surinamese who are famous. I cut the photo from the front cover of a magazine. Taken at night, it shows her standing on the balcony of one of Rio de Janeiro's old colonial palaces. Her head is half turned towards the camera. She is laughing and leaning back against the stone balustrade between two dwarf palm trees. Her black hair is pulled back tightly and shines like the painted hair of a Russian doll. Her face is vital and radiant. Behind her left ear she wears the huge moon like a white carnation.

Before she returned to Surinam for good she would drop into Mambo Racine's when she wanted a break from the formal world of ballet. We became close after exchanging intimate confessions one drunken night. Did she have any skeletons in her cupboard? Of course. A whole cemetery of them. Untold stories rustling and groaning in their coffins. Luckily the dead tell no tales or there would be a lot of bad news.

I first met her in Paramaribo in the eighties. I had gone there to consult my grandfather Papa Bones after becoming involved in yet another of my disreputable incidents.

Papa Bones used to ply his trade in the corner of a rum shop off Gravenstraat. He was a tall gangly black man with a long neck who wore a white Aertex shirt, open at the collar, and whose skin glistened permanently in the heat. His trade was to buy the spirits of the dying. He collected the names from hospitals or homes or street corners and added them to his list. What he did with them no-one knew. He had been known to rub people's names out or add them if there were problems with payment. He was also rumoured to own a copy of *Skrekibuku*, the Shriek Book or the Book of Terror, an ancient book of Dutch creole spells from the seventeenth century. So no-one messed with Papa Bones.

I found him sitting in a corner with his usual glass of rum. His eyes were bloodshot. There were three people with him, a couple and their niece. He introduced me. Pa Tem and Tanta Marti were in a merry mood. They were migrating to Amsterdam for a better life. Pa Tem was an affable, bulky creole. He was accompanied by his big ebony-complexioned wife who wore a slightly mad ill-fitting straightened wig. Papa Bones then introduced me to their niece Elissa. They called her Ella. Her skin was the colour of crème de cacao. She was sitting on a high stool in an off-the-shoulder dress printed with allamanda flowers and she wore yellow sling-backs on feet that were disproportionately, almost comically long. She acknowledged me with a smile and a nod. For my part, one look at her brought about an extinction of the mind and all rational thought and induced a buzzing in my ears.

Papa Bones was drunk.

'Elissa dances with the Ballet Rio.' He gave her a lascivious once-over and placed his gnarled hand on his crotch. 'She has come over from Brazil to say goodbye to her uncle and aunt.'

'Yes. Our Ella can surely dance.' Tanta Marti beamed with pride as she moved her hips in affirmation of the dancing spirit. Her enormous bottom was articulated in such a way that it seemed to move separately from her top like the understructure of a crinoline. Pa Tem patted his wife's bottom.

'We Surinamese ain't got much.' He chuckled. 'But bottoms we got. Bottoms we got in abundance.'

The three of them said their affectionate goodbyes to Papa Bones and made their way out. I watched Elissa go. She left behind her a trace of the scent of fresh lemons. There was a casual artistry in her walk. As soon as they had gone I told Papa Bones about my troubles.

He frowned and shook his head as he poured himself more rum.

'You must leave. Go to Europe. Don't go to Holland. Holland has too much connection with us here in Surinam. Our old colonial masters. England is your best bet. There is a place called Mambo Racine's in London. They have plenty of Surinamese and Guyanese and folk from the Caribbean. Plenty of illegal immigrants.' Papa Bones's face cracked open into a broad grin. 'People who just pitch up in England for a holi-stay. They will give you work.'

Which is how I came to be living in cold-arsed England. But let me return to Camden Town and the café.

I had just settled down to write and was tossing up which of two visions of the world to adopt for my fiction, the one that celebrates the marvels of reality or the other that doesn't, when into the café walked Victor Skynnard – a well-meaning man who makes your heart sink whenever he appears. In his usual state of despair and despite the expression on my face indicating I did not wish to be interrupted, he dragged a chair over and started his outburst without even pausing to say good morning.

'You can't imagine the government's ingratitude towards me. I've spent months devising a way to pay off the national debt. For god's sake, it's into the trillions now. You'd think that in the present economic climate they would listen. I had the perfect idea which I offered to them for a reasonable fee. Hair. Hair and nails. They're growing all the time. They grow even after you're dead. Surely someone could harness that power and link it to the national grid. Or take electric cars! Stop income tax and give everyone an electric car. I can't remember the details of the plan now but it would have worked. The Chancellor of the Exchequer didn't so much as acknowledge my letter. Now look at me. Skulking in this café. Can't even afford to pay for my toast. Could you lend me a couple of quid for one of those chocolate muffins?'

He went and hovered by the plastic display cabinet of stale croissants and pastries. I was barely listening. I realised that Victor Skynnard might be the random thread with which I could begin to unravel the whole fabric of the tale. I ordered myself another black coffee and started to write straight away. What is someone to do who has neither a conscience nor a heart? Order breakfast, of course. Then write a book. It's one way of getting up the world's nose.

Baron S.

Part One

I am drawn to peoples in revolt ... because I myself have
the need to call the whole of society into question.
Jean Genet

Chapter One

Let me introduce you to Victor Skynnard, the mixed-ability parasite, radical socio-irritant and spiritual bomb-thrower who came into the café that day.

After leaving the Head in the Sand café Victor headed straight home and sat in front of the computer in his study. The thin academic and scribbler leaned back and picked up the cheque that his father-in-law had given him, examined it and placed it back on the desk. The cheque was for less than he had hoped.

The house where he lived in Camden Town was part of a terrace of down-at-heel, white-painted houses with steps leading up to the front door and paint flaking off the portico pillars of the porch. Enter almost any such dwelling and you are likely to come across one of those pale utopian spectres from the mausoleum of seventies radicals. Enormous uncurtained windows let in the baleful light of morning. Skynnard's complexion in the pitiless daylight was tallow. His greying hair formed a cobweb of light frizz so pale as to be almost colourless, like a dandelion puff-ball. His forehead, high enough to have been elongated by a distorting mirror, puckered with concentration on nothing in particular. The room was high-ceilinged and draughty. A sepulchral white marble mantelpiece overhung the gaping black square of an empty grate and an old sofa stood in the centre of the room covered with a damson chenille rug. Around the room, on the wooden floor and sofa, enough books were strewn to make you think a library had vomited. In the midst of it all reposed Victor

Skynnard in the full bloom of his obscurity. In a city teeming with venture capitalists, business magnates and hedge-fund managers there he sat, a communist wrong-footed by history. The world had not gone the way he had planned for it.

What is a revolutionary to do when there are no revolutions? How to overthrow the state when nobody else is inclined to do so? Victor continued to wrestle with a complicated mass of ideological problems which most of the world had long given up trying to solve. He picked up the cheque again and stared at it for a while, his pen twitching faintly but uselessly between his fingers like a divining-rod.

'Oh, what's the use?'

He groaned and shoved the cheque back in the desk drawer. Then he threw himself full length on the sofa, put his feet up on the arm and grabbed a bag of crisps from the small table at his side. He shut his eyes and munched half-heartedly. The current plan, from his hatchery of bad ideas, was to take the medieval legend of Parzival and rework it into a modern play. Until such time as revolution was in the air again, Victor had decided that theatre was the fashionable powerhouse of radical ideas and creativity. Some years back he had written his PhD on Parzival, tracing the legend through Cuchulain and Adonis all the way back to that radiant stranger Dionysus himself. He would transform the material into a biting comment and social satire on the state of society today. It was settled. He would become a political playwright of great savagery and international renown.

The gods thought otherwise.

However, beneath Victor's high-domed brain-pan there did exist a rich interior life. Victor settled down to the comfort of one of his daily reveries. He would join the Labour Party. He would join it solely in order to undermine it from within or to resign from it in a blaze of publicity. He imagined himself rising to his feet to address the local members in some room or other – he had no idea where these people met.

'You stupid, hypocritical and murderous shites,' he would begin.

'The Labour Party has embroiled us in tragic wars and drowned us in debt.' He could see before him the startled faces of the local activists and held up his hand to show that he would brook no interruption. At that moment a potent mixture of real indignation and hatred for the government lifted Victor off the sofa and on to his feet. He put down the packet of crisps and started to pace around the room. He was not sure how he would continue his speech but he had the advantage of infinite rehearsal in these one-sided flights of oratory. When he got stuck he rewound the fantasy back to the beginning. He needed to make sure of his facts. Victor's memory was an area where the real, the half-remembered and the totally imagined all shuffled around together.

He had not progressed much further than 'hypocritical and murderous shites' before the fantasy ground to a halt. He repeated the phrase several times and assured himself that he would work out the rest later, outlining in painstaking detail the follies, past mistakes and hopeless future of the Labour Party. Not that he wanted any of the other parties either. They were all as bad as each other. He saw himself returning to his place at the meeting amidst the awed silence of the audience. Or perhaps cheers would be better. No. He plumped for silence. Gradually, people would rise to their feet and confess to their short-sightedness and their mistaken commitment to whichever policy he happened to be attacking. Somehow, in his imagination, the occasion became confused with the sort of meeting held by Alcoholics Anonymous or the Quakers.

Having single-handedly destroyed his local branch of the Labour Party, Victor got to his feet and went down to the kitchen to look for a plum. He took one from the bowl of fruit on the dark wooden kitchen table and returned to his study to stare with morose irresolution out of the window. There had been a downpour earlier and a ghost rain hung in the air. A few orange leaves from last winter lay like sodden cornflakes against the railings of the small park opposite. He watched a squirrel move across the wet grass with the jerky arthritic movements of an old 16 mm film. Victor frowned. He was in debt. The bills had been mounting up since the collapse of his last venture which was to set up a desktop publishing house on the internet called Dot Communism. It was the most recent in the motorway pile-up of his hopes. It occurred to him that should capitalism collapse it might sweep him away with it, dependent as he was on his well-heeled father-in-law.

Just then his wife Mavis, a thin woman whose every variety of smile managed to express anguish, popped her head round the door.

'How's it going?' she cringed slightly as she enquired.

'Fine.' He continued staring out of the window as if she had interrupted him at a crucial point of creation. Mavis waited for a few respectful moments and then discreetly withdrew.

*

As soon as Mavis left the room Victor turned away from the window and went to study his father-in-law's cheque once more as if the amount might have increased. It had not. For a few minutes the master-builder of imaginary solutions was stumped. He spent a while hoping that Vera Scobie, his close friend and a woman for whom he had much affection, would die suddenly leaving him a shed-load of money. Vera was his political mentor, advisor and co-activist.

Since his youth Victor had moved in and out of various political groupings, all of them radical in one way or another. Rumour had it that in the seventies he had been a member of that mysterious cadre in Bradford which everyone had heard about but nobody could find and which always produced the most astute revolutionary analyses of current events. At a time of strikes, mass unrest, police raids and urban bombings their manifestos were published in a highly prized but irregularly produced newsletter. In fact, Victor had never been a member of that group, but had assiduously promoted it and had greatly admired it without really knowing anything about it – although he had been quietly gratified once when a young woman, a complete stranger, accosted him, assuming he was one of the founding editors, and screamed accusations at him that the same newsletter had ruined her life.

After flitting from one revolutionary group to another, he finally ended up becoming associated with an obscure caucus affiliated to some Situationists who lived in Woking.

This particular splinter group was best known for insulting everybody. They got furious at the least little thing. They expelled everybody – it was all in tune with some idea of keeping themselves politically as pure as crystal. They hoped to build a society which would be a shining example of this crystal ideology – although, naturally, they would be the first to put the boot into any such edifice. One of them was an architect – a utopian architect, you understand – he never built anything, obviously. That would have been entirely against the ethos of the group. He only made plans. He was expelled though, in the end, because a friend of his built something. Anyway, nobody could keep up with the level of purity demanded by the group. In the end there were only three of them left. They were against work. No-one was allowed to work because it contributed to the capitalist economy. They were supposed to live on their wits. The girlfriend of the leader did earn some money. She did horoscopes for horses and greyhounds and sold them to racing magazines so punters could see whether or not the animal was having a lucky day. The remaining three quarrelled with everybody at the drop of a hat. Victor was used as a sort of dogsbody. He himself was expelled after he had been unable to come around to the leader's flat and help him mend a fuse.

'I was printing the pamphlets,' apologised Victor.

The leader screamed at him, 'You think I can't recognise people like you who would betray us at the decisive moment?'

But despite the vagaries, fluctuating fortunes and now near extinction of the political left, Victor had never quite been able to rid himself of the simple idea that capitalism was unjust. The great capital cities of the western world, London, Paris, New York, seemed to him like illuminated ships leaving harbour, the more fortunate immigrants clinging to the sides for the journey as the spangled vessels departed leaving untold millions behind in the darkness. And at times when he was sitting on his own in front of his computer, he was troubled by the change that had taken place in the world since the days of his youth. A system which he believed to be the cause of much suffering seemed now to be accepted as the only way of conducting economic and political affairs and it was spreading everywhere. The revolutionary ideas of his own youth were to the current generation a puzzling and ghostly manifestation of some long lost period of history. Capitalism was widely taken to be as natural as the air that people breathed and it saddened him that people mistook it for freedom.

The upshot was that Victor became anguished by the loss of any ideal by which he could live. He was confused by the pony-tailed hedge-fund managers and punk investment bankers who were hang-gliding to work; the global head-hunters with aviator dark glasses and red braces who sang gangsta-rap lyrics in their lunch breaks and exchanged high-fives with street gangs as they roller-bladed into the City. Whenever these people flaunted the Orwellian slogan 'Hey, business IS socialism', somehow he did not believe it to be true. He was politically lonely. Politically forlorn. There was no party to which he could attach his name. And so he worked away on his own in that chilly Camden room refusing to settle for existing evils and working out how to replace them with new ones of his own design.

It was at times like this that Victor turned to his mentor. One of the few people with whom Victor shared a political framework was the actress Vera Scobie. Considerably older than him, she was his most illustrious contact in the world of theatre, a celebrity whose political activism was known throughout the country. He had met Vera when he was a student at Cambridge, a contemporary of her son Mark, whom he had come across once or twice before latching quickly on to his mother. Vera had taken Victor under her wing and encouraged his political development and forays into playwriting. Despite the generational difference they became staunch allies. She had even appeared in one of his plays. One factor in particular bound them together.

Some years earlier, in the late eighties, Vera had divulged to him a great personal secret. It happened during an intense period of rehearsal. She had invited Victor to her house in Kent for the weekend so that they could work on the text together. When he arrived, the cleaner told him that Vera was in bed suffering from a migraine. The cleaner was clearly worried although, in fact, like many actresses Vera was as strong as a horse.

Upstairs, Victor found her in bed. The bed-head was piled with cream lace-edged pillows that matched the duvet. Dried flowers, a half-drunk glass of wine, scripts and a pen were on the bedside table. Her glasses were on her nose. Victor looked at the famous face resting against the pillows. She had good bone structure and paper-fine skin over which stretched a crazy paving of lines. She leaned back against the pillows and patted the bed for him to be seated.

'Victor. I'm sorry about this. I've had a terrible shock.' She reached for a tissue and blew her nose. 'I'm very upset about something. Come in and sit down. I think I can trust you.' Her husky gut-bucket voice had a catch in it. 'I'm sure I can. After all, you were a member of that famous Bradford group in the seventies that was so wonderful, weren't you.' She took his hand. 'You must never tell anyone about this.' She took a gulp of last night's unfinished wine.

Vera's first marriage had been to a high-flying left-wing barrister who went on to become the Attorney-General. They had one son, Mark. In the seventies Mark Scobie became involved with the revolutionary politics of the times and had been active in a clandestine group of saboteurs and urban bombers in Britain. Although Vera held up her son as a paragon of revolutionary virtue, Victor gained the impression that she was secretly rather afraid of him. The urban guerrilla group operated in England and was linked to, amongst others, the Brigate Rosse in Milan. In August 1971, when the international police hunt for these bombers was at its height, an unexpected visitor from the intelligence services turned up at the Attorney-General's office and asked to see him as a matter of urgency. The short, squarely-built young man with a pink complexion had just started his career in intelligence. He was clearly uncomfortable.

'I'm sorry to interrupt you, sir ...' The caller went on to introduce himself and explain his presence.

'My name is John Buckley from the Secret Intelligence Service. This is embarrassing for all of us ... and very embarrassing for me to have to tell you. But here's the situation. Special Branch and MI6 have been working with our Italian counterparts for some time. There is about to be a series of coordinated arrests for recent terrorist attacks in Britain and Italy. One of the people at the top of the arrest-list is your son Mark.'

The Attorney-General said nothing but rose to his feet and walked towards the window. Buckley waited for the Attorney-General to absorb the shock before he continued:

'It would be very awkward for the government if the son of such a highly placed official as yourself were to be arrested for trying to overthrow his own father and ... the state. To use a tabloid expression, sir – this is a tip-off. I am asked to advise you that your son Mark should leave Europe immediately. On no account can you allow him to warn any of his contacts and comrades otherwise all deals are off. Nor will he be able to return to England in the foreseeable future. I'm really sorry to be the bearer of such news. It must be very distressing for you.'

Vera Scobie was extremely practical in a crisis. As soon as she was told the facts she picked up the phone and arranged a one-way ticket to Australia where she had friends. She then contacted Mark in Milan. After a furious conversation with his father, Mark agreed to leave. The following day he was on a plane to Sydney.

'And I had to play Medea that night at the Apollo,' Vera continued. 'Can you imagine?' She put her hands up in an expressive gesture to cover her eyes then placed them palms down on the coverlet. The hands were delicate and wrinkled. She threw Victor an angry look. 'Frankly I agreed with everything they were doing anyway. He was right to attack the establishment. He was a revolutionary.' She sighed. 'But we didn't want him serving a long jail sentence. What would be the point in that?' A look of regret passed over Vera's face followed quickly by a look of determined common sense. 'Of course he wanted to warn the others. But his father spoke to him and managed to make him see reason. He had one friend in particular – you might know him. Hector Rossi. A lovely boy. I adored him. Long flowing hair. Passionate. Serious. Absolutely committed. Unfortunately, Hector spent a long time in jail in Milan because of it all. I always felt bad about that. It's all water under the bridge now. Hector is back living somewhere in Kent, I believe. But Mark still has to stay away. It's so unfair.' She shook her head. 'It left such a hole in my life. I've just heard that Mark has been hospitalised in Perth with peritonitis. And I can't be there with him. I feel terrible. I've only managed to get over to Australia twice in the last ten years. There is still a warrant out for him over here, I believe. I didn't want to burden you with this but I had to speak to someone.'

Vera's eyes moistened with tears. Victor was something of a weed in the battlefield of political honour. He listened in alarm, his raised eyebrows winching up his forehead to give him the air of a startled peahen. However, then and there he swore every sort of solemn oath that he would keep the secret. Vera rapidly pulled herself together and they settled down to work on the text. When he left the house the next day Vera seemed to have recovered her spirits. She saw him off waving a pair of scissors at him as she clipped the dog roses framing the door of her house in Tenterden. He walked down the path to the garden gate. Since the death of her Attorney-General husband she had shared her life with a radical journalist twenty years her junior, but he was away in South America covering the story of a coup.

'I've just heard from Alex,' she called after him. 'The president of wherever he is has been shot. I hope he's all right. He's so brave to be there.' She stood in the doorway waving goodbye. 'Thank you for everything, my good friend. Victor you must keep writing your wonderful plays. And not a word about our secret. I've told Mark what a staunch comrade you are.'

That had all been several years ago. Now, as Victor studied his father-in-law's cheque he thought of asking Vera for a loan but decided against it. She could turn quite vague and irritable at times.

Unable to make up his mind what to do Victor retreated into

another of his heroic daydreams. This time he found himself conducting a citizen's arrest on the foreign secretary in the full glare of lights and television cameras outside the Foreign Office. He was arresting him for war crimes in Iraq and Afghanistan. The minister's Special Branch minders stood in his way. Victor explained in a loud voice that he had a legal right to do what he was doing and that the Special Branch must step aside. Step aside they did, bowing to the law. At that point the prime minister appeared and Victor took the opportunity to arrest him too. With a startled minister on each arm he tried to lead them away to the nearest police station. The fantasy faltered a bit at this stage and Victor had to start it again until he reached his favourite point where the minders stepped aside and the small crowd cheered him on. He revisited that point in his daydream several times.

After a while the apocalyptic dreamer fell fast asleep where he sat on the sofa. During his sleep he was betrayed by his subconscious and dreamed that he was taking Prince William and Prince Harry on holiday and looking for somewhere to buy them fish and chips.

Chapter Two

Hector Rossi needed a breath of fresh air. He excused himself and stepped out into the street. A sweet metallic odour from the workshop hung in the air where he stood. The smell reminded him of his youthful days as a printer in Italy. On Saturdays he attended a copper-engraving and etching class in Folkestone. Fine particles and the cinnamon smell of copper dust had made his nostrils tingle and given him a sneezing fit. That day he had been trying to master the art of using the burin, a sharp tool held in the palm of the hand which is used to push through the copper engraving plate. It removes a small amount of copper that twists away like an apple paring. But the burin had slipped and gouged a lump from his thumb. He wrapped a tissue around the cut.

Across the road from Hector a shopkeeper with a pale gibbous face sat wedged in a chair on the pavement reading a newspaper. The dark interior of his second-hand shop was stacked with dusty old furniture, grimy crockery, oddments and sundries. Hector's mood dipped. The sight of all those remnants of past lives oppressed him and he felt suddenly suffocated by the unchanging face of the town. Stacked against the shop front was an array of different-sized mirrors with curly metal frames. Hector caught a glimpse of his own reflection – an unexceptional middle-aged man in blue shirt and trousers. His brown hair, streaked with grey, lay swept back behind his ears like two bird wings. The slanted reflection made him appear to be standing at an angle to the pavement and to the rest of the world, leaning away backwards with his head towards the sky.

He decided to leave the class early and walk home to Hythe along the seafront. The walk might help him shake off this feeling that his life had silted up and he was being buried alive.

The previous week a small incident had unsettled him and remained in his mind. He had been returning home on the train. Just as the train was leaving Ashford station and before it had gathered speed there was a disturbance at the other end of the compartment. When Hector looked up he saw a tall, good-looking man with silver hair and a handsome silver waterfall of a moustache arguing fiercely with the ticket inspector. Both men were partly obscured by the half-open doors that linked one carriage to the next. The folding doors swung open and shut with the swaying movement of the train. The inspector's voice was raised in anger:

'Well I'm telling you to leave the train at the next station if you have no ticket. Are you going to pay for a ticket? If not I'm going to take your name and address.'

'You're not taking my name and address and I'll leave the train when I want, you shitty little arsehole,' yelled the passenger.

Suddenly the train door opened and a roaring wind entered the compartment. Hector saw a brown suitcase fly out and tumble down the grass embankment. The next minute the silver-haired man leaped out after it, his black raincoat billowing out behind him. Leaning backwards the man staggered down the bank too fast to keep his balance. He skidded on the tall grass, put his arm back to save himself and sat down heavily on the slope. Turning towards the train he caught Hector's eye. His face was alive with a mixture of fury and laughter. For a second he looked at Hector and raised his eyebrows as if in a challenge or invitation. A minute later the man was out of sight.

Hector walked home from his engraving class slowly. For some time now he had been feeling paralysed by an enervating discontent. He regretted the loss of all the revolutionary possibilities of his youth; that search for justice which he seemed to have exchanged for everyday realities; realities that had the warmth and smell of freshly baked bread but did not seem to be enough.

To his left on the English Channel a fluffy grey angora haze blotted out the horizon. The milky sea gave slow sluggish sucks at the shore. Hector was hoping that the walk might shift his headache. The headache was nothing much, a sort of malaise, probably the result of tension at home. When he reached Hythe he stood on the low stone promenade looking out over the blue and orange pebble beach. He stood there for nearly half an hour.

*

It was two o'clock in the afternoon before Hector let himself quietly into the house.

For several days his wife Barbara had been walking around the house wearing her silence like a bridal gown. He could hear the floor in the bedroom over his head creak accusingly as she moved from the dressing-table to the window. She let out a variety of audible sighs. Under this pressure he remained politely upbeat and resolutely unapologetic.

The problem had arisen two weeks earlier when he told her that he was going up to London to see an old friend. Probably he shouldn't have told her. He knew she would react badly. She was always fearful that he might become involved in some sort of political activity, frightened that his past would catch up with them. He had gone up to her workroom to tell her.

Barbara's hobby was furnishing dolls' houses and selling them. The back room was a city of miniature houses. The room had a workbench where she sewed the curtains and glued tiny pieces of broken furniture together. He watched her for a minute or two as she worked. His wife was a short, squarely built woman with a straightforward moral face and short feathered hair that was turning from blonde to grey. She bent down to adjust the placing of a tiny table then straightened up and looked directly at him.

'Which friend?' Already she sounded grim.

The shutter on the window was only partly down and the sunlight shone on her face so brightly that he could see the light fuzz of transparent hairs beneath her chin.

'Khaled.'

'I thought you'd put all that behind you. You swore that you would always put your family first. You, me and Dawn. Before anything.'

'I do.' He became annoyed with himself for the pleading tone in his voice.

'Who else are you going to see there?'

'Nobody.' Stubbornness set in. 'For goodness' sake. I'm going to see Khaled. He's in England for the first time for years. We're going to see the Albrecht Dürer exhibition at the National Gallery. I suggested that because I want to see the engravings. Nothing more. Anyway, I'm going. I'm just letting you know.'

Barbara was still in bed when he left to go to London.

'OK. I'm off now,' he said airily, poking his head round the door of the darkened bedroom. The lightness of his tone belied the weightiness of the atmosphere between them. She turned over in bed away from him to face the wall.

*

They had arranged to meet inside the gallery in case it was raining. The exhibition room was warm and smelled of beeswax polish. Hector's shoes squeaked as he walked around. There were not many visitors but he worried that he might not recognise Khaled after so many years. He studied the wood-carvings and engravings on display. One copper-plate engraving interested him. It was called *The Knight, Death and the Devil*. He went up close to examine the techniques which enabled Dürer to engrave the horse with such magnificent swirling lines.

There was a tentative tap on his arm. Hector turned. The man who faced him had the same slim figure as the Khaled he had first met in Paris, but now he stooped a little and his receding hair was streaked with grey. The long humorous lop-sided face, one eyebrow higher than the other, was still the same. The two men embraced. Khaled spoke first.

'Good to see you. You've put on weight.'

'It was the prison diet in Italy.'

Khaled threw back his head and laughed.

'That's no excuse. That was light years ago. Shall we look round the exhibition a bit then go and have coffee or a meal or something?'

*

They first met under a brilliant blue Paris sky on 13 May 1968 – the day on which a whole nation decided to leave the beaten track. No-one had seen it coming. There had been a few skirmishes throughout the city a few days previously and then millions of workers took to the streets. From the police helicopter hovering overhead it looked as if someone had sprinkled multi-coloured hundreds and thousands in the streets below. Hector was eighteen and on his way back to England from Italy where he was an apprentice printer. He caught the mood of exhilaration as he found himself lifted up and carried along in that outburst of pent-up hope for a new future. Medical workers in their white coats, printers, drivers and workers from the Renault factories had taken over the streets of Paris, each group singing its own songs. A man dressed in a white clown costume clambered onto a traffic bollard with a whistle and pointed the way ahead for the demonstrators. For Hector everything felt clear. His head caught fire and his heart opened up. It was one of those rare moments when people feel they belong to something bigger than themselves, a Dionysiac explosion.

The march swung round past L'Eglise St Ambroise and Hector was swept along with it. The huge studded doors of the church were open and a wedding was taking place. The bride was visible at the altar in her white dress. Some people broke away from the demonstration and went into the church shouting: 'Don't do it. Come and join us. Join the revolution.'

To Hector's amazement the bridegroom exchanged brief glances with his bride-to-be and they joined hands and ran together up the stone aisle and out of the church into the open air. The marchers hoisted them up and the couple were carried along on the shoulders of an enormous cheering and baying crowd. The bride leaned backwards in her white dress trying to hold on to the uplifted hands of the crowd and at the same time hold down her skirts, but every time there was a glimpse of her white stockings and garters the crowd roared approval.

Next to Hector marched a young man with a light brown skin, wearing a *djellaba*. There was a look of triumph in his eyes. After a while he introduced himself:

'*Je m'appelle Khaled. Khaled. Je suis arabe.*'

'You're a what?' Hector Rossi had been in Paris only two days. His ear was not attuned to the language.

'*Je suis arabe,*' Khaled yelled over the noise of the singing crowd. 'I am an Arab.'

'Oh.' Hector laughed. He had collar-length tawny hair and pale brown Italianate eyes. His gaze was direct and curious. They shook hands. 'My name is Hector. You speak English then?'

'I should. I was at school in Berkhamsted until I was twelve. My stepfather is a rich Arab banker called Eddie Sursok. You might have heard of him.' Khaled held up his hands to his head and wiggled his fingers like devil's horns. 'I personally am marching against him and all he stands for.'

The two young men became instant friends. They were exuberant. That afternoon they went back and smoked *kif* in Khaled's shabby apartment which smelled of used cat litter.

'How did you come to go to school in Berkhamsted?'

'My family is Palestinian. They escaped to Tunisia in 1948. I was born there when my mother was only sixteen.'

Khaled put some Arab music on his old record player and explained how his birth had been a major scandal. He spoke about it with equanimity, shrugging as he told Hector that he did not know who his father was but rumour had it that he was a Scottish soldier, one of the British army left behind to mop up after the North Africa campaign.

'It was a huge disgrace which drove the family briefly to Paris where we lived in luxury in the Avenue Foch. When I was about two my mother, who was still very beautiful, married Eddie Sursok from another wealthy Palestinian family. We went to live in England until I was twelve when that marriage broke up. I was sent to school in Lebanon but hated it. At fifteen I went back to live with my grandparents in Tunisia then came to the Sorbonne as a student. That's me. *C'est moi*.'

That evening the two of them, still chattering, were out of breath as they made their way through the back streets towards L'Odeon Theatre.

'I don't want to stay at the Sorbonne,' Khaled announced. 'I want to go back and see what is happening at home. I live in Tunisia. Apparently loads of resistance fighters are passing through on their way to the Palestinian camps in Jordan.'

'Things are moving in Italy too.' Hector spoke seriously as if the weight of the world were on his eighteen-year-old shoulders. 'I'm apprenticed to printers in Milan. When I go back I shall work with the anti-fascists. I would join the Italian Communist Party but it's a bit stick-in-the-mud.'

It was eleven o'clock at night when they reached L'Odeon. Hundreds of students and demonstrators were pushing past the theatre-goers and pouring into the building. Khaled and Hector joined them. Inside it was warm and dark and full of people. The interior of the theatre was a seething indistinguishable mass, a swarm of humming bees in the darkness of a hive. A young student spoke from the centre aisle of the theatre. Someone else answered from one of the gilt-edged boxes. The debate flowed backwards and forwards. Arguments swirled to and from the balconies.

Working lights lit the stage and a thin man with a delicate face stood there giving instructions to the theatre electrician. At that moment the dim lights of the auditorium came on at full strength illuminating the flamboyant portraits on the ceiling, figures from mythology inspired by Aeschylus, Shakespeare and Aristophanes.

'Did you ever see *Les Enfants du Paradis*?' Khaled pointed to the stage. 'That man on the stage is Jean-Louis Barrault.'

The man on stage in the grey suit gave a cursory look around the auditorium before leaving. Later Barrault was to describe how hurt he had been by accusations that his theatre was for the bourgeoisie and how he had turned the theatre over to the mob for fear that they would otherwise tear it to pieces. For a month Barrault's theatre was occupied and used as a forum for housewives, shopkeepers, factory workers and intellectuals. Barrault was sacked for turning on the lights.

'In Paris lightning struck,' said Barrault. 'The storm came from far away and it is still wandering around the world.'

By the end of June it was all over and Paris had returned to the daily grind of rumbling metros and commuters travelling to and from work.

'The mistake was to take over the theatres,' said Khaled when the two friends next met in the Palestinian camp at Irbid. 'We should have taken over the law courts.'

*

It was October 1970, a month after Black September, when the two met again in Jordan. At Khaled's invitation Hector arrived at the Palestinian camp in Irbid by truck late one night. Someone took Hector to one of the tents and showed him to a camp-bed the width of a stretcher alongside the thirty other young soldiers who slept there. Despite being wrapped in two blankets he was freezing cold. He shivered with excitement. At last he was on the front-line of a just war. Two youths waited outside with their hands on the pins of their grenades in case Hussein's army or the Bedouins arrived. Somewhere behind his head he could hear the torrent of an icy running stream. That night he could not sleep and spent most of it propped up on his elbow staring through the open flap of the tent. He watched as the black sky became tinged with blue and the Milky Way dissolved into an Arabian morning.

Early next morning Khaled approached him with his hand held

out. He wore a green combat shirt and camouflage trousers. Khaled was now a commander in charge of fifteen men. Hector noticed a new gravitas about his friend since their time together in Paris. He invited Hector over to a trestle table where they tucked into pancakes, lettuce, boiled eggs, cheese and sardines. Globules of light filtered through the trees and bobbed around on the rough wooden table-top. Hector fished in his pocket to find the 'permission' papers signed by Arafat. Khaled waved them away.

'I know. I'm to take care of you and see you across the border when you leave. The Syrian border is like a sieve. Any amount of people come streaming through. But you have to know when. Sometimes the authorities shut down the exit points.'

In the bright sunshine the two of them talked against a constant drumming noise from tents flapping in the breeze. 'Jumping Jack Flash' by the Stones blared out from a radio. Khaled was tired from being on duty all night but his manner was open and friendly:

'What's happening in Europe?'

'Bombs and strikes all over the place. Northern Ireland has gone up in flames. Have you heard of Gladio? It's an Italian government plan connected with NATO. It's neo-fascist. I'm involved in organising a defence in Milan to fight against it. Some comrades have gone underground. That's why I'm here. You said come for a visit but I also need training with arms and explosives.'

Khaled grinned at the earnest face of his friend who still wore his dark honey-coloured hair at the collar-length fashionable in Europe.

'You look like Mick Jagger. Where did you get that jacket? I want one. I can organise arms training for you. Just the basics anyway.'

They were like lovers, serious and chaste but speaking only about explosives: Kalashnikovs, grenades, rocket-launchers, remote control mechanisms, gelignite, fuses. The conversation resembled the language of love with its meaningful glances, tenderness and offers of help, tips and advice. It was love, in its own way.

At that moment the exchange was broken by a boy of not more than fourteen who passed behind Khaled, swinging his rifle as casually as a young girl swings her handbag, and who clipped him playfully on the back of the head. Khaled leaned back in his chair and acknowledged the boy with a friendly touch on the arm then turned to Hector. He gestured around him at the other young soldiers.

'For me, this was bound to happen. Everything was so dull when I went back to Tunisia after Paris. I was helping out as a waiter in my grandparents' hotel in Sfax.' Khaled pulled a face of mock despair. 'Tunisia is a nation of waiters. Head waiters, hotel waiters, restaurant waiters, café waiters. I was in a café with a friend one day when a hump-backed old waiter in a black jacket passed by our table. "That's my destiny if I stay here," said my friend. "Your family is rich. But I will end up like him." I just said: "Let's go."' Khaled laughed. 'It was a hot afternoon. I went back to the house and grabbed some stuff. I set off with that same friend while my grandfather was snoring on his back taking his two o'clock siesta. We jumped on a train. Ticket inspectors always look the other way for people like us. Twenty-four hours later I was here with the *fedayeen*.'

Later that morning a young *fedayeen* called Wazir taught Hector some elementary techniques with munitions. Hector pushed his hair behind his ears and squatted in the sand behind the tents. The grit penetrated his clothes and a warm breeze blew tiny dust-devils into his face. Wazir showed him how to load and handle a variety of handguns; how to make incendiary devices with non fire-suppressed fertiliser, sugar and sulphuric acid, and how to use them to set off gelignite; how to make clock-timed devices with resistance wire and batteries. Hector wanted experience with machine guns but there were none available so he learned how to make up cartridges for shotguns. He practised pouring small amounts of grey glittering gunpowder into cartridge cases and rolling the wad of thick tissue to insert in the cartridge, tamping it down to make sure it was a tight fit. Then came the little balls of shot. Then another wad of tissue and finally the rest of the cap was fitted over it. That night in the tent with the help of a torch under his blanket he studied the notes and diagrams he had made, panicking that he would get it wrong and forget how everything worked.

Two days later Khaled himself drove Hector to the border and they said goodbye.

'Good luck. I'll keep in touch whenever possible,' said Khaled, his asymmetrical face breaking into a grin as he waved goodbye from the window of the truck. 'Send me that Dusty Springfield album.'

*

Many years later, when Hector looked back on the way they all gambled so freely with their lives – tossing cigarette packs, cartridges and grenades between each other as casually as if they were fielding in a ball game – he reflected on how those brushes with death seemed to give the young fighters an airy elegance and lightness that made them almost skyborne – as if they were eating air. Fleet, breathtaking decisions were taken easily with a light heart and unshakeable certainty. They were not weighed down with personal plans. They possessed nothing. Hector wondered whether that lightness existed amongst them all because they had no future.

*

Hector and Khaled ambled through the gallery studying the exhibits. Khaled called Hector over to look at a wood engraving.

'Here. Come and look at this.'

The work that had caught Khaled's attention was entitled *The Four Avenging Angels of the Euphrates*. Khaled raised a quizzical eyebrow.

'Do you still feel the same about things?'

They sat down together on a bench in front of the artwork and regarded the scene of angels bent on slaughter. Hector shifted his raincoat from over one arm to the other.

'I'm not active now but I believe in the same things.' He looked at Khaled and smiled. 'Once the political bug has bitten it's impossible to remove it from the bloodstream. I feel sorry for youngsters now. They have nothing to believe in. It's not their fault. A huge sand-blanket of commercial pragmatism has fallen over them. Still, you can't buck the times you are born in. I've learned that people are more like their times than like their parents.'

Khaled got to his feet. Hector stretched and joined him. Khaled noticed an unfamiliar scar on Hector's lower lip.

'What's the story with the scar?'

'The Italian police. They gave me electric shocks. I bit through my lip. The ridiculous thing is that it happened when I was anticipating another shock and before they actually gave it to me. I'm fine except that I can't bear to use an electric toothbrush or shaver.'

Khaled put a hand on his shoulder.

'I'm sorry. We all had problems in those years.' He stopped and frowned for a moment. 'The trouble is that when you've invested your suffering in an idea, you become unwilling to give up that idea. Everything in the world just seems to confirm it.'

*

They found a cheap Italian restaurant just off Leicester Square full of bright plastic surfaces, fairy lights and cheerful clatter. Khaled broke off part of a bread roll and dipped it into his minestrone as he spoke:

'I left the Middle East for good after Beirut in 1982. My wife Nabila was killed there. It was hopeless. We'd all been heading into a web of treachery and deceit woven by the Israelis, the Jordanians, Bedouins, Syrians, Lebanese Phalangists – the whole blasted lot of them. Fatah was corrupt.' There was an air of humorous exasperation as he spoke. 'I should have realised that in the very beginning when I saw the Palestinian taxi driver calmly taking down the picture of King Hussein stuck in the front window of his cab and replacing it with one of Yasser Arafat as he neared the camp.'

Khaled exhibited a moment's bitterness.

'The invisible Palestine. The phantom nation. The fulcrum around which the whole of the Middle East turns. Everybody is frightened of a people without a country. I had a dream just before I left. I dreamed of graves falling from an aeroplane. And suddenly I saw all my comrades as if they did not have their own shadows, the shadow of a human figure, but instead they had the rectangular shadow of a grave at their feet. I looked down at my own feet and saw that I still had my own properly formed shadow. I left while there was still time.'

A Ukrainian waitress with a chalk-white face and a vicious slice of red hennaed hair that swung across her forehead cleared their plates. Khaled smiled a sad one-sided smile then immediately cheered up.

'I married again ten years ago. I'm living in Hamburg. We have three children. I'm happy. I speak good German – with the verbs at the end of the sentences. I work for a software company. It's not much. And I'm a cinemaniac now. I love movies. I swap old for new. Well, we live in the age of image. Now I understand why all those photographers got us to stand on a rock with a Kalashnikov and the desert sun setting behind us before they flew off to cover the Oscars.' He shook his head in rueful amusement.

'What about you?'

Hector frowned.

'Well, it's a long time since revolution was in the air – and a lot of air freshener used by governments ever since to get rid of the aphrodisiac smell of it. What am I doing now? Just working quietly in a small firm of printers and bookbinders in Kent. I'm still married to the same woman, Barbara. We have a young Down's syndrome daughter. She came late and she's adorable. My wife says that we were all losers with pie-in-the-sky ideas – that all revolutionaries end up dead or in jail and that after every revolution comes the guillotine. I used to argue with her. I don't any more.'

'Have you given in to her ideas?'

'No. I'm just frightened of having a stroke.'

They laughed. Hector paid the bill while Khaled put on his jacket.

'What brings you to England?' asked Hector.

'I thought it was time to find out about my real father. The Scotsman. I have children now and they should know their true history. Apparently my father was already married when he met my mother and he had a son in Scotland before me. What is really driving me is that I have this brother – a half-brother. I want to find him. I'll give it a shot anyway. I'm going to see Eddie Sursok, my ex-stepfather, while I'm here. Always good to see how the other half lives.'

Outside the two men exchanged mobile numbers.

'You see that cinema?' Khaled pointed over at the Empire. 'Once in the eighties I came to England. I took my mother to the movies. Standing in the foyer of that cinema was the notorious leader of the Lebanese Phalange, the group I hold responsible for killing my wife. He went up to the cashier's desk and bought a ticket for the movie. Why should I have been surprised? Terrorists go to the movies. Of course they do. Terrorism is only a part-time occupation. Terrorists live most of their life outside their balaclavas. A few hours later he was probably giving orders to the Druze militia back in Lebanon. I was close enough to have killed him. But I just went in and watched the movie.'

They embraced with affection as they said goodbye. Hector watched Khaled's back as he disappeared into Leicester Square underground station.

Chapter Three

Hector made his way to Victoria station. When he arrived there he first thought that the crowd milling around the station must have come from a football match. Then he realised it was the tail-end of the May Day demonstration in Hyde Park. Abandoned placards and damp leaflets littered the station entrance. Police vans remained parked out of sight in side roads.

He caught the 3.15 to Ashford. A small group of demonstrators clambered into the compartment with him. They were young, fresh-faced and carried a banner that proclaimed them to be Kent Valley Anarchists. They had painted their faces and wore bright woolly hats and rainbow-knit scarves. Two of the girls had nose-rings and long hair plaited with pinky-orange twine that made their heads look like unravelling baskets of raffia. The group exuded a wholesome type of rebellion, a mischief that belonged to the time of the hobby horse and the Lord of Misrule. There was a gaiety and innocence about them. They ignored the thickset middle-aged man with the leather jacket and the scar on his lower lip who sat in the window seat.

Hector tried to read his newspaper. Spermatozoa of rain wriggled along the glass window by his side. After a while he shut his eyes and leaned his head against the warm glass. The image of his old second floor apartment in one of the poorer quarters of Milan floated into his head. The front door of the apartment was open.

During his apprenticeship Hector lived in a scruffy part of town near the Stazione Porta Romana. That was where he returned after visiting Khaled in Jordan.

The apartment was inhabited by a succession of students and activists who had painted it dark red throughout. Beneath the windows stood enormously thick black-painted radiators whose thermostat didn't work properly so that they became ferociously hot in winter. The varnished wooden floors were old and scuffed. From somewhere the students had acquired a giant moth-eaten Russian bear, an example of botched taxidermy which stood about seven feet tall and still wore its muzzle. It guarded the hall and sometimes served as a hat stand or somewhere to chuck a winter scarf. The flat buzzed with activity. These were the young activists at the heart of the merry-making of the time: revolutionaries pulling insurgency out of the top hat; throw-it-all-up-in-the-air chancers jostling on the revolt and encouraging crises. Ceaseless rebellion. Members of the Brigate Rosse and the Ponte della Ghisolfa anarchist group came and went; some visitors were young workers from the Fiat factory; full-time conspirators; part-time conspirators; all alchemists of revolution. The commonplaces which their parents had learned from the Second World War – that peacetime was to be cherished – had not been passed on to them. Everywhere was the vague desire for confrontation and disorder. What had been passed on to them by their parents and the movies were the stories and experiences of fascism, and they felt the winged beast still breathed close behind them ready to take flight again.

One of Hector's flatmates in Italy was Mark Scobie, son of Vera Scobie the actress. His PhD studies on Garibaldi required him to travel back and forth between Milan and London. Mark had a wide, pale heart-shaped face. He wore black-rimmed glasses. His face was beautiful and unearthly. His complexion was waxen and his hair was thick and black and rose in a straight square block from his forehead. He spoke quietly in a way that managed to be both hesitant and absolutely assured. Because of his well-heeled background, Mark felt it more necessary than most to prove his revolutionary credentials. In England he sometimes organised meetings in his parents' Chelsea house. The others in his political group were impressed and rather enjoyed it when his mother's famous face peered around the door and asked if they would all like tea. They excused themselves for this bourgeois lapse by pointing to the fact that his father, despite being a lord and holding high office in government, was the direct descendant of one of those Cromwellians who ordered the execution of King Charles I.

In June 1971 Mark informed Hector that they must leave the flat in Milan empty on 17 July for a month. Other comrades needed it for some operation or other. Hector arranged time off work and returned to England. He spent less time in London on this occasion. Back in Kent a romance blossomed between him and a nurse called Barbara. On 12 August 1971, Mark contacted Hector and told him it was safe to go back. Hector made the journey to Milan on his own but with his heart reinvigorated by this new love affair.

To get into the old tenement apartment residents used a small entrance set into a pair of great arched wooden doors which opened on to a courtyard. These huge doors, patterned with bronze studs, were only used when a vehicle of some sort needed access. It was midday. Cooking smells greeted him as he entered the yard. He went up the stairs to the second floor and was puzzled to see the door of their flat partially open. There was no-one inside. Hector entered to find a tin bath full of blood standing next to an armchair under the window. A dark blood-soaked cloth hung over the side of the tub. At first he did not realise what it was. Perplexed, he walked over to examine it. For a moment he thought that someone must have been dying clothes or making banners. The liquid had spilled onto the floor. It was black with huge crimson clots in it. It was only when he pulled his foot up and the congealing blood stuck to the bottom of his boot, gluey and elasticated, that he recognised what it was. A tingle of shock moved through the flesh over his jaw and down his arms.

In an instant everything was transformed. Through the window he could see a baker's van and other traffic moving normally along the narrow Via Mantova. It was like looking at a previous life from which he was now excluded. He tried the door to Mark's room. It was locked. Hector picked up his bag and rushed out. As he ran, the strap of his bag caught the Russian bear's outstretched paw in the hallway. The huge bear rocked on its plinth and crashed to the ground. Hector leaped down the stairs two at a time and ran out into the bright light of day.

He dashed to a nearby house in Via Decembrio. The occupants were preparing to leave for a Popular Unity carnival and were listening to news of a kidnapping and murder on the radio. Breathless, Hector tried to tell them what he had found. There was a crash and the noise of splintering as the front door was broken down. Nine armed *carabinieri* in flat-peaked caps and uniform burst into the room brandishing pistols and told everyone to lie on the floor. Hector was in a state of paralysis as he was dragged off into the police van with blood still on his boots. Somebody was yelling that there was an informer amongst them.

*

The body of the murdered man had been found by the roadside not far from the Stazione Porta Romana. He belonged to the Agnelli family who owned Fiat. Both the jugular and the carotid artery had been severed with one jagged cut. A further wound showed that someone had jabbed the knife blade right through the man's open mouth and palate. The murderer had tugged the knife out and struck again. This time the knife blade thrust right up into the brain. It had been wrenched out to one side so hard that the handle snapped off. Fragments of teeth had flown out and bits of grey cerebellum were mixed in with the blood. Although the knife handle was found nearby in the gutter forensic experts assessed that the murder had taken place elsewhere.

*

The police station where Hector was taken was a five-storey building constructed around a courtyard of dove-grey stone. He was frog-marched up three flights of stairs. They put him on his own in a bare cell with no furniture. In the August heat sweat rolled down the back of his neck and made Hector wish he'd cut his hair. He tried to lever himself up to see out of the small barred window but the window ledge sloped downwards and he could not get a grip on it. At that moment all the enthusiasm he had felt at meetings, the excitement of being swept along with unknown comrades, his passion for justice and equality, evaporated. There was no public, no platform, no singing of the Internationale, no support of any kind. He was on his own and not immune from the shock of arrest.

The interrogation room was on the fourth floor along a harmless-looking corridor. There was a small barred and wire-netted window high up on the right hand wall. The only furniture was a wooden table and three chairs. It had the simplicity of a peasant dwelling or a Van Gogh interior.

On the first day of Hector's interrogation a bluff young Englishman with a florid pink complexion introduced himself as John Buckley, a junior member of staff from the British embassy. The man was short and had a pleasant reassuring manner. He asked Hector a few questions. Hector's brain was a busy spider running around weaving together his story, patching it up where there were holes, even creating snares to trap his interrogators. His own clothes had been taken from him and he was wearing a misshapen shirt and a pair of ill-fitting trousers. They were soon joined by an Italian inspector with grey pomaded hair. The inspector sat at the table and took over the interrogation. He noted down the details of Hector's actions on the day of his arrest. Hector explained that he had just that day returned from England. He did not admit to entering the flat. He said he had gone straight to the Via Decembrio.

On the second day when he was brought into the room the Englishman was no longer present and he was faced with a different inspector, a man in his forties with a face like an eighteen-pound hammer. Two jailers stood on either side of Hector. On the table stood a magneto or dynamo. The magneto had been adapted from one used for small marine engines. Bulky and ugly, it squatted on the table in front of him like some mysterious car part. They had told him to undress down to his underpants and his clothes lay in a little pile by the chair. Until the first shock was administered Hector somehow thought that he was about to be subjected to some sort of outdated medical examination. But then his hands were suddenly seized and handcuffed behind the back of the chair. Two electric leads were connected to the dynamo. The police officer hand cranked it to generate an electric charge. When he realised what was about to happen his diaphragm contracted in uncontrollable spasms. The two jailers had strapped him into the chair. The wires were first of all applied to his tongue. A searing pain exploded like a car crash in his head and his mouth filled with the acid taste of metal. Apart from the shock itself he feared memory loss and brain damage. He looked down and saw the two alien stumps of his bare knees trembling. He was given two more shocks. Someone brought in his boots still with dried blood on the soles and placed them beside the magneto. Once he saw that they had his boots as evidence he told the truth about entering the flat and discovering the bath of blood. He knew nothing more. He was shown a list of names, some of which he recognised, and told that if he signed a statement saying they were involved in the Agnelli murder he could go free. It was the first he had heard of the Agnelli murder and his interrogators could see from the shocked look on his face that he knew nothing about it. But they insisted he sign all the same. There were no witnesses to see whether or not he signed in exchange for his freedom. He managed to refuse and pretended to faint. After that they left him alone. That afternoon he was charged with conspiracy to kidnap and murder and was transferred to the San Vittorio jail.

By the time he was brought to court in a mass hearing with other members of the Brigate Rosse and the Ponte della Ghisolfa, most of whom he had never seen, Hector was weak and disorientated. The appearance in court was chaotic. The authorities had constructed a vast cage over the dock in which the defendants made their appearance all together. People were shouting and yelling. Ventilation fans wafted hot air through the court. Hector could not see his lawyer anywhere and felt sick with apprehension and powerlessness. Supporters in the public gallery fanned themselves and gestured wildly to the defendants. He was struggling to keep his footing in the crush of some thirty people in the dock who were calling out to relatives and comrades. The two defendants next to him had been badly beaten during interrogation and were screaming slogans. Hector's lawyer arrived at last and grinned encouragingly at him. They were all remanded in custody until the trial. Eventually, after six years in jail on remand, Hector was acquitted of all charges and returned to England. Mark Scobie, he heard, had escaped the round-ups in both Italy and England and disappeared. He was pleased for Mark's sake.

*

Hector was half asleep but aware that he was still on the train. The Dürer woodcut of the angels floated in front of his eyes. Terrorists are avenging angels, he thought. Self-appointed, of course. Avenging angels are never elected and always at risk of burning their wings. Now he saw that the actions and ideas with which he had been involved were mere tracer bullets, brilliant flak against a dark sky, brief manifestations against a world enveloped in its own daily concerns. He had expected the sparks from those revolutionary fireworks to leap from bank to bank and cathedral to cathedral, law court to law court, school to school, generation to generation in one huge conflagration. That had not happened. The whole period was just the flash of lightning which momentarily lit up a dark landscape, the shining edge of a dark cloud.

The train stopped and the group of demonstrators grabbed their belongings and tumbled out.

The compartment became quiet again. Hector forced himself back to reading the *Kent Messenger*. On the second page there was something about an explosion at the electricity sub-station in Dartford. A small bomb had caused some damage there the day before and there were likely to be widespread electricity cuts in

Kent. He hoped it was not going to affect his train. Barbara would be even more annoyed if he was late back.

As the train continued on its way something caught Hector's attention. A glimmering white shape lay on the ground beside the track. For a moment he thought with shock that it was a naked body sprawled on the muddy embankment. Then, as the train rattled slowly alongside he realised that it was the great blue-marbled body of a dead white hog. The long carcass stretched out peacefully on the ground just in front of the brick support wall of the bridge. As the train passed Hector was close enough to make out the colourless lashes of a half-shut eye.

He changed trains at Ashford and caught the small train to Sandling. The walk home from the station refreshed him. Soft damp breezes gusted over the hedgerows as he made his way along the country lanes. He puzzled over the fierceness which seemed to take hold of him in the city. As soon as he returned home and took breaths of the country air all those feelings began to dissolve. It occurred to him vaguely that the word politics came from the Greek word 'polis' for city. Politics had to do with cities. In the country, surrounded by nature, it seemed possible to look at the world with different eyes.

*

Dawn ran from the kitchen to greet him. She had on a baseball cap, bright clothes and new trainers. Both he and Barbara had refused to let her be dressed in the dowdy middle-aged clothing sometimes given to Down's syndrome children. He knelt down and she hugged him. Her blue eyes brimmed with affection under their slanting epicanthic folds. He brushed her lank hair away from her forehead. Her nose was running. She laughed with an infectious gurgle.

In the kitchen Hector began to rake the ashes in the grate. Dawn knelt on a chair at the kitchen table and carried on with her drawing.

'What are you drawing?' he asked.

'God's face,' said Dawn.

Hector frowned, irritated that she was being exposed to religious ideas at school.

'Do they teach you about god in school?'

'Yes.'

He felt the pettiness of what he was about to say but could not stop himself.

'Even if there is a god nobody really knows what he looks like.'

Dawn continued drawing, ferociously grinding her crayon into the paper.

'Well they will in a minute,' she said.

Hector threw coal from the scuttle onto the unlit fire and backed away from the cloud of dust that billowed up from the grate. Kneeling in front of the hearth he remembered something from his school days. He had returned to Rome for a year with his Italian father after his mother died. The first thing he had learned about at school in Italy was the pantheon of Roman gods. He had taken an immediate and violent dislike to the Lares and Penates, Rome's deities of the hearth. In fact, at the age of twelve, he had been shocked and infuriated that gods should even exist for such a dull and inglorious arena as the household. Gods of the washing-up and scrubbing brush? The hearth and home? They had none of the adventurous scope and panache of the other gods. He found the whole idea of them offensive. Now, as he looked at Dawn making a pattern in the ashes of the hearth with her foot, he was not so sure. Perhaps they were the only gods worth their salt after all. He could hear Barbara moving around upstairs.

'Shall we take mum up a cup of tea?'

'Yes.'

'What's the time?' he asked.

'I don't know,' she beamed. 'The time's in the front room.'

'Do you want to watch children's telly because if you do we'll have to move at the speed of light. The programme is starting in a minute.'

Hector pushed open the door to his wife's workroom. Dawn put the tea on the table. Barbara ignored Hector.

'Thank you, Dawn. Don't forget the Maypole fete tomorrow. You can put out some clean clothes to wear.'

'What is the speed of light?' asked Dawn on the way downstairs.

'Something that goes very very fast.' Hector bent down to switch on the telly.

'Faster than the speed of dark?' she asked.

'I'm not sure. I've never thought of that.'

Chapter Four

Victor Skynnard awoke with a guilty jump as the front door banged shut and Mavis left the house. She taught piano to various pupils around town. Victor tried to settle back down to his work. All told it had not been a creative morning. No new neural pathways had opened up. There had been no unexpected synaptic linkages, no images from the underworld of his subconscious apart from the unwelcome intrusion of the princes of the realm. He popped a marshmallow into his mouth. How would he describe his day? Mediocre, so far. He toyed with the idea of writing to the Honours Committee at 10 Downing Street, recommending himself for a gong, and then, when it was offered, publicly turning it down in a sunburst of glory.

There was a blockage in Victor's creative energy. When these blockages occurred, they affected the hydraulics of his writing in such a way that his creativity sometimes spurted out sideways in the form of anonymous letters to political leaders. During the war against Iraq he had, in his impotence and distress, fallen back on making obscene phone calls to the Ministry of Defence from a public call-box in a fake northern accent. One evening he ran out with a spray can and painted 'Poodle Must Die' on the corrugated iron fence round a building site. It felt like an act of courage. On the whole he believed that when it came to the end of the day, if Members of both Houses of Parliament quietly packed up their belongings, went home and never returned, the world would be a better place. Would it make any difference? The country was already a bird's nest of laws, a haystack of legislation.

At the precise moment when the doorbell rang Victor, with a rolled newspaper in hand, was absorbed in the chase of a bluebottle that had flown in a few days earlier in the mild weather. He was trying to persuade it to exit through the bottom of the open sash window. The fly had been stationary on the window pane wringing its hands for some time and obtusely refusing to take up the possibility of escape. It had stopped buzzing some days before and crawled here and there always just out of reach.

Victor opened the door and a gust of rain came in. Standing on the doorstep was a middle-aged man wearing a heavy black leather motorcycle jacket, leggings and a red and black crash helmet. The pale visitor took off his helmet. He wore thick black-rimmed spectacles. The man's hair was black but a grey streak rose up from the centre like a badger's marking. His mouth was wide and thin. When he spoke his voice was soft, almost apologetic.

'Victor Skynnard?'

'Yes.'

'Mark Scobie.'

For a few seconds the name meant nothing to Victor. Then, in a balls-shrivelling moment, he realised who was standing on his doorstep. A smile tried to force itself through the layers of dismay on his face but failed, only resulting in a nervous twitching of his lips. Victor tried to sound calm.

'Good god! What a surprise! How are you? Is it safe for you to be here? How wonderful. What about the police?'

'Is it OK to come in?' The accent had a slight twang which Victor guessed must be the result of his years in Australia.

'Of course. Of course. Sorry. Christ. How amazing. I can't get over this.' Victor glanced quickly up and down the street and then asked: 'Is everything OK?'

From his smile it was clear that Mark Scobie was aware of Victor's trepidation.

'Come in to the front room where I work.' Victor stood aside.

His hands were trembling slightly as he opened the door to his study. The leather-clad figure went in ahead of him.

Victor's first thought was to try and get this man away from the house as quickly as possible.

'You're lucky to catch me,' he said looking at his watch and inventing an appointment. 'I've only got about ten minutes before I have to go out. Well, well. This is so extraordinary. I can't believe it.'

Victor wrung the hand of his visitor with unnecessary vigour. The truth was that, despite his political convictions, Victor did not want a terrorist or even an ex-terrorist or a putative terrorist staying in the spare room. Not these days. This was no longer the seventies. It had been bad enough then. Didn't this man understand that the whole international picture had changed? He cast an infuriated glance at the visitor. What the hell was he doing back here? Squad cars might come screeching to his door any minute. He, Victor, would be put under surveillance or house arrest. He would be taken to Paddington Green top-security police station. He began to invent his cover story. All he knew was that this man was the son of a famous actress who happened to be a friend of his. He knew nothing about his past. Victor could feel prickles radiating from the top of his spine. How quickly could he get himself a radical lawyer?

Mark put his crash helmet down on the sofa and took off his leather jacket before stretching wearily. He seemed tired. The leather gear creaked as he sat down.

'Look. I'll be quick.' He smiled. 'I haven't contacted my mother. I wasn't sure where to go then I hit on the idea of coming to you. A while ago she gave me your address and said you were a reliable comrade. Can you get in touch with her for me and tell her I'm in England? That's all I'm asking. I don't know if it's OK to go to her place or not. I haven't met the guy she's been living with since my father died and I'm not sure about him.'

'Yes. Of course I can.' Victor's brain was seething with escape plans – his own escape. He managed to plaster a fake smile over his face. Mark Scobie continued to talk in a level tone.

'The person I most need to be in touch with is Hector Rossi. If it's difficult for me to stay at my mother's he will find somewhere for me to go. Do you know where he is these days?'

'Er no.' Victor's heart sank. He wanted nothing to do with all this. Hector Rossi was another well-known name from the seventies, a man who had spent a long time in jail. 'Surely they wouldn't do anything after all these years. The police, I mean. Have you ... um ... eaten?'

Victor could have kicked himself for mentioning food or anything that would keep the man there longer than necessary. All sorts of thoughts were tumbling through his head. Supposing he, Victor, were charged with being an accessory to something. He could be charged with harbouring a criminal or worse, conspiracy or aiding a terrorist. Why had he opened the door?

Mark nodded. 'I grabbed a kebab on the way here, thanks. But I'm knackered. I've just biked over from Holland. Mind if I have a bit of a kip on this sofa?' He was worn out and looked pale. Suddenly he put his feet up, boot-heels on the arm of the sofa. He rested his crash helmet on his stomach, placed his head against the other arm and went almost immediately to sleep. Victor stared at him with outrage then quickly checked his pocket for his front door keys and let himself out. He must find Vera straight away.

As he left the house Victor felt himself to be riding the horse of a great decision. He headed for the telephone box at the end of the square. No point in making traceable calls from his own line. Panic is a great energiser. His legs began to run of their own accord.

*

Victor finally traced Vera Scobie to a picket of about ten people outside the newly refurbished Royal Academy of Dramatic Art in Malet Street. Vera was wearing an expensive beige trench coat with a scarf tied round her stylishly cut grey hair. She was busy handing out leaflets to passers-by. Sheltering under part of the porch were five Uzbeks whom Vera had brought with her. The women wore headscarves with big roses printed on them. They all looked gloomy. As Victor approached, a young square-chinned actor in a state of great agitation was talking to Vera about a failed audition:

'You see I assumed the audition was going to be on stage at the Aldwych, but something was going on there and we couldn't use the stage. So I had to do the audition in a tiny office upstairs crammed with furniture. There was hardly room to move and I was playing the part of a Chinese emperor who had epileptic fits. I went into the first fit and knocked some letters off the table including a very important one, about the theatre's annual grant. I was just about to have the second fit when the director asked me to stop. "That's fine, thank you," he said.'

'I shall phone him,' said Vera huskily, 'and explain your political background. No-one unfamiliar with the works of Rosa Luxemburg should be allowed to appear in that play.' She turned away and called out to anybody who might be listening:

'Save our profession.'

Victor approached her and from ten feet away she started proselytising in her gorgeous smoky voice.

'Hello there.' She turned to him. 'How lovely that you came.' She addressed him with misty-eyed warmth. 'Do you realise that our noble profession is being sullied?'

'No. What's happening?' asked Victor.

'I have just discovered that the mealy-mouthed governing board of this treacherous school, where I myself trained, has given in to the multinational corporations and agreed to train their management personnel. They now do not only train actors. They are training politicians and businessmen.'

'That's awful.' Victor was indeed taken aback.

'Yes. Can you believe it? They are accepting money to train businessmen in how to walk and gesture authoritatively; to look as though they are listening sympathetically to clients; how to persuade people to buy goods through seductive voice technique; and how to train politicians in the use of body language so that they look sincere and as though they are not lying. It's disgusting.'

'Save our profession,' she called out again. It began to drizzle. Someone handed her an umbrella.

'Thank you.' The reward was a dazzling smile.

'We must start a newspaper. We have to do it. It should include articles from theatre in other countries. An international paper. You could write for it.' For all her renown there was something direct and unpretentious in her manner. 'We have to denounce injustice everywhere.'

'I don't feel like doing that at the moment,' Victor demurred.

'Why ever not?' For a moment she looked dismayed. Then she brushed away the inconvenient reply. 'Well you could do it later. And perhaps you could think of somebody else meanwhile, until you are ready. We need to spread the information about what is really happening in our profession.'

She continued like this for some minutes before pausing and seeming to examine his face in great detail.

'It is Victor, isn't it?' she said. He had forgotten how short-sighted she was. She continued evangelising:

'The prime minister is a philistine. He has no depths. He lacks wisdom. If he had depths he would love the arts.'

Victor lowered his voice.

'Vera. I need to speak to you urgently.'

'Just one minute.' She fished up her spectacles which were on a black cord around her neck and put them on. Then she rested the open umbrella on her shoulder and went to fetch herself a placard from the few that were resting against the glass front of the drama school. They had become wet and torn. She gave a placard to Victor. Her gloves were damp.

'Here you are, Victor. What are you doing here?' But before he could answer she raised her voice and called out in her famously throaty voice:

'Keep big business out of the arts.'

She turned towards Victor again. 'Did you know Victor that, to our shame, Hitler was trained by an actor in gestures of oratory? Let us not repeat that ignoble episode. We must keep big business and charlatans out of the arts. Business has got in everywhere.'

Victor managed to take her arm and lead her away from the group.

'Vera. Listen to me. Your son Mark is here.'

'What?' She immediately came down to earth. She lowered the placard and looked at him in disbelief.

'Mark is here. He's in my front room. I'm sorry to break it to you like this but I'm not sure what to do.'

'Well you must hide him.' Vera looked aghast. 'I must come and see him straight away. No I'd better not. It's not safe. I'm too well-known. What's he doing here? Why didn't he tell me?'

'I don't know. He wanted me to tell you. He wasn't sure he could trust Alex.'

She bridled at this reference to her partner.

'That's ridiculous. Of course he can trust Alex. Alex knows everything. Alex is absolutely reliable. Alex thinks that what he did was splendid. He has the greatest admiration for him. Let me tell the others that something has turned up and I have to leave. One minute.'

'Keep the boardroom out of the stage,' she yelled as she rushed to put down her placard. Victor ran behind her.

'He wants to get in touch with Hector Rossi.'

She stopped.

'I'm not sure that's a good idea.' She bit her lip and took Victor by the arm.

'I've just remembered. I've got the Uzbeks with me. Go and tell Mark that I can't come just now. Tell him that I have people from Uzbekistan staying at the house. They've been tortured. It's not safe for him to come there just yet. You must keep him at your place until I say it's safe. Dear Victor. You must be our go-between.'

On the tube train as he hung on to the overhead bar Victor assumed a brave stance, upright, head thrown back, chin thrust forward – the sort of stance you might assume if you were up to your neck in a rapidly rising tide of shit.

He checked that there was no sort of surveillance in the street and then let himself into the house.

Chapter Five

While Vera Scobie was demonstrating outside the drama school, her partner Alex Hamilton was sitting at the kitchen table of their house in Tenterden. The table was cluttered with scripts. The radio murmured in the background. He drank some half-cold coffee from a bowl as he looked through the newspaper. Several ashtrays were full to overflowing with the stubs of cheap Uzbek cigarettes. A pair of Vera's spectacles lay upturned on the table amongst scattered pamphlets, unopened bills and envelopes. It was a relief to have the house to himself for a while.

His partnership with Vera had lasted amicably for fifteen years. It was a good match of status. Both prided themselves on their radicalism. Alex himself cut an attractive figure, slim, debonair and well-proportioned with a light step. His dark hair almost reached his collar in a way that managed to be both respectable and a touch bohemian. He enjoyed his reputation as a progressive journalist, clear-headed and humorous. He nurtured that secret internal image every man has of himself – handsome, honourable and brave.

In half an hour he was due to meet John Buckley from MI5. Such meetings two or three times a year were routine. Alex maintained the contact for professional reasons, but he also enjoyed Buckley's company. Buckley had risen to become one of the top men at MI5 and Alex felt gratified at being one of the privileged few allowed a discreet glimpse into the power-filled arena of the secret services. He was often surprised by his contacts there. They seemed more broadminded than the stereotype would suggest. He looked forward to these meetings with Buckley. Buckley was a witty and erudite conversationalist.

However, a telephone call from Vera had put his midday appointment with Buckley on a different footing. Vera sounded breathless and upset when she phoned from London. She knew about his lunch engagement and wanted him to find out from Buckley whether there was still an active warrant out in England for her son Mark's arrest.

'It's urgent. Can you find out if the police and secret services are still interested in him? But be discreet when you ask.'

'Why do you need to know that after all this time?'

'I can't speak right now. I'm surrounded by Uzbeks. I'll tell you everything when we get home.'

'I'll do my best but it's Special Branch who have that sort of information not MI5. Buckley isn't the man to ask but I'll try to find out what I can without being too obvious.'

'Do what you can.'

Alex stood up and went to the kitchen window. The helper had left some sort of stew on the Aga and he lifted up the lid of the pot and breathed in the steamy aroma of beef goulash. Then he wandered into the living room. They had built two extensions onto the rambling sixteenth-century house. The living room was part of the original building and was a little cramped and dark. The ceiling was low and the windows overlooking the garden were small. The wallpaper had a regency stripe and the walls were crammed with photographs of Vera playing various classical parts, framed playbills, sundry awards, designer sketches of costumes and a large oil-painting of her as Madame Ranevskaya in *The Cherry Orchard*. He looked at the clock. He was to meet Buckley at one o'clock in the Crown and Castle pub at Smarden.

Alex opened the door into the quiet hum of the pub and saw the rotund figure of Buckley studying the large plastic-covered menu. His neatly clipped white hair surrounded a patch of pink freckled scalp. There was a deliberate devil-may-care look to his open jacket which he wore over a white poplin shirt with a solid red tie. He had to sit sideways with his legs crossed to make room for a paunch which escaped flamboyantly over a low belt. As soon as he spotted Alex, he put the menu down and pointed with pleasure to a half-empty glass of white Belgian beer.

'I chose this pub because they do *Blanche de Bruges*. My favourite. Can't often find it.'

Alex fetched himself a Glenmorangie from the bar.

Buckley was in a jovial mood.

'How's Vera?'

'She's in good form. Demonstrating about something or other as we speak.'

'Beware bohemians with guns,' Buckley chuckled. 'Well, she has her causes. Having a great enemy is almost as good as having a great friend. Mmmmn. Giving your life for an ideal? I think we are all too sensible, too pragmatic for that these days. That notion has been tidied away for good. You must understand, Alex, that every revolution finally capitulates to the suffocating intrusion of comfort.' He waved his hand in the air. 'Explain that to Vera, if you would. In the end people succumb to the temptations of law and order and the cosiness it can bring.' He looked down again at the menu.

Alex laughed.

'You've probably got a point. How are things?'

Buckley pulled a face.

'I've had to spend the morning trawling round private schools for my son.' A waitress came round from behind the bar and took their order. Buckley took a sip of his beer.

'You knew Hector Rossi, didn't you?' Buckley enquired out of the blue, dabbing the froth from his mouth with a napkin. 'His name came up on the radar at GCHQ the other day which was a bit of a surprise. In connection with a Palestinian activist. He wouldn't remember me but I cut my interrogator's baby teeth on him thirty-odd years ago. I was young and undercover at the British embassy at the time, attached to the consulate in Milan. He thought I was a diplomat representing his interests. They called me in to help with one of his interrogations. Frankly, I rather admired him. He was full of all that hope you have when you're young. Torture and hope create a furious tension. But he was very honourable. Tried not to give anyone's name unless the evidence was waved under his nose.'

Alex was disconcerted that Buckley should bring up an area of subject matter that he himself had been about to raise. Buckley looked directly at Alex and continued:

'Well at least he believed in something. More than anyone does nowadays. I quite miss the Trots, communists and anarchists who wanted to overthrow the state. They were at least secular.' Buckley put the menu down and looked around for a waitress. 'Ironic, really. Everything we feared from communism is being brought about by capitalism: bland uniformity, cloned cities, secret prisoners, omnipresent surveillance. Perhaps fate has a sense of humour after all.' He raised his white eyebrows and shot a rueful look at Alex.

For a few seconds Alex wondered if Buckley might not be more radical than he let on, a possible Philby or Burgess or Maclean.

'I do know Hector Rossi, yes. Haven't seen him for a long time.' Alex put his whisky down on the table. 'That's all very old hat isn't it? Nobody could still be looking for any of that crowd, surely? They're more or less pensioned off.' He decided against mentioning Mark Scobie's name. He liked Buckley but needed to remember that the sharp-eyed, cordial man at the table was a practised interrogator, smooth, friendly and fatal. Buckley beckoned to the waitress for another beer and placed his order.

'No, Hector Rossi is of no interest really. It was only the Palestinian connection. I agree with you. His sort are the dying embers of a conflagration. Of course, it's impossible to know whether they've been extinguished for good or whether some breeze will whip up the flames again – the past attempting to be reborn. We try to keep an eye open for any resurrection of the terrorist left but on the whole I think their time is over.' Buckley sighed. 'They used to say that communism was the last manifestation of Christianity in the western world.'

'I'd forgotten your father was a minister,' said Alex. 'You sound quite wistful.' He paused. 'Are you saying you miss the Cold War?'

'In a way, yes. I was used to what the two sides stood for. The American kind of power is to do with wealth, display. The Russian idea was of power for its own sake. Almost mystical. Purer. Much more dangerous. It works against the desire for money and what money can buy. That's why the Americans never understood it and were so frightened by it. Orientals understand it. The English have never gone for the big idea. It's the Russians who love a big idea. Just now their big idea is kleptocracy.'

Alex tried to steer the conversation back to the British radicals. He wanted to find out more specifically about any arrest warrant for Mark Scobie. Having decided to say no more about Hector he suddenly found these words slipping from his lips:

'I can certainly find out what Hector Rossi is doing these days. He lives not far from here in Kent, you know.'

'So I gather,' said Buckley.

An odd spurt of professional rivalry flared up between the two men as to who knew most about Hector Rossi. Alex could not resist saying, 'He's probably still in touch with the Brigate Rosse. They're beginning to be released now. And the remnants of the Baader-Meinhof.'

Buckley patted the head of a dog that wandered past.

'Oh it was only the Middle East contact that alerted us. I'm sure you can imagine there's been a mad focus on the Muslim world lately. It's been a helluva scramble. Now we're running all over British universities trying to recruit Arabic speakers. We've even had to dig up some of the old Foreign Office Arabists. Do you happen to know if Hector Rossi speaks Arabic? He spent some time in the Middle East.'

'Haven't a clue. I can easily find out if you want. I know where to find him.'

'Thanks. I'll take you up on that if necessary.'

Buckley was looking around for the waitress to see what had

happened to his order. He pushed the condiments across the table to make room for his food. Then he chortled.

'I remember how our director-general loathed those seventies left-wingers. He saw them as some sort of political herpes: small, painful, untimely eruptions which were difficult to control. The only thing that would be of interest to us these days is to know whether any of those people link up with the Islamists. That's why we keep an eye on them. If they made common cause in some way or other then we would need to know about it.'

'Hardly likely, is it? Utterly different politics. It's more likely they'd be at each other's throats. I can't think of any reason on earth why they would work together.'

'Never rely on reason.' Buckley looked hopefully towards the waitress. 'It's reason that enables us to misunderstand the world with such shrewdness and sophistication.'

The barmaid arrived with Alex's salmon steak and an apology for Buckley:

'Your steak and kidney will be along in a moment, sir.'

Buckley went on:

'Since Iraq the Intelligence Services have lost credibility. We have to claw it back somehow. We need long-term infiltration of Muslim groups as we did in the old days with the miners' unions, but unfortunately that takes time. The president of the miners' union in the sixties was one of ours, you know.' In the midst of the man's affability and irrepressible good humour, Alex caught a glimpse of a cold and planetary mind. He understood that Buckley saw his department as the engine of the ship of state, running smoothly under his stewardship, below decks and out of sight. As far as he was concerned, governments could come and go, and he resented any interference from what he regarded as an ever-changing passenger list of parliamentarians. Buckley's food arrived.

'Do you want wine?' Buckley asked. 'I think I'm going to stick with my beer.' He flicked his napkin open, put it on his lap and looked down at his plate.

'Damn it. I thought it said steak and kidney pudding on the

blackboard. I've got steak and kidney pie. I prefer the pudding. It absorbs the gravy better. Makes it nice and soggy. The pastry seems just to repel the gravy and get unpleasantly wet.' He pulled a childish face of despair and looked over to where the bar staff busied themselves behind the counter. He decided against complaining and tucked into his food.

'Mind you, parliament has been on our side recently – for once. Given us the new terrorism laws and so on.'

Alex tried stepping up on to the moral high ground.

'Why do you people always want more powers?'

'Oh, nothing sinister. It just makes life easier. Makes people happier. Governments are supposed to aim for the happiness of the common man aren't they?' He looked around the pub. 'My god this music is awful. What is it?'

'Abba. Doesn't it make us slide nearer to being a police state?'

'Oh that's a bit melodramatic. What we do affects very few people directly but it lets things run smoothly. It's the Jeremy Bentham idea – a society constructed on the model of a prison. The perfect prison is structured so that people believe they are being watched at all times.' Buckley paused and toyed with his fork before continuing. 'To maintain order in a liberal society the population needs to believe that any person could be under surveillance at any time, subject to ID checks, DNA databases and so on. People internalise this and police themselves. Look at the way people slow down when they see speed cameras. I'm all for a quiet life although I suppose it could all lead to a police state.'

'I thought you were a cheery optimist. You're confusing me.' Alex laughed. Buckley smiled back at him.

'Confusion is not a bad thing. It's not doubt that makes a man mad. It's certainty.'

As he spoke there was a clattering crash and conversation in the pub came to a halt as everyone looked towards the flustered and red-faced waitress who had dropped her tray. Buckley turned back to Alex.

'So – enough of the world of spooks. Tell me what you and Vera have been up to. Give me some news from the world of glamour.'

'Vera is about to start work on a new play by someone called Victor Skynnard. A political pal of hers.' Alex had another stab at gaining information. 'You don't seriously think there's still any interest in Hector Rossi or any of his pals do you? If there is I might think of doing an interview with him – comparing today's terrorism with his or something. Would there be any warrants or anything still outstanding on any of them?'

'Shouldn't think so. Special Branch deals with all that. We don't get our hands dirty.' He glanced at the clock behind the bar. 'I must be going. I want to catch the next train from Ashford if it hasn't been cancelled.' He groaned and put down his napkin. 'Tragedy lies in the fact that we are not entirely masters of our own destiny. It's the transport system that will probably do us all in in the end rather than fundamentalist Islam.'

Alex stood up. 'I'll get this.'

'Thanks. They keep on at us these days about our expenses.'

'Are you going back to the office?'

'No. As a matter of fact I have a meeting at MI6.'

'I always think of their building as the "Graham Greene building". It looks like a secret service hangout.'

Buckley gave a humorous snort:

'Most people say that those tinted green windows look like a tart's sunglasses.'

Alex watched the silver Saab scrunch its way over the gravel out of the car park and on to the road. As he walked over to his own car he felt an unexpected twinge of envy at Hector Rossi's history. Hector had fought for something he believed in. Hector had been tested in a way which felt more admirable than his own journalism. He only ever watched and commented from the sidelines without putting himself at real risk. Buckley clearly knew about Hector's recent movements. They must be watching him. Alex got in his car and sat in the driving-seat for a while with the door open and one foot on the ground. He considered alerting Hector, then, in a spirit of meanness, decided against it.

When he reached home he found that Vera had already come back and gone out again.

*

'This is typical English countryside.'

Vera tried to appear calm. She had arranged to take her Uzbek guests for a drive through Kent but was so distracted by the news that Mark was back in England that she was hardly aware of where she was going and became lost down some minor roads near Lympne. She pulled up in woodland and the Uzbeks piled out of the four-wheel-drive looking disgruntled. Vera climbed down from the driver's seat.

'I was brought up in this part of England. The great English actress Ellen Terry used to have a house nearby. I'll take you there.'

Vera swept her hair back and pinned up some stray ends, looking round to try and ascertain where she was. The woodland next to the road was fenced off. Her brown and white Borzoi dog pranced behind her. It was a skinny dog and behaved nervously as it bounced towards the high metal fence and away again. Despite her radical politics she had bought the animal through sentimentality because of the Borzoi's association with the old Russian aristocracy. Like them it turned out to be highly strung, impossible to train and a terrible scavenger. She called it back as it tried to eat the unpleasant remains of something in a ditch.

Vera was unaware that the wire-fenced border marked the end of a wildlife safari park. Just then a rhinoceros thundered past on the other side of the fencing. Short-sighted Vera peered in the direction of the fence and mistook the creature for a horse. She let out a light nostalgic laugh and turned to the Uzbeks.

'I spent half my childhood riding those.'

The Uzbeks looked confused.

'Come with me. There should be a wonderful view of the county from the top of this hill. Kent is known as the garden of England, you know.'

Vera beckoned them to follow her further up the road and climbed over a stile leading them along an upward-sloping footpath. She tried to concentrate on her visitors and ignore the anxiety in the pit of her stomach.

The previous day she had sat drinking coffee in her sitting-room and asking the Uzbeks about the hardships endured by her fellow artists over there. She had been reading about conditions in a newspaper: there was the violinist who fell off his chair in the overture because he had not eaten for days; the actor suffering from paratyphoid who froze to death in his dressing room; the stage manager shot in the wings by the secret police; the pianist who had to stop because her fingers had frozen rigid during the concerto; the dresser in the costume department who died because of vermin in the clothes. Vera's temperament was mercurial. When her heart was touched she responded immediately with great generosity. Without hesitation, on this occasion, Vera got up, went to her desk drawer and wrote an enormous cheque which she handed to the leader of the group.

But now, with the wind blowing in her hair, she was preoccupied with thoughts of her son and wanted to be rid of the Uzbeks. Half-way along the public footpath and before they had come to the view she suddenly snapped: 'Well, I think we've seen enough countryside. Let's go back now.' They all trailed back along the muddy pathway. 'Another day I'll take you to see Ellen Terry's cottage.'

The wild-eyed Borzoi was rolling ecstatically on the ground. His long hair was caked with mud as he scrambled into the driving-seat ahead of her.

'You're filthy. Get out!' she screamed and pushed the dog into the back with the Uzbeks.

As she walked up the front path to the house, with the Uzbeks traipsing behind her and the dog skulking alongside, she stopped to finger some of the dog roses in the hedge. A press photographer who had been waiting at the gate took a series of photographs.

'I long to be an ordinary woman,' she sighed. 'But throughout my life it seems to have been impossible.'

Chapter Six

Hector was at home in the kitchen when he answered the call on his mobile. He did not immediately recognise the caller's voice, but as soon as the caller identified himself Hector walked quickly out of the kitchen hoping that Barbara would not overhear him. His heart beat a little faster. After arranging to meet he switched off his mobile.

'But you said you'd take Dawn to the doctor.' Barbara stood up from bending over the washing machine. She looked exasperated. Hector had forgotten. He looked up at the kitchen clock. There was just time to do both.

'I'll bring her back by half past ten,' he said. 'Oh and I've got to go into work for a couple of hours at some point this morning. I'll do the weekend shopping before I come back.'

*

It had been over two hours since the phone call. Mark Scobie had asked him to find somewhere safe to stay. Hector drove along the road to Dungeness and parked the car by the Costcutter shop in Littlestone. From there he walked along until he came to a row of holiday-let homes. A narrow tarmac road separated the houses from the pebble beach. There was something desolate about the white-painted guest-houses which were all empty at this time of year. A long row of them in a muddle of different architectural styles stood on one side of the road facing the sea. Opposite them on the beach huddled a cluster of bleak beach huts. Two old fishing boats leaned sideways on metal winching tracks that led down to the sea.

Hector stopped next to the endmost house. There was a paved patio in front of the house surrounded by a low concrete wall. The white-painted concrete felt damp. He walked down the front path and peered through the window. It looked empty. He went round to the back. Quickly, the old squatter's skills came back to him. The lock on the back door was brittle with age and gave easily with a push. 'Christ. I'm middle-aged. What am I doing?' He thought of Barbara at home tending to Dawn and giving her tea with a piece of Battenburg cake.

The damp chill of the empty house engulfed him. There were patches of moisture on the tiled kitchen floor. He walked through to the front to the sound of his own footsteps. Behind the glass-panelled porch stood two mildewed armchairs with wet patches visible on the red upholstery. A blustery wind outside rattled the window frames, so that despite the chill it felt strangely safe and sheltered inside. This place would have to do. He walked back down to Costcutters and waited.

At exactly eleven o'clock he saw a motorbike approaching in the distance from the direction of Dungeness. Hector felt a prickle moving up from the back of his neck behind his left ear to the top of his head, as if an insect were walking along the inside of his skull. The rider dismounted, parked the bike at the roadside and came over. He lifted the visor of his crash helmet. Hector barely recognised him. The heart-shaped face had lost its clear definition and grown puffier and coarser, although those black-framed glasses were the same. The two men held each other in an awkward embrace. A look of exhaustion passed over Mark's face and his shoulders sagged for a moment.

'Have you found somewhere?'

Hector felt suddenly protective towards his old comrade. He looked across at the row of empty holiday houses.

'I'd like you to stay with us but my wife is desperate to leave that part of our life behind. I daren't risk it. I've had a look in one of these houses. Most of them are empty this time of year. It's not The Ritz but I hope it will do.'

'Great stuff.'

'I can bring you bedding later. A sleeping bag or something.'

The two men walked around the house inspecting the facilities. Mark tried to switch on a fan heater. The electricity was still on. Upstairs the beds had mattresses but no other bedding. After a while, when they came down again, the small front room felt warmer.

'Why did you risk coming back?'

Mark looked at Hector with weary resignation.

'My best friend Sam Jones has just been arrested in Australia. We worked together for ten years in the touring theatre group I founded. At one point he left to spend time in Afghanistan. His wife is Afghani. He joined Islam. You might have seen his picture in the papers – a bluff-looking Welshman with a beard. Good bloke. You'd like him. Last month he was charged with conspiracy to cause explosions at the American embassy. I had to leave.'

'Is there still a warrant out for you here? By the time I was released you'd disappeared. Your mother never gave anything away. She just said "Australia". I don't think she wanted me to be in touch.'

'I'm not sure about any warrant. The others have all been out for some time now, haven't they? Do you see any of them?'

'No. I've pretty well lost touch.'

Mark looked through the window and scanned the road outside where his motorbike was parked. Two large suitcases were strapped onto the passenger seat. Beyond the road the wind whipped the grey wave-tops into white froth.

'I'd better bring my bags in. And the bike. It feels very strange to be back. For the time being I don't want to be seen with my mother. She's too well known. There's press around her.'

Hector decided to challenge him on the question that had haunted him for thirty years or more: 'Did you know anything about the Agnelli murder?'

'No. Absolutely not.' Mark spoke with quiet certainty.

Hector relaxed in the presence of Mark's calm. It was the same soft voice and steadfast unflappability that used to reassure him in Italy, although he sensed a new harshness in him. They went into the kitchen. Mark picked up a kettle and examined it. It was furred and needed descaling. He shook the contents out into the sink and turned on the tap. The cold water rattled the metal sink.

'Well, guess who I've just seen,' Mark grinned. 'Victor Skynnard. Do you remember him? The quickest way I could make contact with my mother when I arrived was through Victor Skynnard.'

'Oh my god. Victor Skynnard.' Hector began to laugh. 'The only man in the history of the counter-culture who mimed taking drugs. Well, oddly enough, I saw Khaled again the other day. Everyone's turning up at the same time.'

'Is Khaled over here? That's interesting. I know some people here who'd like to meet him.'

'Does your mother know you're in England?'

'Yes. I'm meeting her later. She was shocked. She'll have had time to calm down by the time we meet. Thanks for all this, mate. Much appreciated.' He turned to look appraisingly at Hector. 'Do you still feel the same about things?'

'Khaled asked me that.' Hector smiled. 'I do but the world has changed. Definitely not a revolutionary situation any more. Not even suitable for propaganda of the deed. We did our bit. Capitalism won.'

Mark stared out of the window. 'Oh I don't know. Maybe it just needs one more big shove. Look how it's collapsing worldwide. But true, the baton's been handed on to a different generation. A different set of people. The swing doors of the world's jails let some out as they let others in. Our lot are coming out now and the Muslims are going in.'

'They're not anti-capitalist.'

'Some are. More than you might think.'

Hector looked at his watch.

'Listen. Will you be all right here for a bit? I have to go into work for a couple of hours and then pick up some shopping. I have a child, a little girl with Down's syndrome. We have to organise things around her needs. I'll come back later tonight with a sleeping bag and food and stuff. I'll whistle at the back and knock twice. Be careful about putting the lights on. People might notice. These houses are usually empty at this time of year. And don't phone me at home. My wife will get suspicious. Text me if you need anything.'

'Sleeping bag would be great,' Mark smiled. 'I'm used to roughing it in Australia. I don't expect I'll have to do all this for long. But better safe than sorry. Do you know this guy Alex Hamilton who is my mother's partner? I presume he's OK.'

'He's fine. On our side I think. I've met him a couple of times.'

Mark checked his motorbike from the window. 'By the way, do you know anyone who can do passports these days?'

'I might do. Don't know if the guy still does them. But I know a fisherman working out of Dungeness who could take you across the Channel for the right price.'

'Good. Might need someone like that.'

Mark went and fetched his bags. Hector left him manoeuvring the burly motorbike through the back door so that it was safely hidden in the hall.

*

Hector whistled as he drove his old Renault back to Hythe. He felt buoyant. It had been an ordinary Saturday morning and then life had opened up in this unexpected direction. Seeing Mark again and breaking into the house had brought back that old sense of adventure, of having his mettle tested. It produced in him an excitement and flamboyant daring as if he were part of the hunt or the chase again. He picked up some shopping and headed for the printers.

That morning Hector had arranged to go into work and tackle the backlog of student PhD theses that needed binding. The only other person present in the open-plan workspace was the plump receptionist. After making himself coffee he stood at the long table under the neon strip lighting and started cutting and gluing pages.

The doorbell jangled. An elegant woman in her fifties wearing a lime green dress walked in and went over to the reception desk. She had wide, slanting sloe-black eyes and sleek black hair pulled up into a French knot. A spike of hair stuck out at the top like an Indian feather. She asked to look through a folder of various type settings for funeral programmes. Hector was struck by the particular grace of her hand movements as she flicked through the brochure.

'What date do you need the funeral notices by?' asked the receptionist.

The woman threw the receptionist an embarrassed look. Her expression was both amused and shamefaced.

'Actually, my mother is not dead yet. But the doctor has warned us she is dying. I was passing your print shop and I thought I'd check whether you did funeral programmes. It's a bit premature.'

Hector stopped work. The woman looked directly at him. Her face lit up suddenly with a smile. His heart lifted and he smiled back. Something shifted in his solar plexus. Hector watched her make her way down the high street. There was a confidence in her walk; a physicality that reminded him of a different century and a different continent. He wanted to run after her but she was already out of sight. Back at his workbench he opened the PhD thesis he was binding. On the front page was typed a quotation from Neruda: 'I want to do with you what spring does with the cherry trees.'

Ten minutes later he abandoned work. Instead of going straight home he followed the route she had taken down the high street, but there was no sign of the woman.

*

When he arrived home Barbara was hanging out washing in the garden. Hector stood sipping a cup of tea. He was aware that an element of chance had entered his life and that things were reconfiguring in ways that he could not entirely grasp.

Chapter Seven

It was evening when Hector returned to the house on the Littlestone coastal road. He grew uneasy at the sight of a dim light visible through cracks in the downstairs shutters. The other houses on that stretch of road were in complete darkness. He went round to the back with the sleeping bag under his arm and gave the arranged whistle and knock. After a few minutes Mark opened the door. Without the bulky armoury of his leather biking gear Mark had the familiarity of the figure he remembered from his youth.

'You can see some light from outside,' warned Hector as he followed Mark into the front room.

The light came from the gas fire which was hissing in the chimney breast and from the table lamp next to an armchair. The shock of seeing other people seated there made Hector's heart leap for a moment but he managed to conceal his surprise. There were two men seated in armchairs. They got up when Hector entered. Mark introduced them:

'This is Shahid.' A short young man of Asian descent with a beard and long girlish hair that almost formed ringlets proffered a hesitant hand.

'And this is Massoud,' said Mark turning to the second man, a robust genial man of about forty with a grizzled beard and great warmth in his smile. They all sat down, except Hector who remained standing.

'What is going on?' Hector looked from one person to another.

'Do you remember me mentioning a Sam Jones in Australia who converted to Islam and who was arrested in Perth?' Mark leaned forward in his chair. 'Well these are good friends of his who want news of him. That's all. I'll go and make us some tea.'

Mark got up and went out into the kitchen. The gas fire hissed continuously. The shadows of the three men were thrown large against the walls. Hector listened uneasily. His attitude hardened into distrust as he looked from one man to the other:

'I'm afraid I'm a convinced atheist myself.'

Shahid tossed his long black hair back over his shoulders and laughed. There was a light in his dark eyes as he jabbed his finger towards Hector.

'It's possible to be a believer and a revolutionary, you know. You should check out the website. Nida'ul Islam. It's Australian. Sam Jones helped us set it up.'

Hector looked sceptical. Shahid's elated high giggle annoyed him. Shahid continued:

'Mark told us you were a reliable comrade of his. Islam is not just a religion. It's a political ideology similar to yours. Look. Communism didn't work. Capitalism doesn't work. The only solution left is Islam.' He laughed again and his eyes widened. 'We're jumping into the void left by the Soviet Union. You wait and see. It will be the sword of Islam that slashes the bellies of the fat. It's an amazing feeling when you understand that – when the walls of everyday life fall down and there is exposed in front of you a sort of uplifting glory – a massive feeling that you yourself can stream out into eternity and join with Allah.'

Massoud gave Hector a sympathetic look and remonstrated with Shahid. He spoke with an even stronger Lancashire accent than Shahid's.

'Don't bend the poor man's ears like that. He just came for a cup of tea and to bring his friend a sleeping bag.'

But Shahid's eyes were gleaming in the light from the gas fire. He leaned forward in his chair, his long hair streaming down in front of his shoulders. He waved his arms around in the air.

'No. No. Shut up, Massoud. Let me go on and explain to him. Everything falls away from around you. All materialism, even anything to do with your family. It is you and Allah alone in clouds of glory. Did you see that young Muslim sentenced to death for the Bali bombing? On television I watched him. He was radiant as the judge read out the sentence of execution. Euphoric. He turned and gave a thumbs-up to the public assembled behind him. He was longing for death, for martyrdom. Fearless. Ecstatic. As I watched him I saw the bricks of the judicial court around him crumble in the face of his belief. The court of God was smiling on him. The power of those earthly judges completely evaporated. They executed him. So what?' Shahid gave a shrill laugh of delight and jumped up. 'All man-made institutions shrivelled and withered at that moment, brother.' He snapped his fingers in a derisory gesture. 'He is in heaven. That martyr has transcended it all. There is nothing anyone can do against the power of such beliefs. It is unconquerable. When your life means nothing compared with the ... glory of Allah. Then it is easy to throw your life away. Look at what happened in Mumbai.' Then Shahid added slyly, 'I believe you've done the same sort of thing in your time.'

Hector was taken aback and angry that Mark had landed him in this situation. He was about to protest that his actions hadn't resulted in indiscriminate slaughter when Shahid changed his tone to become more conciliatory.

'Look. I'm sure you once had these same feelings. What you only dreamed of we made happen. The attack on Wall Street? Our actions need to be spectacular, designed for the media age.'

'Wall Street didn't collapse because of the attack on the Twin Towers. As far as I know it collapsed under the weight of its own corruption.' Hector could hear the tone of priggish disapproval in his voice.

Mark came back in with mugs of tea on a tray and handed them out.

'If you had to choose between Islam and capitalism then which would it be?' Massoud turned to Hector with a broad smile as he stirred his tea.

'Neither. I would choose some form of libertarian and democratic communism.'

'That's so last century,' said Shahid. 'That's so over.'

Hector was stung.

'For argument's sake let's say you have to choose one or the other. Islam or capitalism,' Massoud pressed him. Out of a sort of perverseness and to his surprise Hector heard himself saying, 'I'd choose capitalism. Almighty power is always barbaric. No exceptions. Execrable. God's the worst. A total totalitarian.'

Shahid lowered his eyes to hide the scorn in them. He shrugged his shoulders.

'They say all people become conservative as they get older.'

Hector suppressed a rush of fury. He had no wish to become embroiled in an all-night argument. He finished his cup of tea and stood up.

'Mark I have to go. I want to see my daughter before she goes to bed. I'll come over and see you tomorrow.' He turned to the others. 'Sorry about this everyone but I must go. Good to meet you all.' Hector raised a hand in farewell. The others remained seated and raised their hands in response.

Hector drove as far as Dymchurch before he pulled into the side of the road trembling with rage. He got out of the car and crossed the road to climb some steps and stand on the high concrete sea wall. To his annoyance he recognised in Shahid something of his younger self: the fervour, the exultant righteousness, the willingness to sacrifice, the ardour of shared beliefs, the millenarian glint in the eye, that last push to utopia. To his left he could see the lights of Hythe further along the coast. There was a warm rain-bearing wind in his face. In front of him the sea was an enormous blackness which marked its presence now and then with a shushing sound. He realised how much he missed the great transforming idea – the intoxicating idea that explains the whole world – that touch of the gods. Enthusiasm. *En theos* – the god within. Hector's head was spinning. He walked back to the car and drove home.

At home Dawn was still up and in her pyjamas. She was laying out her school photographs on the dining room table. She pointed one out to Hector.

'Mum doesn't like that one.' Her tongue lolled as she talked.

'How do you know?'

'She said she was going to get it blown up.'

Hector laughed. 'Do you want me to carry you upstairs to bed or are you too big for that now?'

'Carry me.'

He felt her warm face resting on his neck. She smelled of soap and milk. He took the hairclip out of her hair and put it on the bedside table before putting her into the bed and pulling the duvet printed with pink panthers over her, tucking it in at the sides.

After she was asleep he phoned Khaled on impulse to tell him what had happened.

Khaled was laughing.

'Leave them alone. Don't have anything to do with them. They're crazy. Especially don't try and argue with them. You'll never win. Like Jehovah's Witnesses, they never give up. What makes people turn to religion? At least we were secular. By the way, do you know where I am?'

'No.'

'I'm in Notting Hill in my ex-stepfather Eddie Sursok's house. He invited me to stay the night which was surprising as I hadn't seen him for years and he seems to be a recluse now. Anyway, tomorrow I'm going north to try and track down my half-brother. Go to bed, Hector. Forget the crazies and try to get a good night's sleep.'

Chapter Eight

Khaled had been accurate in his judgement of Eddie Sursok as a recluse. Sursok was a heavy, brooding man with a laid-back walk and black eyebrows like two brush-flicks of Chinese calligraphy; a slow-moving titan who dealt in excess; a melancholy despot who wore a trademark loose shirt that almost reached his knees and which billowed slightly as he walked. When Khaled was shown into the spacious kitchen area in the basement of the house Sursok was sitting in a large wicker chair wearing a silk dressing-gown and paisley socks, gazing over his stomach at the wood-burning stove. He nodded towards Khaled and beckoned him to sit down. Nothing was said. The wood crackled in the flames. The room was pleasantly warm. Sursok was adream and remote. After a while he asked Khaled how his mother was and then lapsed back into silence. Khaled refrained, out of politeness, from enquiring whether the turmoil in international banking had affected Sursok's private finances. Eventually, Sursok got up, pointed out where Khaled would be sleeping and padded away over the stone flags to disappear into some other part of the house. Khaled made his way to the bedroom. He found the house oppressive. The floors had been gutted leaving an enormous well in the centre of high brick walls. High in one wall was a solitary window. In the dim light Khaled felt his way along the iron gallery and up some metal steps to his room. He drifted into a restless sleep.

Sursok's nickname was Midas. The financial deal that clinched his fortune was the sale of his family bank in Syria to HCB. Having worked behind the closed doors of the world's most powerful banks he finally moved from Lazard's investment bank to an arm of the Dutch HCB bank in London. He was made one of its vice-presidents and used his investment to become HCB's largest private shareholder.

For several months Sursok had been suffering from insomnia. The sleeplessness was not related to finance. It was stoked by the fear that he was not revered enough by everybody. Sitting on the edge of his bed that night Sursok stared ahead in the unyielding grip of envy. The man stalking his thoughts was a banking colleague on the executive board of HCB called Johannes Caspers.

Sursok's growing obsession with Caspers was provoked by an odd rivalry. Eddie Sursok hosted parties. He did not attend them himself. This was no surprise to people who had known him from his youth. As a young man he used to pay for orgies in which he did not take part. To control them was enough. These days his parties were for private clients and for corporations. They were competitive celebrity events judged by the wattage of wealth in attendance. Over the years, Sursok's parties had become the object of much speculation in the press. How much did he spend? Which tycoons and magnates attended? The events received double-page spreads in the *Tatler*, *Vogue* and *Harpers and Queen*.

A year earlier Sursok had entered into light-hearted competition with one of the Russian oligarchs. The oligarch entertained his guests with a huge retro Soviet-style party. A version of the Red Army Choir sang and Soviet-style guards strolled up and down with white wolves on leashes. Sursok retaliated by hiring Salton Heath for the weekend, a vast tank-training ground scarred with caterpillar tracks. His party organisers recreated the Kosovo war zone with camouflage and flak jackets as requirements for the guests. Helicopter trips over the area were arranged. Tanks were provided which, depending on the outcome of the games, could eventually be blown up. Party-goers all agreed that there was something unbelievably sexy about the combination of mud, camouflage gear and exhausted officers reviewing battle tactics in the military tents provided. Sursok was gratified to have been considered the winner in this competition.

This year, however, Sursok's event organisers had made a spectacular bungle of everything and he felt humiliated. They had hired a specially adapted twenty-thousand-square-foot warehouse in Rotherhithe. But the theme of the party was a mish-mash of circus, geisha girls and *fin de siècle* Paris. Besides which the media, in the light of the credit crunch, had turned against these displays of conspicuous consumption. The press response had been scathing. The tabloids ran headlines like '*Sir-Put-A-Sock-In-It Eddie*' and '*Sur-plus Moneybags Party from Hell*'. The broadsheets and glossy magazines were equally dismissive.

Johannes Caspers, his colleague on the executive board of HCB, was also famous for hosting parties. His gatherings attracted the intelligentsia. Caspers was a warm-hearted benefactor to Nobel laureates, musicians and painters of international standing. Opera and ballet were his great passions. In the programmes of the Royal Opera House he was frequently acknowledged and thanked for his patronage.

Eddie Sursok pulled out the notices sent to him by his clippings service and laid them out on the bedside table next to him. His party had been a fiasco. The black hairs on the back of his hands stood up as he read the coverage. The word 'vulgar' cropped up more than once. The word 'philistine' particularly stuck in his craw, giving him a physical feeling of choking. Quite by chance the event shared pages with glowing references to Johnny Caspers, who had organised bank sponsorship for a new and much-praised production of *Così Fan Tutte* at Covent Garden. Comparisons were made between the two men. Caspers was referred to as a man of culture and intellect. The sight of Caspers' picture smiling up at him from the newspaper snagged at Sursok's heart. He tried to push his feelings of anger down. For Sursok it was the live burial of jealousy. Resentment glowed inside him like the embers of a fire.

He went to bed and lay there awake. The next morning was Sunday. By ten o'clock Khaled had left. Sursok was still in bed. For months he had been brooding on how to reclaim his reputation. That evening was to see the first of his attempts to match Caspers in terms of intellect and culture. It was an area new to Sursok. He had donated a room to the British Library. There was to be a dinner there in his honour. He would make one of his few public appearances.

Chapter Nine

That same Sunday morning Johannes Caspers was at home in Chiswick working on the guest list for one of his country weekends. His son Felix lounged on the sofa. The sun caught the highlights in Felix's blond hair as he flicked through *GQ* magazine. Caspers glanced over at him. These days there was a persistent tension between father and son. Caspers tried not to let his disappointment with Felix's choice of career show too much but the truth was that it puzzled and depressed him. Felix had refused to go to university and instead had become a pilot, which seemed to Caspers a second-rate profession unworthy of his son's talents. As an adolescent he had seemed so full of promise.

As he looked at his son's fresh, slightly spoiled face, Caspers remembered the particular summer at their country home in Wiltshire when things had started to go wrong. Felix's mother Lillian was serving wine to some guests near their small outdoor swimming pool. Felix was about fourteen. He had gone for a swim. He came out of the pool with tendrils of his fair hair darkened by the water and sticking to his forehead and neck. One of the guests leaning forward to help Felix out of the pool was the architect Michael Feynite.

'Oh, your hand is all cold and wet,' Feynite laughed as he took the boy's hand. Felix's white skin glistened with drops of water and beneath his ribcage the dip of his stomach was pulsating. Caspers could remember the look of admiration on Feynite's face.

'Look at that skinny torso.' Lillian Caspers was standing on the grass smiling as she placed her hands on either side of her son's wet ribs.

'You look like the poet Shelley,' commented Feynite.

Felix was tall for his age and slender. How could the boy be so slim? It gave him an ethereal quality. If he was a girl there might have been worries about anorexia. Felix was almost too perfect. He seemed like an affront to the gods.

That Friday evening at dinner Felix looked particularly charming with his dark blue prayer hat jammed over his fair curls. Opposite Felix sat Michael Feynite, someone Caspers had known from the years when Feynite was the youthful lover of a famous ballet critic.

Feynite leaned across the table and tried to engage Felix in conversation. Caspers could remember the whole exchange.

'What are you going to do when you leave school?'

'I don't know yet. I might go and work in Surinam for my gap year before university. Dad still has family there.' The Caspers family originated from the long-established Jewish community in Surinam.

'Ah yes, of course, the Third World,' said Feynite, with a hint of scorn. 'The finishing school for the British middle classes.'

Felix had looked at Feynite with puzzled curiosity for a moment then turned away a little uncertainly. A young man with tight wavy hair and a sly smile had joined the party. He was a university student and sat next to Felix impressing him with stories of his Oxford escapades. The two of them began to grow boisterous and noisy as they exchanged anecdotes about yobbos and chavs and losers and the poor in general.

Michael Feynite was now quite drunk on Polish vodka. He faced Felix.

'I see your private school is raising you to be a snob.'

Felix flushed and defended himself then turned back to his friend. The dinner party had reached the stage, during dessert, when it generated a steady warmth like a banked down fire.

'Would you all like to come into the music room?' Johnny Caspers stood up smiling after coffee had been served. 'Felix has promised to sing for us before we are entertained by the professionals.'

The song was called 'The Lightning Tree'. Felix did not seem at all shy. He sang with passion and vehemence in a tuneful voice that was piercing and frail as crystal:

> In the middle of a field stands a lightning tree
> Its limbs all torn from the day it was born
> For the tree was born in a thunderstorm.
> Grow grow the lightning tree
> It's never too late for you and me.

The guests smiled and applauded Felix who went over and sprawled on the sofa with his head against his mother's arm. Then everyone settled down to listen to two members of the Royal Opera Company sing the duet from *The Pearl Fishers*.

At the end of the evening they had all gone back inside after saying goodbye to their guests. Felix could hardly wait till his parents had shut the front door behind them. The boy stood in the spacious hall its walls covered with family photographs, portraits and paintings. Before they had time to switch the hall lights off and go into the front room, he turned to them, an extraordinary livid pallor on his face and his lip trembling:

'You've brought me up to be a snob,' he said with an anguish his parents could distinguish even in the dim light of the hall. 'You sent me to a school that would ensure I became a snob.'

Lillian tried to put her hand on his shoulder. He shook it off. 'But darling we are just trying to give you the best education.'

'No. Everything you do and say is snobbish. That man Feynite was right. You're always on about the right kind of people.'

His parents were taken aback. Their son was staring at them, his eyes darting from one to the other as if two dangerous strangers had walked through the front door. Later that night they heard him sobbing in his room. His mother tried to go in but he had locked the door.

'Oh go away. Get away from me.' His voice sounded high and childish.

It was from that night on that Caspers' relationship with his son had started to deteriorate.

Felix began to spend time with Michael Feynite, the very man who had accused him of snobbery. Feynite introduced him to a drag-act pub on the Isle of Dogs and Felix was enchanted with the risqué, illicit excitement of it all. Feynite also introduced him to some gay activists who lived over a radical bookshop in Camden.

Before long Caspers noticed that his son was beginning to get a certain look in his eyes: a clean, morning-fresh look; the look of someone who is beginning to believe in something. He was disturbed that Felix was disappearing for whole weekends attending loved-up raves, but other parents of teenagers reassured him that this was par for the course.

*

One night when his parents were at the opera Felix went upstairs and put on a white towelling dressing-gown. He went into the bathroom. The cleaner had been. It was spotless. There was a shiny green sink with tiny bars of soap, thick green hand towels hanging on the rail and a thick green spongy carpet underfoot. Upstairs, each of the bedrooms had the same décor: floor-length floral curtains with a ruched pelmet and matching floral coverlets on the beds. It all felt sound-proofed. He felt that even if he screamed the sound would not be able to penetrate the weight of the silence.

He sat at his mother's dressing-table and applied water-based white make-up all over his face. He made his eyes the shape of almond kernels, outlining them with black eye-liner. Then came the lipstick and the brilliant red rosebud mouth and an eye-mask of red blusher powder that he applied with a soft brush. He leaned back from the mirror. The trick was to keep his face tilted downwards to conceal the Adam's apple. There was a special cream he had heard about that helped with any five o'clock shadow but he did not need that yet. As soon as the make-up was complete he experienced a calm elation.

He realised that he should have put the make-up on after he dressed so as not to soil the dress. The scarlet silk evening gown belonged to his mother. He held it up to examine the huge loose sleeves. That day he had taken five-foot lengths of black hair from the school drama cupboard. The extensions were fastened to a small black cap with stripes of fake hand-sewn pearls which had been used by the boy playing Juliet in the school play. He pinned the hairpiece on and flirted with his reflection. A geisha shot back a knowing look from the mirror which gave him the uplifting sensation of a cocaine high. He stood up and thrust out his pert butt. For a while he remained posed like that with his head at a slight tilt, his finger held to his chin.

He muttered some words that he vaguely remembered hearing a rabbi recite once:

I am the rose of Sharon and the lily of the valleys.
As the lily among thorns so is my love among the daughters.

He did not know how long he had been standing there. In a sudden panic lest his parents return, he ran to the bathroom and slapped onto his face the greasy cleansing cream from a Max Factor jar also borrowed from the school drama department. He scrubbed his face clean with cotton wool. By the time his parents returned Felix was back in his jeans, sprawled in front of the television, eating potted shrimps and watching Holby City.

Later there was a terrible row at the Caspers' house, when Felix refused point-blank to go to university. His father was appalled, but Felix insisted he wanted to do something practical and useful. He enrolled with British Airways to train as a pilot. As Caspers looked over at his son, now absorbed in his magazine, he wondered how Felix, with his sharp angelic features and delicate body, could be responsible for piloting the huge weight of an aircraft from continent to continent.

*

The phone rang and Johnny answered it. It was Stephen Butterfield, one of his banking colleagues on the executive branch of HCB.

Butterfield was at Heathrow airport and wanted to come and see him straight away.

Unexpected calls from banking colleagues on a Sunday had become more frequent since the downturn of the global economy. Twenty minutes later Johnny answered the ring at the door to find Stephen Butterfield standing on the doorstep dressed in a black pin-stripe suit and tie and carrying a briefcase which contained his laptop. Caspers was surprised to see that he carried with him a tightly furled four-foot-long scarlet umbrella that was completely out of character and made him look a little mad. A small suitcase on wheels stood at his side. Butterfield was out of breath and apologetic.

'I hope you don't mind my turning up unexpectedly like this. I've come straight from the airport.' Caspers stepped back, withdrawing instinctively from the terrible innocence that always seemed to be plastered over Butterfield's face.

'Not at all. Not at all.' He gestured for Butterfield to come in and placed a solicitous hand on his arm as he led the way into the living room. The room was furnished with enormous comfortable sofas upholstered in plain cream-coloured material. Stephen acknowledged Felix with a nod and a smile and sank into one of them. Felix regarded him with barely concealed distaste. Caspers went over to the decanters on the dresser.

'Can I get you a drink?'

'Oh ... er ... thank you, Johnny,' said Butterfield gratefully in his mild voice. 'A whisky would be very nice.' He leaned forward, hands clasped in front of him, his thick neck bunching up at the back over his stiff white collar.

As Caspers poured the drink he glanced with concern at his colleague. Apart from the turmoil in the banking industry it was only six weeks since the brutally sudden death of Stephen's wife in a boating accident. Caspers had not seen him since the funeral, when the gentle, heavily-built man had wandered, stunned and bereft, amongst the mourners in the rain. His thin fair hair seemed to have become colourless overnight. Rain and tears were caught in his pale gingerish eyelashes and on his puffy cheeks as he nodded his head in acceptance of condolences.

Caspers guessed that this visit was triggered by loneliness or some sort of trouble at the bank. Butterfield was based in the main Amsterdam headquarters. He handed him a heavy tumbler of whisky.

'How is Amsterdam? I wanted to talk to you about the bid for Sarcele. It's been in our sights for some time. It could become a giant company on the NASDAQ. Bigger than Microsoft – but no-one wants to take risks at the moment. The other thing we need to talk about is the Sursok shipping deals. They could incur massive losses if not properly handled.'

Butterfield looked up:

'Oh. Could you help me have a look at Sursok's shipping deals? It's just that my ... er ... mind hasn't been quite on the ball lately.'

His bottom lip quivered and there was an oddly childish expression in the small blue eyes that was both pleading and full of wonder.

'I've fallen in love.'

Caspers tried to conceal his shock. Even Felix looked up with curiosity. Butterfield continued, blurting everything out in a rush, staring straight ahead:

'Don't misunderstand me. My marriage to Margaret was good. I suppose we had become complacent, but there was never any question of infidelity on either side. Little irritations, you know ... just the normal sort of thing.' He looked up at Johnny and paused before saying, 'I haven't had feelings like this ... for thirty years. It is like being reborn. She's an American ... Hetty, that is. And she's a September 11 survivor. She was on the ground floor of the second Twin Tower. She just got out in time.' A look of sympathetic awe came over his face.

Failing to find the right words for the situation Johnny turned his whisky glass in his hand and went to sit down on the sofa opposite. For the next half an hour, he listened to Butterfield's quiet outpourings of love; how he had met Hetty Moran by chance in the gym of the Grosvenor House Hotel; how they had immediately hit it off; how her vitality had made him feel alive again; how sympathetic she had been on hearing of the death of his wife; how he wrote lengthy emails to her almost every day.

Caspers regarded Butterfield gravely throughout all this. He stroked his beard to conceal his embarrassment.

'Well. This is a surprise. I really don't know what to say.'

'No ... no. Well. There's nothing to say really.' Stephen smiled at the ineffable workings of destiny. Then he looked at Johnny in an expectant way, as if seeking approval. Johnny responded:

'Look, that's ... mmn ... splendid. You must bring her to meet us some time. We're having a weekend party in Wiltshire in a couple of weeks to celebrate Arnold Thorpe's Nobel laureate. Why don't you come and bring her along? I'll make sure you are sent an invitation with the details.'

'Yes. Fine. Thank you. That would be lovely.' Stephen finished his drink and got up to leave. 'She's going to come to Amsterdam with me and I'm taking her to Paris for a weekend too.'

Half an hour after Stephen had gone Lillian Caspers returned home from a flurry of shopping and heard the news. She put her carrier bags down on the kitchen table and fastened a loose strand of hair behind her ear. Her brown eyes shone with indignation.

'How awful,' she said. 'How could he? So soon. How awful. Don't you think that's awful, Felix?'

Her son raised a supercilious eyebrow and yawned to demonstrate his indifference. He picked up his magazine and continued to read.

Chapter Ten

When the phone rang Victor was still in bed. It was his father-in-law Lord Pankton.

'I phoned because there's a banker chap called Eddie Sursok. He's funding a new wing of medieval literature at the British Library – just up your street. I mentioned that you were a specialist in the field in case anything might come up for you work-wise. There is a dinner in his honour at the library tomorrow. Would you like me to arrange for you to come along?'

Victor pretended to have flu. He mumbled his apologies from under the bedclothes.

'Never mind, old chap,' said Lord Pankton. 'I'll go along and put in a good word for you.'

The chairman of the British Library, Lord Dinwell, had been astonished but grateful to accept Eddie Sursok's offer of donating a specialist room to the library. Sursok had never before shown any interest in the intellectual life of the country. The board decided that the new 'Sursok' room should house a collection of rare medieval books and manuscripts. The dinner, with Sursok as guest of honour, had been arranged by the library to coincide with the exhibition of painted glass from ancient Antioch. It was a subtle reference to Sursok's Syrian-Palestinian background.

Guests were invited to stroll around the exhibition before being summoned up the flight of stairs to lunch. The meal was to take place on the upper level. Tables were laid within sight of the great glass-enclosed columns of the George III collection. Each table seated eight people and was laid with a fine linen tablecloth, silver cutlery, elegant glassware and magnificent sprays of white waxy flowers in silver jugs.

As Sursok mounted the escalator escorted by Lord Dinwell, he was unpleasantly surprised to see the jaunty square beard and gleaming brown hair of Johannes Caspers on the ground floor immediately below him. Caspers, drink in hand, was immersed in conversation with his son Felix. At that moment Felix Caspers looked up. There was something wild in his blue eyes. His blond hair was crinkly and his open lips were glistening and red. He nudged his father who also looked up and waved a hand at Sursok. It had not occurred to Eddie that Caspers might be invited or that Caspers himself might be a donor to the library. Sursok was even more unsettled to find that Caspers and his son were seated opposite him at the table.

Apart from the chairman, the other guests at Sursok's table included a property developer and his wife; the TV historian, windbag and chronic show-off, Robert Sharp; Lord Pankton, octogenarian philanthropist and Dr Mahjoub, an eagle-eyed Palestinian historian.

Sursok was seated next to Lord Pankton. The ageing peer had wads of hair, huge hanks of it like frayed hemp sprouting from his balding head. He had yellowing teeth and exuded a warm aura of rotten sentimental humanity.

The kind-hearted aristocrat took it for granted that Eddie Sursok was genuinely interested in rare medieval books. In fact, Eddie Sursok hardly ever read a book, either ancient or modern. Lord Pankton turned his beneficent gaze on him trying to find common ground:

'My son-in-law is a medieval scholar you know. Victor Skynnard. Have you heard of him?'

Sursok shook his head.

'No. No-one ever has.' Lord Pankton sighed. His bald dome radiated perplexity. 'He's a political radical so I still have to support him financially, of course. He's started writing plays these days.

He has a mentor – the actress Vera Scobie, another radical. She encourages his playwriting. All the same ...' His voice petered out and he shook his head and smiled benevolently at the antics of his son-in-law.

As soon as the other guests took their places at the table Robert Sharp the TV historian fell out with Dr Mahjoub the Palestinian historian. Sharp was unable to resist one or two pointed jabs at his rival. He held his head cockily to one side.

'I hear the way some Palestinians got rich was by selling villages to the Israelis.' His small mischievous eyes flickered between Dr Mahjoub and Sursok. Then, seeing Dr Mahjoub's furious reaction he patted him on the arm and said, 'Don't look like that. I'd have done it myself.'

One or two people glanced over at Sursok to see if he had heard the remarks but Sursok was leaning back in his chair seemingly relaxed and smiling at his host. Lord Dinwell rose to his feet from the snowy mountain range of crested napkins around him and tapped a spoon on his glass for silence:

'Before we eat, may I just say briefly that this dinner is in honour of Eddie Sursok. He has recently become one of our most generous benefactors. I wish to express my thanks on behalf of the British Library for his contribution to the intellectual life of the country. Will you please raise your glasses for a toast?'

Everyone except Eddie rose to their feet. Eddie remained seated. He wore his trademark collarless loose shirt which hung below his coal-black jacket. His complexion was dark yellow ochre. The shadow of a beard made his jaw look as if it were smeared with coal dust. He felt awkward at having all eyes fixed upon him. Public occasions did not suit him. However, he managed to acknowledge the compliments with an ungainly nod. He was not at all put out when Dr Mahjoub asked him: 'How is your son Khaled these days? I met him many years ago. Is he still working for the PLO and Fatah? Or has he progressed on to Hamas?'

Eddie smiled.

'Khaled is not my son. As it happens I saw him last night briefly.

I'm not sure what he is doing now. He is Hyppolita's son – my first wife. I don't see her. She's gone to ground somewhere in Surrey.'

Lord Pankton joined in the conversation, cocking his head sideways to give his good ear the advantage:

'Oh is your son a terrorist? What a coincidence. My son-in-law is a Trotskyist. Victor Skynnard. Do you know him at all? The actress Vera Scobie is a great pal of his. She's a radical too. She was kind enough to appear in one of his plays. A huge flop. Did you hear about it? Apparently it went down quite well in Germany. You see the Germans like all that high-minded abstract stuff. The Germans don't mind being bored. They think it is all part of the experience. The French don't mind being a bit bored. But the English can't stand it.'

The dinner party had loosened its stays. Guests chatted amiably amidst a debris of crumbs, candles, half empty wine glasses and rumpled napkins. Coffee was being brought around and served to those who had ordered it. Then, in all innocence, Johannes Caspers leaned forward across the table and dropped a small bomb in Eddie Sursok's lap:

'Tell me Eddie, I've always had an interest in etymology. Does the word Palestine come from the same root as Philistine? Would it be correct to refer to you as a Philistine?' He looked around the table laughing.

Few people noticed the extraordinary transformation that came over Eddie Sursok's face. Those dining across the table from him could see the tiny capillaries under his skin begin to fill with blood. At first the effect on those fine blood vessels was almost imperceptible but gradually, as the engorgement increased, patches of darker red began to show unevenly under his left eye and on his right cheek. Soon four or five patches on his face became suffused with darkness. He had pushed his chair back and was staring down at his lap. The lividity spread over his features, reached full strength and began to fade again.

At that moment Felix Caspers, who had been in a sulk until then because he had forgone an evening clubbing to accompany his father, noticed the silver jug of white blossoms decorating the table and drew his father's attention to them. Caspers leaned forward and touched a spray of the waxy flowers with genuine appreciation.

'How beautiful. White mariposa flowers aren't they? It's the national flower of Cuba. Stands for the purity of ideals, rebelliousness and independence.'

Johnny Caspers smiled.

'Poor old Cuba will be like Las Vegas before long.' He turned to the property developer at his side.

'Some beautiful property to be had in Havana when the time comes.'

Dr Mahjoub sipped his coffee and said with a touch of ice in his voice:

'Yes indeed. Poor Cuba. Waiting for the iron hand of American freedom to fall on it. Whenever Americans use the word freedom what they actually mean is capitalism. It is capitalism that Americans want to spread around the world not freedom. I'd rather be in jail for the rest of my life than infected with the American idea of liberty.'

The TV historian immediately disagreed in his petulant squawky voice:

'Oh pooh pooh. You're caught up in this hysterical hatred of America like everyone else. We live in the age of hysteria and exaggeration. Hysteria impregnates our lives. Soap-powder ads jostle next to warfare programmes so there's no difference in value. Everything is reduced to hysterical information to feed our hysteria. And you've fallen victim to it.'

The two men fell into a heated argument with the Palestinian historian's sharp pointed beard raised as if he was about to stab his opponent with it.

Eddie Sursok's attention was elsewhere. His chin was sunk in his chest and he was gazing ahead of him with the fixed stare of a child violinist. Eventually, he looked up and regarded Caspers with a sort of fascination. He hardly took in what was being said around him but he managed to smile and nod when guests thanked and congratulated him. People were getting to their feet. After a while

95

he rose, stumbling a little, and left with them to look downstairs for his driver.

As Sursok was driven away there was a disturbance outside the library. Felix Caspers had been taken violently ill and was vomiting into the kerb while his father tried to hail a taxi.

Chapter Eleven

On Sundays Barbara took Dawn with her to work. As soon as they left Hector drove over to Littlestone. Mark opened the back door, his hair still damp from the shower. Without his glasses the pale circle of skin around his eyes made him look owlish and vulnerable.

'Sorry. Come in. I've only just got up. We stayed up late talking after you left.'

They went into the front room. To Hector's relief there was no sign of the other men. The shutters were still drawn and the room smelled of stale smoke. Mark switched on the light. Hector confronted Mark straight away.

'What on earth are you doing with those people? I hate religious fundamentalism of any sort. I hate religion.'

Mark smoothed back his hair and smiled.

'Me too. But sometimes they attack the same things that I want to attack. You can make strategic alliances for particular targets. Look at the attacks on Mumbai. It was the hugely wealthy hotels and western bankers that were targeted. It was not dissimilar to what we targeted in the seventies. Do you want tea?'

They went into the kitchen. Hector persisted:

'Those people are nuts. What we did at least had its basis in popular support. It was some sort of search for justice or equality. Times are different now. It's not what people here want.'

'True. What people here want is to crawl through shopping malls like maggots through a dead sheep.'

'If shopping makes them happy, why not? You're out of touch.'

'I disagree. It is exactly the right time to have more attacks on the capitalist system. It's already rocking. A few more shoves might send it over the edge. Are you trying to say that you don't want to help me, comrade? That's OK but just tell me outright. I took a big risk coming back. I need to know where I stand.'

'No. Look. I'll always ... I'll do whatever I can. I just think you're climbing up the wrong rope.'

Mark rinsed out two cups at the sink and continued, calmly, 'I was hoping that you'd be involved in something I'm setting up. It is exactly the sort of thing we both believe in. Unless you've changed, of course. My pal Sam Jones in Australia was planning an operation in Amsterdam when he was arrested. The target is the HCB bank. That's something you'd approve of surely. There are plenty of other comrades and brothers in Holland, not just Islamists or jihadis but non-religious radicals in Dutch universities who see the HCB bank as a legitimate target.'

Hector began to feel claustrophobic in the house.

'Do you fancy going for a walk?'

'Let's go.' Mark pulled on his leather biking jacket.

The two men walked along the coast road. Ahead of them the bay curved round in a huge sweep. The sky was blue. At the end of a spur of land the squat towers of Dungeness power station stood outlined against the long white-fleeced sky. The morning mists had lifted and the sun was shining. Mark kicked a pebble towards the beach.

'Did you read about the explosions at the electricity sub-station in Dartford?'

Hector stopped in his tracks and looked at Mark in dismay.

'Was that something to do with those guys? But that was idiotic. For fuck's sake. Why?'

'Practice.'

Hector stood still and shook his head. A family of three came towards them, their hair blowing in the breeze. The mother held the back of the saddle as her blond son wobbled by on his bicycle.

Mark waited till the family had passed.

'So you're no longer prepared to fight for your beliefs. You were once.'

'There's nothing worth fighting for just now. Times change.'

Mark spoke with cool venom:

'Well I'd still like to see the whole system crash and burn in flames. And I'll do what I can to bring that about. I still nurse that feeling. It's my core. People might think of it as a tumour inside me. I don't care. It's grown so big that if it was taken out I would probably die anyway. Why do they think that it's only Muslims who feel like this? Yes. I fucking hate religion too but not as much as I hate capitalism. So I don't mind if a bunch of maniacs blow things up even if I don't always agree with their reasons.'

Hector was taken aback by his ferocity.

'So you agree that those guys are maniacs, then?'

'Yes. And I don't give a shit. Good luck to them.'

They walked on in silence until Mark calmed down. Hector challenged him:

'We didn't target innocent people.'

'We kidnapped and killed.'

'I didn't.' Hector suddenly stood still and looked at Mark with suspicion.

Mark stopped in turn and saw Hector looking at him.

'Come off it, Hector. You weren't averse to attacking people you saw as collaborators. You were quite proficient with guns and explosives if I remember rightly. The Alitalia offices? The Alitalia flight? Banco di Roma? They just got you on the wrong charges.'

'Banco di Roma had a history of fascism in Ethiopia.'

'The HCB bank has a similar history in Indonesia and Surinam. See what I mean?'

'No-one was hurt at the Banco di Roma.'

'Luck.'

'Luck plays a part in every story.' Hector was ruffled. They continued walking.

'Oh how we used to say we would never get old and lose our passion,' Mark mocked. 'Well I haven't lost mine.' He turned to confront Hector. The sunlight made the sea sparkle behind him. His features had a certain relaxed clarity because his face was in the shade and he did not have to screw up his eyes against the sun. He put his hand on Hector's shoulder.

'You mentioned Khaled yesterday. Ask him. He's Eddie Sursok's stepson isn't he? Ask him what Sursok and the HCB bank have been doing in various parts of the world. In fact I'd like to speak to Khaled when you can get hold of him.'

Hector said nothing. Mark stared at the ground and then said with a knowing smile, 'Shahid was right, I suppose. He said everyone drifts to the right as they get older.'

With some anguish Hector recalled how once, in what now seemed to be another age, he had sat with Mark on the bed in their Milan flat with the stuffed Russian bear looking down at them both from the hall. The two of them made a vow. They swore an earnest oath: that they would never betray each other and that they would never give up their beliefs when they got older.

A steady wind blew in their faces. They walked on past Derek Jarman's tarred plank cottage with its bright yellow-painted window frames. Hector remained silent. Finally he spoke:

'Those guys hate unbelievers. They'll shaft you.'

'Sam Jones was a convert and I have the information and contacts they need. There are more British white guys than you might think who have converted. I'm not one but I'm indispensable to them at the moment. I can follow the target, for instance, without looking suspicious.'

'Which target?'

There was determination in Mark's voice as he continued:

'We're targeting a man called Stephen Butterfield who is a top executive for the HCB bank in Amsterdam. It's a kidnap. You talk about popular support. Have you any idea how much bankers are hated at the moment – with their bonuses and executive jets and high-flying lifestyles? People would welcome their come-uppance. And this time I've made sure it will work. He won't get hurt. It will be coordinated with a series of bombings at the HCB bank at night when the bank is empty.'

Hector regretted asking. They passed a fisherman in his garden. He stood behind a tarred fence. His boat was winched up on one side of the house. The fisherman himself seemed arid and dry, pale as the dusty stones. He leaned on a rusted rake. They acknowledged him as they passed.

'That's someone who'd take you across the Channel if you pay him well enough,' Hector muttered, against his better judgement.

Ten minutes later they reached the power station. There was a bench near to the wall outside one of the three reactor buildings. The two men sat on it. Behind them sunlight caught the spectral white brilliance of a seagull's flight as it skimmed against the grey of the power station wall. Hector wished Mark had not told him anything. He looked at his watch.

'I'd better be on my way. I've got stuff to do at home.'

They started to retrace their steps along the bleak road. When they reached the house at Littlestone Mark said, 'I'm going over to Holland to do a recce on the bank and some surveillance on Stephen Butterfield.' He grinned. 'Are you with us or against us?'

Hector felt drained. He found it impossible to refuse his old comrade outright.

'I'll let you know.'

'Soon.'

'Yes.' Hector gestured towards the house: 'Try and leave the place looking as if no-one's been there. The lock's bust but otherwise clean up where you can.'

'Tell Khaled I'd like to see him. The others would too. He might be interested in what we're doing.'

'I doubt it.'

Mark did not look round as he went in the house.

*

Hector returned to the empty house in Hythe.

He sat in the front room and stared at the ashes in the grate in

a whirlwind of confusion. At two o'clock he pulled on his jacket
and left the house. He flung himself into the car and started to
drive without knowing where he was heading. Ten minutes later
he found himself on the A20 to Dover. He roared up the steep hill
overlooking St Margaret's Bay. On top of the white cliffs he pulled
over onto a patch of litter-strewn asphalt near the cliff edge where
a small crowd had gathered.

A group of Morris men had assembled by the cliff-top barrier.
A small boy, his faced daubed with black, his forehead bound with
a fluttering yellow handkerchief, was handing out promotional
leaflets to the few people who had come to watch. The Fool who
accompanied the Morris men was lounging against some railings.
He wore a black tailcoat, black leggings, white trainers and a crooked
top hat from which sprouted a sheaf of tall feathers. In one hand he
carried a pig's bladder on a stick and in the other a long skinny pipe
of a trumpet. Without warning he executed an extraordinary leap
and blew a harsh note on his horn.

The Morris men shuffled into formation and started their
stamping dance, banging on tambourines with the bells on their
legs jangling.

To his surprise Hector realised that one of the people watching
the dancers was the woman he had seen at his print shop. She wore a
loose fawn mackintosh. Her bright headscarf was tied in an unusual
way with the points at the top in a Brazilian or Caribbean style.
One hand supported her chin and she was absorbed in the dance.
Hector moved towards her. She looked up as he approached. Hector
underwent a rush of attraction to the woman.

'Excuse me. I saw you in my print works the other day. But I
think I've met you before.'

She smiled and then looked back at the dancers.

'I was a dancer. You might have seen photos of me. I used to be
with the Royal Ballet a long time ago.' She pointed to the Morris
men. 'I can't resist any sort of dancing. Even this.'

'I think I know you from somewhere else.'

He caught a momentary look of alarm in her eyes before she turned back to watch the dancers.

'Would you like to come for a coffee?' he asked when the dancing had finished.

'Why not?'

She followed him in her own car. In his car mirror Hector could see the skinny dancing figure of the Fool silhouetted against the Dover cliffs and fields, his coat-tails flying in the breeze. He felt as if he had been taken over by some inexplicable force and had relinquished responsibility for his own actions. Somewhere in the rolling hills and fields to his right, he realised, Barbara and Dawn were tugging potatoes from the dusty earth. He felt liberated from hearth and home.

Chapter Twelve

Together Barbara and Dawn trudged over the furrowed land to the far end of the field. The day was warm and the benign soil underfoot was a dusty pinkish brown. Dawn wore a short denim skirt and a stripy tank top. Her straight toffee-coloured hair was lank and floppy. Her gait was clumsy and there was a determined expression in her slanting blue eyes as she strode forward.

It was Dawn's task to wait with a sack at one end of the field while her mother worked her way along one furrow and back along the next picking the new potatoes and putting them in a trug. Then Dawn emptied the trugs into the sacks which she did slowly but with great care, diving to pick up any potatoes that fell to the ground.

Barbara stood up to ease the ache in her back. Most of the pickers were the wives of ex-miners trying to earn a little money after the closure of the Kent coal fields. She looked out over the fields. The women formed ragged lines across the hillsides. From a distance they looked like an uneven shuttle on a loom slowly weaving their way backwards and forwards across the land.

At lunchtime they stopped and gathered together in small groups. Sandwiches burst from wrapping paper blooms. Madge, an ex-miner's wife with a strong twisted face, smiled down at Dawn:

'Are you off to the grass toilet then, Dawn?'

Dawn nodded and put down her sack full of new potatoes. She made her way to the overgrown patch of land behind them and squatted to piss in the tall seeding grass. It was a lavatory made of wild flowers with wondrous green wallpaper. The humming of bees and insects filled her ears. Pollen tickled her nose. Stalks tickled her bum. There was a pause before the waters came and then the hot smell of urine on grass as she shifted her feet trying not to piss on her new trainers. When she went back to join the others they were already munching on their sandwiches and pouring tea from a Thermos. A skylark spiralled its way up into the blue sky singing. Madge looked skyward following the bird's ascent:

'Hark at that skylark, drib drib drib. Did you watch Celebrity Spies last night? They had a special version for May Day.'

'No. I don't like that guy whatsisname. The presenter.'

White plastic knives buttered buns.

'On May Day you're supposed to bring a white pig into the house and feed it all day with bread and butter or it will turn cannibal and eat its piglets. When the colliery was working my George wouldn't go down the pit if they passed a pig on the way to work. It would mean a pit disaster. Same with the trawlermen and the fishermen. See a pig and they'll turn back. My nan says pigs can see the wind. She used to frighten us with stories about a boar that ran through the skies in a storm. That's how she kept us quiet. That and the gin.'

Since the pit closures the women's husbands were mostly unemployed or doing casual work, ditching and hedging. Madge fished in a carrier bag for another bun. When the women finished eating they lay on their backs in the sun.

'Did you know that pigs can get sunburn? And there's wild boars in Ashdown forest now.'

'Who says?'

'It was on telly. They escaped from some boar farm in Tenterden during that hurricane in the eighties. Been breeding. There's quite a few round about these days. They're all over Kent and Sussex in the woods. There's some in Devon as well.'

Barbara levered herself up onto her elbows:

'That's funny. My husband was on the train the other day and says he saw a dead sow lying on the embankment.'

'Sometimes the wild ones try and mate with the domestic ones.

They're wanting to breed. That's when they're dangerous. That's probably what happened. A wild one must have killed a tame one.' Evie shaded her eyes from the sun and looked across the field. 'I wouldn't mind mating with a nice wild husband – if I could find one.' She was laughing.

Madge put her hands on her hips:

'Never mind finding a husband. How to become a widow, that's what I want to know. I want my husband gone and I want everything that's left, the money, the house, my son, everything. And I've worked out that a hitman is less expensive than a bloody lawyer.'

The other women laughed until the tears rolled from their eyes.

A shadow of anxiety passed Evie's face.

'I worry that all this is going to come to an end soon. The other farmers are using these gang-masters to bring them cheap labour from abroad. Ukrainians. Albanians. Poles. Look down over there. That farmer used to rent out holiday caravans. Now the whole caravan park is used to house east Europeans. But what with this credit crunch they're likely to lose their jobs too.'

The women strained their eyes and looked down in the distance to a field of caravans with groups of men standing around.

'Oh well. Everything is changing these days.'

The sun had begun its slow descent westward. The women went back to work. As the afternoon progressed Barbara kept stopping and straightening up. Dawn waited patiently at the end of the field screwing her eyes up against the sun. The clock moved ever more slowly and the afternoon's end seemed to recede away from the workers as though they would never catch up with it. They were scattered now, bobbing like lost swimmers in the billowing Kent fields.

In the van on the way back the women pondered over whether they would still have jobs when the season came for Brussels sprout picking. Back at the White Horse pub the van dropped the workers off at Eythorne. Since the pit closures the whole district had an air of dull neglect. Barbara helped Dawn fasten her safety belt and they drove home. She asked her daughter, 'What's your favourite lesson at school these days, Dawn?'

Her bulbous jaw and enlarged tongue sometimes made Dawn's speech difficult to decipher but her answer was quite clear.

'Dinner,' she said.

Later that evening when Dawn was in bed Barbara went upstairs. The dolls' houses all around her looked both mysterious and cosy in the lamplight. She started stitching some upholstery for tiny sofas and chairs. She worked away as if she were finally able to stitch some safety into her own life. She was still working when Hector quietly let himself back into the house.

Chapter Thirteen

There was no-one to whom he could tell everything.

They lay naked, face to face on top of the double-bed in the darkened room. The affair was still new enough for them to spend time looking into each other's eyes. Hector stroked the curve of the woman's body, the smooth dip from the waist to the rise of her hip, and then brought his warm hand to rest in the hollow of her back. He had not been looking for an affair but it had released in him a wave of euphoria. He pushed a strand of dark hair away from her face and smiled at her.

'How did this happen?' he asked. The strand of black hair fell back across her face. He traced the curve of her mouth with his finger.

'I don't know.' She smiled and shrugged her shoulders.

'And how can you convince me you're not working for the police?'

She giggled and put her leg over his, entwining them together.

'Of course I'm not. What about you? You could be.'

He chuckled.

'Not likely given my history.'

She turned her head on the pillow and smiled at him.

'On the contrary. You're just the sort of person they would recruit. Nobody would suspect you.' She pulled on the lobes of his ears. 'You won't even tell me your address and home telephone. I've only got your mobile number and the number at work.'

'That's not because of my political activities. That's because of my wife.' Again he pushed the strand of hair from her face. 'I thought I recognised you from somewhere.'

'I didn't recognise you.'

'Well it was a long time ago and you couldn't have seen me more than two or three times in that house in London. I spent most of the time in Milan. And, if I remember rightly, you were always off somewhere with the ballet company.'

'Tell me again what you did in Italy.'

He fingered the tiny mole on her top lip and sighed:

'Maybe you've fallen in love with the young man I used to be.'

She scrambled on top of him and lay with her chin on his breast bone.

'No. I love you as you are now. The man you are now.'

He shifted her gently to one side and sat up.

'All right then,' he said. 'I'm going to tickle your feet to see how long you would last under interrogation.'

They took it in turns to tickle each other's feet to test their will-power until their stomachs ached with laughter. Then they play-wrestled for a few moments. She pulled the pillow down in order to settle more comfortably.

'You have to be able to resist interrogation by chat as well as by torture. Interrogation by chat is a skilled art.' He grinned and rolled over on top of her again. It was true she was slow to arouse. Slow as the rose adagio she told him she had once danced. He had to work for a long time. And she did not bother to do much in return. What didn't give her pleasure, she didn't bother to do.

'That's nice. Go on doing that,' she said. 'Go on. Just go on doing that. That's it. That's it.'

They lay on top of the bed with their limbs plaited together like dreamy milk-fed infants. After a while she said:

'I'm getting cold. I'll go and make us some coffee.'

He ached when he had to detach himself from that body. He watched her stand up and stretch. She flicked her black hair over her shoulders and looked round at him with a smile. He watched the naked figure go to the door.

'You still have the body of a fourteen-year-old,' he had said in amazement when she first undressed. 'You're so bendy and pliable. Can I have a photograph of you dancing? I'd like to make a print of it.'

By the time she came back with a mug of coffee in each hand Hector had switched on the bedside lamp and was reading a book he had found at the side of the bed. He did not hear her come in. The years in jail had taught him to become lost in books very quickly. She handed him his coffee.

'I hate other people's kitchens,' she said as she lowered herself back onto the bed. They had borrowed a friend's dull flat for their rendezvous. 'You don't know where to find anything.'

'I have to go in a minute.' He sat on the edge of the bed sipping the coffee. It was dark outside now.

'I thought you said your wife had taken your daughter away for the weekend.'

'She has but she might be trying to phone me at home on the land-line. My daughter likes to say goodnight. She's the most precious thing in my life.' The mention of his wife and daughter suddenly reminded him of Mark and their fierce argument on the road to Dungeness. He became agitated and looked around on the floor for his clothes.

'I'll give you a lift.' She rolled off the bed and started to dress.

'No don't give me a lift. You said your car lights weren't working. I don't want you to get into trouble.'

Her eyes grew big with astonishment and laughter as she turned to face him.

'Is this the same man who had convoys of police chasing him down the autobahn from Hamburg to Munich at a hundred miles an hour? The man who blew up an Alitalia airplane on the ground?'

'Just an incendiary – a flash and a lot of black smoke. The plane was empty at the time. Most of the serious bombings in Milan like the Piazza Fontana bombing were carried out by agents provocateurs on the extreme right. We were infiltrated.'

He recalled the cheery face of the police informer who had penetrated their group in Milan all those years ago. In a moment of paranoia he was suddenly not sure of anything or anybody, even her.

'There were infiltrators everywhere in those days ... in England too.' She sounded hesitant, her voice small and diminished. She helped him button up his shirt.

'I can't believe this is the same man who's worrying about my car lights. I'll give you a lift,' she said firmly. He watched while she brushed her hair with practised hands, holding the hairpins in her mouth, and twisting the hair again and again into a knot on the top of her head.

'Drop me by the Imperial Hotel then. I've left my car there.'

She pulled up in the hotel car park to let him out. He leaned back in through the window and bent his head to kiss her on the neck and then on the lips.

'Your neck and your breasts smell of lemons.' Then he smiled. 'You've given me back my youth,' he said.

'If your wife ever found out about this affair, would you admit it?' She looked up at him enquiringly.

'Only if there was evidence. Anyway, you are married too.'

She looked away for a moment.

'Yes,' she said. 'I am married too.'

'Still to that same man? Donny. I remember him vaguely. Michael Feynite used to call him "the radiant stranger".'

She looked back at him and he saw something impish sparkle in her dark El Greco eyes at this description of her husband.

He waved her a kiss as he drove away. She waited a few minutes before driving away herself.

There was no-one to whom she could tell the whole truth either.

A Word from the Narrator

Sitting here in the Head in the Sand café I have to admit to an attack of the hots when I write about Ella in Hector's arms. I've always carried a torch for her. In fact, writing it made me push my black coffee aside and rush off home to have sex with my own wife Ma Brigitte. Luckily we live nearby in a fashionably converted slaughterhouse – you know, revealed brickwork and so on. Yes. That's what happens to writers. I'm not the first and I won't be the last to excuse myself in the middle of describing that sort of scene. Not that jealousy would do me much good. Ella long ago lost her heart to someone else.

Ma Brigitte did the honours. My wife is a tough-talking woman with long red hair. She's always weighed down with heavy gold necklaces and earrings and swathed in a purple shawl. In her youth she too was a virtuoso dancer, known for rubbing hot peppers into her genitals to liven up her sexual partners. Afterwards she fed me with rice and black beans, coconut meat, grilled corn and my favourite smoked mackerel. Then she sent me back to work.

I know full well that narrators, like assassins, are supposed to keep in the background but I flout that rule when I feel like it. I see nothing wrong with the narrator occasionally showing the reader what he is doing in the same way that an architect might escort his client around a building in progress. Being a narrator is like being some sort of god. The characters, poor souls, are human. The odds are against them.

Let me take time by the tail and swing it round my head for a minute.

Part Two

Of all history I understand nothing but revolt.
Flaubert

Chapter Fourteen

One May morning in 1970 Ella de Vries, at the age of seventeen, waited on the platform of Preston station for the 11.35 AM train to London. She wore a pale primrose yellow dress that made her dark eyes and hair seem blacker than ever. Her hairline was low, her black eyes slanting and wide set. She had an attractive forward-thrusting mouth with a small mole above the top lip that made both men and women want to kiss it and she carried herself with the classically straight back of a dancer. The other members of the Royal Ballet had finished their last touring date in Manchester the previous night and returned to London. Ella was the youngest member of the company. She had made the unnecessary detour to Preston for reasons of love.

To fall in love is to nurture a secret. Even a stranger can sense it. One or two of the passengers on the platform caught the glint of self-contained excitement in her eyes. She had told nobody that she was going to Preston or why. Her mother used to complain to Ella's father about this trait in her daughter:

'Why is she so secretive?'

Ella sat down on the wooden seat and placed her bag on the ground beside her. Soft breezes lathered her face. Diadems of raindrops from an earlier shower trembled along the edge of the station sign. The green telegraph of spring signalled from tree to tree behind the station buildings opposite. The whole world around her felt aphrodised.

The young man who was the unknowing cause of this turbulence was nowhere near Preston. He was leaning against the green table in a Soho billiard hall, smoking in stereo with a cigarette in each hand and one behind his ear. A quiff of gleaming chestnut hair fell over his forehead as he waited for the golden explosion of whisky to enliven him with its rush through the body.

Ella had not expected to find him in Preston. But she had been unable to resist a quick visit to the city. He had spent some of his childhood there and that was enough for her. In the manner of the lovesick she wanted to breathe the air he had once breathed and roam the streets of the city where he had once lived. Calf love, the adolescent crush of a fanzine reader – whatever it was, her fate had been sealed by the sight of a coltish ankle a few weeks earlier.

The slow milk-train from Manchester to Preston early that morning creaked and groaned as it set off. The empty compartment reeked of stale cigarette smoke. There was a small mirror over the seats under the rack and Ella pushed her tongue under her top lip to examine the mole there, always fearful of it growing bigger. She stretched out face-down on the seat, one leg dangling to the floor and let the rough fabric prickle her cheek. Dust from the upholstery made her nostrils tingle. She examined the pattern of the material in the dim light. It was dull and regular with the rusty red markings and dark blue design of cheap carpeting.

After a while she lowered the thick leather belt a few notches to open the grimy window and lean out into the fresh dawn air. The train rumbled past a huge ruined red-brick cotton mill standing by a canal. Early morning sun caught a multitude of broken window panes, as many square panes as a slab of butterscotch. Sunlight flared off the glass, flashing and distracting attention from the burnt-out dereliction of the interior. One half of the building still functioned as a work place. A grubby white sheet hung from one of the windows. On it was painted in black capital letters: HILLYARDS WORKERS OCCUPATION. SUPPORT DEMOCRACY AGAINST CAPITALISM.

Ella withdrew back into the carriage and sat down. The mounting industrial unrest that was rumbling through Britain, the strikes and mountains of rubbish in the streets, had failed entirely to penetrate the enclosed world of ballet. Ballet had its own history that wove its way untouched through revolutions and wars.

Twenty minutes later the train pulled into Preston and Ella set off to explore the streets. Even in the sunshine, the Victorian red brick buildings exhaled an air of industrial exhaustion. The terraced houses were low enough for a wide stretch of sky to be visible over the roofs. After walking for ten minutes she came across a junior school. In the playground knots of children formed and re-formed like viziers plotting and conspiring at court. She rested her head against the iron railings and watched them. Perhaps this was the school he had attended.

He told her once that he had been cast as Tinkerbell in the school play. The teacher must have had a sense of humour. The Tinkerbell costume for the fierce-eyed little boy consisted of steel toe-capped boots, thick socks and short trousers over which jutted a crepe paper tutu. His close-cropped hair, like iron filings pulled upright by a magnet, earned him the nickname 'Bristle-Bonce'. For the performance he had been given a big school hand-bell which he rang vigorously every time he came on stage demanding that people believe in him. The audience laughed whenever he appeared. This he could not understand. It left him feeling mildly affronted. He felt that people should accept divinity when they saw it. Later, he set fire to the school toilets.

That was another of his attractions. Ella fell in love with him, as Dido had with Aeneas, because he was a box of stories.

Ella's aimless wandering around Preston lasted for two hours. Then she made her way back to the station. She reached the station with a sense of mission accomplished, satisfied that the energy she had expended in going to Preston would in some magical way bring him back. Because Donny McLeod, the young man who was the cause of all this turmoil, had disappeared.

For Ella de Vries falling in love had been a sudden and violent descent, a plunge downward into passion. As soon as she set eyes on the pale narrow face and the down-slanting green eyes she fell in love with him. For her it was like the shock of seeing a wild animal let loose in the drawing-room. She saw no warning signs in the crescent-shaped dent on his forehead or the unnerving thinness of his lips. When she first set eyes on him it was as if the top of her head came off and she rose straight up to the ceiling. She felt that her bloodstream had been irreversibly altered and started to flow in the opposite direction. It was an encounter from which there was no withdrawal.

Now she sat on the station bench flicking through the newspaper. In the distance a toy-sized train waited on a glinting skein of railway lines for the signal to change. To encourage an interest in dance the Royal Ballet had sent some of the younger members on a tour of the north to perform excerpts from both the classical and modern repertoire in schools. Ella passed over the news items: the Vietnam war protests; the bombings in Ireland and London; the sombre warnings of growing unrest over the Industrial Relations Bill. She turned straight to the arts' review section. The paper had sent its main ballet critic to cover the last date of their tour. It had been easy for the young dancers to pick out the critic from the rows of teachers and schoolchildren assembled in the school hall. He looked like a banker, immaculately dressed, balding with a pinkish face and silver hair. He sat in the front row, notebook in hand accompanied by a young blond man with an angelic face. Ella turned to the inner pages and read the three sentence review of her performance as the Partisan in *The Green Table*:

'Elissa de Vries moved with grace. For so young a dancer there was something elemental in the performance. I was reminded that there is danger in the body.'

Ella put the newspaper in her bag, feeling elated. She made up her mind to go straight to class as soon as the train reached London. It seemed that love had fertilised everything around her; love had decked the trees with bud-sprays, blossoms and green foliage; love caused the bee to nuzzle the flower stamens in the hanging basket over the Waiting Room behind her. She drew a deep breath as if she wanted to fill her lungs with the scent of spring.

Minutes later the toy-sized train that had been waiting on the points metamorphosed into the huge steam train with buffet cars that glided slowly in front of her and came to a halt. She hoisted up her bag, climbed on board and was already dozing when they passed the fading adverts from a defunct industrial era painted on the brick buildings alongside the railway line: 'Percy Brothers – Hotspur Press'; 'Uncle Joe's Mint Balls Keep You All Aglow'; 'Hearsey's Removal Firm – Careful Since 1890'. All the heart had gone out of them.

The train rocked her and she slept until she reached London.

Chapter Fifteen

The love explosion happened like this.

One day after rehearsal at Covent Garden Ella de Vries leaped up the rackety stairs to her flat two-at-a-time clutching tea-bags and a packet of biscuits. Ella shared a flat in Old Compton Street with an American girl called Hetty Moran. The flat was on the second floor above an Indian restaurant called 'Shafi's'. It smelled permanently of curry but the rent was cheap and it was close to Covent Garden. There were two adjacent flats on the third floor divided by a partition wall in a botched conversion job. Both flats had cream-painted front doors made of plywood which stood at right angles to each other on a tiny landing. Ella walked daily to class or rehearsal through the Soho streets, surrounded by smells of rotting vegetables, freshly ground coffee, and garbage. The flat adjacent to Ella's was rented by Cyrus Vance, one of the accompanists at the Royal Ballet School.

At the top of the stairs she knocked on Cyrus's door. His flat was the smaller of the two, a poky L-shaped room with two narrow beds set against the walls. Both beds were covered with what looked like grey prison-issue blankets. He had somehow managed to cram in an upright piano opposite one of the beds. A bleary-eyed Cyrus opened the door. He had short wavy marmalade coloured hair and a pale face. The skin around his lips was raw red from a bad cold and from too much rough kissing of other male mouths. He took the shopping which she handed him.

'Oh you are a bona palone. Come in and have a cup of tea.'

The room reeked of Vick's vapo-rub and frowzy blankets. Cyrus had been in bed for three days with flu. Ella sat on the edge of the bed as far away from him as possible.

'Are you feeling better?'

He snuffled. His eyes streamed.

'Not much. How's *Aida* going?' Ella was on loan from the ballet company to dance the part of one of the slave girls at the Royal Opera House.

'It's OK. My mum came to see it. All she said was, "You can see everything through that dress."'

'Mothers. You can't please them,' Cyrus sniffed.

Wearing jeans and a red polo-neck sweater, Ella sat on the edge of the bed trying not to breathe in his germs. Then out of the blue came a fierce knuckle-rap on the door. The rap turned into an impatient thumping. The door nearly gave way. Cyrus put his cup on top of the piano and crawled over her outstretched legs to open the door but before he could reach it the flimsy lock broke and the door flung open.

Framed in the doorway was a young man, lean and blazing with energy. He was supporting himself against the door post with one hand while the other nursed his raised ankle. He looked momentarily nonplussed at seeing Ella as if he had expected to find Cyrus alone. His hair gleamed a dark reddish brown, the colour of a Highland peat burn. It rose at the front from a widow's peak into a shining chestnut sea-roll. His complexion was clear and pale. His shirt collar was open. All the vitality was in the hazel-green eyes, which flashed with curiosity at the sight of Ella. For her it was the strangest thing, this almost visible life-force that streamed from him. It was like the radiant attack of a young god and she shrank back as though it might burn her.

He hopped in awkwardly and hobbled over to the bed, wincing and smiling. Ella stood up, allowing him to sit down.

'The police is after us. Ah've twisted ma foot,' he said laughing.

Cyrus stood with an amused grin on his face, arms folded. He introduced them.

'Donny. Ella. Ella. Donny.'

Donny nodded towards her, groaned and rolled over on the bed, then shot upright again holding his foot with both hands. He wrested his shoe off and pulled down the sock to inspect the damage. The ankle was slender, coltish and ended in a strong slim foot. He twisted it this way and that gingerly. There was already some swelling around the joint. Ella stared at the bony excrescence peeping from the sock. It reminded her of a horse's hock or the bone spavin of a goat. She sat down suddenly on the bed like an unstrung puppet. Donny bent over to examine the injured foot. A strand of shining hair fell over his forehead in a question mark.

'Look after your feet. First rule of a soldier.' He winced as he moved the foot.

'And dancers,' she said. 'I'm a dancer. We have to look after our feet too.' He stared at her with interest for a moment. Then, still massaging his ankle, he turned to Cyrus:

'Can I get out by the fire escape?' He gestured with his head towards the window.

'You can get out on to next door's roof.' Cyrus turned to Ella. 'Run into your flat and see if Betty Bracelet is in the street.' She looked bewildered.

'Betty Bracelet. Lily Law. The police,' he explained. She ran into her own flat and looked out through the window, then came back.

'I can't see any police.'

'Good,' said Donny. 'Give us a hand.'

Cyrus held his arm as he limped and hopped towards the window, holding his shoe in his hand. He scrambled out onto the roof:

'See you later.'

They watched him disappear over the rooftops.

'Who is that?' asked Ella.

'Donny McLeod. I met him about a month ago.' Cyrus mopped his nose with a tissue and gave a hoarse cough. 'Do you know what "rolling a queer" means?'

Ella shook her head. He raised his eyebrows and rolled his eyes at her ignorance.

'Well, there are guys around Soho who pretend to give you the come-on. Then they get you on your own, beat you up and rob you. I brought Donny back here one night. I suspect he was planning something like that. But anyway as soon as we got back here we started chatting and he stayed for his supper. I think it was the piano that saved me. That and the bacon sandwiches. He had this menacing light in his eye until he spotted the piano. Then he asked me, "Can ye play that thing?"

'I didn't want to play. I thought if I turned my back to him he'd attack me. Then I thought, oh what the fuck. I lifted the lid and began to play some Chopin. I turned around and there was this look of horror on his face. He shoved me sideways off the stool and said, "I don't know what sort of fingers you've got but mine are the one and ninepenny sort." And he began to pick out some boogie. So I said, "Oh, I can do that." And I started to bang out a honky-tonk version of "When All the Saints ..." You should have seen the grin on his face. You've cracked it, Cyrus, I thought. Not much chance of sex but at least you won't end up a corpse. I offered him a joint but he likes booze. So we started popping open some beers.

'"Wait here a second," says Donny, and runs out into the Soho night. Ten minutes later he reappears with some drumsticks. Where the hell he got them I don't know. I played and he beat out the rhythm with his drumsticks on the side of the sink and then on the top of the piano, on the bed, the floor and any other available surface. And we start up a bit of a session. Then one of the waiters comes up from the restaurant and says we're disturbing the customers downstairs. So I tell Donny to keep it down a bit. And he goes mad. He bounces up and kicks the door shut in the man's face: "Fuck them. I like din. I am a fucking roarer. I am someone who loves clamour," he says. And he pushes me out of the way and starts to hammer the piano and sing at the top of his voice.

'"Don't do that," I'm saying. "They're my landlords. I'll get thrown out."

'"I don't give a fuck." And he goes and puts his foot down on the loud pedal and goes on bellowing at the top of his voice. There's something about him that's making me laugh. "This is just what I'm like on a couple of beers," he says. "Two whiskies and I go for the jugular. Two whiskies and Mr Puma appears." And he leaps up and performs a little tap dance and sits down again. Anyway the end of it all is that we're both screaming with laughter and he's dancing around and singing some obscene song he learnt in the army as a boy soldier and I'm frying up bacon for bacon sandwiches.

'"I was going to kill you," he tells me, wiping runny butter from the corner of his mouth with the back of his wrist. "But seeing that you are a musician you were spared." We're both doubled up with laughter by now. I don't know what's going on. "I'm going to come up again and we can play some more," he says. Then he gets all enthusiastic. "Get a drum kit," he says.

'"From where?"'

'"I don't know. Somewhere."

'"I don't know where to find a decent one that's cheap."

'"Ah. Bollocks. I hate people that say they can't do things. Find one. Steal one. Hijack a band." And then he grabs his jacket and gets up to leave. I ask him where he's living.

'"In a train at Victoria station. It parks up in the sidings at night and I sleep there. In the morning I get up and use the wash-and-brush-up in the station and go to work."

'"Where do you work, then?"

'"Building sites. I prefer them because when the work's finished the workforce moves on. Everywhere else the workforce stays stuck in the same place and the product moves on. I like to keep moving."

'"I'll give you the phone number here if you like."

'"Fuck off. I hate telephones. It's like talking to a fucking shoe or something. You think – I hope nobody can see me talking to this lump of plastic. Look, I'll just come back some time." He spun a drumstick into the air and caught it and put it down on the bed.

'"Look after these drumsticks for us."

'And he was off down the stairs two-at-a-time. I didn't see him again until just now.'

That's the man I'm going to marry, thought Ella.

Chapter Sixteen

When she danced as a child what was most noticeable was her gift for stillness.

In the winter of 1959, when England had not yet shaken off its post-war austerity, three examiners for the Royal Academy of Dance sat behind the table at one end of a draughty south London hall. An icy morning fog swathed the streets outside. Some children were late because of cancelled buses and there were arguments between mothers in the changing-room as to whose turn it was to go into the examination hall next. Parents unwrapped their offspring from scarves and coats and rubbed their blue fingers and feet to bring back the blood. That December it was so cold that the examiners kept their coats on in the hall. Their breath steamed out in wisps as they looked down at the marking papers and up again at the performing candidates. Behind the upright piano Mrs Patrick kept her woollen mittens on to play. Her permed hair was dyed black and she wore bright red lipstick with wartime bravado, although the war was long since over. Number five on their list for the Grade II exam was Elissa de Vries, aged six.

The examiners noted that the child had the sinuous grace of a cat. Her straight black hair was cut in a pudding-basin style with a fringe. Her skin was the colour of agate. Her obsidian eyes were wide-set. One of the examiners wondered to himself whether she might not be Mexican. Another thought that the wide slanting eyes might be from somewhere in the orient. She wore a black swimming costume and over it a short, home-made, ill-fitting tunic with a slit down each side. Her scuffed ballet shoes had turned from pink to grey. The pale face and intense eyes gave an impression of mischievous remoteness as if she belonged elsewhere or was entirely focused on her own inner life. She barely looked at the examiners but concentrated on executing the steps which she did reasonably well.

When one of the examiners asked her what she would like to do next, she thought for a moment and then replied:

'Walk on my hands.'

'I mean what other pieces have you prepared for us?'

The child looked far away, up at the high windows which were still covered with a mesh of wire netting to protect them from bomb damage. She had lost interest in the examination. What she wanted was to be either a trapeze artist or an acrobat. She enjoyed flipping onto her hands, arching her back and then letting her elbows give slightly until she found the correct balance to walk forward. She wanted to show them how she did it. The examiners waited. Mrs Patrick leaned round from behind the piano and hissed loudly, 'The Sailor's Hornpipe', and began to play.

Ella danced the hornpipe with reluctance. She disliked the dance with its folded arms, mock salutes and mimed gestures of looking out to sea. She preferred the gaiety of the polka where she could spin and whirl using the space of the whole room. The pinched frown remained on her face all the way through the hornpipe. It lost her marks.

Deportment: 80%

Steps: 82%

Dance piece – hornpipe: 54%

'You must teach her to smile,' said Mrs Patrick afterwards to Ella's mother, a cockney woman with wide cheekbones and blue eyes, who was leaning against the wall smoking a cigarette in the swirling fog. 'She's not going to get anywhere unless she learns to smile.'

And so Ella's mother set about teaching her daughter to smile.

'She's a solemn little creature. Solitary. Like her dad. I can't always make head or tail of her,' said her mother to her sister Doris as they washed dishes.

However, amidst the calm stillness which had been so striking to the examiners, lay a degree of recklessness and abandon that would eventually reveal itself.

*

Every Thursday after school Ella's mother took her to a dance class at the Cambridge House Settlement for Underprivileged Children in the Walworth Road.

'It's not that we're underprivileged,' she said to her neighbour. 'It's just that it's cheaper than anywhere else.'

The classes were held in a shabby building owned by Cambridge University. Light blue paint peeled off the front door. There Ella learned ballet and tap-dancing. In the basement of the building was an unheated kitchen, a cracked sink, an old wooden table pale from scrubbing with too much bleach, and a few rickety chairs. Sometimes when one of the girls went down to fetch a glass of water she would find an obscene note left on the table or a crude sexual drawing. It seemed that a paedophile – maybe more than one – frequented the premises, which were used by several charitable organisations. The adults tut-tutted but did nothing. The children went down to look and have a snigger. Most of them had seen men exposing themselves on a bomb site or in a dark alley or had experience of an uncle gripping their thigh too tightly. A little molestation was the norm in that part of south London. Nobody took a lot of notice.

Ella's teacher was Miss Dolores Beer. She had crinkly hair and a manner both diffident and gushing. 'I was trained under Biddy Pinchard,' she would say to the mothers as her eyes misted over with admiration for her revered teacher. 'Biddy Pinchard would never allow anyone to chew gum in class,' she said reprovingly to her pupils. The mothers hoped their daughters would escape the drab environs of south London and become Bluebell Girls or Tiller Girls and move into a world of elegant stage-door Johnnies and afternoon teas at The Ritz.

Miss Beer's troupe was booked to perform in Manor Place Baths, Camberwell. In winter the swimming pool was boarded over and a boxing ring erected on top of it. Amateur boxing matches took place there for all ages and weights. Miss Beer's troupe was to provide the pre-match entertainment in the boxing ring. The baths were in a dank old building half a mile from the Elephant and Castle. The building also housed the public wash house where the air was hot, steamy and filled with the tang of chlorine, wet clothes and disinfectant.

Ella had rehearsed a short ballet solo. She watched from the side as the other children went on first with their tap-dancing routine. Their arms swung from side to side in unison as they sang:

'Hey neighbour, say neighbour

How's the world with you?' Clickety-clack. Clickety-clack.

Something had gone wrong. The tap shoes did not sound right on the canvas of the boxing ring. In fact, they did not sound at all. Confused by the muffled noise, the tap-dancers broke rhythm like a troop of soldiers breaking step to cross a bridge. They tip-tapped to a halt and stood looking at each other. An anguished Miss Beer, near to tears, gestured desperately for Ella to go on next.

Ella climbed in the ring and stood, as she had been taught, with one foot crossed behind the other and her arms curved at her sides. When the cue came and she started to dance it was as if the music had suddenly overflowed and caused her to move.

Half-way through her piece there was a disturbance. A skinny boy of about nine, ready for combat in his blue boxing shorts and gigantic boxing gloves jumped up from the front row of the audience and dashed towards the ring. He put his boxing gloves up to the sides of his head like two enormous Mickey Mouse ears, pulled a terrible face and capered up and down on the spot in a wild parody of her dance. An attendant grabbed him in a neck-lock and hauled him away.

Ella finished the piece. Sporadic applause echoed through the hall. Miss Beer, already distraught by the silent tap-dancing, tried to make the best of the incident to Ella's mother:

'She was very heroic to carry on. Very professional. That's what I was always taught to do if anything went amiss. Just keep going. I trained under Biddy Pinchard, you know.'

Ella slipped away to the deserted stage at the end of the hall where the boy had been confined. The black curtains hanging at either side of the stage smelled stale and musty with disuse. The boy was sitting swinging his legs on a bench in the dark wings. She could barely distinguish his features in the gloom. They stared at each other. He pulled another terrible face and after a minute or two she backed off and returned to the others.

*

As a child, Ella was convinced she could break the laws of physics. She had heard about, although not seen, a doll – some sort of little mannikin – that could not be knocked over and which always bounced back upright. Ella was convinced that, given the chance, she could knock it out flat. She longed to see one, knowing without doubt that should she ever come across one of these resilient creatures she would be able to deck it for ever. She had also heard about the secret of perpetual motion and was sure she could solve that. She would lie on the floor of their council flat for hours trying to make four pencils resting on each other in a square click around for eternity. It never worked but she always felt that she came close.

Later on, when she became a dancer, it appeared as if she was almost able to break the laws of physics or at least bend them to her will: the forces of gravity, spin and friction all came under her control.

*

Ella's father came from Surinam. Her parents met at a tea dance in the Locarno on the Strand. Alice Pimms soon fell for Hubert de Vries. He was a man with gentle manners who danced with a timeless grace that made her feel that she was floating across the floor. He had come over from Surinam via Holland to work as a clerk for a Dutch sugar company. Unbeknownst to either of them, his tuberculosis was already well advanced when they married. Six months after the wedding he jerked up in bed with a coughing fit. When Alice switched on the bedside lamp she found their pillow streaked with dark blood. Hubert was sent to a sanatorium in Surrey. Four months after he was admitted, Ella was born in Camberwell's King's College Hospital.

Every other Saturday, the 'fever bus' left Trafalgar Square to take relatives of the patients to the sanatorium. For two years Alice de Vries caught the bus and took Ella along. A nurse would wheel her husband along the paved walkways to where she sat waiting in the grounds with the baby in her arms. She was anxious about letting him hold her for too long and tried to pull Ella away after a few minutes lest the child too became infected.

For most of her childhood Ella's father was in and out of hospitals and sanatoria. Sometimes he was allowed home for a few months. At one point they performed an operation to remove his left lung. The doctors warned him never to return to South America. The climate, they said, would kill him. Alice took odd jobs waitressing and managed somehow with the help of her sisters.

One September afternoon Alice and her sisters decided to take Hubert out for a picnic in some woodland near Chislehurst. Ella saw her father standing a little way apart under the trees. Suddenly, she saw him as a stranger might and understood that a stranger might find him a little frightening. She saw that he was alien to the landscape. Amongst the slender birch and silver beech trees he looked so un-English. He was lost in thought. Alice had brought his winter coat along even though the weather was not yet cold. Tuberculosis and the operation to remove his lung had twisted his spine into a question mark, so the ill-fitting herring-bone coat hung loosely from his shoulders. His complexion was dark and sallow. His eyes were circled with black. Ella had inherited his slender arms and obsidian eyes. She felt a rush of affection for him and ran over to give him a hug. He bent his head and butted her lightly with his forehead. He had learned long ago never to kiss his child directly or even breathe on her.

'All right. All right. Run along now,' he said and patted her on the shoulder. He rarely spoke. He conserved his energy. Often his speech was preceded by a cough or he would clear his throat. He was thin and gaunt and seemed somehow removed from the robust fair-skinned English family into which he had married, and who now sat chatting and joking apart from him surrounded by the debris of the picnic.

Chapter Seventeen

One year later there was a rupture in Ella's life. While her father was in the sanatorium Alice too became seriously ill and was hospitalised with a series of operations for appendicitis and then peritonitis and septicaemia. In a flurry it was arranged for Ella's uncle to take her back to Surinam until her mother was well again.

Pa Tem or Uncle Pa as Ella called him was nothing like her father. The siblings in that family had a kaleidoscopic mix of racial features, African, Amerindian, Dutch and Indonesian. Pa Tem looked more African. He spoke both English and Dutch creole. Ella's father Hubert was slender and had an Amerindian's lighter skin colour.

They disembarked at Paramaribo on a Carnival weekend and the city shook its old bones in readiness to greet Ella with its salt-laden trade winds and well laid out grass-edged streets. But the alien heat and the wind which carried strange stagnant smells made her nauseous. Pa Tem and his official wife Tanta Marti lived in a white wooden box of a house off Gravenstraat. Tanta Marti welcomed her at the door wearing a bright skirt and stiff head-wrap that scratched Ella when she bent to embrace her. At the back of the house was a small patch of lawn.

'You can play here on the grass as much as you want,' said Tanta Marti.

Ella looked down at the tough wide blades of coarse tropical grass:

'This isn't grass. It's leaves,' she said.

The next morning Ella was unable to eat the paw-paw, fresh guava and bakes that were put in front of her. Her face was a smooth rink of glycerine tears.

'I want my mother,' she said.

'As soon as your mummy gets better you will go back to her.'

'What if she dies?'

Tanta Marti looked at the child with concern. She wiped her hands on the back of her hips:

'I'll tell you what we will do today. I'm going to take you to visit a friend of mine who will know all about your mother.'

The heat pressed down on Ella as she followed her aunt through the streets. Tanta Marti took her hand as they entered a small rum shop.

'Ella, this is my old friend Papa Bones. He has a list of everyone who is going to die. He can tell you about your mummy.' She gave Papa Bones a meaningful look and put money on the table. He beckoned Ella to sit on his lap. His eyes were glazed with rum. He mumbled something in Dutch creole and pulled four grubby lined sheets of an exercise book from his pocket. On each line was written a barely decipherable name.

'What is your mama's name?'

'Alice de Vries.'

Papa Bones went through the list naming each name in turn and looking questioningly at Ella after each one. He reached the end of the list:

'Your mama's name is not here so she can't die yet.'

Tanta Marti beamed.

'Thank you, Papa Bones. You should join us in the Wie Eegie Sanie independence movement. My husband is a member now.'

'I don' business with politics.' Papa Bones looked over at Ella who was standing by the door. He whispered in Tanta Marti's ear:

'That chile is danger. She attracts danger. Or she attracted to it. Or she cause it. I don't know which.'

Tanta Marti looked perplexed. She was about to ask Papa Bones what he meant when an agitated brown-skinned woman with a jangling harness of cheap gold jewellery rushed into the shop. The woman pushed Tanta Marti aside and sat down opposite Papa Bones. Without waiting to introduce herself she launched into a confession that in her youth she had had affairs with two South American lovers. Both of these men had died and now suddenly they were coming back and fondling her at night. Tanta Marti hovered nearby to listen.

'What parts do they fondle?' asked Papa Bones. The woman touched her breast and pointed further down.

'I will come to your home tonight and throw holy water on whatever parts the dead men play with.'

Tanta Marti thought she saw Papa Bones give her a sly wink as she steered Ella away and through the door.

Outside Carnival was underway. Ella gazed with delight at a group of Djukas dancing to a powerful drumbeat. The dance required great stamina. They crouched low to the ground with raised knees that looked like the bent legs of black spiders. Their feet drummed on the ground as they passed. After half an hour the baking heat made Ella wilt and she was sick at the side of the road.

*

Uncle Pa took Ella with him to the interior when he visited his mistress. The night before they left Tanta Marti smashed some plates against the kitchen wall.

'Don't worry,' said Pa Tem to Ella. 'Tanta Marti is vex. She havin' a little tantrum and throwing some crockery about de place.'

They travelled by boat. Uncle Pa's consort was a Trio Indian woman called Suki, dark and fiery with eight children, some by Pa Tem. When she spoke her own Trio language it sounded to Ella as if she were shouting. But there was an immediacy in her glance and a tremendous vitality and vigour about her that appealed to Ella. One of her daughters, Marijke, was the same age as Ella. The two little girls fell in love with each other the way children do and played together. Ella loved the physical freedom of running around all day naked apart from her panties.

Two soldiers from the nearby camp arrived at the house. The dogs barked as the men walked down the slope. They asked if they could borrow one of Pa Tem's planks. Both men wore standard baggy camouflage trousers, heavy boots and army olive-green T-shirts. The soldiers were part of an army contingent that had been sent to the interior to suppress the independence movement that had spread there. They said they needed a plank because the ground near the camp was marshy.

Pa Tem's planks were kept lying across the wooden roof-poles under the open eaves of the palm thatch roof. They were there to serve as coffins should any of the family die. The sergeant was a burly man of African descent. He pointed to the plank he wanted and then swung himself up on the beam to help Pa Tem heave it down from the roof.

'You must be fit,' panted Pa Tem.

'I should be,' replied the sergeant as he manhandled the plank down to the ground. 'I'm an army sports instructor.'

The two soldiers hoiked the plank onto their shoulders and pushed their way past Suki who was making lemonade.

'Bring me some of that lemonade. Bring it to the camp,' ordered the sergeant as he left. Pa Tem grumbled as he watched the men make their way along the track from the house:

'Dese people does come and tek wha' dey does like.'

'That ground is not marshy. It hasn't rained for months,' commented Suki. She watched the men go. 'We will fetch the plank back when they leave.'

She held three lemons in each hand which she had picked from the lemon tree at the back of the house. Now she went over to the wooden table to squeeze them. She added water and spoonfuls of sugar, beating it all together with a spoon in a battered aluminium bowl. She poured the liquid into a red plastic jug leaving the thick white pulp and pips floating on top:

'Ella you must take these to the sergeant.' Ella sensed that Suki resented her for not working as hard as the other children. She was not an unkind woman but her manner was brusque. 'Don't leave the jug behind. It's the only one we have. Put on your dress. You can't go just like that in your panties. The track by the creek will bring you to the road and you can see the camp from there.'

Suki's scolding tone filled Ella with apprehension. Wearing her blue cotton dress she set off with the red plastic jug, determined not to spill the juice, and walked along the trail down to the creek. One of the dogs trotted a little way behind her dashing off sometimes to follow a scent.

Half-way along the trail Ella came to a halt. From somewhere nearby there came an ominous sound which she could not identify. The reverberating noise grew louder. At first she thought it was an animal growling. She looked up. Some way ahead of her and to her left was a dead giant mora tree. Ten feet up on the trunk was what looked like a seething black ball, two feet wide, whose shape was constantly changing. It hung tenuously from a deep cleft in the tree. The noise was appalling. One sentinel bee darted out and buzzed angrily near her face before returning to the nest. Several other bees flew out of the nest and back in a trajectory of fury. The humming black ball-mass of creatures detached itself from the trunk and became airborne, flying towards her, a long black cloud stretching and shrinking as it drew near her. She threw down the jug of lemonade. Something like a tin-tack drove into her head and then another, then several more down her arms. Instinct told her not to move. The dog, however, began to run towards the creek. Angered by the movement the swarm wheeled with one mind and attacked the dog en masse. The dog yelped and leaped in the air. It howled and shook its head as the bees swarmed into its mouth and over its eyes. It tried to continue running but the ferocity of the bee-attack overcame it. Soon Ella could only see a dog-shaped mass of seething bees on the ground. Somewhere underneath the dog was twitching and quivering uncontrollably. Finally, it stopped and the bees crawled here and there clambering over each other.

Ella remained motionless despite the fact that there were one or two bees in her hair. The swarm suddenly became calm. The air was filled with the scent of lemon. The bees began to circle around her head in a black corona. Instead of the angry buzz the air was filled with a benign hum. Several bees filed slowly up her arm without stinging her. She looked at the jug and the spilt lemonade. Lines of bees were steadily entering the jug, stumbling over the pips and lemon pulp. After ten minutes the swarm re-grouped. The wild bees continued to circle Ella's head before flying back to the segmented honeycombs in the crevice of the tree. She did not dare look at the corpse of the dog.

When she returned home she told Pa Tem what had happened. Suki dabbed some concoction made from cinchona bark on the stings and put her in a hammock. Pa Tem looked at her with anxiety:

'That chile gat fever. How come she survive? Those were killer bees – the ones that come over from Brazil. Look at what they did to the dog. She lucky she alive.'

Suki shrugged.

'Maybe she's mistress of bees.'

A few days later the body of an Amerindian was discovered nearby. He had been beheaded. Pa Tem's plank was found at the scene covered in blood. The children gathered round in wide-eyed silence. Pa Tem came over to Suki and spoke in a low voice:

'I think I should take Ella back. Things aren't right here. I'm responsible for her. I don't know what's happening with the army. It's something to do with the independence movement and I don't know which side the army is on. I think that army sports instructor who came to the house might have something to do with all this.'

Suki narrowed her eyes with scorn:

'This ain' nothing to do wid no independence movement. The soldiers don' like we Indians. That's de trouble. They does kill us for fun.'

Outside a gentle rain was falling. Suki looked out of the window. Her eyes softened with sadness:

'Dead man's rain,' she said. 'It's the sort of rain that falls when a good man dies.'

That night Ella lay in her hammock looking up at the grey planks which would serve as her coffin should the need arise. She crossed her arms over her chest and imagined she was already dead and encased in a plank coffin. For a few days she lost faith in words and stopped speaking. The whole panoply of human speech seemed to be a covering up of something else; some other reality about which she had not been warned.

'She gone quiet,' said Pa Tem. 'But her daddy is a quiet sort of chap. Mebbe she take after him.'

It was Marijke who kept her anchored to the human race. Marijke had the inspired idea of joining her in the world of silence. They created a life together without speech. Gradually, playing and miming turned into a game. Marijke communicated warmth and fun and beamed pleasure through her eyes. After a while Ella began to speak again.

It took a week for the boat to arrive that would take Pa Tem and Ella back to Paramaribo. About two hours into the journey they heard gunfire. The toothless old boatman laughed at Pa Tem's nervousness:

'That's not the military. That comes from further downriver. Plantation Roorak. There used to be a leper colony there years ago. Some lepers escaped and tried to make their way back to Paramaribo. They drowned. Their spirits are said to wander around looking for the way to Paramaribo. People fire off guns to frighten the spirits away. Nothing to worry about.'

*

News came that Ella's mother was well again and Ella could return to England.

'We'll see you again,' said Tanta Marti as she delivered Ella into the hands of the stewardess on the docked ship. 'Tell your daddy when we save enough money we comin' to live in Holland.'

Tanta Marti stood waving at her niece from the dock as the *Nieuwe Amsterdam* sounded its melancholy horn and departed for Liverpool.

Chapter Eighteen

On her return Ella found that they had moved to a council estate in south London. Hubert had come out of the sanatorium and sat on the steps of Lambeth Town Hall until the council officers heard his case. He explained that he was an immigrant, married with a child and suffered from tuberculosis. Within weeks they had been allocated a flat on the second floor of a council block.

*

Twice a week Ella attended a local ballet class where she could immerse herself in the silent language of dance. That was where she felt most at home. There was only the squeak of shoes, the scratching scrape of toes dipped into the rosin-box and the familiarity of the teacher's voice counting the beat or calling out instructions for an enchaînement:

'Glissade. Assemblé. Glissade. Assemblé. Pas de bourrée. Coupé.'

If the steps were complicated the teacher would ask Ella to demonstrate or take the lead. She was not among the brightest at school but her body seemed to have an intelligence of its own. When called upon she could execute the steps, seemingly without effort, and then go back to leaning on the barre and day-dreaming.

One Saturday, when she was thirteen, she came home from ballet class and lazed on her bed. Gradually, she became aware of intimations of some seismic spinning centrifugal force like the deep tugging pull of a magnet in the dark lower anterior of her body. She put her hand down and rubbed herself between her legs. The feeling intensified until it became unbearably delicious and culminated in an eruption of concentric waves of pleasure, as if a stone had fallen into the blackest and deepest of pools and a goldfish was dancing in the centre of the blackness. After that, she discovered that she could make love to almost anything: pillows, hot-water bottles, cushions, even the back edge of the sofa while her parents watched television.

Alice worried that her thirteen-year-old daughter seemed possessed by a sort of lethargy. Apart from attending school and dance class Ella did nothing. She stayed in bed all morning at weekends. She lay in the bath for hours at a time listening to Top of the Pops on a portable radio, her hair floating around her like black seaweed, until the water grew first tepid then cold. Sometimes she drained the bath and lay there as if in an enamel coffin. Late one winter afternoon, when it was growing dark, her mother walked into the bathroom to put out fresh towels. Ella lay prone in the bath. The only light came from the glowing orange bar of the Radox heater fixed to the wall. Although she said nothing, Alice was startled by the beauty of her daughter's limbs and underwent a sense of shock at the sight of that perfectly proportioned body glimmering in the dusk.

'Get out of there. That water's getting cold. You'll catch your death.'

Ella stood up like a statue with the water dripping off her and Alice handed her a towel, feeling uncomfortably like a retainer in service.

At night in bed Ella ran her hands over the smoothness of herself, enjoying the relaxed pleasure of caressing her own flesh, the curves and dips of her body as she moved and stretched.

Chapter Nineteen

Ella knew that her father was going to die when he started to sing. Alice was away at her sister's house in Kent. When Ella went with him to the shopping centre at the Elephant and Castle he took her arm and stopped frequently. He sang or hummed under his breath. The doctor had told her that people do this when their heart or lungs are failing. It is an instinctive way of regulating the breath. Sometimes he whistled, which served the same purpose. One day when he and Ella were at home together he stood at the sink washing up with a tea cloth tucked into the waist of his trousers. He addressed by her full name as he always did.

'Elissa, your daddy is dying. You must help your mother. She has been a good wife to me.' Ella looked at him but said nothing. She helped him dry the dishes. When Alice returned she bustled around with silent anxiety, tending to her husband, who now sat motionless in his chair for most of the day gazing straight ahead of him.

On the day he died Ella was given the news by her headmistress at school and ran all the way home, anxious about her mother, but also curious at this new experience of death. From the courtyard she looked up to see her mother by the window-sill watering the flowers. Smells of cooking drifted from the windows of the other flats. She dashed up the stone stairs of their block. The door of the council flat was open like the flap of an advent calendar revealing the cheery interior. As she rushed in her mother turned towards

Ella with a look of worry and sadness on her face. She held Ella in a warm embrace.

'What are we going to do now?' said her mother.

A month later some sort of solution presented itself.

'We want to enter Ella for a scholarship to the Royal Ballet School,' said her dance teacher. Alice was doubtful. Dancing seemed a precarious sort of existence. When her sister Doris came to visit, Alice consulted her about it.

*

The two sisters looked alike. They were both sturdily built with frank open faces and Anglo-Saxon blue eyes. Doris sat in the kitchen with all her shopping around her in white plastic bags that bulged out on either side of her like water wings. Alice complained: 'I don't know what to do with her. She keeps her nose in a book all day so she can't see the dust. I don't know why she reads.' Alice was a practical woman who suspected that all forms of intellectual activity were some sort of disease. 'You pick up a book and the next thing you know you've wasted three hours.' Alice took a basket of plastic clothes-pegs out onto the tiny balcony, put a couple of pink pegs in her mouth as she pinned up the washing and came back inside with some dry clothes.

'You can do some of this ironing for me if you like – while you're sitting there doing nothing.'

Doris unfolded the ironing-board, picked up the iron and examined it.

'Steam iron, eh Alice?' she chuckled. 'We're living in the fast lane now.'

Alice took out her sewing-box and fumbled around in it looking for some blue thread to stitch a patch on Ella's jeans. The potatoes bubbled on the stove. Doris flipped a pillow case over and began pressing the damp corners, while the steam iron sighed its regular mechanical sigh like someone breathing in an iron lung.

'Maybe she likes reading. She's clever. She's got your brains.'

'I wondered where they'd gone.'

'My friend Terry's got a daughter like that. She's studying something at a university.'

Alice broke off the cotton with her teeth.

'Studying what?'

'Something with a terrible name.'

Alice put down the jeans, went over to the stove and prodded the potatoes with a fork.

'These potatoes are devils for not breaking up.'

'Potatoes are devils,' agreed Doris. She watched while Alice juggled pots and pans, releasing clouds of steam into the fizzing bubbling chemistry of her kitchen.

'Mind you, they say bread is life but so are potatoes,' said Alice. 'I miss my Hubert you know. He was a lovely man. Even though we had our differences. He liked rice.'

'Did you ever think of leaving him for anyone else?'

'Not really. Why change one kitchen sink for another?'

'What was wrong with him in the end?' Doris asked.

'Same old lungs.'

'Lungs are terrible things,' said Doris. 'What happened to that friend of yours in hospital?'

'She's dead too.'

'What from?'

'A clogged something. Pass me the masher. Mind you, I believe in anastasia for the old. Anasthaesia or whatever it is.'

Doris passed her sister the potato-masher from the drawer. Alice drained the potatoes in the sink and began to mash them.

'I wouldn't mind leaving London you know, now Hubert's gone. I might come out your way. Move to Kent. I wouldn't mind Kent.'

'You'd miss London. You love London.'

'London was all right till they got rid of the fog.'

Alice stopped mashing for a minute and glanced out of the window: 'What I love is seeing that washing dancing on the line. I love all that fresh air and wind and the sea and the countryside. I could get a little job working in the fields. Fruit-picking. Do they still have hops?'

'No. Hop-picking is more or less over now. That's all gone. We pick whatever is in season. I like it all right but it doesn't pay.'

'Dinner's ready,' Alice called out to Ella who was still in bed.

Ella wandered in still wearing her nightie at midday, yawning and rubbing the sleep from her eyes with the backs of her wrists. She pushed her long black hair back with her hands.

'Look at that lovely hair,' said Doris admiringly.

'Go and put something on. Brighten yourself up. Dinner's on the table.' Ella drifted out again. 'She gets that sallow complexion from her father. When she was little I had to put rouge on her cheeks in case people thought I was a bad mother.'

'It's lunch now.'

'What is?'

'Dinner. It's lunch in the middle of the day and dinner in the evening. You've got to keep up with the times, Alice.'

'Well, when I was young it was dinner at lunchtime and supper at dinnertime.'

'Is Iris coming over?' Doris enquired about their younger sister.

'Yes. She's coming tonight. We'll all have to sleep in my bed. Oh poor Iris. What a life. She's had a terrible time since Albert died. First Albert dying. Then that mother-in-law chasing her down the street with a carving knife. Then the dog died and all her hair fell out. That was all her dreams through the mangle. But she's the youngest of us and I still feel I ought to protect her somehow. If only she wasn't so stubborn. Her place is a mess. All the carpets are damp. I tried to show her how to use the gas card when Albert died. You're meant to put it in and press Button A. She doesn't understand it and she's got no intention of understanding it either. She's just waiting for big hands from the sky to help her. And she's got this hand-written notice pinned to the wall: "Beware the fury of a patient woman."'

'She's got low self-esteem,' said Doris. 'That's what's wrong with her.'

'Where did she get that from?' puzzled Alice, as the two of them laid the table.

That night Ella woke suddenly and sat up in bed. She thought she heard wolves howling. Then she realised it was screams of laughter coming from her mother and her aunts all in the one bed next door. Through the wall she heard her mother repeating a favourite joke from a comedian she had seen at the Camberwell Palace.

'He came on dressed as a housewife in an apron and said: "Here I am slaving away over a hot stove and there he is in that nice cool sewer."'

Ella listened to the howls of laughter ricocheting around the room.

*

When Ella won the scholarship to the Royal Ballet School, Alice and Doris went for a walk in Battersea Park to talk it over. They sat on a bench next to a Barbara Hepworth sculpture, at the edge of a pond. The abstract sculpture had an oval hole in it. A brisk wind corrugated the surface of the water.

'I suppose she might as well go. She's got dancing-mad feet,' said Alice. 'She'd have to board.'

'Does she want to go?'

'Oh she's dead keen as far as anyone can tell. You can't tell anything with her.'

'What about money?'

'She'd get a grant, apparently. The scholarship pays the fees. If she goes I'll definitely move down to Kent near you so you'd better start looking out for a place for me.'

Doris was munching a sandwich and staring with suspicion at the sculpture:

'What's that supposed to be?'

'It's a sculpture.'

'I could have done that.'

'No you couldn't. It's art.'

Doris pointed at a brown speckled duck that was paddling towards them across the water:

'Now that's beautiful. And it works.'

'Yes, Doris. But that's not art. That's an animal. What do you reckon, then, about Ella?' asked Alice.

'I suppose she might as well go.' Doris threw the bread crusts on the water.

*

That September Alice moved to the village of Eythorne near Dover and Ella went to board at the Royal Ballet School in Barons Court.

Other students found her remote. She hung around on the edge of the group but spoke little. The girls sometimes went shopping en masse to Carnaby Street where they bought Mondrian style minidresses, pill-box hats and patterned tights while Chubby Checker and Beatles music blared out from the shops. Ella went with them to coffee bars, played the juke-boxes, and shopped with them for sexy underwear, camisoles and suspenders. She took part in the fun when they came back and laid out everything on the beds to inspect the haul, or when they pranced around doing the Twist. But the others never felt that they really knew her.

'Where is she from?' asked one of the other students.

'I don't know. Someone said Mexico.'

'She's not Mexican. She's about as Mexican as Baked Alaska. She's got a London accent.'

'She's sort of coffee-coloured though. And those dark eyes.'

Ella's progress as a dancer, however, was clear to everybody. She had certain inborn advantages: strong slender ankles and an instep with the strength of steel. She had both stamina and flexibility. Her dancing seemed entirely spontaneous and she had an instinctive use of variety in musical phrasing. It was no surprise to anyone when, at the age of fifteen, she was offered a place in the corps de ballet of the company. She was given special permission to reside at the school until she was sixteen. She settled down at the Royal Ballet to gain in strength and experience. Other dancers in the company also found her difficult to befriend. They put it down to her youth or shyness. There was something hidden about her. No-one could tell when something upset her. She just smiled and lowered her eyelashes.

'I'm OK,' she would say after a fall or some other setback in class.

Ella struck up one close friendship outside the company. She met Hetty Moran at the Saturday jazz-dance classes, which she could not resist attending despite being warned that contemporary dance might interfere with her classical training. Once a week she sneaked away to dance to the rhythms of samba and Cuban salsa. Hetty worked as a secretary in the offices of an American pharmaceutical company, Merkel, Sharpe and Dolme. She attended dance classes in the hope that healthy exercise might offset her habit of smoking twenty cigarettes a day. From the beginning Ella admired Hetty. She warmed to Hetty's wise-cracking humour, her quick grasp of things and penetrating intuition. Hetty was a slim blonde who bubbled with vitality. She was one or two years older than Ella. There was a kind of unreflective outgoing generosity about her; a daring and panache that impressed Ella. To Ella, the American girl felt like a breath of fresh air, bold and liberated compared with the residual stuffy post-war Britishness that clung to the ballet school and the company. She and Hetty fell into the habit of going to a café and drinking iced coffees together after class. One day Hetty asked Ella if she would like to share her flat in Old Compton Street. And Ella moved in.

Chapter Twenty

'Welcome home, honey.' Hetty threw open her arms to indicate the small space which they would be sharing.

It was only eighteen months since Hetty Moran had quit Omaha, Nebraska for good.

They say the wind never stops blowing in Nebraska and on the day that Hetty Moran decided to leave the wind was as hot and steady as the blast from a hair-dryer. On that particular day Hetty carried inside her all the restless and chronic impermanence of America. She had gone for a job interview at the new Novotel. The road leading from the Novotel back into town was deserted. The hotel was the only finished building in a new development on the outskirts of town, a monolith that rose up against the blue sky in the middle of nowhere, surrounded by vacant ungroomed lots scattered with builders' debris and tufts of seeding grass. Wild goldenrod sprouted from surrounding patches of rubble.

Hetty Moran was all spruced up for her appointment but when she turned into the wide asphalt forecourt of the fifteen storey building she suddenly changed her mind and sat on the low wall outside instead. She bent to light her cigarette. The wind blew a double helix strand of blonde hair over her eyes. Two sharp pincer lines formed a frown on her pretty, featureless face. She scowled and pushed the hair out of her eyes. She drew slowly on her cigarette and squinted up at the building. Balconies jutted out all the way down one side like rough concrete vertebrae with the blue sky showing in between. For nearly half an hour she waited there in the sun smoking first one cigarette and then another until the time for the interview had passed. Then she flicked the butt of the last cigarette away, picked up her shoulder-bag and walked slowly away from the hotel back towards the road.

Now there was just the kerb and the road and the enormous Nebraska sky. The silence pressed on her ears. A vehicle passed by with a muted hiss on the smooth road making its way from somewhere in the outer suburbs to the shopping mall a mile away. Just once she looked back at the hotel and its ratchet silhouette. She thought half-heartedly about what excuse she might give her mother for not attending the interview. She could say that the interviewer had never turned up or that there had been a road accident on the way there. She would tell her friends something else, perhaps: that she had been offered the job of assistant manageress but turned it down. She concentrated on walking. The sides of the road were no longer paved so she had to tread over dry brown earth and patches of grass. Nobody walked in those parts. If you didn't drive you didn't exist. Soon she was covered in a light film of sweat. Her white cotton blouse clung to her chest. She preferred to keep her eyes lowered to the ground. Whenever she looked up, the huge sky and wide open space of the empty plains made her feel fearful and exposed, with nowhere to hide.

It was a relief when she reached the top of a slope and the familiar outline of the Bass Pro store which had replaced the old grain elevator came into sight on her left. The hot gusting wind became stronger, and all of a sudden it was blowing all around her like hysteria looking for a victim. She felt the first signs of a panic attack; palpitations kicking in her chest like an unruly foetus. Hetty tried taking deep breaths, gulping in the air, but that only made her heart pound more and made the surrounding emptiness seem to invade and become part of her.

Now the wind from across the plains was moaning in her ears. She tried not to look at the vast expanse of land around her. It made her disorientated, as though she had lost the boundaries of her body and was made of air. To ground herself and make herself feel real she clenched her fists until her nails dug into the palms. Quickly she sat down at the roadside, welcoming the feel of the gritty earth beneath her, and fished in her bag for a Valium. A few minutes later she took another of the small yellow pills. After a while she became less agitated and decided that she could manage the walk home. She stood up. The silence settled back down over her. All she could hear was the sound of her own breathing and the scrunch of her footsteps. The whole of America might have been a sound-proof chamber through which no sound from the outside world penetrated. 'Sheeyit.' She cursed as her ankle turned over on the uneven ground. But she felt calmer now, despite the sensation that she was walking in a mirage, moving forward without making progress.

*

Where Hetty Moran lived was on the south side of Omaha, in a sprawling wasteland of cinder-block houses behind the old meatpacking factories. It was Nebraska in the sixties. The stores had broken fluorescent lighting and the diners served greasy food on faded Formica tables. Omaha was known for its granaries and for producing Malcolm X. Hetty did not care much about either. She lived with her mother in an apartment over a pet food shop on Grenadine Street. When she finally reached home, instead of going through the front door next to the store entrance, she climbed the iron fire-escape at the back of the house and let herself in that way.

Her mother was sitting, legs apart, watching TV on the old battered settee, lank brown hair done up like a child's in two side-bunches. Without taking her eyes off the TV she fumbled under her bulky backside and pulled out a bunch of letters which she waved at her daughter.

'What's all this crap? You writin' to people sayin' you engaged to a Japanese pilot who's crazy about you and waitin' till you're twenty to marry you and take you back to Tokyo?' She gave a derisive snort and chucked the letters on the floor. Hetty grabbed at the letters pale with anger. Her voice slid upwards:

'You been in my room again?'

'If you call that pigsty a room, yeah.'

'You are so much of a fucking cow it's not true.'

'Raised on a Nebraska dairy farm, honey. At least cows are honest. You don' open your mouth 'cept to give birth to a big lie out of it. You should sleep well you lie so easy.'

Ma Moran's podgy hand dived into a packet of popcorn and she leaned forward to gaze intensely at the screen. After a couple of minutes she raised a face round and pasty as uncooked pizza dough and looked at her daughter with dislike:

'What happened with the job?'

'They cancelled the interview. The woman didn't turn up.'

Ma Moran blew a disbelieving hiss out of her mouth.

Hetty crossed her arms and stared fixedly at her mother.

'Has it ever occurred to you that with a mother like you I might just kill myself?'

'Sure. Go get a noose and get the chair ready.' Her mother chuckled.

Hetty's eyes narrowed.

'Your ass is so big and bulky it looks like you're still wearing diapers. You smell like it too.' She slammed out of the room. Still staring at the TV Ma Moran yelled after her:

'You better pull yourself together and get a job, young lady. This is real life, you know. This ain't no dress rehearsal.'

Hetty flounced into her own room and changed her clothes. She sat on her bed and laced up the trainers. It was at that moment she decided to leave Omaha for good. She pulled her hair back with both hands and twisted it deftly into a pony tail, placing her sunglasses so that they perched like a black butterfly on top of her head.

In the kitchen the yellowing old box freezer rattled and whirred. Hetty lifted the lid and took a quick slug from the frosted bottle of vodka that her mother always kept there. The vodka hit the back of her throat like iced gasoline. Grasping the letters, she slipped into her mother's bedroom. The windows were open. Cheap curtains that hung on wire over the window were blowing in the breeze. She ripped up the offending letters and tossed them on her mother's bed. Her heart thumped with that particular shame which comes from having your camouflage spotted. Then she opened the bottom drawer of the dresser and took out her mother's fifteen welfare books, each one laboriously forged with a different name. These she stuffed into a large brown envelope which she put in her shoulder bag. A minute later she had gone, banging the back door behind her.

The neighbourhood baked in the afternoon sun and the asphalt road surface turned soft in the heat. This was the dead-end of town. The blind eyes of the boarded-up shops depressed Hetty Moran as she walked towards the Welfare Office. It was housed in a three-storey brick building the colour of dried ox-blood which had once served as a grain depot. Hetty went up the front steps and pushed open the doors. Inside there was no air-conditioning. Sitting behind a counter in the main hall was the receptionist, a gingerish dry-skinned woman in her forties with hair set square and firm like a loaf of bread. Hetty approached her with an exaggerated demeanour of respect. In her hand she held the brown envelope stuffed with her mother's forged welfare books. She opened her eyes wide.

'Excuse me ma'am. I'm sorry to trouble you, but I found these in the street outside and I thought I should bring them in. Think they might belong here.'

'Well, thank you, dear.' The woman's frown deepened as she looked through the contents and saw the forged welfare books, all in different names, clearly faked and all with the same address in Grenadine Street. She reached for the telephone. Outside, Hetty skipped down the steps.

She looked back at the converted grain depot, certain that she belonged somewhere altogether more glamorous than Omaha, Nebraska. Houston appealed to her. She had seen Houston on TV, a huge insectivorous city, with its giant gelatinous buildings and corporate sky-line; a city of glacial ice-lollies in the desert. She went to the bus station and checked the timetables. Not until it was dark did Hetty creep back into her own home.

Nembutal snores issued from her mother's bedroom like the

creaking of a door. Straight away Hetty began packing. She put her favourite clothes into a suitcase. She went to the medicine cabinet in the bathroom and emptied it of first-aid kit: bottles of Valium, Librium, Diazepam, Ritalin, Nembutal, Benzedrine, Mogadon and anything else that she could find. She tip-toed into the kitchen and found her mother's handbag and chequebooks, which she transferred into her own purse.

At the bus station she used one of the cheques to buy her ticket. The Greyhound bus pulled out of Omaha bus station headed for Kansas City, Oklahoma City, Dallas and Houston. Hetty watched each identikit neon-lit pod town as it came and went by; an endless sequence of interconnected shopping centres linked by a mesh of highways, billboards, motels and fast-food outlets. Her heart was set on Houston.

*

Hetty liked her uniform as a hospital cleaner in the private maternity home on the outskirts of Houston. It consisted of a small white cap and a blue and white overall. She was full of enthusiasm and eager to do well. It was her job to hoover the thin blue carpeting in the corridors. She also had to wipe down the tubular legs of the beds with disinfectant and clean the telephones by the patients' beds.

She was glad she was not one of these new mothers. They looked big, milky-breasted and misshapen from the waist up, and reported that they felt uncomfortable and sore from the waist down. She cleaned around them as they drank their required tumbler of water or slept humped up in the bed.

Each patient occupied a private room. There were ten such rooms on every corridor with a nursery at the end where the babies were put. Hetty let herself in to the nursery quietly in order not to wake the babies. A soft smell of disinfectant and baby-powder clung to the shiny pastel walls. There were ten cots but only six were occupied. All of the babies were asleep. She stood looking at them. The clock said ten past twelve. Then the clock said fifteen minutes past twelve and suddenly she was leaning over one of the cradles. Hetty pinched the baby's nostrils together in a firm grip. The baby lay still for a few moments and then squirmed. Hetty looked towards the door and put her other hand over its mouth. She watched with interest as the baby's back arched and its arms swung out from beneath the light covering sheet. She held on to the baby's nose, gripping it with casual indifference and regarding the infant with curiosity. Then, noticing that her fingers were becoming covered in the baby's dribble, she took her hand away in disgust and wiped it on her overall. The baby gasped and screamed.

At that moment the doors swished open and a nurse came in. Hester experienced the sort of thrill that comes with a near miss. She smiled at the nurse. She had neither smothered the child nor been caught. It was like a game of grandmother's footsteps. She had not been detected. She was innocent.

The nurse smiled back and lifted the wailing infant from his cot.

'I wasn't sure what to do when he started crying,' said Hetty, smoothing the baby's soft cheek gently with her forefinger. 'I didn't know if I was supposed to lift him out.'

'Oh no. You're not supposed to touch them.'

'Goodness. Just as well I didn't. Poor little mite.' Hetty put her head on one side and smiled at the shrieking baby. 'Oh what's the matter?' She shrugged with helplessness and looking directly into the eyes of the nurse said: 'Don't you just feel for them?'

She felt uneasy about the incident even though no-one had seen her. Two weeks later she went into the supervisor's office looking tearful and said, 'I'm really sorry but I will have to leave. I hate to do this so soon after I've started. But my father is a Vietnam vet. He's been in an asylum for ages because of what he saw out there. Flashbacks and stuff. He's coming out now and my mom needs me to help at home. I really don't want to leave. I'm so sorry.'

*

Hetty's next job was as a receptionist for a large pharmaceutical company in mid-town Houston. She was a popular addition to the firm with her friendly grin and willingness to help.

'Sure, no probs,' she would say when asked to take over somebody else's shift at short notice.

The building was in a skyscraper complex built around a gigantic central paved patio; a dehumanised space where nobody walked. She worked on the twenty-seventh floor. Through the window Hetty could see a thousand windows glinting in the sun. The scale dwarfed humanity. Omaha seemed like hicksville in comparison. She spent more time than was strictly necessary in the ladies' bathroom, with its shining sinks, its marble-clad floors and jasmine-scented air-conditioning. She liked flicking the mascara on her eyelashes in front of the mirrors there.

Very soon she caught the eye of a middle-ranking married executive called Hank Stanton. She flirted with him but held him at bay. He developed a mild fixation on this new receptionist. When he was due to be transferred to London he asked if she would also like a transfer. He said he could fix it for her. A month later, Hetty was at the hairdressers in Ducane Street with a white towel around her neck, breathing in the sharp scent of astringent while having her hair streaked with ash-blonde highlights and undergoing a facial detox and manicure.

'I've just been given a modelling contract in England,' she told the beautician. 'I'm really nervous. I hope I can do it.'

'I'm sure you'll be fine,' the hairdresser reassured her.

Two days later, Hetty sat in the JFK departure lounge. Hank and his wife had left for London two weeks earlier. Hetty arranged herself in what she considered to be a model's pose. Her mother's words echoed in her head: 'This is real life, you know. This ain't no dress rehearsal.'

But Hetty was not bothered about any dress rehearsal. Life for her was just the lighting technical that would illuminate her in whichever pose took her fancy: glamour, grief, or heroism. For Hetty Moran, all virtue was a pose.

Chapter Twenty-One

On arriving in London after her love-struck visit to Preston, Ella hurried straight to class in Floral Street. Approaching the studio she could already hear music from the piano tinkling like ice cubes. She was late.

For Ella class was a sanctuary. It had the simple austerity of a nunnery. The floor of the studio was plain blond wood. The barre reached around three sides of the room. The fourth wall consisted entirely of mirrors in which the dancers could watch and correct their positions. Some dancers fell in love with their mirror selves and always looked sideways at their reflection, but Ella used the mirrors only to straighten the line of an arabesque or correct the curve of an attitude. There was nothing flashy about her technique. It consisted of unerring simplicity, plus a sense of abandon. In class all concentration was on the body. Nothing ornamental or decorative obscured the shape of those bodies. The dancers wore no make-up. Their hair was scraped back with differing degrees of severity, giving them an air of chaste sexiness like acolytes of some Eleusinian sisterhood both ascetic and erotic. In the cloistered seclusion of the studio all secret passions, yearnings and furies were transmuted into dance.

'I studied under Diaghilev,' the elderly Russian teacher, who walked with the help of a silver-topped cane, was saying as Ella came in. Ella apologised for being late and took her place at the barre. 'He taught us zat dancing is prehistoric. Animals dance. You are always half-way between ze animal and ze human. Dance is our craving for expression after we leave behind ze patterned instincts of animals. Here you think only with your body. We live only through ze body.'

It was generally acknowledged that Ella was one of the most promising young dancers in the company. She had a tensile strength from knee to solar plexus to neck that gave her a near perfect geometric line. Her sense of balance was such that she rarely drifted a centimetre one way or the other, which would allow gravitational torque to pull her over.

Cyrus was playing for the class that day. Above the piano in the corner hung a large portrait of Nijinsky painted entirely in various shades of blue and mauve, the legs muscled like sticks of blue plaited barley sugar. Cyrus nodded his head to acknowledge Ella. She warmed up briefly on her own before joining the class.

'Petits battements and battus, please,' shouted the teacher.

Ella held onto the barre with her left hand. She enjoyed this exercise. It produced a delicious conflict of sensations. Standing on her left leg, right arm raised, right foot resting against the left ankle, she began the slow sensuous stretch of the top half of the body led by the arm, arching her torso first towards the barre and then sideways away from it. At the same time her right foot beat rapidly against the ankle of the left foot, fluttering like the wings of a baby bird. The teacher came over and adjusted Ella's posture, pulling her thigh round a little.

'Relevé,' shouted the teacher, and the class rose obediently together. 'Demi detourné.' The class spun in unison to face the other way and repeat the exercise on the other side.

For the next hour Ella subjected herself to the familiar pain of muscles stretched and worked to their limits. After twenty minutes her legs felt like lead weights. Before long she was coated in a film of sweat and feeling sick. She waited for the brief gap between each exercise which allowed her diaphragm to expand and contract, giving her back her breath. Her left calf seized up with cramp as barre work finished and the students moved to work in the centre of the room. She rubbed her leg and flexed it.

During the arabesques the teacher's eye was drawn critically to Ella as she struggled en pointe. Then came the enchaînement.

'Lift zat left leg higher at ze back Ella. Higher. Higher. Keep ze back upright. Shoulders down. Now express something. Enjoy it. You must dance this enchaînement like you are a queen bee mating with ze sun.'

Everyone was tired, sweating and panting by the time they came to the révérence at the end of the class. Some students stood and flopped over to let their arms rest on the floor. Others leaned against the barre with heaving ribs. Révérence was the expansive bow to each section of the audience with which every class ended.

'Let zem see your neck,' said the teacher. 'In ze révérence ze audience want to see your neck.' And she opened her arms elegantly, turned her head and leaned it backwards to demonstrate how to expose the neck. 'It is possible to speak with a turn of ze hip too,' she explained, 'to walk in one direction towards a love in the grand circle box on one side of ze auditorium and suddenly turn teasingly away to someone in ze box on ze ozzer side.' She demonstrated. 'Leave ze turn of the head away from him until the last minute.'

The class undertook a mass flirt as they turned from one side of the 'auditorium' to the other.

'Good. Good. Class finished.'

The students curtseyed their thanks and applauded the teacher.

Cyrus collected up his sheet music as the dancers flocked past him up the stairs.

'I'm not coming home just now,' he said to Ella. 'I'm going over to Richmond this evening to do two more classes and earn a bit of spondulix. You'll have to tell me all about the tour later when I see you.'

As he went up the stairs Ella asked:

'Have you seen Donny since I've been away?'

Cyrus avoided her eyes and looked coy as he ran his hand through his orange hair:

'Oh. Crazy Horse. Lethally sublime Donny. The lame god of light. No, I haven't.'

*

Ella's black hair was still wet from the shower. Fronds of it stuck to her forehead and neck as she climbed the stairs to her flat. At the top her heart made an extraordinary swivel inside her chest. Coming from inside Cyrus's flat she could hear a tune being played tentatively on the piano. She stood still for a moment with her ear to the grubby cream-painted door. The smell of curry drifted up the stairs. Notes on the piano were being picked out delicately and slowly like someone exploring a thought. It was not Cyrus. Cyrus had gone over to Richmond. She held her breath and listened. There was silence. Then the music started up again. She knocked. The music stopped immediately. She knocked again. There was no reply.

'It's me,' she said.

The door opened suddenly. Donny stood there.

'Oh it's you.' He wore jeans and his feet were bare.

'Can I come in?' He stood back and she stepped into the tiny flat, which smelled of curry and damp washing. Donny's socks and a washed shirt were drying over the piano stool. There was a plate of half-eaten baked beans on the floor. She bent to move some clothes off the bed so that she could sit down, causing Donny to suffer the kind of sexual shock that can beset a young man confronted close-to with such a figure. Ella's breasts were outlined under her nylon sweater, two delicate drooping bluebells above a slender stalk of a waist. He looked away, embarrassed and disconcerted.

'Will ye have a cup of tea or what?'

She noticed that he was snaggle-toothed. His top two front teeth crossed slightly at the bottom.

'Please.'

He whistled a jaunty tune and stood with his back to her, tapping his foot and looking through the window at the fire escape while he waited for the kettle to boil. She sat on the bed. He gave her the tea and settled down on the other bed with his legs stretched out and feet crossed, watching her drink. He leaned his head against the wall where the wallpaper was streaked with grey marks from head-grease. With his chin sunk into his breastbone he stared at her. She looked up from her tea and caught his gaze.

'Is my hair a mess?' She pushed the still wet strands of black hair away from her neck, tossing her head back so that her throat was exposed.

It was then that Donny McLeod instigated that most delicate and subtle of courtships – courtship by insult.

'You look like a piece of cheese after the rats have been at it.'

Her eyes shot open with surprise. There was a pause.

'You look like a gangster's dog,' he persisted.

'No I don't.' She flushed and laughed, entering into the flirtatious spirit of it.

'Could this be the face that sank a thousand ships?'

'What a cheek.' She puffed up with delight and her eyes shone.

He leaned forward. Now there was a look of intense excitement in his eyes, and he watched her every move like a cat waiting for a crumpled ball of paper to be thrown. She finished her tea and put the cup on the floor. With each gruff insult, accompanied by a warm and mischievous glance, he edged nearer to her.

Suddenly his leg was over her thigh.

'And you've got a mouth like a plasterer's bucket,' he whispered, his breath tickling her ear so that she shivered with delight. She was giggling. There was a hand under her shirt moving up from the waist. The more grievous the insults he whispered into her ear the more she laughed. His voice had grown throaty and gruff. Rust-coloured sideburns scraped against her cheek. His lips had the bitter liquorice taste of roll-ups. His weight was on her. Something inside her was unspooling. Then came the tugging off of jeans and the throwing aside of shirts and skirts. The smell of him was the strong smell of a goat, and tumbling through her head went pictures of ungulates, fetlocks, horse-hooves, deer, goat-foot, hock-joints, amber eyes with elongated pupils and childhood pictures of Billy Goat Gruff. She dug her fingers into his back to gain some purchase on his body and struggled to achieve for herself that dark inner whorl whose spiralling sensation would culminate in a delicious cuntquake. It eluded her.

They pulled on their clothes in silence. Donny sat on the bed and rested a green and gold tin of Old Holborn tobacco on his lap. He rolled himself a cigarette. Ella leaned back and embarked quite naturally on her first post-coital chat.

'Cyrus had bad flu that first time I met you. He was off work for ages. He says he still feels wobbly.'

'Ah, but that's middle-class flu. That's different. They can stay off work for six years 'cos what they're doing is not very important.'

'Is Cyrus middle-class?' She pulled her black hair back and twisted it into a knot on top of her head.

'Well he plays the piano as if he is.' Donny blew a smoke ring. He offered her the tobacco tin and she shook her head.

'Cyrus says you are a bit irresponsible,' she said slyly.

'Of course I am. Responsibility makes arseholes of us all.'

'Why were the police after you?'

'What we do sometimes, for a laugh, is we lie in wait for some raving punter who's wandering around Soho. You can spot them a mile off. They've got that look in their eyes. We ask him if he wants to see a blue film or a live sex show. Then we take him up to the fifth floor of this derelict building and take the money off him and run down the other stairway. Turns out the guy that day was a policeman. He flashed his card and came after us.'

'Cyrus told me that you planned to go north again to work.'

'I just told him that. I don't make plans. Plans are things that put a brake on your life. I just tell other people I've got them in order to shut them up. There's cheese in the kitchen if you want it.'

'Are you a vegetarian?'

'Only when there's no meat. I don't like cheese. It's like eating the sole of somebody's foot.'

'That's what I like about you. Straight from the shoulder. No bullshit.'

'Wrong again. I'm pure bullshit.' He went over to feel his socks and shirt to see if they were dry. They were still damp. He pulled them on.

'You'll get pneumonia.'

'No I won't.'

'You shouldn't put that shirt on if it's not dry.'

'I've only got this one shirt. Which is OK 'cos I've only got one body.'

'Why don't you iron it dry?'

'Because it would make me look too handsome.'

He stood in front of the mirror and ran a comb through his hair.

'In fact, I'm so handsome I might have to start stalking myself.'

'Delusions of grandeur?' Ella teased.

'Maybe. But I bet my delusions of grandeur are better than anyone else's.'

'But you are good looking.'

'No I'm not.' He looked at her with an expression of amusement. 'I'm just alive. That's enough small talk. I'm Donny McLeod. Profound statements only, please.'

He was looking round for his jacket.

'Are you going then?'

'Yes. I've got a meeting somewhere in the city with a big bottle of wine.'

'Can I come?'

'No.'

'Why not?'

'Because I'm like a ship and I don't like fucking limpets trying to stick to me. I have to keep removing them because they slow down my journey.' He put on his jacket.

She got up. He was moving towards the door.

'Will I see you again?'

'Of course you will. What's your name again?'

'Ella.'

'See you tomorrow then, Ella.'

He was gone and Ella, undone by the goat-hock ankle, began to love most what she could least possess.

Chapter Twenty-Two

After he left, Ella let herself back into her own flat. The room had retained all the stuffy warmth of the afternoon sun. It was like walking into a block of heat. She went and looked in the mirror. Then she sat down on the bed. Her head felt as though it were on upside down. And something had happened to the floor. It had dropped. Her feet no longer seemed to touch it. She felt fretful, as if something irrevocable had happened; that she had been branded and was no longer free. She went over to the window and flung it open to the warm evening air. An odd character, half musician, half tramp, was playing his recorder in the street below. Fastened behind each ear were two red carnations. Their long stalks swung like antennae as he moved his head. The fluting sound of his recorder spiralled upwards towards her. She looked down Old Compton Street. There was no sign of Donny.

The flat Ella shared with Hetty consisted of one main room containing two single beds, one under the window and one against the partition wall. Ella slept under the window. The first thing she saw in the mornings was Hetty's hand reaching out and fumbling for the pack of cigarettes on the floor. The girls had done their best to make the place cheerful. Both beds were covered with colourful patchwork bedspreads. A small circular table stood in the centre of the room. The tiny adjoining kitchen contained a Belling stove and, against all hygiene regulations, a toilet and bath.

Before Ella went on tour there had been a minor spat between the two friends, when Ella found money missing from her purse. Hetty swore that she was just about to return it. Hetty didn't really steal, she filched. She was so sunny in her treachery that Ella soon forgave her. Besides, Hetty could exhibit an easy generosity and affection when it pleased her. On one occasion she gave Ella a beautiful skirt and blouse that she no longer wanted:

'Here, have these, honey. I really don't need them.'

Ella tried them on. A cigarette dangled from Hetty's lips as she narrowed her green eyes to take stock of Ella in her new outfit.

'Oh you look darling. They suit you.'

Sometimes Ella was not sure where she stood with her friend. There was a feeling of impermanence about her; of insidious waters; a mosaic of sunlight wavering on the blue surface of a swimming pool.

Cyrus too had mentioned a puzzling incident. Cyrus had been out with Hetty and some actor friends at a restaurant after the show. For no good reason, Hetty had suddenly thrown a glass of wine smack into the face of the mild-mannered young actor sitting opposite her. It came out of nowhere. They were not even having an argument. After she had done it she sat with a strange smile on her face.

'You bitch,' a bearded gay actor sitting next to her exploded. The young man looked dismayed and hurt as the wine dripped from his chin on to the tablecloth. She apologised, but the other diners noticed that she cast her eyes down at the table as if she wanted to laugh.

'What on earth made you do that?' asked Ella.

'Sweetie. I couldn't resist it.' She made light of the whole incident. In that way, Hetty sometimes revealed her fangs.

*

Two hours after Donny had left, Ella lay on her bed in a high-alert dream state. Hetty let herself in with a pile of shopping.

'Hi. I'm back. Has anyone called for me? It's so hot. I'm just going to take myself a quick bath.' She dumped the shopping on the table and went straight into the other room. Ella heard clothes being discarded on the floor of the tiny bathroom.

When Hetty came out of the shower, Ella was standing on the

bed with her ear pressed to the partition wall. Hetty wore a brightly patterned kimono. She unwrapped her head from a towel and a cataract of damp blonde hair fell to her shoulders.

'What are you doing?'

'Listening,' said Ella.

'For what?'

'To see if anyone is in there with Cyrus.'

The bed sagged as Ella jumped off it. Hetty rubbed her hair with the towel.

'Honey, shall we go have an Italian? I don't feel like cooking.'

Half an hour later they were sitting at their favourite table in the window of Luigi's, a small restaurant in Greek Street. It was dark outside. The bottom of the window was nearly the same height as the table. Ella sat with the large plate-glass window to her left. Hetty was facing it. Hetty suddenly shrieked and pointed at the window.

'Hey Ellie. Look at that.'

A man's head was bouncing along the bottom of the restaurant window. No torso was visible. He must have been crouching on the pavement outside and progressing in a sort of Cossack dance movement. Both index fingers were inserted in the sides of his mouth, elongating it to make a mad, humorous face. Hetty laughed out loud. The head disappeared without explanation into the night. Ella ran to the door and looked out in the street. There was no sign of him. She came back.

'That was Donny.'

'Who's he? He looks wild.'

Ella hesitated for a moment and then chose not to tell Hetty what had happened.

'A friend of Cyrus's. Cyrus calls him Crazy Horse.'

Hetty twirled strands of pasta around her fork, then shoved it in her mouth. She took a gulp of wine.

'Crazy Horse was a Sioux from Nebraska. That's where I'm from. He used to paint his face blue when he went to war, with tiny white dots for hailstones so that his enemies came face to face with a blizzard. Anyway, you must introduce me to Donny. He sounds a trip.'

*

Although Hetty had a sense of fun, she was pragmatic in her choice of partners. She sought out men of financial stability. Hank, her current boyfriend, was a balding executive who wore navy-blue nylon socks and whose white shirt smelled of Paco Rabanne after-shave. He was married. There was a photograph of him with Hetty taken in America, before he was posted to England. In the photo Hetty stands with her arm around Hank's waist. The bobby-soxiness of her blonde curls was that of a girl-next-door model on the front page of *McCalls* magazine. She was leaning her head against Hank's shoulder.

But Hank and Hetty had broken up acrimoniously. Somehow or other that very same photograph of the two of them had mysteriously been posted to Hank's wife. Hetty pleaded innocence.

'Hank. How could you think I would do such a thing?' Her eyes filled with false, fiery tears as she spoke. 'Someone at the office must have sent it. I don't know who. They must have been jealous of us and got hold of the photo somehow. I kept it in my bag. I left the bag on my desk. Anyone could have taken it.'

For a while Hetty stayed off work. She hung around in the flat looking through newspapers for another job. Meanwhile, Donny had disappeared again. Ella waited on tenterhooks but there was no sign of him. One evening she saw him making his way down Wardour Street. He strode along as if he were on parade.

'I was going to come up, eh. But I had a date with a magistrate.'

Ella asked him round for a meal. Finally, she confided in Hetty and told her what had happened.

'That's wonderful, Ella sweetie. I'll cook.'

*

Donny arrived in a clean shirt and new jacket. He seemed stiff, unsure of himself and hostile. He had made an attempt to flatten his hair down with some grease but it still sprang up. The girls brought in plates of spaghetti and a dish of runner beans.

'What's this?' He regarded the food with suspicion.

'Spaghetti.'

Hetty opened a bottle of red wine:

'There's no dope so we've splashed out on some wine.'

'That's what I like to hear – the words "splashed out".' Donny gave up trying to use a fork and spoon and tackled the spaghetti with a knife and fork. 'I'm all in favour of squandering. If I found I was dying and I still had a couple of pence in my pocket I would crawl to a news-stand and buy a newspaper. I couldn't bear to save money by mistake. Look.' He pulled his jeans pockets inside out to show their emptiness.

As the evening went on he relaxed and gained confidence. Rocking back in his chair he embarked on stories which made the girls laugh:

'When the magistrate asked me why I was sitting on top of a wall at two in the morning with two Burtons' suits over my arm, I told him that I was practising my golf. The magistrate didn't get the joke. Dumb as a box of hair. But I suppose it's the job of some people to make the world a duller place. The ditchwater brigade. How do you like my new jacket?'

Hetty eased back in her chair and lit a cigarette. Ella found herself overcome with shyness. Hetty was relaxed. Ella felt that her own tongue was nailed to the bottom of her mouth; a clockwork tongue that clacked now and then, incomprehensibly. Hetty noticed.

'Ella is a bit in love with you, you know,' she remarked with gay malice.

Donny's eyebrows shot up and he looked at Ella. The wine was working on him. He became expansive.

'So she should be. What's wrong with that? On the other hand ...' His mood darkened. 'If music be the food of love, shoot the pianist, I say. Where is Cyrus, by the way?'

'Working.'

'At the ballet school?'

'Yes.'

There was an awkward silence.

'Do you know what the Russians say when there's a silence like that at the table?' Donny grinned.

'No. What?' Ella was clearing the plates.

'They say, "A policeman has just been born."'

'Did the police ever catch up with you that day?' asked Ella.

'No. Thank fuck.' Donny nearly lurched backwards off his chair.

'Do you not like policemen?' enquired Hetty.

'Not particularly. That's why I prefer cats to dogs. You don't often see a cat on the end of a policeman's lead. Dogs are collaborators.'

Hetty handed Donny a cigarette from a pack of Marlboro. He lit it and leaned back in his chair, looking at Ella as she came back from the sink to the table. She wore a blue summer dress. Her black hair was tied loosely at the nape of her long Modigliani neck. She smoothed her dress over her knees. He spoke quietly, looking away from her.

'If you have to choose between love and liberty, choose liberty. The desire for love and the quest for the grail are at odds with each other. And I am for the quest. Actually I'm addicted to the fucking quest.' Then he looked down with an odd, coquettish expression in his eyes. 'If you want to be free, you can't be passionate.'

Hetty was smiling.

'So what was this obscene song Cyrus was telling us about?'

'What song?' Donny looked mystified.

'Cyrus told us you sang a filthy song you'd learned in the army.'

'I don't remember.'

Hetty and Donny helped themselves to more wine. The two of them became more expansive as Ella retreated into herself. Donny regaled them with stories of the dole-hoods, the ne'er-do-wells and mystery-hunters of Soho. Then he went on to tell them about the army.

'For recruiting they always use a drummer and a flautist. I was only fifteen and I fell for it. But as soon as I hit the parade ground I knew I had fallen amongst madmen. All those red-faced sergeants bawling and screaming in your face. Why couldn't they have some manners? If only they could have said, "Would you mind very much coming to attention" or, "A little right turn here wouldn't come amiss," I might have cooperated.'

Coils of blue cigarette smoke rose into the air. From somewhere outside in the street came the sound of music from a barrel organ. The ashtray overflowed. Ella pushed the bottle away with a shake of her head.

'No more wine thanks. I've got a dress rehearsal of *Coppelia* tomorrow.' She hoped to sound impressive, but the information didn't seem to affect Donny, who was laughing at something Hetty said.

She went to open the window and returned to sit down. Hetty had lit a candle, although the summer evening was still light. The candle began to gutter. Donny jumped to his feet. Keeping a delicate beat with his arms as if he were conducting a band he performed a neat little dance step and began to sing quietly in a tuneful voice:

Eyes right,
Foreskins tight
Arseholes to the rear
We are the boys
Who make no noise
When we're on the hunt for cunt.
We're the heroes of the night
And we'd rather fuck than fight.
We are the Foreskin Fusilliers.

The two girls sat astonished at the table. Donny bowed and sat down again.

'I was a boy soldier. That was our anthem,' he announced.

Hetty tossed back her hair and began to laugh. Soon, she and Donny were convulsed with hilarity.

'Well, thanks very much ladies,' said Donny, finishing the dregs of his wine. 'I'm away back to my mobile home. I'm residing in *The Flying Scotsman* tonight.' He turned to Ella with old-fashioned politeness.

'Will I come and collect you after your rehearsal tomorrow?'

'I don't know when we'll finish. Wednesday's better. I'll come to the pub in Floral Street after class at two o'clock. How are you going to get back now? It's late. The tubes have stopped running.'

'I'll get a taxi.'

'I thought you said you had no money?'

'Look. Getting into a taxi when you have money is no fun. Getting into a taxi when you have no money and then announcing to the driver that you're Mr Micawber and hoping that something will turn up is great fun.' The laugh-glint was back in his eye.

'Och. I'll walk. Thanks again, eh? That was magic.'

As he opened the door to leave they could hear Cyrus playing a melancholy tune on the piano.

'We should have asked Cyrus,' said Ella as they washed up.

'I don't think so. Cyrus could be a rival.' Hetty looked sideways at Ella then gave her a hug.

'Oh honey. I don't know what made me say that. I'm sure it's not true. Donny is cute.'

*

Bare light bulbs framed the dressing room mirror. Ella leaned towards the mirror to fix her black eye-liner. The light was harsh. She drew long Nefertiti lines to accentuate her dark eyes and then stared at her face, dissatisfied. Ella wanted to be a bubbling blonde with green eyes like Hetty. Next to Hetty's effervescent gaiety at dinner Ella had felt gauche.

It was the dress rehearsal for *Coppelia*. Ella had been chosen as one of the leading couple in the Hungarian *czardas*. The call for the corps de ballet came over the tannoy and the dancers ran down the stone stairs. The wings of the theatre were dark and draughty. The dancers assembled off-stage, next to the huge scenic flats which smelled of fish-glue, paint and turpentine. It was chilly there and Ella's arms came up in goose bumps. She did not feel like dancing. The orchestra struck up with the first shivering flurry of violins. Then came the long drum roll. Ella aligned herself with her partner and ran onto the blue-lit stage to take up her position facing the dark gulf of the empty auditorium.

Once she embarked on the movements and executed the first steps of the dance her gloom fell away. With every flirtatious step she grew in confidence, expressing the seductive movements through her waist, shoulders, neck and the angle of her head. The music communicated directly to the body, beyond the reach of words, and she was left with the pure pleasure of dance. In the auditorium the director noted the twisting hips and torso that marked Ella out as a young dancer of provocative sexuality. He looked at his assistant and they exchanged approving nods.

By the end of the performance Ella was elated, her blood was racing and her spirits restored.

Chapter Twenty-Three

Ella reached home after the dress rehearsal to be greeted by chaos. Cyrus was standing on the landing with two friends. A glance inside his flat showed Ella the state of his piano. The wrecked instrument hung on its side, a spray of wooden struts tipped with ivory bursting out of the piano case like so many mad tongues. Bedding was strewn around the room. The black plastic piano stool had been slashed, exposing the cheap grey flock stuffing which spilled out like scum. His two friends moved around restoring the furniture to its original position as best they could.

'What happened?' She feared it had something to do with Donny.

A pale-faced Cyrus, his watery blue eyes rolling around in his head, tried to explain.

'I came home. The door was bust open and four guys were sitting in the flat. I don't know who told them I lived here. One of them had a scar like a ravine down one side of his mouth. He was grinning at me.

'"We've come for the party," he says.

'"There is no party," says I.

'"There is now," says the guy.

'I'm trying to keep it cool. So I say: "OK. There's a party. Not much to drink here though."

'"Then I'll have to stab you." The guy pulls out this steel knife and puts it on the bed beside him. And this other guy with goofy eyes and a knitted V-neck pullover picks up the knife and runs his thumb along the blade and says: "It seems that we know where you live." I could see the zipper on his flies was broken.

'"What do you guys want?" I'm asking.

'"Heroin," says Goofy. "Smack. Barbs. Nembutal. Benzedrine, Mogadon. Uppers. Downers. Anything you've got."

'"Or a party," says the guy with the scar.

'"I haven't got anything."

'"Well fuck off out of it then before we kill you."

'I take off down the stairs and I can hear them smashing everything up behind me.'

That night Cyrus came to stay next door with the girls.

'Oh it's all too much for a white lady,' he moaned, as he settled down on the floor in a sleeping bag.

*

Ella put all worries about events at home behind a steel bulkhead and concentrated on dance. She was the youngest dancer ever to have been chosen to understudy Ondine. In the spacious neon-lit rehearsal room next day she focused with rigour on the instructions from the choreographer.

The costume for Ondine was nothing but gleaming white tights, a white body stocking and pointe shoes dyed white with white ribbons. When she danced, Ella looked like a sculpture that had just stepped out of a block of rough stone and come to life. She looked like stone dreaming.

The choreographer worked through Act One with her until he was satisfied.

'We will leave that for today. Fish-dives everybody please. Ella you need to work on your fish-dives. Everybody find a partner please.'

He watched Ella as she practised her fish-dives, opening the arch of her arms as she swooped towards the floor to be caught by her partner. Her dark eyes flashed with pleasure. Even the risk of being dropped seemed to exhilarate her. They ended up on the floor laughing as her partner lost his balance. With typical stubbornness she insisted on doing it again. And again. And one more time. She had forgotten entirely about events in the flat.

A major new production of *Swan Lake* was planned. It was taken for granted that Ella would be promoted from the corps de ballet to dance the part of one of the four cygnets. It was the traditional first step for any dancer whom the company wanted to groom as a prima ballerina. Meanwhile, in the current production of *The Sleeping Beauty* Ella enjoyed being part of the corps de ballet, merging with the others in the living labyrinth that formed itself into an intricate moving maze around the principal dancers. The discipline of blending in with the others had its own satisfactions.

*

The Sunday after the break-in, Donny, Ella and Cyrus decided to eat breakfast in the Quality Inn on the corner of Coventry Street. Ella was studying the statue of Eros with interest. Eros was poised in the ballet position 'en attitude en l'air', but he was leaning forward too much. In real life he would over-balance, she thought. As they walked down Wardour Street, Cyrus grabbed Donny's arm: 'That's him. That's one of the guys that broke in and wrecked the piano. He looks as if he's just been getting his script from Boots in the Dilly.'

Donny turned and saw a thickset man in his forties coming towards them. He wore a dark shirt nearly long enough to conceal the broken zipper on his trousers.

'Hey. Wait a minute there, cha.' Donny blocked the man's way.

The man stared at Donny from boiled eyes. Then a smile cracked open an enormous chasm in the man's face revealing one or two blackened teeth and the black and silver of amalgam fillings.

'You gotta problem?' asked the man.

'You broke ma pal's piano the other day. And I like to play piano.'

The man looked at him with an impenetrable stare. Then he caught sight of Cyrus and a flicker of some half-remembered incident passed over his face.

Donny made a grab for the packet in the man's hand.

'Is that heroin, is it? Och you shouldnae be doing that. That'll do you no good at all. Give me that stuff.'

It took the man an eighth of a second to pull the knife from the waistband under his shirt. The blade shone dully in the sun. Its point rested on Donny's shirt, pressing into his stomach just above the navel. Cyrus and Ella stayed motionless. The street was busy. Passers-by streamed around the frozen tableau, oblivious to what was happening in their midst.

'Don't do that.' Ella's voice sounded tiny. They were in a cavern of silted time where everything had slowed down. The people passing by were in a different time zone where speed was still normal.

And then something extraordinary happened. Donny became completely relaxed. With the knife still resting on his belly he smiled and opened his arms wide in a sort of invitation. As he held his arms outstretched, an almost tangible warmth flowed from him that seemed to engulf the other man. The man's wrist trembled and then started to shake violently. Almost imperceptibly his hand began to turn downward, as if some invisible force were deflecting the blade away from Donny's stomach. Donny continued to smile. The knife fell from the man's grasp and dropped with a clatter to the pavement. The man fell to his knees. He was crying. Donny kicked the knife into the gutter.

'Come on,' said Donny. 'Leave the cunt.' The three of them moved on leaving the man on his knees on the pavement.

'Where did you learn to do that?' asked Ella later over breakfast.

'I don't know. Nowhere,' said Donny.

*

Ella was at home darning the feet of her tights when she received a phone call from one of Hetty's ex-workmates at Merkel, Sharpe and Dolme.

'How is Hetty's hearing?'

'What?' asked Ella.

'Her hearing. You must know about that. That's why she's off work. She's going deaf.'

'What?' Ella was shocked. 'I don't know anything about it.'

'She's been off work having tests. It's been going on for ages. Didn't she tell you? When she was working here some of her friends tried to help. We practised with her while she learned how to lip read. Two of the girls in the office have even been learning sign language so that when she finally loses her hearing she can still communicate with us. She's being incredibly brave.'

That night, while they were sitting at the table, Ella asked Hetty about her deafness. Hetty breathed in sharply and held her hand to the top of her breastbone. The speed of her lateral thinking was dazzling. Her mind moved as fast as a scramble of spiders. She breathed out slowly. Her voice deepened.

'Honey, I didn't know how to tell you. I didn't want to worry you when you were busy rehearsing. A while back I was diagnosed with a condition that causes progressive deafness. It's incurable.' She gave a little shrug, accepting her fate with no hint of self-pity. 'Caused by a virus in the middle ear. But I've just discovered I'm going to be all right. I saw the consultant at the hospital today and by some sort of miracle it seems to be clearing up of its own accord, which is almost unheard of. The tinnitus is receding. It was pretty scary at the time.' She sighed and looked at Ella with a rueful expression. 'I never told you but that's why Hank and I broke up. He didn't want anything more to do with me. He couldn't handle it. We'd planned to get married. He was going to divorce his wife. But he couldn't cope with the thought of being with a disabled woman; having a deaf partner.'

Hetty wiped her mouth with a napkin and pulled a small brave face. There were tears in her eyes.

'Never mind. That's life. The consultant wants to write up my case in some magazine called *The Lancet*. So maybe some good will come out of it all. How about us taking in a movie to celebrate my recovery? I'm so relieved. The girls at the office will be thrilled when they hear. They've been so sweet. Can you imagine me featuring in *The Lancet* as a medical curiosity? Now guess what sweetie. I've been introduced to Eric Clapton and been invited to go backstage to see him on his next tour.'

Hetty's first priority was to eradicate her own history by moving her story on to the next extraordinary episode. Hers was the peculiarly American belief that she could leave history behind and remake herself in whatever form she chose. When Ella told Donny about Hetty's condition, the miraculous cure and Eric Clapton's invitation, Donny's forehead creased into a sceptical frown.

*

Cyrus no longer knocked on their door. He avoided the girls. They heard him chatting with friends through the partition wall, or caught the sound of his footsteps running up and down the stairs, but he no longer dropped in to see them. It had taken him a while to understand that an affair had developed between Donny and Ella. When he realised, his heart sank into the grey dead-dog realm of jealousy. In class his face was closed and tight-lipped.

Ella, for her part, tried to adapt to Donny's elusiveness. She never knew when he would appear or vanish. He would go missing for days and then suddenly turn up again at the flat laughing and joking and rolling his Old Holborn cigarettes. His sudden arrivals were as surprising as his unexpected disappearances:

'Come with me. Quick. I've just seen this painting in the National Gallery. A Goya. You must see it, Ella. Quick. Put your coat on. We'll go now. Now. Now.'

*

One night there was a violent storm. A long-haired Geordie youth with a pockmarked face rushed up the stairs at midnight to tell Ella that Donny was being held in the police box next to the all-night coffee stall at Charing Cross. There had been a fight.

'What happened?'

'Ah divvent kna. Someone starts arguing and jabbin' two fingers into Donny's chest. Donny went on a radge.'

Ella threw on a coat and rushed down there, shouldering her way through the crowds outside the Whisky-a-Gogo. From inside the club she could hear a faint but frenzied drumming and the clash of cymbals. Gusts of rain swept over her like a yard brush as she ran through the streets. Her hair was plastered to her head. On the embankment by the coffee stall a large group had gathered. People watched, mesmerised, as the sturdy police box began splintering from the inside. Two policemen waited. Donny eventually emerged into the arms of the police in a halo of street lights and rain, with the dancing glint of rapture, bliss and brutality in his eyes that bode no good for anybody.

'Christ. It's like getting into a fucking beehive,' he said, as he was shovelled into the hump-roofed Wolseley police car. He did not see Ella standing in the crowd. Two minutes later he was out again. The police had left the car door open while they answered some query from a passer-by. She watched Donny vanish into the night.

*

Donny strode alongside the river feeling triumphant; possessed by that moral anaesthesia which occurs immediately after a fight. The fight had been exhilarating, a burst of nonchalant savagery. Golden elvers of reflected light wriggled in the black water of the Thames beside him as he walked along the embankment. The downpour had stopped but the road was still wet. The sound of police sirens in the distance made him cross the road and head for the back streets. Violence was a purgative. It was his own personal violence for which he alone was accountable, a joyous explosion into a fight. His head was clear. His forehead stung. He felt refreshed and began to whistle as he walked along.

*

An enigmatic smile. Flawed topaz eyes. Bright sunlight and then the sudden darkening of the room. That night Ella dreamed that Donny appeared in her flat or some dark space that was also her flat. She was surprised and delighted to see him.

'Whenever you are here I want to dance,' she said. She raised her left arm in a tango or flamenco gesture and experienced the slow burning pleasure of dance. She was flattered that he had bothered to come all the way from his strange northern country. Suddenly and unexpectedly, he too began to dance, shoulders moving, fists still furled. Just as suddenly he stopped and lay down. She realised he must be exhausted from the long journey and lay down next to him.

*

Cyrus recovered from his jealousy quickly and struck up a short-term friendship with a cheery young bar-tender with a fleshy behind who wore plum velvet flares. He would come round to Cyrus's and they would smoke dope together after work. But Cyrus was still drawn to Donny and assuaged his feelings by becoming Ella's confidant. She and Cyrus fell into the habit of drinking cups of tea and talking endlessly about Donny. They consoled each other by poring over what they knew about him, which turned out to be very little. He came from the north of Scotland. He had joined the army as a boy soldier at fifteen and then abandoned the army to go wandering. At one time Ella became so unhappy with his frequent disappearances that she thought of saving up her money and going away, but her hate was carved on ice and when Donny turned up again it melted with the spring sunshine.

'Just give me some warning when you're going,' she said.

He looked surprised:

'I don't get any warning myself.' He spooned honey into his mug of tea and tried to explain. 'Look. I'm a gallivanter. You can't plan gallivanting. You can't say, "In July, I'm going gallivanting." It's a thing that comes over you.' He raised his arms and announced with mock theatrical panache: 'People try to bind me but the bonds and withers just fall away from my feet. I ricochet between the azure vault and the gutter.' Then he said with casual arrogance: 'All the same, if it would make you feel better I will marry you. Would you like that?'

'Yes. I would like that,' said Ella, aglow with happiness.

'And you can have the whole of the sky as a wedding present,' he said.

Chapter Twenty-Four

Hetty had decided to house-sit for a friend in Muswell Hill. The wrecking of Cyrus's flat had made her feel unsafe in Soho. When Ella visited Hetty to tell her that she and Donny were to marry, she found Hetty lying on the sofa with two circular moistened pads covering her eyes. Hetty groaned and got up to make coffee:

'Oh God, Ellie, it seems I've been sleep-walking again.'

Ella looked at her in surprise:

'I didn't know you did that.'

'I haven't since I was about six.' She gave a wry smile. 'I thought it was something I'd left behind. It must have been all that rumpus with Cyrus and the flat that triggered it off again. Here, have a doughnut.' Hetty caught a drip of jam from her doughnut and licked her finger.

The front room where they sat drinking coffee had an old-fashioned air. There were bamboo plant-holders dotted around containing tall leafy plants, a leather pouf, metal tongs, an old pair of bellows, a bronze toasting-fork and a poker all in the Victorian tiled fireplace. Behind Hetty's head a Tiffany table lamp stood on an Indian brasswork coffee table.

'That lamp is gorgeous,' said Ella. Hetty turned to look at it. The lampshade had the brilliant colours of a dangerous insect: emerald green, creamy apricot and caramel. Hetty fingered the patterns, outlined in black like the markings on a butterfly wing.

'I know. I might just have to take it with me when I go,' she laughed. 'Actually, Ellie, a policeman has just been round. It was pretty bad. Apparently, I was out in the middle of the road last night and had no idea.'

Hetty picked up a card and showed it to Ella. On it was the telephone number and extension of Detective-Sergeant Alan Forbes.

'The policeman was kinda cute. Dreamy brown eyes with long lashes. He didn't have to come round. He came off-duty and told me what happened.'

*

At two o'clock the previous morning residents in the area would have been surprised to see an odd procession making its way along Muswell Hill Road. A young woman in an ankle-length, white nightdress walked steadily along the pavement followed by a small Panda police car driving at funeral pace just behind her. The woman was barefoot and the nightdress fluttered behind her under the orange sodium light of the street lamps. The stretch of road where she walked was long and deserted. Beside her, tall dark trees interspersed with silver birches loomed over the fencing that separated her from Highgate Wood.

Every now and then the police car accelerated gently and drew ahead of the woman so that the bulky policeman in the passenger seat could twist himself round to study her more closely. He judged the woman to be about twenty years old. She had a sweet face and a firm chin, held upwards in a way that made her look both vulnerable and defiant. A river of dishevelled blonde hair fell to her shoulders. The police officer wound down the car window to take a better look. The breeze rushing through the tree tops immediately filled the car with a whispering sound like the distant sea. Some way off in the warm night could be heard the pop-popping of a Vesta motorbike. The girl looked neither right nor left. She seemed unaware of the dark whispered counsel of the trees beside her. The overweight officer felt a surge of protective lust.

'What do you reckon?'

D. S. Alan Forbes lifted his foot from the accelerator and allowed the car to drop back once more behind the woman. Forbes was of a slimmer build than his colleague. He had the square jaw, dark brown hair and conventional good looks of a male model in an old-fashioned knitting pattern.

'Better keep with her,' he said.

The officer in the passenger seat took off his peaked hat. The rhubarb pink skin of his balding head was blotched with pale brown freckles. He rubbed his forehead to erase the indented line left there by his hat.

'Yes. I wouldn't mind a piece of that.'

Forbes turned his head away. The salty whiff of shrimp on his colleague's breath made him feel nauseous.

The police telephone exchange had received an anonymous call from a woman saying she had spotted the sleep-walker when she was driving home. She had not liked to wake the woman because she had heard that waking a somnambulist ran the risk of precipitating a heart attack. She gave details of where the woman was walking and advised them to get there quickly. Six minutes later, the patrol car turned the corner and spotted the figure in white a hundred yards ahead of them. From a distance she looked like a walking candle.

Suddenly, the sleep-walker veered left into a side street. The car followed. She went up the steps of a large house, pushed open the front door, went through and banged the door shut behind her.

'Now what?' Forbes was tired. During the day he was undergoing intensive training for his transfer to Special Branch. 'We'd better wait for a few minutes and see if she comes out again. We ought to check on her and maybe advise her to go and see a doctor.'

They sat in the car. Forbes could not wait to leave life in police uniform behind and become a fully-fledged member of Special Branch. The training excited him.

He went back over the events in his training that morning. He had done well in the improvisation exercises, but then he had an advantage. Before he became a police officer he had started off as an actor with Hornchurch Repertory Company. When it became clear that he would never make much progress as an actor he left the theatre and joined the police force. In his initial training he became interested in the psychology of police work. They were trained to grin. They were trained to use humour and sympathy as a way of defusing tense situations. It was amazing how many cons came quietly after a friendly joke. He preferred that aspect of the work to the physical challenge of the dawn raid. He'd been on one or two of those and always hung back as far as possible. The time was chosen when people would be at their most vulnerable, four or five in the morning. The plan was to batter the door down and conduct what was called 'twenty-five seconds of fury' to terrorise the family. That usually shook them so much that the police could get what they wanted or carry off a suspect in his pyjamas. Alan Forbes decided that he was better suited to infiltration and undercover work and applied for Special Branch.

That day the Special Branch trainees had been encouraged to divulge any weaknesses they had in order that they could not be blackmailed. There had been a hilarious session when the new recruits admitted to all sorts of things: a history of shoplifting; carrying knives; using pornography; indulging in transvestism; all kinds of previous criminality. They were then trained to use those weaknesses as part of their operational kit. Trust exercises were set up – that sort of team-bonding was fashionable. A psychologist had come in to train them in the art of infiltration: 'You have to gain the confidence of your prey. Share any intimate details of your own life; marriages, misdemeanours, infidelities, regrets and petty crimes. Make the subject identify with you. Identify with the subject. Appear to agree with the subject's opinions, their politics, sympathise with them, laugh with them. Have an affair with the subject. That's how undercover agents work. Now we will do some improvisations.'

With his actor's background, Forbes had excelled in the improvisations, pretending first to be a junkie and then a transvestite.

The overweight police officer yawned and got out of the car to stretch his legs. He had put on unwashed socks that morning and his feet fizzed in his shoes like old yoghurt. After a minute he strolled up to the front door, radio in hand, and examined the flat numbers. Then he returned to the car.

'The house is divided into flats. I can't tell which flat she's in. We'd have to wake everybody. Better send someone round in the morning.'

'I'll drop round myself,' Alan Forbes yawned. 'OK. Let's go.' The car reversed and made its way back to the end of the street, accelerating as it pulled away.

The police would have been even more surprised had they been able to see what happened then. As soon as she was inside the house Hetty Moran ran up the stairs and let herself in to the first floor flat. Without switching the light on she darted to the window and stood to one side behind the curtain so that she would not be visible from the street. She watched the two officers sitting in the car. When she saw the policeman approaching the front door she dashed to her bed and crept between freshly laundered sheets which were stiff and white. She lay motionless for a while, heart thumping with anticipation, as she waited for the doorbell to ring. Nothing happened. She propped herself up on her elbow, listening intently. On hearing the police car drive away she was half-relieved and half-disappointed. She checked the window, then poured herself a vodka and took it into the front room.

After a while she pulled the curtains shut, switched on the table-lamp and went to stand in front of the large gilt-edged mirror that hung over the mantelpiece. The top of the mirror leaned forward a little from the wall. In the lamplight the room reflected in the mirror seemed unfamiliar and mysterious. Hetty preferred that reflected room to the real one in which she stood. She examined her own image: a pretty face with no strong features and a torrent of blonde curls. She felt empty. A wave of disgust came over her. She needed some Dionysiac remedy for the dryness and desolation that plagued her. A tug of envy pulled at her stomach when she thought of Ella and Donny. After a while she went to bed.

The engaged couple came round a week later. Hetty cooked for them and admired Ella's sapphire ring.

'Oh it's gorgeous, honey,' she crooned.

*

Donny McLeod knocked on the door of the first floor flat in Muswell Hill and Hetty opened it. Hetty's hair was piled up untidily. She wore a pale blue polo-necked sweater and had a lighted cigarette in her hand. The hoover which she had left on blared hoarsely in the background.

'Did I leave my tobacco tin here, hen, when Ella and I were here the other night?'

'I don't know. Come in and have a look.' Hetty pushed some loose strands of hair back over her shoulders, yawned and switched off the hoover.

'This place is a tip. I'm just cleaning up.'

Donny came in and looked on the coffee table, under the table and on the mantelpiece.

'Nah. No luck. I must have left it somewhere else. Shame. I liked that tin.'

'Here, have one of these.' She tapped a cigarette out of a packet of Marlboro. 'I'll make some tea.'

She came back out of the kitchen with two cups of tea.

'What time is it?' She looked preoccupied. 'Sorry if I'm a bit all over the place. I've been trying to cope with some bad news from home.'

'Oh aye.' Donny sounded wary. He disliked hearing bad news.

Her expression changed, as quickly as fleeting clouds from pain to stoicism.

'Never mind. It doesn't matter. Just the usual demons that continue to haunt my family in the States.' Hetty pulled a grim face and sipped her tea.

'They should come over here and join my demons. My demons are having the time of their lives.' Donny lit up his cigarette. Hetty gave a rueful smile:

'Sometimes I wonder if I'm clinically depressed.'

Donny looked at her askance:

'Why do you have to be clinically depressed? Why can't you

just be fucking ordinarily depressed like the rest of us? Where's the sugar?' She handed him the bowl and he put four teaspoonfuls into his cup.

Hetty laughed, then her lower lip suddenly trembled uncontrollably.

'I'm sorry.' Her voice slid upwards tearfully. 'But my dad's just gone back into a mental hospital.' She bit her lip and twisted her head to one side, shaking tears out of her eyes like transparent jewels. 'Christ. What's wrong with my family? I need some medication myself. Do you take pills ever?' She wiped her nose with the back of her wrist.

'Nope. I don't need tranquillisers. I just make do with a wall to smash my head against every now and then.'

She came and stood in front of where he sat on the sofa. Hetty's eyes were the colour of mineral chrysoberyl: a greenish yellow or gold. They changed colour with the light, as if they could reflect back at people what they wanted to see. She looked directly at him, breathing so rapidly that she was on the verge of hyperventilating. She folded her arms across her chest looking distressed and gulped:

'Donny, can I ask you a favour?'

'What?'

'Could you give me a hug? I really need one right now. I really need to be in your arms for a few minutes.'

He put down his tea and stared at her with distaste, as if she were a hair in his soup.

'Fuck off. That's all I fucking need. Mata Hari from Minnesota or wherever the fuck you're from. I'm away.' He rose to his feet with a gesture of irritation and made for the door.

Hetty, changeable as the skies, immediately metamorphosed into a pragmatic, calm and dignified young woman. She sat down on the bed and patted it, indicating that he should sit down beside her. He remained standing.

'OK. I'm sorry Donny. I'll tell you why I'm upset. I've never told Ella about all this. My dad served in Vietnam, OK. He was a colonel in the Third Commando Division. When he came back my mother couldn't handle him. He had these rages. He was hospitalised. Then one day last summer my mother came out of the wash house and found him hanging from one of the apple trees in the orchard at the back of the house.'

Donny was still staring at her:

'How picturesque of him.'

'She had to cut him down. He survived. He's been in and out of mental hospitals ever since.'

There was now a look of open dislike on Donny's face. Hetty shrugged and raised her eyebrows in mild disdain.

'OK.' She stood up, smoothing her skirt, and said with composure, 'I really don't mind if you believe it or not, sweetie. That's up to you. I have to get on with the hoovering.'

He put out his cigarette still looking at her.

'You know what you're like – a fucking film-set. All façade. You're all front. Behind you is just fucking emptiness. You're like the set of an American Western, very convincing from the front, but at the back it's just a flat one-dimensional film-set supported by struts and looking out on to nothing but bare earth and emptiness.'

Donny made for the door. He turned to look at Hetty. Her face had become stiff and turned grey like a stone angel. For a moment the stone angel with its ancient pitted face of porous lava rock and cavernous eyes stared back at him. Then Hetty smiled her golden smile. She could have been awarded a billion-dollar contract for smiling. She pinned back some loose corkscrew strands of hair, turned away and switched on the hoover.

Chapter Twenty-Five

Ella told her mother about Donny and the wedding plans. She took Donny down to Kent to meet Alice, who waited for them on the doorstep. Alice now lived in a small miner's cottage. There was an air of desolation about the place. The cottage had once been condemned and was almost entirely held together by plaster and by its dull pebble dash exterior, but Alice liked having a garden where she could hang her washing. Two horses grazed in an adjacent field. Her sister Doris lived in nearby Elvington and they worked together with miners' wives picking fruit and vegetables on a local farm. Ella noticed how shy and flustered her mother looked as she welcomed them in. She seemed older and diminished in some way.

'Come in and have a cup of tea and a bite to eat. How's the dancing?' her mother asked.

'It's fine.'

After eating steak and kidney pie and salad in the kitchen, they went into the small sitting-room. The room had been tidied, the cushions plumped, the carpet swept. There, with great courtesy, Donny asked Mrs de Vries for permission to marry her daughter, while Ella sat on the settee in silence turning the pages of a mail order catalogue.

'Yes. I suppose that's all right if that's what you both want.' Alice wiped her hands on her apron. 'Now then, what about some pudding?' She turned to Donny, who was looking out of the window. 'I'm sorry. I shouldn't have given you salad. You're a working man like my brothers. My mother wouldn't have known a salad if she saw one. Nobody had ever heard of egg mayonnaise in our house.'

'What's that railway-line doing there?' asked Donny peering through the window.

'Oh that's just a little local line that brings the coal wagons from Tilmanstone Colliery.'

Donny smiled:

'We used to have a line just like that when I lived in Dalkeith. I helped deliver the milk churns.'

Alice was pleased to find common ground:

'We had milk churns when I was a girl. Some of the miners' families still use them round here. The miners are getting ready to go on that big protest march in London. They've hired buses. I'm helping to sew their banners. You should see the work in them. All that beautiful stitching. I love sewing. My best friend Emmie was apprenticed to do church embroidery. I love to see the banners in a procession. Mind you I don't know what's happening with all these strikes. I might even go for the liberials next time. Or do I mean liberians? The ones in the middle of conservative and labour.'

Donny laughed a gurgling laugh and nearly choked on his tea.

'I don't know,' he said. 'They all get on my nerves.'

The laugh was infectious. Alice laughed with him. She began to feel more at ease and risked teasing him.

'Oh you've got nerves, have you? You're lucky to have nerves. We couldn't afford them in my day. Nobody had nerves then. Or am I being spiteful? We cockneys can be spiteful, you know. If we see somebody wearing gloves we say it's because they haven't got any fingers. Now do you want another cup of tea before you go?'

Alice watched Donny open the gate and let Ella through. He was pointing at the grazing horses and Ella was laughing at something he had said.

*

After they'd gone her sister Doris's face peered tentatively around the door.

'How did it go?'

'I think it went off all right.' Alice was sitting in front of the television. 'Move the cat off that chair and sit down. He seems all right. At least he's not posh. Since she started moving in that other world I've always been frightened that she was going to bring back somebody who was so la-di-dah I couldn't understand them. Like that play I went to see the other day up in London.'

'What was that?'

'Age Concern didn't want their tickets so they gave them to us. What did we see? Oh what was it called? It had a funny name and it was by someone. Adrenalin, was it?'

Alice fished for the programme in her bag.

'Here it is. *Andromache*. I might as well have stayed at home and cut my throat with a rusty razor.'

'I know what you mean,' said Doris. 'They took us to see *A Midsummer Night's Dream*.'

'What was that like?'

'All right but there was a bit too much Shakespeare in it. Is she happy, do you think?'

'Ella? Oh, she's happy as a butcher's dog. She doesn't say much. She never was forthcoming.'

'Seventeen is young to be married. But I suppose then she'd have time to get a divorce and marry someone else. What did you give them to eat?'

'Beef pies and salad. And then some plums and custard.'

'That's not much.'

'You can talk. You can't cook anything. You'd burn water.'

'Well I hope she'll be all right.'

Alice shrugged and handed everything over to fate:

'You can't stop them. They do what they like anyway. He's got a lovely laugh, though. He could warm the world up with a laugh like that.'

Chapter Twenty-Six

Students and members of the company took it in turns to perform the steps diagonally across the brightly lit top-floor studio, while others leaned against the barre watching or limbering and stretching.

Ella had tied the arms of her grey cardigan around her waist to make a flap at the back. Her black hair was pinned on top of her head but a crest of it had come loose and quivered as she moved. She set off across the room making the infinitesimal adjustments required by inertia, spin and the friction of her pointed toe on the floor. With the dancer's instinctive understanding of gravity and balance, she managed to achieve four pirouette turns, giving her spin back to the earth which was also spinning in the same direction. The slenderness of her legs belied their muscular strength. When she leaped into the air, her legs scissored open in a grand jeté and she seemed to hang there allowing the earth beneath to change its orbital trajectory by one tenth-of-a-billionth-of-an-atom's width to accommodate her landing.

One of the other dancers was looking out of the studio window on to the street.

'Who is that man who looks like a young Gary Cooper? I keep seeing him hanging around.'

'It's Ella de Vries's boyfriend. I think she's going to marry him.'

'Really? She's a dark horse, isn't she?'

Donny was waiting outside the pub opposite the studio. It was a December mid-morning of furious bright blue skies and sleet-cleaned streets. Tiny flakes of snow spangled his collar-length hair and lodged in his moustache. A knife-whetting wind sliced at his face. He pulled the collar of his jacket up for protection. His toolbag, containing a level, a string-line and a trowel, rested at his feet.

Class finished and minutes later Ella was running up the road towards him. She had wound a red woollen scarf around her neck. There was always the fear that if she kept him waiting too long he would disappear. They had planned to go Christmas shopping. Jingles and tinny carols piped out from shop doorways into the streets.

As they made their way towards Oxford Street, they could hear in the distance the sound of chants and echoing shouts through megaphones. The noise grew into a roar. They turned a corner to find themselves confronted by a flood of people and the ebullient swirling energy of a huge demonstration. An elderly man marched by, his cheeks crimson with cold like the last flare of sunset. Donkey-jacketed stewards gestured for demonstrators to keep up with the marchers in front. The air was filled with the shriek of whistles. Workers' banners swung high along the street. Office workers hung out of their windows looking down on trades unionists, communists and Trotskyists marching together, yelling 'Kill the Bill' in unison. People handed out leaflets.

'Come and join us,' enthusiastic demonstrators beckoned to the onlookers.

A phalanx of miners under the ornate banner of their branch of the NUM, and accompanied by the braying of a brass band, marched past Donny and Ella as they stood on the pavement and watched.

'Perhaps that's one of the banners mum helped sew,' Ella said, as the miners swung past. Behind them came a group of jaunty actors with a banner that said: 'Save Our Profession.'

Ella recognised the familiar face of a leading actress.

'Look. I think that's Vera Scobie.'

Wearing a black knitted beret and high-collared winter coat, the actress with fine features and swimming-pool blue eyes was walking backwards leading a small group and conducting a chant:

William Shakespeare, William Blake
We are marching for your sake.

The actress then proceeded to make a speech through a megaphone which was drowned out by the colliery band.

A scuffle broke out nearby. A young man with a mane of light brown hair was bracing himself against two policemen as they dragged him towards a police van. Placards and poles were being thrown at the police line. The police lost their hold on the young man who ducked back into the crowd.

There was a look of dislike on Donny's face.

'Come on. Let's get the fuck out of here,' he snarled.

'What are they demonstrating about?' asked Ella.

'Fuck knows. Having moral principles is against everything I believe in. I am against anybody who is *for* anything. War I don't mind. It's patriotism that I hate. Flags and shite. I hate things to do with flags, parades, glory and honour. All I want to do is wander about the earth. I don't give a shit about nations or politics or anything. Come on.'

The shouts of the marchers receded behind them as they made their way back through the Christmas shoppers.

Ella hurried behind him trying to keep up as he pushed his way ahead.

'What do you believe in then?'

'Nothing. Children. The innocence of children. Humanity. Die for an idea? What a load of fucking shite. You can be imprisoned by an idea. And all the wankers who have ideas try to slaughter you. Which ideas, anyway? Communism? Paradise? Ideas are things that are all alike. That's why I like children. They don't say go and die for this or that. They've got too much sense.'

He pushed open the swing door of a pub.

'Come on. Let's have a drink? We'll go shopping later.'

Chapter Twenty-Seven

Entering the pub was like diving underwater into a brown river. Donny dumped his toolbag by his feet at the bar. Only one other customer sat in the corner. He was a fat, bald, snub-nosed man, a cheerful pub regular who raised his glass of beer to Donny. He had wispy grey hair and a smooth face; half cherub, half satyr. A cigarette drooped permanently from his lips which gave him an air of whimsical, disrespectful humour. Donny greeted him.

'Hello, Sil.'

Ella loosened her red scarf.

'Can you get me a lemonade. No. I'll have a coke. I've got to be back in the theatre in a couple of hours. If I have alcohol before a performance I fall over.'

Donny downed his double whisky, enjoying the sensation as it cut a warm channel through him. He ordered another. The pub door swung open and seven or eight demonstrators crowded in. The first one was out of breath and laughing. He was the one they had seen escaping from the police. He tossed back his lion-head of tawny hair and examined the rip in the sleeve of his pale brown sheepskin jacket.

'I got away but they tore my fucking beautiful new jacket.'

A serious, pale young man with black-rimmed glasses who had come in with him was not concerned about the fate of the jacket. His voice was almost apologetic and he was well-spoken. His brow wrinkled and he lowered his voice.

'You must be careful. You don't want to be picked up just now.' Donny took a step towards the group.

'What are you lot all doing in the pub? You should be on the street. There are two thousand Tupamaros guerrillas round the corner waiting for you to lead the revolution. What am I to tell them – that you've gone to the pub and Che Guevara's gone to his mum's for his Sunday dinner?'

Hector Rossi, the young man with the sheepskin jacket, laughed and pushed his fingers through his hair making furrows. He spotted Donny's toolbag.

'Were you just on the march?'

'No. I wasnae. I am one of the working men who doesn't give a fuck!'

'Are you in a union?'

'Am I fuck. I'm too anarchistic even to be in a group of anarchists. And I don't vote. If I did I'd do it the same way I do a lottery – shut my eyes and put a little cross wherever my hand ends up.'

'You have to take sides sometime. On something. Surely.' Hector Rossi was smiling.

'Never. I'm against everything.' There was humour and a challenge in Donny's eyes. 'And it's because I never take sides that I'm more moral than any of youse lot. I'm honest. And that's the only morality there is.'

'You're an individualist then, or a nihilist,' someone said from the back of the group.

'Neither. I'm a fucking optimist. I'm hoping that one of you seekers after justice will buy me a drink. Look. I don't like belonging to gangs.'

A voice piped up from the middle-aged man in the corner of the room: 'Hear. Hear. Hermits of the world, unite.' Sil raised his glass.

Donny looked over at him and gave a shout of pleasure.

'Cheers Sil. Now that's the type of guy I like. Pure crank.'

There was uneasy laughter from the protesters, caught between the paradox of Donny's warmth and his intractable savagery.

'Were you on the march?' A buck-tooth girl wearing a square-shouldered fake fur jacket turned to Ella.

'No. I'm a dancer with the Royal Ballet,' said Ella as if that absolved her from any such activity. The girl let out a snort of disdain:

'Oh my god. You have to be a real bourgeois to go there. No ordinary people go to the ballet.'

Donny took a dislike to the girl.

'Well I love it when people dance. Are you a student?'

'Yes.'

'Well get back to your fucking thinketeria. No ordinary people go there either.'

Hector went to the bar. His geniality had a steadying influence on everyone. He offered Donny a drink.

'What are you having?'

Donny looked him up and down.

'Are you a penniless student too or can I have a scotch?'

'No. I'm a printer – well, an apprentice printer. And you can certainly have a scotch.'

Donny raised his glass. The earnest bespectacled young man with black hair moved through the others to stand next to Donny. He introduced himself.

'Hello. I'm Mark Scobie. Whereabouts do you work?'

'Haringey till tomorrow, then it's wherever we get sent.'

Mark shook his head.

'Things are going to get very tough in the building industry if they bring in this Industrial Relations Bill.'

Donny regarded him with impatience.

'Look. Don't talk to me unless you can say something cheerful, pal. I don't like talking to some cunt who's moaning "Beware the Ides of March" all the time. Hang on while I deal with this thing that's tugging at me.'

Ella was pulling on the sleeve of Donny's donkey jacket.

'Are you going to stay? Because if we're not going shopping I'm going back to the theatre. I didn't have much time anyway.'

'I'll walk you back there.'

'No. It's all right. You stay here if you want.'

She gave him a light kiss on the cheek and went to open the pub door. A gust of icy air blew in. Hail-stones rattled and bounced off the pavement like grain. She wrapped her red scarf around her neck, pulled up her coat collar and disappeared into the street.

Mark Scobie frowned as he continued with his denunciation of Edward Heath's government. After a few minutes Donny interrupted him: 'The trouble with you, cha, is that you introduce railway lines into the conversation. I like a conversation to blossom and grow in all sorts of unexpected directions. I don't like it when you've already planned what you're going to say.'

It was three o'clock and the publican was turning everyone out.

'Do you want to come back to our place and talk some more?' Mark Scobie's tone was exceedingly polite.

'Not particularly. But if you're offering me a drink, the answer is yes.'

*

Mark Scobie rented a house in Bethnal Green. Hector kept a room there but he spent most of his time in Milan. The house was gloomy and unheated. Uncarpeted wooden stairs led up to the bedrooms and a flat at the top. On the ground floor there was a communal sitting-room which contained two decrepit musty-smelling sofas. Maroon and brown Indian cotton covers had been thrown untidily over them and there were several large beanbag cushions on the floor that functioned as chairs. A paraffin stove stood in the centre of the room and there was a black and white TV in the corner. The kitchen on the same floor served as a general meeting place for the household, a fact marked by the endless piles of dirty coffee cups. From the hall it was possible to look down the stairs and glimpse a damp basement room with rotting carpet, a Gestetner printing-machine, an old typewriter and agit-prop posters tacked onto the walls.

The group of demonstrators and their new-found companion bought chips to eat on the way home. Conversation raged all the way back on the tube. Donny had brought a bottle of whisky with him. He was strap-hanging and taking nips from the bottle at the same time. He looked round at the seated passengers, the apathetic stares and slumped postures. Then he addressed the compartment in general.

'It's bureaucracy that I hate. I hate bureaucracy. Every time I see a form I tell lies. I can't bear to have anyone write down my name. I would like nothing better than to burn every single piece of paper with my name written on it. Create disorder. Confuse the bastards. May they die. May they die an agonising death. Soon. Everything's the wrong way round. Why can't we have a society where the bailiffs come and give furniture to people who haven't got any money instead of taking it away?'

His humorous energy was infectious. Strangers started to laugh and join in the conversation. Before long the whole carriage became unexpectedly intoxicated.

Discussion was still in ferment when they entered the house. The main room smelled of joss-sticks, dope and old carpet. A few people sat on the floor or sprawled on the sofas. The youth whose jacket sagged with the burden of its badges sat down cross-legged on the floor to roll a joint.

Donny tossed a chip in the air and tried to catch it in his mouth.

'Personally, I always use violence to obtain my objectives. And that's what will happen when I die. People will stand up and have one minute's violence.' He let out a cackle.

Mark went down to the basement to roll off some pamphlets on the Gestetner. Hector was on his knees in the front room trying to light the paraffin-stove. He pushed his hair back so that it wouldn't catch fire.

'Violence is fine. Sometimes it's the only way to get justice. I don't have a problem with that.'

Donny stood watching him.

'That's not what I'm saying. I don't do things because of right or wrong. Or justice or any of that crap. I don't believe in any fucking cause. Whatever I do I'll do just for the hell of it. D'you understand me?'

The yellow light from the stove illuminated the steady intelligence of Hector's eyes. His manner was open and honest. He looked directly at this new acquaintance.

'I do believe that if you want to buckle down with ordinary people and push for justice you might have to make some sacrifice – give yourself up to the greater good. A revolution would always have to come first. I think, anyway.'

Donny swayed in the centre of the room as he lit a cigarette.

'What revolution?' His mood darkened. There was menace in his voice. 'You want action. I'll give you fucking action. I trained as a soldier. But don't talk to me about sacrifice or redemption or any of that shit. You can get your own redemption through your own fucking illusions if you want. Illusions are people's security. Most people would rather have security than the truth.'

The stove puffed out a tiny mushroom of smoke and the room filled with the sickly smell of paraffin fumes. Donny looked round for an ashtray.

'Oh I see you use this whole carpet as an ashtray.' He flicked his ash on the floor.

Hector shook his head and laughed.

'You're drunk. Try and be reasonable for a minute.'

Donny gave him a scathing look. He held up his fist, scrunched the burning stub of his cigarette into the palm of his hand and then opened it and shook the stub onto the floor.

'Be reasonable? What a cuntish idea. Why live in an iron cage when you can get pissed and be free? You and your reasonable fucking world. I don't belong to it. Do you understand that? It's reason that causes all the violence in the first place. There's always violence at the heart of reason. The only thing that guides me in life is ... the latest hit song. Or any song that I've liked.'

He stepped back and tripped into a giant blue beanbag that swallowed him into its folds.

'I am the barley god. The honey god. I am the god of fucking

Mondays,' he shouted out from the centre of the cushion. After a few minutes of struggle, Donny fought his way out. His eyes were liquid and mobile. He staggered to the sofa and sat on it leaning forward with his jacket collar bunched up behind his neck. He addressed the floor with a mutter.

'There's something about all this endless sympathy for the poor. It gets on my nerves. What's wrong with being rich? Why not be rich? Good luck to them.'

A girl in a long skirt with a great Botticelli cloud of ribbed dark brown hair and racoon eyes appeared from upstairs. In her arms she held a purring tabby cat.

'What are we going to do with this cat when you and Mark go back to Italy, Hector? I'm going to my parents in Leeds for Christmas and then back to university. There will be no-one in the house. He's a lovely cat. I'd love to take him with me. I'm going to miss having a cat but I can't afford to feed him.'

Donny was on his hands and knees crawling over outstretched legs in search of packets that might contain a cigarette.

'Then get a dead one,' he snarled. 'A dead black cat. Jimmy Hendrix for instance.'

'Is Jimmy Hendrix dead?' enquired Hector. 'When did that happen?'

'While you were winding up the fascists in Italy,' said the girl. 'Choked on his own vomit or something. As you do.'

In response to the conversation, someone put a Hendrix album on the record player. Hector could hear the guitar screaming as he went downstairs to the cramped basement, where Mark was operating the Gestetner, his hands covered in ink from the roller. The table was a mess of pamphlets and placards and pots of paste. Mark fastened the template onto the machine.

'Has it occurred to you that Donny could be useful? Demolition firms have access to explosives. But he's been in the army so he might be right-wing. I can't quite tell where he stands.'

'I don't think Donny's right-wing,' said Hector. 'He's just an ordinary working bloke. But we've only just met him. It's too soon to include him in anything. We don't know him well enough.'

Hector went back upstairs. Donny was putting on his jacket.

'I'm going out to get some fags,' he said, pointing at the black and white telly. 'Don't let Lassie die while I'm out.'

'Bring us back some then.' Hector delved in his pocket for money.

'Who said I was coming back?'

'I thought we had to keep Lassie alive till you got back.'

'I've changed my mind. I'm not coming back.'

'You can kip here if you like.'

'No thanks, mate. I'm going for a walk.' He flashed his snaggle-toothed smile. 'Anything might happen when you're walking. Life is beautiful then. The flame of life. The spirit of life. That's all I want. Nothing else. And a packet of fags.'

Hector saw him out and went downstairs again to Mark in the basement. He leaned against the door jamb.

'You know what? I think he's all right. Why don't we ask him if he and his girlfriend would like to have the flat upstairs. Rebecca is going back to university. It'll be empty. It would be good to have someone in the house. I'm mainly in Milan. You're backwards and forwards between Milan and here. And that way we'd get to know him a bit better.'

'OK. You'd better run after him. We don't know where he lives.'

Chapter Twenty-Eight

The Soho period came to an end that winter. Cyrus never recovered from the gang invasion of his flat and went to live with friends in Clerkenwell. Hetty decided to stay on permanently in Muswell Hill. Donny and Ella accepted the offer of renting the top flat in the Bethnal Green house.

'How does Mark manage to keep paying for this house?' Ella asked the student with the Botticelli hair who was vacating the top-floor flat. The girl looked surprised.

'Didn't you know? Mark has rich parents. His mother is Vera Scobie the actress. His father is the Attorney-General or something. They have a house in Chelsea and one in Kent. Mark is dead embarrassed by having rich parents. He thinks of himself as a revolutionary. Apparently he's written a statement to a lawyer disinheriting himself and saying he will not accept any money or property left to him by his parents.'

'Fucking hell!' Donny stopped struggling with a table and rested it on the banisters. 'I thought there was something I didn't like about him. Why doesn't the cunt give the money to me?' He swore as the table started to slip from his grasp.

Ella and Donny settled into their new home. They decided to wait until the ballet company's summer break before they married. Donny was restless. Sometimes he worked on demolition sites, sometimes as a bricklayer or labourer or scaffolder. Between jobs he spent hours in the National Gallery gazing at paintings, or went on boat trips as far as possible down the river to where he could see the estuary or any other escape route. For a while he went north to Barrow-in-Furness to paint the hulls of ships in Vickers shipyard. Then he came south again, commuting every day to work in Harlow New Town. Unrest was spreading throughout Europe. The newspapers and television reported firebombings and exploding incendiary devices. In Ireland, the IRA stepped up their operations. In West Berlin, the Baader-Meinhof group had attacked three banks. In Italy, the Brigate Rosse undertook a series of bombings and bank robberies. In England, the targets were Conservative ministers, army recruiting centres, banks and the offices of big business. Adrenalin-fuelled outlaws took on the state. Scotland Yard formed a new bomb squad.

One morning, a young policeman strolled up to Donny as he waited on the concourse of Liverpool Street station amid a throng of commuters.

'Excuse me, sir. Can I have a look in that bag?'

Donny glanced down at the toolbag resting at his feet. He leaned against a pillar, his head on one side, and regarded the policeman with curiosity:

'No,' he said.

'Now don't be silly, sir. Open the bag.'

Donny said nothing. A smile darkened his hazel eyes. The policeman shuffled uneasily.

'Open the bag at once please, sir.'

'I said no.'

The policeman tried a joke.

'Come on, let me have a look. What have you got in there? The crown jewels?'

'I'm not telling you.' Donny looked around him at the throng of other passengers. 'I'll tell you what.' He pointed to a well-dressed businessman reading *The Daily Telegraph* with his briefcase at his feet. 'If you go and look in that man's briefcase I'll let you look in my toolbag.'

'Just cooperate please, sir. Open your bag.'

'No.'

'Don't be foolish, sir. If you don't let me look in the bag I shall have to call for assistance.'

'Well you'd better hurry up.' Donny pointed up at the station clock. 'My train is due in and I'm going to catch it.'

The policeman walked away muttering into his walkie-talkie. Donny went to catch his train. As he walked through the ticket-barrier he looked round and caught the policeman peeping at him from behind one of the station's pillars.

*

One evening, Donny came home white-faced and threw down his toolbag. That afternoon a man had fallen twelve feet from the scaffolding planks onto a concrete reinforcing rod that skewered him through the groin and balls. Donny had made roll-ups and held them to the man's lips until the ambulance arrived. When he reached home Donny slid down against the wall, exhausted. In a moment he was sitting on the floor fast asleep. A flurry of resentment ran through Ella. His work was dangerous and paid little. It was a life of torn muscles, splinters and tiny triangular lumps of flesh gouged from his knuckles by spanners. His muscles ached from carrying planks and ladders. In winter freezing bricks stuck to his hands, taking off the top layer of skin. Once he took Ella's hand and guided it so she could feel the solid raised lump on his shoulder where the scaffolding tubes rested. She fingered the contours gingerly beneath his damp checked shirt. On that job he lifted between five and ten tons of steel a day. Sometimes she came in late after a performance and looked at him laid out on the bed, too tired to undress, his body spread out like dried mud-flats: hands creviced, muscle fibres split, his face, under streaks of cement-dust, leaden and drained as after sunset.

However gently she woke him, he always jumped awake with a terrible start as if the death-boat were coming. He endured endless and frightful headaches. Because of the headaches he couldn't bear to have the light on when they watched television. She had to do whatever she needed to do by the light of the telly. But then she too had aching muscles, and her feet were sometimes bruised and bleeding. She would lie on the sofa next to him with her head on his shoulder and feel his arm around her, his shirt gritty with dust, the acrid smell of sweat wafting over her as they lay half asleep in front of the television. Sometimes they lay like that all evening, dozing, waking and dozing off again.

Ella looked down at him asleep on the floor sprawled against the wall. She tied her wrap-around cardigan more tightly around her waist. Then she went into the kitchen and put his meal back in the oven. She was still wearing her black footless leggings from class as she stood at the sink in the bruised light of evening. Staring down into the sink she was amazed to discover angels' wings amongst the potato peelings.

*

'Is Donny going on strike?' Hector asked Ella.

He had arrived back from Milan sporting a white shirt and fashionable striped tie with a big seventies knot. He was setting off for the launderette with a black plastic bag full of washing. 'One-and-a-half-million workers will be on strike tomorrow. Are you joining them?'

He smiled and points of light danced in his eyes. She thought how different he was from Donny.

'I don't think so.' Ella looked doubtful. 'We're doing *Romeo and Juliet*.'

*

Donny did go on strike the next day, and the day after that, and for several more weeks he continued to strike all on his own when everyone else had gone back to work. He drank bottles of wine and watched old black-and-white movies on the television. One day he took off for the Tate Gallery. Strolling around he came to an area cordoned off from the public. He slipped through an empty gallery and found his way down a flight of stairs to the dimly lit basement warehouse where thousands of paintings were stored. Around him lay dozens of canvases framed and unframed. For a while he wandered amongst them. Then he came across one particular painting that caught his attention. He sat down on the floor to gaze at it. It was a painting of a large black panther with yellow eyes surrounded by scarlet and purple fruits. Donny was hypnotised by it. He leaned back against two crates that had been used to transport the paintings. He snoozed. Somehow the alarm had been set off. Guards searching the building discovered Donny asleep, legs stretched out in front of him, with one arm hanging casually over the frame of a painting. He was surrounded by large members of the cat family, as if he lay in the feline embrace of spotted, striped, and amber-eyed jaguars, leopards, tigers, lynxes and cheetahs. He was escorted off the premises.

Another day he phoned Ella from the zoo.

'I've discovered what animal I'm like. An ocelot. It's just the same as me. It's hiding behind a tree looking at people.'

Chapter Twenty-Nine

Whenever Mark Scobie returned from Italy he signed on the dole and immediately set about working on Claimants' Union business. He wrote and printed out pamphlets and attended meetings. He kept the door of his room upstairs locked. Occasionally he would come and talk to Donny. He had the habit of pushing up his heavy black-rimmed spectacles with his thumb, revealing the indentation they left on his nose. Sometimes Donny would go downstairs to the basement when Mark was printing out stuff on the Gestetner and lean in the doorway with a mug of tea while they chatted. Mark's waxen pallor highlighted his intense manner.

'I was married,' Mark explained in his soft voice. 'But marriage didn't fit with what I believed or what I was doing.' He tried to explain his actions to Donny.

'I told her, "I'm sorry, but I've come to realise that the institution of marriage is utterly against my principles. It's a fundamental building block of capitalism; a system that I loathe and despise. I want to dedicate myself to overthrowing it. It deforms us all. I can't stay married and be true to my beliefs."'

Donny looked at Mark with suspicion. He stubbed out one cigarette, lit another and changed the subject.

'Listen, Mark, what we were talking about earlier ... fund-raising, you call it. Robberies, I call it. If I do what you are suggesting you'd better understand that I'm organising it. Anything I do, I do on my own or with someone of my choosing. I take responsibility for myself and no-one else. I don't trust anyone. Other people let you down. I'll carry it right through. I know someone who can fence the stuff in Germany. You can have the money. I don't care about that. I'd just do it for the craic.'

Mark took his glasses off and rubbed his eyes with the heel of his hand. He wore jeans and an ill-fitting black leather jacket. For the first time he broke into a shy smile.

'Thank you. You see we want the politicians and judges and businessmen to experience directly the consequences of their actions. They get away with everything. You'll be helping in a good cause. It's about justice really. But we need funding.'

Donny replied with casual insouciance, flicking his ash on the floor.

'Fuck your fucking causes. What's justice anyway? Revenge in a suit and tie. I don't want to make the world a better place. What would I be against, then? I don't want the money. I just want to see if I can do it. That's all. You can have the money and do what the fuck you like with it. You can buy all the guns you like and have as many revolutions as you want. I don't give a shit. OK? Think about it.' He looked at his watch. 'But right now I'm away to watch Monty Python on the telly.'

Donny loved television. He was transported by it. His infectious laugh could be heard all over the house. He lost himself in it. He was married to it.

'I watch television until I am hypnotised into nothing,' he said.

When the end of the day's programmes was signalled by an ever decreasing dot of light on the screen, he used to sigh with bitter fury and say: 'Well, that's it. Everything's dead now. Another fucking day of torment to be faced.'

Sometimes Donny would come home at two or three in the morning and shake Ella awake. His destructive vitality was unflagging. He would pace energetically around the bedroom, talking for hours, skidding between joviality, wonder and menace until she became exhausted. Every time she tried to fall asleep he woke her up to share some joke or impart some new thought. Once he clutched his head in despair saying: 'No-one can move fast enough. What's wrong with everybody? No-one can keep up with me. The whole fucking world is asleep. And I'm flying.'

In the mornings, after one of these episodes, her eyes felt dry in their sockets. She felt empty. Weightless. Exhausted. A shell of herself.

But sometimes the position was reversed, and Ella found herself looking at him while he was asleep, his head against the pillow, and she would hold her breath as if she were in the presence of a rare wild beast that was unaware of her being there.

Chapter Thirty

The robberies Donny executed were simple, bold and conducted without force, guns or masks. As the police acknowledged, they were daring. The first one was in New Bond Street. Blue diamonds were the target. With hindsight the shop-assistant in the carpet-muffled precincts of the well-known jeweller's shop should have guessed that the hand reaching out to examine the precious gems was not the soft-skinned one of a wealthy man. There was grime in the crevices of the knuckles and one or two livid triangular notches in the fingers. But sales assistants in Bond Street jewellers are trained in deference and understand that the rich come in many guises. This customer had taken three of the most expensive blue diamonds from the tray to inspect them in the light from the window by the door.

Donny learned something interesting about himself on that occasion. The minute the gems were in his hand, he had become paralysed, frozen to the spot as he stood facing the assistant in front of those cabinets full of glittering jewellery displays. Time stretched endlessly around him but his legs did not respond to the brain's instructions. It was as if he himself were entirely encased in finely-blown transparent glass and unable to move. He could feel his heart thumping. Then he spoke.

'Thank you very much. I'll be keeping these.'

It was speech that released him. Words were the hammer which smashed the glass and allowed him to step out as if he had been miraculously unfrozen and released from an ice prison. He ran out of the shop clutching thirty thousand pounds' worth of diamonds in his fist.

Around the corner, Sil waited in the getaway car, his trademark cigarette drooping from his lips. The engine was idling when Donny flung open the door of the passenger seat and threw himself in.

'Move. Move!'

The car pulled out into the West End traffic.

'What do you think of my disguise?' said Sil.

Donny, still out of breath, turned and looked at Sil.

'What fucking disguise?'

Sil took one hand off the steering-wheel and pointed to his head. He was wearing a Jewish skull cap and smiling complacently.

'Orthodox Jews don't do robberies,' he said.

Donny let out a yelp of laughter. Both men began to shake with mirth. Soon tears were streaming out of their eyes. Sil glanced at his young friend. There was a vividness about him. Thousands of pounds' worth of diamonds were clutched in his hand. The skin of his face was clear and glowing with excitement. He looked young and alive, as if he had just been reborn.

Donny tossed back his gleaming chestnut hair and let out a roar of laughter.

*

The first Ella knew about it was when she was woken early in the morning three weeks later. She sat up as Donny came into the bedroom. In the dark, he was pacing back and forth. She switched on the bedside light and Donny began to fling handfuls of fifty pound notes into the air until the room was a blizzard of notes.

'That can't be your wages,' said Ella in alarm.

'Oh can't it?' he said.

He opened the bag fully and pitched more notes into the air. There was an expression of grim satisfaction on his face as he told her about the diamonds. They had had to wait three weeks for the stuff to be fenced in Germany. He tipped the bag upside down over his head, until for a moment he resembled the bride at a Greek wedding.

Then he threw the bag into a corner and collapsed diagonally on his back across the bed. Within minutes he was asleep. Could there ever have been a more dangerous smile on the lips of a radiant hoodlum? He too looked like a dancer, sprawled there, arms flung back, one leg bent at the crook of the knee. Ella got out of bed and examined the scattered fifty and twenty pound notes. When she tried to get back into the bed she found he had left her no space to get in. For the rest of the night she lay curled up in a foetal crouch in a corner of the bed amid the leaf-fall of ten thousand pounds' worth of notes. In the morning, Donny got up to go to work as usual.

'I don't want you doing this any more,' Ella announced in a huff.

He grabbed a few notes, stuffed them in his pocket and swallowed the last of his tea.

'Suit yourself. Tell Mark to come up and take the money. It's for him.'

After he had gone Ella snatched up two hundred pounds or so for herself and sorted the rest into piles. She knocked on Mark's door. Mark mumbled something from the other side. He had a girl with him. She called through and told him that his money was waiting upstairs.

Then Ella made her way to the shops in the West End and bought a brown velvet-trimmed winter coat with a fur collar from Fenwick's. After that she walked down to Freed's in St Martin's Lane and bought three new pairs of ballet shoes, four soft primrose silk leotards and some expensive pale yellow tights. She walked past Leicester Square, up Regent Street and into Oxford Street. In Selfridges she looked for a wedding-dress. She tried on several in the wedding department of the main store but they were too ornate, so she went to Miss Selfridge and bought a white lace minidress and a wide-brimmed white felt summer hat with a border of flowers.

*

A week later Ella looked out of the window and her stomach churned.

A police car was crawling slowly along in the street below. It stopped a few houses away. Ella was seized with fear.

'Donny. Donny. Quick. Look. It's the police.'

They snatched some clothes, ran downstairs and climbed out of a back window into the unkempt garden. The light was fading fast. They had left the lights on in their own flat upstairs. The rest of the house was in darkness.

'We'll go to my mum's.' She was breathless as they ran through the back streets to the tube station. The shock of bolting gradually receded. They stopped running and walked. By the time they reached Victoria station it was nine o'clock at night. Donny said, 'Aw fuck it. Let's go home.'

When they returned there was no sign of a police car.

*

The younger dancers in the company were rehearsing a showcase and Ella was cast as the Herald of Spring in the ballet of *Hiawatha*. As the weeks passed her anxieties over the robbery abated. She devoted herself fully to dance. The new ballet outfits raised her spirits. The other girls envied the expensive pale yellow silk tights and soft mimosa yellow vests that contrasted so strikingly with the shining blackness of her hair and elvish eyes. It was difficult for people to take their eyes off her when she danced. The seventy-year-old choreographer, whose stiff mask of a face could have been carved from a totem pole, stood with the director of the company watching her as she worked.

'Needs to work on the placing of her arms. She has real *joie de vivre* though,' he whispered to the director, who nodded agreement. Ella danced as though she had escaped from the weight of the earth. When she arched backwards she was as pliable as a sapling. Her partner, a pompous boy with over-muscled calves who wore his hair in a pageboy bob, supported her. His warm sweaty hands gripped her waist in preparation for the lift.

'We must do something about that awful boy,' whispered the choreographer.

On stage Ella had an understanding of the space surrounding her. She enjoyed creating her three-dimensional shapes in relation to it. Friction, spin and gravity; energy, mass and light; the embodiment of the geometrics of crystal structures brought to life.

'You're so good I could kill you. How do you do it?' Manuela, who shared Ella's dressing room, teased her with mock envy. Ella liked Manuela. They had been at ballet school together. Manuela's soft eyes suggested something biddable about her. Her shoulders were rounded, her mouth often slightly open, and she was sometimes told off for slouching at the barre. When she danced there was something casual and slapdash about her movements. Manuela had already changed into her day-clothes and was hanging her costume up next to the row of swan headdresses with their black frowns. She came over to kiss Ella goodbye. Ella smiled and leaned her face into Manuela's soft breast: 'Bye, Manuela.'

Without warning the two girls exchanged a passionate kiss.

'Oh wow.' Manuela rolled her eyes and crammed her hat on her head. 'Better get back to my boyfriend.'

'Me too,' laughed Ella.

All the dancers appreciated the individual and secret beauty of each other's bodies. It bound them together in some way.

Chapter Thirty-One

Hetty perched on the sofa looking radiant. Her gold curls were cut short and she wore a grey suit with a diamante bluebird brooch on the lapel.

'Oh how hilarious. Donny should learn to behave himself.' Hetty gave a chuckle. 'Sometimes I wonder if Donny is capable of killing someone.'

Ella was wearing a loose top, black tights and stripy leg-warmers. She jutted her chair back on two legs. Hetty sipped her tea and looked around the sitting-room.

'You should get a carpet for this flat, honey. There's a roll of blue carpet in the house in Muswell Hill I could give you. No-one's going to notice it's gone. You might as well have it.' Hetty sounded practical and well-grounded as usual. She continued with a voluble stream of talk.

'Well. My news. I have this new beau. He's a real sweetie and he has a title. I managed to pry him away from his girlfriend who was in a terrible state and not doing him any good at all. A total addict.' Hetty rolled her eyes. 'Incoherent. Clearly coked to the eyeballs all day. I told him she would destroy him. He's so grateful to me now. Did I ever tell you that I have some sort of British aristocrat ancestor? Sir Tony Hardwicke.' On the spur of the moment, Hetty dipped her ladle into a soup of false ancestry. 'He was a relative of the Dukes of Cumberland or something. He was probably deported to the States for something vile.' Hetty chuckled again. 'We never really knew much about him.' She pulled out a cigarette and lit it. Her eyes shone with a strange mixture of earthiness and disembodiment. She took a deep breath and sighed.

'You're lucky that you're going to be married. I'd love to be married. I wouldn't care what he'd done. Do you have cookies or coffee or anything?' They went into the kitchen. Hetty wandered around picking up and examining some of the blue-and-white-striped crockery.

'You know that old broderie anglaise Victorian nightie your mother gave you? The one that belonged to your grandmother. There it is hanging over the back of that chair. Do you think I could borrow it? He's invited me to somewhere called Chatsworth for the weekend in a month's time. It belongs to the Duke of something or other. Devonshire, I think. The Rolling Stones are going to be there and loads of hoorays. That nightie is so cute. It looks like an heirloom or something. I could use it.'

'That nightie can be quite cold. I wore something cotton and caught a chill the other day.'

'Well don't breathe your germs over me.' Hetty held her hands up to guard her face. 'I nearly died of pneumonia once. I was on life support in Houston for a week. I'll make sure I keep warm. Let me borrow it anyway.'

Hetty stood up and cupped her hand under the long cylinder of ash.

'Where are your ashtrays?'

Ella gave her a cracked ashtray and paused in the doorway.

'Actually I was thinking of taking that nightie with me when Donny and I go away on our honeymoon, but I haven't got the dates yet so maybe I'll hang on to it. I've got other pretty ones I could lend you. I'll go and find them.'

'Do you want a white one or a blue one?' Ella came back into the room unexpectedly and caught Hetty with the Victorian nightie half-stuffed into her bag. Hetty took it out hastily and threw it on the table.

'Oh, what am I doing? Sorry sweetie. I'm all over the place. I've been having trouble with my ears again. I wasn't thinking.'

Ella ignored Hetty's sleight of hand with the nightie. What was pressing on her mind was Donny and the robberies. In the end she sat down and confided in Hetty.

'It's not just Donny.' Ella enjoyed being the melodramatic one for a change. 'The other guys in this house are revolutionaries. Donny has done it to help fund whatever they're doing. Don't tell a soul but I'm sure they're involved in these bombings.'

Hetty's forehead puckered as if someone had pulled a fine thread to cause a frown. She responded with the pragmatism of a practised illusionist.

'Don't tell anyone about that, honey. If there is anything going on when you're married you can't be asked to give evidence against Donny. Now then, have you got everything ready for the wedding? I insist you give me that nightie. I'll bring it back before the big day.'

*

In the wedding photograph, Donny and Ella are standing on the steps in front of the registry office. Donny's chestnut hair is collar-length. He has rust-coloured sideburns and a heavy bandido moustache. He is standing with his head cocked slightly to one side like a bird. The sleeves of his suit are too short, exposing his wrists below the cuffs. He is wearing a silver tie and squinting a little as if the sun is in his eyes. Ella is wearing a white lace minidress and a hat with a big pink rose pinned to the wide brim. She is directing a wide, vague smile at the camera. There are only five people present: the married couple; the witnesses Cyrus and Hetty; plus Alice de Vries, who is wearing her best suit with a shot-silk scarf and a hand-made hat with flowers cut from blue felt.

Ella looked at the marriage certificate.

'I didn't know your name was Dughall. I thought it was Donald.'

'They called me Donny to distinguish me from my dad. It's Gaelic.'

'What does it mean?'

'Fuck knows. Dark stranger, or something.'

Chapter Thirty-Two

They had to wait for their honeymoon until there was a break in the ballet company schedule. Donny had grown more relaxed and affectionate in the weeks since the wedding.

It was late summer and they travelled north towards the light. They travelled by bus because it was cheaper than the train but as they crossed the border into Scotland Donny became fractious. His legs were cramped and it was several hours before they would reach their destination. The rain started as the bus came into Inverness. By the time they reached the bus station the rain was biblical. Two destroyers grazed on the grey loch. Great sheets of water fell from the sky. They clambered from the bus to the sound of water trickling and gurgling through the city's pipes, drains and stone gutters, as if all the rivers, canals and lochs in Scotland were plotting the ultimate conquest of the land, running in secret through cities, making their own connections, their own plans and conspiracies for a final flood.

Ella and Donny waited by the bus station for a smaller bus that would take them on to the Western Highlands. The wet weather seemed to have revived Donny and he was revelling in the downpour, looking around him, taking in deep breaths of the fresh air. Ella sheltered in a shop doorway encased in a transparent plastic mackintosh with a hood. He came over and pushed the hood back from her face and gave her a kiss.

'You look like a boil-in-the-bag fish, Mrs Lady.'

He moved a few yards away then called to Ella: 'Come and look at this.'

A small boy of about three, dressed from head to foot in a Batman costume, was standing under an arch gazing out in a trance towards the mountains, and humming the Batman theme tune in a soft but persistent voice: 'Na na na na na na, Batman.'

'Magic, eh?' said Donny, squeezing Ella's arm.

*

There was a huge rainbow and then the rain stopped as they travelled westward. The small bus meandered through wide purple brown valleys where there had been no rain and everything was dry. Sullen mountains looked down on them from either side. Then the bus turned a bend in the road and Ella caught her breath. A curdled silver junket of sky stretched far into the distance. Everything was bathed in silver light and the low mountains, lochs and distant islands seemed to float ahead of them. By the time the bus trundled into Lochinver it was eight in the evening and they were the only passengers left on board. The bus dropped them off by a forbidding stone church and abandoned them to silence as it disappeared into the distance.

'Come on Spike,' Donny picked up their bags. 'Let's find somewhere to stay.'

After an hour of trudging around the village they stood facing each other outside the last bed and breakfast to turn them away. There was no accommodation available that night.

'It's summer. I told you we should have booked somewhere.'

'Give me your bag. I'll work out something.'

They walked for half an hour to the cliff top. Up there, what felt like a gale-force wind was blowing. The grass streamed in the wind.

'Fucking hell. This wind's near tearing me face off,' Donny said with pleasure as he walked. The wind whipped the sea. There were white frills on the waves. Ella tried to shelter behind him, following in his footsteps like the page behind King Wenceslas.

'Wait here a minute.' Donny took the bags and disappeared

along a path that led down through some rocks. He shouted from somewhere below her. She trod gingerly down the hillside to meet him. He had found the ruins of an old stone croft on the hillside. He whistled merrily as he laid out their mackintoshes on the ground, fixing them down with stones. Ella was tired. The stone walls sheltered them from the wind. There was no roof. Children must have set light to the place at some point because portions of the crumbling stone lintels and the grass were black and charred. They tried to make themselves comfortable on a floor littered with sheep droppings. A plane passed overhead, its light flashing like the regular sparking of a flint. Donny's eyes were alive with excitement.

'This is better than some old bed and breakfast, isn't it?'

There followed a session of Nordic love-making on a bed of stone blocks strewn with straw. It was too cold to undress. Their rough clothes kissed everywhere except where the flesh joined. Donny's tongue poured down her throat like a long stream of syrup. The dark night sky slipped between her thighs, followed by a river of burning water. All spent and in a tangled embrace of clothes they rolled away from each other. She sat up and began pulling on her woollen leg-warmers beneath her cotton skirt. Within minutes Donny was asleep, with his head cocked against the stone wall as if his neck was broken. She held her breath. In the moonlight his face had a terrible beauty. The only time she could gaze at him properly was when he was asleep. It puzzled her that even when she was with him she felt this yearning for him. His eyes shot open.

'What are you looking at?'

'You.'

'Well don't.' His eyes drooped shut again.

When he woke each morning one eye always blazed open with intense curiosity to find out where he was and start the adventure of life afresh.

Ella was unable to sleep. After a few minutes she stood up, straightened her skirt and left the croft to tread over the coarse animal pelt of the hillside towards the cliff top. Overhead was a wilderness of clouds. The wind had dropped a little. She went to the cliff edge and peered over until she could see the silver ocean fingering deep into the crack of the black mountains. The sea hissed on the beach below. Ella felt calm and refreshed, reborn like a snake that has shed its transparent coil of skin. Then she turned to look up at the sky behind her. A vertiginous attack of terror overtook her. The moon was reeling stark naked through the clouds like a mad woman looking for lovers. Unnerved, Ella ran all the way downhill back to the ruined croft.

By five in the morning it was light again and they were both awake, uncomfortable and stiff with cold against the raw stones. Ella suggested that they find a room somewhere. She began to count out their money. Donny became fretful. He started a quarrel.

'The trouble with you is that you want everything to be safe. You say, "I'd better not do that, I've got to pay the rent." I say, "Fuck the rent, let's just see what happens."'

At Ella's insistence they found a place to stay in a house in the village. The room, at the top of narrow stairs, was tiny and smelled musty. Even the pale ridged wallpaper was damp to the touch. The floor creaked every time they moved and the bathroom boiler was difficult to light. Donny grew bad-tempered. Ella tried to distract him as they lolled on the bed.

'Have you noticed the landlady's dogs? They're gorgeous.'

There were two dogs in the house with long hair the colour of dried bracken. They lounged by the grate of the hearth, rolling their amber eyes at visitors. Donny made no reply. He stared into space.

'Are you going deaf?' she asked after a while.

'No. My brain is just refusing to accept your crappy conversation.'

She kicked at his legs. He stretched and got up.

'Come on, then. Let's go out.'

Donny decided he wanted to walk along the ridge of the mountain tops. Ella stayed below, keeping him in sight silhouetted against the blue sky. Every now and then he waved down at her. She began to run along the small track in the valley below, leaping over stones and patches of flooded ground. After a few minutes she took off her shoes and ran barefoot. The mossy grass and peat underfoot made the ground springy. She ran without stopping or feeling tired. It was as if she were powered by a tremendous energy, buoyant and indefatigable. For half an hour she ran with no awareness of the stones or puddles beneath her feet. Only when she saw Donny begin to make his way down the mountainside towards her did she stop and wait for him. And then it puzzled her that she was not short of breath at all. All was quiet except for the insects buzzing around her in the heather. The silence pressed on her ears.

'I could live here.' Donny stood in the ruddy brown scrub of tangled gorse and heather looking around him at the mountainscape with satisfaction. He slashed at the brambles with his arm.

'What would you do? How could you earn money here?'

He examined his forearm where a bramble had made a deep scratch.

'I don't know. I'd rob and steal. I'd go marauding. Marauding for meals. I'd put on black glasses and a black coat and get a big knife and go up to the sheep and say, "Puss. Puss. Puss," and lure them to their deaths.' Donny stood laughing against the sun.

'But really. How could you live? How would you manage?'

He looked exasperated.

'Look. I don't think about tomorrow or next year. Never did. Never will. I can't think about that. There is no fucking past and there is no future. People are always asking me for explanations. I give them whatever explanations will suit them – to the romantics I give a romantic explanation. To those who need an economic explanation I give an economic one. I create explanations. But there is no fucking explanation.'

They ate sandwiches sitting in bracken next to a tan river with a silver lace of froth on its surface, and then lazed in the sun until late afternoon. Donny wanted to return to Lochinver skirting the black hump of Suilven. That would make it late evening before they were back home. They walked in silence.

Between the two horns of another mountain they came across a lake. The sun was setting in a red volcanic eruption along the horizon casting a dull fiery glow over everything. Around the edges of the lake the ground was marshy. The wind made a herring-bone pattern on the surface of the water. Ella broke off some reeds and tried to throw them against the wind into the lake.

'It's a shame I have to be back for rehearsals on Thursday. We could have stayed another week.'

'I'm not coming back with you.'

'Why not?'

He was standing outlined against the strange red waters of the menstruating lake like some prophetic vision from the past.

'Because I'm going for a wander.'

Back in the rented room Donny lay on the bed naked from the waist up, fiddling with a small portable radio trying to get a signal. His shirt hung over the back of a chair. Ella looked at the white bluebell-veined arm with its deep bramble scratch and ruby-clotted blood.

'Do you want something for that arm?'

'Nope.'

'When will you come back?'

He stared at the ceiling.

'I don't know. Soon.'

'What do you mean?'

'How do I know? Look. I will be back very soon. I just want to look around for a bit longer. Can't you see I'm already travelling?'

*

Hetty stood in the grounds of Chatsworth House. It was five in the morning. She stood at the edge of the field in a black vintage silk dress with a bubble skirt and smoked a cigarette. She had walked some considerable way from the house, until she could no longer hear any sounds of music or gaiety. There was a very light white morning dew or frost on the grass. Her shoulders were bare. One long black strap from the front of the dress crossed over her left shoulder to meet the back of the dress halfway down. After a short while, she continued walking alongside the white picket fence which marked the end of the grounds at the bottom of a valley. As she walked through the grass her footprints darkened. An hour earlier her fabricated story of British ancestry and wealth had unravelled. She was deflated. Someone had denounced her for lying and publicly humiliated her. Her imposture had been exposed. Imitation, the key to nature's cipher, was Hetty's forte. She was an expert in camouflage. Her new aristocrat boyfriend, shocked by the deception, had stared at her on the ballroom floor like a naturalist startled to find that he has been looking at an animal rather than a patterned flower.

The decision taken, Hetty threw her cigarette into the whitened grass and made her way back to the car park of the great house. She chucked her bag into the back and drove to London.

Chapter Thirty-Three

Ella returned on her own from the honeymoon. She was dispirited. In the daytime she rehearsed then went home to mooch around the house. The atmosphere there had changed. A steady stream of young men and women in jeans and burdened with rucksacks came and went. Both Mark and Hector were back from Milan, although Hector was spending most of his time in Kent with his new girlfriend. Donny turned up a week after Ella. Disgruntled, he slung his bag on the bed. The honeymoon had made him more restless than ever. 'What's the matter?' she asked.

'I don't like buying fucking return tickets. In any circumstances.'

But Mark was in good spirits. There was even a vestige of colour in his cheeks: 'It's great having all these comrades from other countries coming to visit us. That way we can link up all across Europe.'

Most of the visitors were from Italy. Several were members of Lotta Continua. Some had links with the Brigate Rosse. German militants leaned across the kitchen table to insist with vehemence that the current crop of German industrialists were nothing more than the reincarnation of the Nazis and must be attacked. They explained their fear that Nazism had not been rooted out of high places, and insisted that there was considerable support for the militants throughout Germany.

Donny referred to all these visitors as 'The Totallies'.

'You know,' he would say with amusement, 'fascism must be totally eradicated. Fuck idealism. All idealism is untruthfulness.'

In fact Donny worked hard. If Ella was not performing in the evening she would cook and wait for Donny to return, listening for the sound of his work boots coming up the uncarpeted wooden stairs.

'What's to eat? I'm knackered.' He flung his toolbag in the corner.

'Don't you want me to give you a kiss?' Ella was laughing as she went to hug him.

'Kiss, no. Egg sandwich, yes. A frog kissed me once and look what happened – I turned back into a common lout.' He kicked off his shoes and stretched out on the sofa. Ella came in with two plates of mince and potatoes on a tray.

'Ah, fucking magic, hen.' He sat up and rubbed his hands together at the sight and smell of food.

Most of the time Donny and Ella ignored the comings and goings below and stayed upstairs in their flat, curled on the sofa, watching television.

'Poverty is OK,' announced Donny. 'The best thing is to have a great idea about making a fortune and then not bother to follow it through. Put the telly on. It's *Caligula*.'

*

Hetty arrived and spent two hours talking to Ella with an intensity unusual even for her. Her eyes were swimming with distress. Ella sat next to her on the sofa. Hetty touched up her lipstick, put the lipstick in her handbag and breathed out a sigh.

'I have to go to the pharmacy for my medication.'

Ella flashed her a look of sympathetic worry.

'Should you be taking medication if you're pregnant?'

Hetty held her hand briefly to the top of her breast-bone, as though suddenly breathless. She ran both hands through her hair, tossed her head back in a way that showed off, with apparent innocence, her cheekbones and gave that familiar brave smile.

'I need my tranquillizers and antidepressants, honey. But maybe you're right. I don't know what to do.' She rolled her eyes.

'Do you want to stay here till I come back? We have a performance this evening. I'll be back later. Donny knows but I haven't told anyone else.'

'OK. Thanks. I think I might.' Hetty gave a rueful smile. 'Saves going back to my empty flat. It's a bit lonely there. I'll put my feet up here and wait. Your eyebrows need plucking by the way. I'll do it for you some time.'

*

It was still light when Donny came home from work. He went into the sitting-room to find Hetty lying on her back aslant on the sofa with her head and one arm hanging over the side. Her blonde curls brushed the dark blue carpet. She had a glistening snail-track of dribble coming from the side of her mouth which was slightly open. A handkerchief had dropped from her hand. Pills were scattered around her. A glass of water stood next to her on the floor.

For a full minute Donny stood in the doorway, looking at the rumpled figure and tear-ruined face in the pale early evening light. He put his toolbag down. She did not move.

'Fucking get up,' he snarled.

There was no response. He repeated: 'Get the fuck up.'

Hetty opened her eyes. The expression on her face was sweet and foul as she raked through her brain for a quick explanation. None came, so she started to gag as if about to be sick.

'Pick up those pills.' Donny's voice was deep and grim. Her eyes filled with tears.

'Oh holy shit. The pills didn't work. I'm alive.' A peculiar talent for believing her own lies made her sound convincing. She gasped and flung herself face down on the sofa. She clutched a cushion, half gagging and half sobbing.

'You have to swallow them first,' sneered Donny, 'not just throw them on the fucking floor.'

Donny picked up Hetty's handbag and tossed it over to her.

'Get up.'

When challenged in this way, Hetty became calm and matter-of-fact. Her tears stopped. For a few moments she stared up at Donny with a sly smile. Then she sat up and shrugged. She began to gather her things together as if nothing had happened. She popped the pills back in their bottle one by one.

'Where's my comb?' She looked round vaguely, found it on the sofa and ran it through her hair. The shallowness of feeling was in stark contrast to the intensity of the demonstration a few minutes earlier. Donny looked at her. It was as if she was a platform from which everything rebounded without reaching the interior. Nothing penetrated. Tremendous exaggeration was followed by staggering superficiality and she already seemed to have forgotten what she had done.

'Don't try that trick again,' he snarled.

'It was just a kinda joke.'

'No it wasn't. Now fuck off,' said Donny.

Hetty finished gathering her things together and walked to the door.

'Could you tell Ella to ring me please?' she said with icy politeness, as she let herself out. Hetty Moran went home, where she remained for a week sequestered with her own fury at Donny for unmasking her charade.

*

'You shouldn't have done that. She might just have been really upset at being pregnant,' said Ella when she came home.

'No she wasn't.'

'How do you know?'

'She's not pregnant. I can just tell.'

Chapter Thirty-Four

The next Tuesday Hetty walked into the New Scotland Yard offices and went up to the reception desk. MI5 had already spurned her offer of information.

Three officers were on duty behind the front desk.

'I have an appointment with Detective-Sergeant Alan Forbes.' She held out the card he had left with her after the sleep-walking episode and went and sat on one of the seats in the window.

The receptionist called his office. 'He will come down and see you.'

Five minutes later the lift doors opened and Alan Forbes approached her. Although she hadn't seen him for some months she recognised the conventional good looks, the square jaw and brown eyes and remembered that he had started out as an actor before he became a policeman. As a member of Special Branch he now wore plain clothes, a casual suit, and had let his hair grow down to his collar:

'Good heavens. You've got long hair.' Hetty gave him a beguiling smile.

'Yes. Part of the job these days. How are you? No more sleep-walking, I hope.' He was relaxed and friendly.

'No, that's stopped. I'm sorry to bother you but I have some information that I think you should have.' Hetty regarded him gravely as she spoke. He nodded.

'I'm afraid we'll have to talk in the canteen? Special Branch are not allowed to take people into their offices.'

Hetty smiled her youthful smile.

'That's fine.'

They went up in the shiny metal lift and sat in part of the canteen that was sectioned off. In the next area was the restaurant which was noisy with clatter. They queued up and he paid for two coffees.

'How can I help you?'

Hetty's demeanour changed to one of anxiety. Her voice was tremulous as she spoke.

'Is it safe to talk here? I'm in a dilemma. I'm not sure if I should be telling you this. I'm not even sure what it is I'm trying to say. And now, all of a sudden, I feel I might be wasting your time. Maybe it's not important at all.'

'I won't know till you try it.' Forbes smiled at her as he stirred his coffee.

'It has something to do with the bombings that have been happening lately. But I don't know what to do as I might be completely wrong. I might know someone who had something to do with it. But I'm really not sure.' She bit her lip and looked at him in anguish.

'Fire away and we'll see what it's all about.'

'First of all, I'd better say that I would never be prepared to give evidence. He thinks I am his friend. I've been in agony about this. It's making me feel really treacherous but I think I'm doing the right thing. It might not be him but I know something is going on in that house anyway.'

'Which house?'

'Well, I haven't actually seen anything. It's only what I've heard. The thing is I'm going back home to the States and I couldn't have it on my conscience that I'd left without telling somebody. It's a house where I've heard people talking about ... explosives and robberies ... Hell. I'm really not sure I'm doing the right thing.'

The Detective-Sergeant took out his pad and a pen from his top pocket.

'Why don't you just write down a name and address. We can investigate. Nobody need know anything about your involvement.'

Hetty hesitated and looked troubled. Then she looked him directly in the eyes and bit her lip before scribbling a name and address down on the pad.

'I hope I've done the right thing.'

'Anything you've told me will be strictly confidential. And thank you for coming in. This might be useful. We'll check it out anyway.'

After she had left, Detective-Sergeant Forbes studied the name and address she had given him. Back in the office he reported what he'd been told to his colleagues. The matter was brought up at the next daily meeting.

*

It is in the nature of everything to be reported, to leave a trace or a trail. Even a pebble has a shadow to remind us that it is there. So does the planet. A fern leaves its trace in the rocks. Footsteps wear out a stone stair. The world is full of signatures. Even an electron, although its path cannot be predicted, leaves a trace of where it has been. But Hetty Moran rarely left a trace when she decided to move on.

Ella tried telephoning her every few days, but Hetty had gone.

Chapter Thirty-Five

The house in Bethnal Green was full of a harsh new energy. There were footsteps running up and down the stairs day and night and the sound of unfamiliar voices and foreign accents in the basement. Students and trades unionists came and went. The mood in the house matched the mood in the country. The government had declared a state of emergency. Six Yorkshire miners arrived at the house to lobby parliament. They slept curled up in sleeping bags on the floor. A Black Sabbath album blasted through the house day and night. All this left Ella feeling restive. The incessant political conversations induced an odd sensation of effervescence in her stomach, making her light-headed and dry-mouthed. It was as if the myelin sheaths around her nerves had been removed, leaving her exposed to prevailing winds. When she listened to arguments about class and revolution she felt a sympathetic rage related to Donny's work and pay. Then her position would inexplicably go into reverse and she would become hostile to whatever they were discussing.

'I'm really not interested. I just want to be a dancer,' she said, when asked for help over some campaign issue or other. One of the miners, with a strong work-bitten face, said: 'We dig the coal that provides the electricity that lights up your theatres, love. Our wages have dropped to nothing.' Then he suddenly gave a sneering smile and grabbed Ella's breast. She shook him off and went upstairs.

That evening Ella looked around the dressing room at dancers pulling their faces this way and that to apply pale pink lipsticks and black eye-liner, and for the first time they annoyed her. The conversation was all about who was playing what in which ballet, or tips on whether Elastoplast, methylated spirits or footbath lotion best protected their sore feet.

'Don't dancers ever go on strike?' Ella asked, as they collected their costumes from the wardrobe department. The others looked at her in surprise.

'Shouldn't think so,' said Manuela, holding a small white feather tiara between her teeth as she fixed her hair. 'Striking's just not what we do. I want to hook one of those bankers that hang round the stage door. How can I bag one if I'm on strike.' She giggled. 'Can you help fix this headpiece?' The other girls continued chatting and adjusting their full net skirts, pinning on headdresses and fastening white ribbons around their ankles. Ella felt a rush of impatience with them all.

'OK. Les Syphilitics are coming,' yelled one of the girls, as the tannoy called them on-stage.

*

At home Ella half-listened to the intense conversations in the kitchen, her feet marking out some new choreography under the table.

Frequent visitors included a gangly young Dutchman with spiky blond hair called Jaap and a local worker at a community playground called Jerry Haynes. Jaap was a veteran of the defunct Provo movement in Amsterdam and had arrived on a white-painted bicycle which he parked in the hall. Jerry Haynes was immediately nicknamed Clark Kent because of his square-jawed good looks. Ella liked him best. Most of the other visitors ignored her. Jerry at least acknowledged her with a friendly grin and he brought with him an endless supply of dope which he shared around. Flicking back his long brown hair, Jerry described what had happened during his last year at university.

'It was amazing. The lecturer just said: "In England, ten per cent of the people own ninety per cent of the wealth of the country" and there was a sort of whoompf as if he had held a match to a build-up of gas. The whole place went up. That guy had been giving the same lecture for years to zero response. This time everyone went wild. They had to call the police onto campus.'

'A policeman tried to search Donny a while back but he wouldn't have any of it.' Ella spoke quietly. For the first time she found people listening to her with approval.

'They would pick on a working-class guy,' said Jerry. 'I don't think people will put up with all this shit much longer.'

Someone had brought a TV down into the kitchen. Everyone in the kitchen gathered around it in silence. The news showed thousands of workers assembled in the Glasgow shipyards. Jimmy Reid, the trades union convenor, was speaking.

'The government has decided to let the shipyards close. But we will not let the yards close.' There was a roar of approval from the shipyard workers. 'Youse have voted to take over the yards and begin a work-in. We will start straight away. No hooliganism. No vandalism. No bevvying.'

'I suppose they have to exercise discipline.' Jerry turned to the others.

'Yes, but we don't,' replied Mark with steady calm. 'We can do things on their behalf. Anonymous targeted actions to support them.'

*

Another visitor to the house was Situationist architect Michael Feynite, a young man with blond hair and classical Grecian features who could have been mistaken for an aristocrat until he opened his mouth.

'I've seen you dance,' he told Ella, in a slight cockney accent. 'I saw you dance in a school in Manchester. I went there with a ballet critic – my lover at the time.'

Feynite had been in Paris in May '68 and still wore an air of subversion. He believed that architecture should be a summons to revolution and spent long hours in conversation with Mark Scobie discussing the works of Debord and Vaneigem. The discussions gave Ella a headache.

'We should provoke something.' Feynite drew on his spliff. 'Until we can build the city we want we should try letting a herd of sheep loose in Parliament Square.'

The presence of Feynite caused ructions in the house. He was despised as elitist. Various political factions clashed in the kitchen. Arguments and fights broke out. It required a tremendous effort for Ella to keep herself focused on dance. Jerry Haynes spotted that Ella was becoming unsettled by the turmoil. One evening he invited her to see a movie with him. Jerry called for her in his old green Simca. It was a hot summer night.

'Will Donny mind us going to the pictures? He's not the sort of guy I'd like to cross.'

'No. He's not bothered.'

Jerry swung the car round into Mare Street.

'I've booked two tickets for *The Seven Samurai* at the Rio. I hope you like it. By the way, did you meet Hector's new girlfriend, Barbara?'

Ella shook her head.

'She seems nice enough. A nurse, or something. They came up from Kent the other day. Is Hector with Lotta Continua in Italy or is he with the Brigate Rosse?'

'I've no idea.' Ella smoothed her skirt down over her knees and looked out of the window. Jerry continued full of enthusiasm.

'Someone said that Donny could get hold of explosives at his work. That would be brilliant. Is it true?' Jerry sounded in awe of Donny.

'I haven't got a clue.' A faint smell of garbage from the Hackney streets floated in through the open car window.

The film turned out to be shot in black and white. It was not at all what Ella had expected. At the beginning there was a lot of yelling and confusion in Japanese and despite subtitles Ella could not follow the story. Then a figure came onto the screen who mesmerised her. It was Kyuzo the swordsman, taciturn and stone-faced, with black hair pulled back into a knot with a spiky tuft sticking out at the back. His prominent cheekbones, grainy complexion and ascetic face reminded Ella in some way of her father.

Ella watched the swordsman practise his art alone in the mist on the hillside. He was mute. He did not smile, and worked in isolation far from the other Samurai. His swordsmanship was the art of deadly precision. When he killed, the blow exploded out of nowhere and blood sprayed from his opponent's neck like grain from a burst bag. She identified with this character. She wanted to dance with the same degree of precision and commitment. She remembered her teacher saying, 'You have to be masculine and feminine to be a dancer.'

She was silent on the way home. Jerry switched on the car radio to hear the news. There was an announcement.

'An explosion has damaged the home of John Davies, Minister of Trade and Industry.'

Jerry let out a whoop of delight.

'They've got John Davies. He's the one who's closing down the shipyards. Do you remember? Tell Donny that someone's blown up the house that belongs to the minister in charge of the building industry. Yippee. Doesn't Donny work for Laing's?'

'Yes. Yes.' She was barely listening. 'He used to. He changes every five minutes.' She was trying to remember the moves that the swordsman had made.

Jerry dropped her off at the house.

*

The next evening, when Ella was at work, Donny came downstairs into the kitchen. Jaap the Dutchman was rocking backwards and forwards on the hind legs of his chair. His boasts about previous revolutionary activities had been grating on Donny's nerves.

'How about coming for a drink, then?' Donny asked. Jaap nodded, grabbed his peaked leather cap and stood up to leave, smiling his endless vacant smile around the room.

Jaap had not been prepared for a rampage. After the first two pub visits, however, Donny's eyes were alight with the anticipation of violent disorder. There followed a whirl of taxi rides, raucous arguments with the drivers, the bright lights of various pubs, threatening encounters and unsolicited exchanges of underwear in different parts of London. Finally, in Camden Town, there was a scuffle in which heavy punches were exchanged. Panting, Donny stood on the pavement with his head to one side challenging Jaap: 'Did you say you were interested in class struggle?'

The fracas had unsettled Jaap but he tried to maintain a level of bonhomie.

'Ya. Of course. That is why I am in England.'

'Then lace up your cunt-kicking boots and come with me. I'll show you some fucking class struggle.' Donny grasped Jaap's arm and pushed him into a taxi. Jaap let out an apprehensive laugh. Before he knew it the taxi was pulling up outside The Ritz.

Joyous, bountiful, grim and gruesome Donny fell out of the cab dragging Jaap after him. He approached the entrance to The Ritz brandishing a blood-stained jockstrap he had picked up somewhere along the way. His own white T-shirt was also decorated with streaks of blood down the front. A blood bubble shone in his right nostril. His eyes burned with an invincible strength. The uniformed doorman tried to stop this force of nature from getting through the swing doors. But into the pink and gold art nouveau of heavenly order erupted Donny McLeod, raw-headed and bloody-boned, for his evening cocktail of palm court orchestral music and good old-fashioned class struggle.

Jaap agonised on the pavement outside as to whether to follow Donny or not. From inside the lobby came shouts and the tinkle of breaking glass. Jaap crept away. Back in Bethnal Green, Jaap told the others what had happened. A mood of self-righteous disdain overcame the people around the table.

'That's not class struggle,' said a thin-faced activist known as Weasel. 'That's just a street brawl. It doesn't achieve anything. There has to be discipline. You have to submit yourself to a party or organisation or whatever.'

Donny, that connoisseur of pure rebellion, became the topic

of conversation. Weasel's lank hair hung around his face like two brackets.

'Donny's a liability. That's not revolutionary behaviour. It's counter-revolutionary. Adventurism.'

There was a sober nodding of heads. It had proved impossible for them to impart to Donny anything to do with ideology. He would not take on that apparatus. As soon as anything became set in its ways, Donny was part of the urge to overthrow it. He seemed to think it was a curse to take sides for any other reason than contrariness. He was against all titanic sterility and preferred to settle for ecstasy, terror, brutality and liberation – all at once and this minute. In his absence, Donny was accused and found guilty of political deviance – individualism and spontaneism – by those sitters round the table.

When Donny came home there was blood in his hair and a crescent bruise under his swollen eye. He put his head around the kitchen door and looked with scorn at the disapproving faces that greeted him.

'Too much Seneca, not enough Caligula,' he announced. 'No risk, no joy.' He slammed the door behind him, then popped his head back in to say: 'Have you ever noticed that when you're lying on the pavement waving your arms the taxis won't stop for you?'

While condemning his behaviour, everyone in the room felt secretly that what they stood for was rigid and harsh and that an onslaught from Donny could sweep it all away letting milk, honey and wine burst through everywhere and that maybe Donny was some sort of wounded god living amongst them incognito.

Upstairs in the flat Donny was in an expansive mood.

'You see, what you have to do,' he said, 'is ride a donkey against the titans in the hope that the braying and confusion will make them run away.'

Ella, wearing shorts and a loose vest, was bathing her feet in a tub of hot water. The steam dampened her loose hair and her face was flushed.

'What's happened to your nose?' she asked.

'My nose?' He touched it and raised his eyebrows in surprise at the blood on his finger. 'Who knows?' he cackled.

Donny gave her a blood-stained, whisky-fumed kiss and switched on the TV, then flung himself on the sofa and lay looking at her.

'You're beautiful. You're so beautiful,' he said in an onrush of love and warmth. Then he lay looking up at the ceiling. 'What nobody seems to understand is that I need to live in a house with seventeen doors so I can get out quickly.'

Chapter Thirty-Six

Michael Feynite the Situationist architect was more tolerant of Donny than the others. One night in Donny's flat he described the surreal graffiti he had seen in Paris in 1968 that persuaded him to join the Situationists.

'I like graffiti.' Donny was cleaning his boots. 'I like it because it has a writer but no fucking author. The anonymity of the murmur, that's what I like. It doesn't matter who's speaking. That's the glory of rumour – there's no fucking flash cunt taking credit for it. Let's go and see if Mark has any cigarettes. I've run out.'

'I've got Gitanes.' Feynite offered one.

'Nah. Mark smokes Senior Service. I like them.'

Mark was working but had forgotten to switch the light on. There was a ghostly crepuscular air to his room and they did not see him for a moment.

He switched on the light and tossed Donny a cigarette. His tone was almost apologetic and he was so quietly spoken that at first Donny did not hear what he said:

'Donny, I wonder if I could ask you something. Can you get hold of some gelignite from your demolition site?'

'What?' Donny frowned. Mark's heart-shaped face was even paler than usual. The bare light bulb over his head moved in the night breeze from the window and made the shadows in the room shift. He looked directly at Donny as he said again: 'I was wondering if you can get hold of any gelignite from your building site. Or dynamite.

We want to set some explosives off outside the Explosives Branch of the Ministry of Defence. A sort of poetic statement. Redecorate the outside of the building a little. It's the Royal Armament Research and Development Establishment at Fort Halstead in Kent. Do you think you'd be able to get your hands on anything?'

'I might,' said Donny.

Feynite was standing in the doorway in a halo of smoke. He winked at Donny.

'Sometimes blowing things up is just a little exclamation mark. It's like the graffiti you said you enjoyed – an imaginative reminder to the authorities that not everyone submits.'

*

The next week Donny came back from work bringing with him eight sticks of gelignite: long sausages covered with waxy greasepaper. He went down to knock on Mark's door. When Mark unlocked it Donny went in and flung the explosives down on the table. Mark flinched. Donny looked at him with distaste.

'Don't worry. They won't go off till the detonators are fixed.' Donny reached into his top pocket, pulled out eight detonators: aluminium tubes about two and a half inches long and an eighth of an inch wide. He put them on the table where they rolled a bit and shone like dull silver pencils.

'Now stop bothering me with all this fucking business. I've had enough,' he snarled.

*

Ella was not due at rehearsal the next day and spent the morning tidying up the flat. It was nearly lunchtime when she went down the two stairs off the landing to see if the hoover was in Mark's room. She had the key. On the table by the bed under the skylight were the sticks of gelignite which she had seen Donny bring back from work. Standing next to them were three packets of non fire-suppressed fertiliser from Boots, several two-pound packets of sugar, two bottles of sulphuric acid, a dozen or so small screw-top medicine bottles with the circular top cut out and several sheets of greaseproof paper. Then she noticed the electric fire which Mark had recently borrowed from their flat. It had been dismantled. The resistance wire from the fire had been taken off and pinned with two metal pins to a large square battery.

She slipped out of the room, her heart beating fast with a mixture of fear and delight. She ran downstairs out of the house and walked towards the parade of shoddy shops. In the small, brightly lit supermarket she picked up two packets of cereal and put them down again, hardly aware of what she was doing. For a long time she stood staring at a shelf of detergents and kitchen cleaner. Then, reluctant to go home, she went to the cinema and bought a ticket for *The Thomas Crown Affair*, which she sat through without seeing anything on the screen in front of her.

When she came back to the house at four that afternoon, to collect her things for the theatre, she peeped into Mark's room with a sense of dread. The table had been cleared. There was nothing on it.

Chapter Thirty-Seven

The kitchen was abuzz with anger, fear and danger.

'They've been arrested.'

Mark was on the telephone talking to a solicitor, one hand over his ear to block out the noise. Six or seven people were standing in the kitchen, their faces tense as they listened to Mark's conversation. Ella paused, shocked, on her way to work.

'Who's been arrested?'

'Jaap and Weasel. They picked up Michael Feynite too. There was a raid on a house in north London. It happened on Wednesday. They've all been charged and taken to Brixton prison.'

'Charged with what?'

'We're not too sure. Conspiracy. Fraud. Deception. Mark's trying to find out now. They've raided loads of places all over London. Someone threw a petrol bomb at the Army Recruiting Centre.'

'No, it was just a firecracker,' said a breathless girl who had just arrived. 'And that explosion at John Davies's house – apparently they used a tiny amount of gelignite with a detonator inside a condom that was inserted into the lock of his front door and held there with chewing-gum.' She gave a sudden giggle.

Mark seemed calm and euphoric. There was an aura of invincibility about him. He put down the phone.

'The solicitor doesn't think they will get bail. What is needed now is for more attacks to take place so that the police realise they've got the wrong people and there are many more of us out there.' He gave a smile: 'Fire-bombing is just one way of serving the community.'

Ella's heart was thumping as she went to work. When she reached the stage door of the Royal Opera House she tried to look calm as she said good evening to the stage-door keeper. She wanted to warn Donny to stay away, but there was no way of reaching him. He was working in Northampton and would not be home till midnight.

*

That night's performance was *Beauty and the Beast*. When it was over, Ella left the theatre without even taking off her make-up. *Beauty and the Beast* was not a ballet she enjoyed. It opened with so many confusing exits and entrances outside the castle that she always feared she would make mistakes and appear at the wrong place. She hurried from the dressing room and clattered down the spiral metal stairway to the stage door. When she emerged from the theatre everything around her seemed bright and unnaturally clear, as if she were on the verge of a migraine. The streets were full of late-night revellers. She dashed down the stairs into the underground. At Holborn station she waited on the draughty platform in front of a poster advertising the Tutankhamun exhibition, feeling that the inside of her stomach had been scraped out. She feared what she might find when she reached home. It was Donny's safety that concerned her.

Donny was already asleep when she let herself in. He had fallen asleep with the gas fire still on. She turned it off and crept into bed beside him. She felt for his shoulder under the sheet and shook him awake.

'Did you know Jaap and Weasel and Michael Feynite are in jail' she whispered.

He lifted his head.

'Good for them. I don't give a shit.' His mouth made a chewing sound and he went back to sleep.

For an hour Ella lay next to Donny in the darkness, staring at the ceiling, unable to sleep for the feeling of free-floating rage at the arrests. Occasionally, the lights from a passing car made a travelling pattern across the walls. She lifted herself up and strained her eyes in the dark to see the shape of Donny's head on the pillow. After what seemed like an age she drifted into sleep.

That night she dreamed she was in the sky trying to reach a circular hole above her. She swam upwards through blue space towards the opening but two doors, like the doors of a tube train, slid shut together in front of her. She turned around in the air and suddenly the whole earth lay bathed in glorious sunlight below her. There was a bear in the sky floating towards her. As she took the bear's hand, they danced floating down to earth together and patches of his fur came away revealing gold underneath. Together they alighted on the flat sand of the shore. She knelt by the scalloped waves and fashioned a heart out of foam and mud. Then she woke.

In the morning she ran downstairs to look for milk in the communal kitchen. The kitchen was deserted. Someone had cleaned up, done the washing-up and emptied the roaches from the ashtrays.

Upstairs she heard Donny singing in the bathroom between spits and gurgles as he cleaned his teeth. He called out.

'I'm tired of this Northampton job. I'm going up to Scotland to see about working there for a bit. I'm only going for a few days. You've got a few days off, why don't you go to your mum's if things are getting a bit jumpy around here?'

She was relieved that Donny would be going away from any danger.

'OK. I think I will. We have a week off while the opera is playing and I haven't seen mum for a while. I'm worried about the others in the house though.'

'Look.' Donny came out of the bathroom with his mouth full of toothpaste froth. 'Don't bother with them. Nothing matters, OK?'

Chapter Thirty-Eight

Ella spent the next week with her mother. She pottered around the Kent cottage, restless and unable to relax, but pleased to give her bruised feet a chance to recover.

On her return to London she noticed something odd as she approached the Bethnal Green house. It was when she crossed the road that she realised the front door had been smashed down and someone had reboarded it with two criss-cross planks of wood. Her key still worked. She let herself in with a sense of foreboding. The house looked different: empty, as though it had been swept out and nobody lived there any longer. There was none of the usual junk-mail and debris cluttering the hall. From upstairs she could hear a woman's deep smoky voice.

'He was always such a wonderful child. Full of integrity. He would say, "Mummy, I can't do such a thing," and I would say, "No darling, then you won't have to," and he was so sweet and I was so moved. I can't believe this has happened. I'm distraught. Do you think we should take this writing-desk? It's worth quite a lot. It belonged to my father-in-law.'

Ella climbed the stairs. The skin on her neck prickled. She stood outside Mark Scobie's room. The door was ajar. The lock had been broken and one of the door panels shattered. From inside, the woman's voice was echoing as if the room was empty. Ella could see in at an angle. It was denuded of most of its furniture. A middle-aged woman with glasses and prominent cheekbones stood running her fingers along the edge of Mark's desk. His bed had gone. The woman wore a brown cape with a check pattern and expensive brown leather boots. As she turned towards the door, Ella recognised Vera Scobie. The other woman was a sharp-faced creature with darting eyes who, Ella learned, was a friend who had come to help.

Vera jumped as she saw Ella.

'Oh my goodness. You gave me a fright.' She swept towards Ella holding out her hands.

'My poor girl. Do you remember me? We have met. I'm Mark's mother.' Vera radiated sympathy as she embraced her. She screwed up her eyes to examine Ella. 'You must be in shock. The police have been here as you can see. Is your husband with you?'

Ella shook her head. She felt sick.

'No.'

Vera raised her hands in disbelief at the turn of events. She put an arm around Ella.

'Try not to worry. Mark has had to go away. Don't ask where he is, dear. I don't know. I'm just getting over the shock myself. And we've just heard that Hector has been arrested in Italy. Mark won't be coming back here so we're clearing things out. This is Molly, a friend of mine who's helping.' Vera frowned as she gazed around the room: 'We must get the place cleaned. You and your husband can stay here as long as you need until you find somewhere else. We wouldn't dream of making you homeless. But we will be giving up the house eventually. It feels unlucky.' She shuddered. 'Now then Ella, would you like us to come upstairs with you to your flat? I'm afraid the police have been in there too. What monsters. I've been saying for years we were headed for a police state. Now it's here. What are we to do?'

Ella nodded. Her heart beat fast and there was a sort of singing buzz in her ears. They trooped upstairs to the top flat. The door had been forced. The flat had been entered and searched. There was a note from the Metropolitan Police Special Branch pinned on the door with a copy of the warrant, granted by a magistrate, to search for explosives.

Vera looked at the note:

'I'll show this to my husband. He's a lawyer. It's outrageous. What right have they?' She consulted her watch looking pale and tense. 'I must rush to the theatre. Will you be all right, dear?'

'I think so.' Ella's stomach tightened into a knot. She came downstairs to see them out.

Ella saw the two women conferring in the street outside before they drove away in separate cars. As soon as they had left she darted back upstairs and went through the flat looking for any evidence that could link Donny with the robberies or the gelignite. She racked her brains trying to remember if they had left anything incriminating behind. When Donny telephoned later she told him what had happened.

'Mark's disappeared. Even his mother doesn't know where he is. There's no-one here. I don't think you should come back.'

He cursed and hung up.

*

The next day Donny was back. He went through the house examining the damage. Ella took him down to see the basement. Everything was a mess, as if the police search had been hurried. The Gestetner machine had been taken away. Newspapers, pamphlets and documents were scattered everywhere. A dirty white T-shirt and a tracksuit lay on the floor. Drawers had been upturned and emptied, ashtrays upset. There were heaps of index cards, scraps of paper and press cuttings strewn about. Upstairs, Donny pushed open the door to Mark's room with his foot. Ella explained that Mark had disappeared, that his mother had taken his stuff and that his parents were giving up the house.

'Fuck them,' said Donny. 'Dirty no-good rat-faced bastards. I hope they don't die before I have time to kill them.'

'Who? The police or Mark or Mark's parents?'

'Everybody.' He kicked at a pile of newspapers on the floor of Mark's room. Ella tried to calm him.

'No point in biting the hand that feeds us. We don't have to go straight away. We can stay here for a bit.'

Donny stood still on the landing, his hands in his pockets, with bitter humour in his eyes.

'Listen. I would bite not only the hand that feeds me but any other fucking hand within tooth-reach: the helping fucking hand; the hand across the sea; the hand out; the hand-up; the upper hand; the hand of God. Whatever hand is fucking available, I will fucking bite it.'

They went on up the stairs to their own flat.

'Donny, I don't think you should have come back ... the police might be looking for you. We don't know where Mark is or what he's said.'

Before Ella could finish Donny turned on her with a look of burning contempt. He looked around their flat. It still bore the imprint of the police raid in the broken locks, the damaged record player and the piles of books that had been taken down and scattered around. He picked up one of the books and let it drop. Ella sensed that he could barely contain his rage at the violation. He pulled on his jacket.

'I'm going out for a few minutes.'

*

When Donny came back, Ella was curled up on the sofa trying to read an old biography of Diaghilev.

He ignored her and walked straight over to the window. The grey evening light caught the top of his head. His hair needed a wash and gleamed dark chestnut. The collar of his jacket at the back of his neck was stiff with dirt. He stared out of the window without seeming to see anything. His facial muscles tightened and then contorted. He held his chin, then moved his hand down slowly, pulling his face into a sort of grimace. There was an earthquake of sadness behind his eyes. He behaved as though the rest of the world had evaporated and he was in the room on his own. The light from the unshaded bulb overhead was harsh and yellow. Ella raised herself onto her elbow and watched him. For a while he stood in the centre of the room just holding his chin and staring at the floor. Then he turned away from the window and pulled out a twopenny piece from his jeans pocket. He spun the coin towards the mantelpiece, with a gesture that was both vicious and dismissive. The coin hit a large yellow vase that exploded into shards. The shattering of that vase seemed to release in him a simultaneous burst of violence. Some savagery emerged from the depth of his nervous system that plummeted him down to the level of the black explosion of a boar.

Ella pulled her legs up onto the bed and leaned back against the wall, keeping absolutely still as he picked up the iron from the floor and flung it with the movement of a discus thrower. It left a black hole in the partition wall. The room began to shatter and buckle. Plaster fell from the ceiling. Ella remained motionless in the eye of the hurricane. The violence did not feel directed at her personally. It was an elemental storm; a frenzy introduced into the world of comfort and security. More plaster and powder showered her head as he hurled a cast-iron frying-pan at the ceiling. The pan fell back and bounced off the bed onto the blue carpet. Picking it up again, he held it over his head and used it to smash the table, which buckled and disintegrated into splinters and matchsticks. The order of the world exploded.

There was a dangerous electrical sweat over Donny's face like the leakings of an old battery. His features twisted into a grimace as he went about the destruction, looking dangerously well, possessed and empowered by some illness of the soul. Ella knew there was no point in speaking or even calling his name. He had retreated into his own interior desert, seeing and hearing nothing around him and with no idea who the enemy might be. Pitiless, holy and horrible, he was in a state of battle frenzy. He started hurling furniture at the window: first a chair which crashed out and fell to the pavement four storeys below; then a bookcase which became wedged between the window frame and the guttering, allowing most of the books to tumble to the ground beneath. His eyes were oddly distorted, one eye open wide and blazing, the other narrowed to a slit. The light caught the horseshoe dent on his forehead. Before he flung it, he gazed at each piece of furniture as if it were both a sacrament and pollution. And throughout all this there was an expression on his face of exaltation, repulsion and mad humour.

Somewhere far below, amidst the sounds of tearing destruction, Ella heard the sound of the front doorbell.

'That's the bell. I'm just going to see who it is.' She edged towards the door and flew down the stairs.

When she opened the front door, brilliant lights shone in and uniformed men wandered up and down the front steps as if aliens had landed or she was on a film-set. She shaded her eyes and saw four police squad cars parked, headlights blazing, with their noses drawn up in a semi-circle around the house. A gentle rain was falling. The drizzle, caught in the headlights, looked like dancing atomic particles. On the damp pavement were damaged books and the wreckage of half the bookcase that had finally fallen out.

'A neighbour called us,' said the local policeman with a radio. 'Said there was a disturbance.'

Ella did not have time to say anything before everyone's attention was distracted by the sounds of continuing destruction inside the house.

None of the police volunteered to investigate. Ella shivered. She had run out without a coat. Everybody looked towards the front door which gaped wide onto the dark interior of the hall. Eventually the sounds from inside ceased and there was silence. Outside there came the gravelly call and response from one of the officers on his radio. Then came the unmistakable noise of someone descending the stairs with uneven steps and the occasional slithering crash. Among those waiting below, tension grew. The police instinctively stepped back and formed a semi-circle some fifteen feet distant from the front door. Ella went and stood with them, taking her place in the middle of the curved line. After a while Donny appeared in the doorway brandishing a piece of broken banister. His body looked odd, all angles, as if he had turned around in his skin. One wild, shining tuft of hair stood up on his head like a jet of black blood. His eyes were mobile as if they had got loose in his face. He looked deranged.

Nobody spoke. After a while he put down his weapon and surveyed the scene in front of him. His eyes focused on Ella, standing in the line of police, with a mixture of surprise and pleasure.

'Ella,' he said. 'You've joined the police force.'

Everyone started to laugh.

Donny smiled with them. He looked over his shoulder and pointed at the open front door.

'That house has had too much to drink,' he said.

One of the policemen spoke into his radio: 'It's a domestic.' He looked at Ella. 'Are you all right, miss?'

She nodded. The other policemen headed for their cars. Each in turn drove away. Donny staggered off awkwardly, as if his feet and knees were turned backwards. He disappeared around the corner, leaving Ella on her own in the dark street.

*

Ella climbed the stairs to their flat. She was exhausted. The curved banisters on the top landing were smashed and broken. In the sitting-room, water from the large broken flower vase on the mantelpiece still purled silently onto the small tiled hearth. The panels of the door were all cracked. The room felt cold and full of a tangible ugliness as if the air had been poisoned by violence. She sat on the edge of the sofa bed and smoothed the coverlet. Puzzled, she noticed that the cheap bedspread was damp to the touch. Then she realised that rain must have come in through the shattered windows. Everything in the room was stiffly rearranged in fragments: vicious shards, jagged splinters of glass, shattered wood, pottery and pieces of plaster were strewn about.

She went over to the window. The bottom end of the bookcase lay wedged in the guttering outside the window. The other half lay in the street below, where it was possible to see pages of the books fluttering here and there. A cold wind blew into the room. The window panes had shattered into the sharp peaks and troughs of a child's drawing of mountains. One curtain, partially caught on the spikes of glass, twisted and flapped. The wind filled the other curtain, making it billow into the room. Ella felt that some sort of wildness from outside had invaded her home. She looked around. Everything was unfamiliar. There was the black outline of a hole in the wall above the skirting-board. Not an ornament remained intact on the mantelpiece. It was as if the room had witnessed the roaring black violence of a mad god. Nearly everything was smashed. The only item that remained undamaged was Donny's beloved television set.

Ella lay on the damp bed. She slept fitfully in her clothes and woke with a start. She looked at the bedside clock. Half past five. The early morning light lit the empty pillow beside her.

Systole: the contraction or period of contraction of the heart. He had not returned. A pitiless bird outside unstitched the dawn with its trilling song.

The next morning, Ella phoned the theatre and told the stage manager she had flu and would not be coming to rehearsal. The inside of her mouth was parched and dry. She lay staring at the wall and the iron fireplace. At around eleven she heard Donny coming up the stairs. He entered the room. His boots scrunched on the broken glass. He fetched a broom and began to sweep. She lifted her head up from the pillow.

'Do you want a cup of tea?' she asked. He looked drained and tired.

'Aye. That'd be a good thing,' he said.

*

Shortly after that episode the electricity board cut off their supply. Ella prepared food and cooked by the light of the gas stove. They had replaced the smashed table with a small trestle-table and they ate by the light of one candle, its flame remaining almost motionless, in the shape of a molar tooth. Donny's face, caught in the pale yellow light, was haggard. Her love seemed to part and stream round him like a river that flows around a rock.

'I have to go away.' He wiped his plate with a piece of bread.

'Because of the police? Do you think Mark might have said

something to the police? If they were looking for you, why didn't they arrest you the other night?'

'They were local police, not Special Branch. The two don't always connect with each other.'

They sat on the bed. Ella stroked his arm.

'We don't know what Mark might have said or done.'

He shook her arm off.

'I don't give a shit. Mark is a cunt, a whole cunt and nothing but a cunt.'

'Perhaps you're right. It would be safer for you to go away.'

'I'm always fucking right.'

'What about us? I want to have a serious talk about our relationship.'

'Oh yes?' Donny raised a challenging eyebrow and looked at her with a humorous glint in his eye. 'Who with? Not me, I hope.'

He gave her a reassuring kiss, hugged her and rolled himself a cigarette.

'Look. I'm not going away because it's safer. I don't give a fuck about safety. I don't like this city. No horizons. Everything's dead here. A wasteland. Nobody seems to be awake in London. Everybody's in some dream. It's a fucking hall of mirrors. A big shopping arcade; all windows, reflections, lights and illuminations. It's one long conveyor belt of tarted-up garbage. We should both leave. I was talking to the trawler men up north. I might try Norway. I need to see horizons. Now then, switch on the telly.'

'The telly doesn't work without electricity.'

Panic bubbled up in Ella. She put her arms round his neck and rested her head on his shoulder.

'How will you keep in touch? I will have left this house. How will you find me? When will you come back? Will you send me a postcard?'

'I'd rather dip my hand in boiling lead than write a fucking postcard. I'll find you through your mum.' He cheered up for a moment and kissed her. 'And if the fucking revolutionaries turn up again tell them how I've been distributing literature to the working class in Bethnal Green.'

'How do you mean?'

'I threw the bookcase through the window, didn't I?'

His guffaws of laughter took some of the pain away. Donny went out and got six bottles of wine. He took out his guitar and began singing 'In the Summertime', imitating Mungo Jerry. After a while Ella danced around the room, partnered by the wild gyrations of her shadow on the wall.

'I love it when you dance like that,' he said. 'We'll be all right.'

Later, when they were lying in bed together, a wind burst through the broken window and extinguished the candle.

Chapter Thirty-Nine

A week later, Donny phoned from Aberdeen to say he'd found work on a trawler. Ella felt a rising anxiety as she asked:

'Shall I come up and see you off? I'm not working till Thursday night.'

'No. No. Let me be. We'll be together again. Soon. Don't worry.'

She could hear the wind behind him battering the window panes of the phone booth, and could only just make out his words.

'Look. I want you to do something for me. There are four sticks of gelignite that I hid under the tiles of the roof. If you go to our window – the one that I broke – and lean out and twist round to look at the edge of the roofing you'll see two loose tiles above you to the right where the gutter is broken. They're under there. I want you to take them to the river and throw them in, at night. Otherwise they can trace them to the site where I was working. OK? They won't go off without detonators. They were going to use it to blow up Fort Halstead or some fucking thing. Have you got that?'

'I think so.'

'Good. Bye then. I'll call you tomorrow.'

'Don't go for a minute.' Ella could not bear for the contact to be broken. She heard the humorous exasperation in Donny's voice.

'I've got things to do. People to see. I'm trying to say goodbye here and you're clinging on to that phone like an octopus. Bye for now. I'll phone you tomorrow.'

Ella went immediately to the window. She leaned out, twisted round and saw the loose tiles. She lifted off the two reddish, cracked tiles and could just see the sticks of gelignite. She retrieved them and put them under the pillow on the bed. Her hands reeked of the oily marzipan and almond smell of gelignite. Ella decided to dispose of them after the show. Then she ran round the house putting the gelignite in various different places. Each time she put it somewhere after ten minutes she would panic and move it somewhere else. In the end, she left it in the wardrobe in their bedroom covered by a dressing-gown. Although she scrubbed her hands, the smell remained and gave her a headache like a bad hangover, so that when she went to class the next day she found it difficult to balance.

*

After class in Floral Street, Ella hurried straight to the Royal Opera House. The new cast list for *Swan Lake* was to be announced. Despite the upheavals at home, she could not wait to see if her name was on the noticeboard. It would be her first step towards becoming a soloist and a principal dancer. The cast list was always pinned up in the draughty corridor backstage. She decided that she would find somewhere else to live and concentrate entirely on her dancing until all this had blown over. She ran her eyes up and down the list. Her name was not on it. Manuela's name was there as one of the cygnets. Ella's name was at the bottom of the list but only as a member of the corps de ballet, not one of the named performers. She checked and re-checked. At that minute the artistic director of the company poked her head around the door of her office and called her in.

'Sit down, Elissa.'

On the office walls hung the black and white posed, signed photographs of Fonteyn and Beryl Grey and Leonard Massine; demure, distant, frozen black-eyed sprites, corybantes and maenads. Ella sat upright on the chair. The director spoke briskly.

'Now Elissa, you have done very well this year. We are very pleased with you. We had a long discussion about the cygnets. You are suited in every way, but in the end we decided that for the look of the production you are slightly too dark to be cast. The director of this production wants all the cygnets to look as similar as possible. It's an entirely aesthetic judgment on the part of the designer and director and no reflection on your abilities as a dancer. I just wanted to reassure you that you're making excellent progress, and perhaps there will be something else later in another production.'

Ella nodded her head in polite acknowledgement. She gave no indication of what she was feeling. Inside she was aghast and her stomach agape with misery.

The director continued: 'Would you pop along to Miss Wren's office? We would like you to attend the Friends and Associates function this year.'

Ella was numb. She avoided the curious eyes of the other dancers around the noticeboard and made her way down the corridor. In a daze she knocked on the door of Miss Wren's office.

Miss Wren was a skinny, flat-chested but efficient woman who wore her black hair in an old-maidish bun and was secretary to the Friends and Associates of the Royal Ballet. She opened the door and ushered Ella into her cramped office. The 'Friends and Associates' was an organisation that supported and sometimes donated funds to the ballet company. Amongst other things, Yolande Wren arranged an annual function. Each year some eminent sponsor of the 'Friends' would throw open his or her house for a bash, allowing sycophantic balletomanes to meet members of the company. The members were mostly grey-haired afficionados who had lost their souls to ballet years earlier.

'Now dear. We would like you to be one of the company who goes to the function this year. It's quite an honour for you to be invited. It will be tomorrow, Saturday. I've checked that you don't have either a matinee or an evening performance.'

Ella was in a trance, half aware of the fan in the ceiling circulating the stale air of the office. The woman went on:

'Lynn Seymour is coming back to the company to dance Anastasia in the MacMillan ballet and she has promised to attend. We will meet at the stage door at one thirty and cars will take everybody there, but you will have to find your own away home. Is that all right?'

Ella nodded. She left Miss Wren's office, went into the Ladies' toilets on the first floor and examined her coffee-coloured skin.

The other girls in the dressing room were quietly sympathetic that evening. Everyone in the company had assumed that Ella would be cast as one of the four cygnets. No-one could understand why she had not been chosen. Ella told nobody the reason. It seemed like some primordial shame and cast a shadow over the whole of her future with the Royal Ballet. It made her feel ill. She went home exhausted and lay on the bed. Her limbs felt like lead. She did not have the strength or will to dispose of the gelignite that night. Before she fell into a black abyss of dreamless sleep she had a hypnagogic vision of a head floating in front of her and mouthing unspeakable things.

Chapter Forty

Ella went through the next morning's class on automatic pilot. After rehearsal she joined Manuela in one of the three cars that took the invited company members to the home of the minister of trade and industry.

Inside the elegant ground-floor Kensington flat, Ella found her surroundings to be petrified in some way, as if overlaid with that golden lacquer that blocks the pores and suffocates the victim. The wealth felt crushing and exhausting, as if the opulence squeezed all the life out of her and left her breathless. She hated it: the beautifully laid table; the subservient Filipina home-helpers; the fresh lilies in the silver jug; the long stiff embossed cream curtains at the windows. Fifteen other dancers from the company were there. She and Manuela sat primly together on a sofa whose pastel-coloured bolsters and hard cushions were stitched and trimmed with gold cord binding. Nothing was out of place. Nothing was comfortable. With expressionless faces, the maids circulated holding trays of canapés. The guests clustered around the company stars.

Manuela leaned over and brushed a crumb off Ella's chin. She whispered: 'It's like being on a life support machine and someone's just switched off the ventilator.'

'How do you do? I'm Johnny Caspers.' A star-struck young Jewish man of about twenty-four introduced himself to the two girls. 'I'm a banker who wishes he was an artist. My real passion is opera but I do my bit for the ballet as well.'

The girls stood up and shook hands.

'This is how half the girls get husbands,' whispered Manuela. 'Merchant bankers. They're always snooping around.'

Just then the minister, tufts of grey hair sprouting from either side of his bald head, made his way over to greet the new guests. His pink hand grasped a mushroom vol-au-vent from a passing tray.

'Are you all right after what happened the other day?' Caspers enquired as the minister shook hands with Ella and Manuela. 'Dreadful business.' He turned to the girls. 'John was the victim of a bombing incident.'

The minister shook his head reassuringly:

'Everything's fine, thank you. It was quite minor – took the paint off the front door, but that's all. Muriel wasn't at home, luckily. I suppose something like that was to be expected. But it's a new departure. It's made Muriel a bit nervous. And it means I have to have protection everywhere I go, which is a bit of a bind. Special Branch are here now.' He nodded over at two men sitting slightly apart from everyone with full plates in their laps.

One of the Special Branch officers caught the minister's eye and came over holding his plate and wiping his mouth with a napkin. He lowered his voice:

'Sorry to intrude, sir. Just to let you know that Nigel is off sick and we've had to take somebody off undercover work to drive your car. His name is Alan Forbes. He'll only be with you for an hour or so this afternoon. I'm apologising in advance about his long hair. Don't want you to think we're reduced to employing hippies. He needs long hair for his undercover work. We'll need to leave in about ten minutes if that's OK, sir?'

'Thank you.' The minister looked at his watch and moved away to greet prima ballerina Lynn Seymour who had arrived late. Ella realised with a shock whose house she was in. She remembered Jerry Haynes in the car going home from the cinema whooping with glee at the news of the bombing. She turned to Manuela: 'I think I'm going. I've done my bit. The cars aren't waiting for us. We've got to make our own way home.'

'OK. I'm going to stay on. See if I can find a rich, stage-door Johnny. I'll see you on Monday night for *Les Noces*.' Manuela moved off to make polite conversation with the balletomanes.

By the time the maid had found her coat and Ella had said goodbye it was also time for the minister to leave. She followed him out. Revolving doors opened from the lobby of the apartment block onto the street. The minister's two Special Branch minders glanced quickly up and down to check the street. One went out in front of the minister and one behind. The first minder held the car door open for him and then went to the back-up car waiting immediately behind. The first car moved smoothly away down Victoria Grove. It passed Ella as she walked down the street, and she caught a clear view of the driver's square jaw as he looked up to check his rear mirror. His long brown hair was tied back. The police driver was Jerry Haynes. An enormous turbine shaft seemed to rotate in her chest and squeeze the air out of her. She turned her face away and began to walk in the opposite direction; Jerry Haynes a police agent, an infiltrator, a spy. Underwater thunder boomed in her ears.

On Kensington High Street Ella hailed a taxi and ordered it to take her to Bethnal Green. She held on to the leather handgrip, trying not to be sick as it raced through the streets. It was four o'clock when she reached the house. Her first instinct was to contact Donny. She ran inside. The house was empty. She dashed upstairs to see if the gelignite was still there. It was. A shocking volt of giddiness went through her head accompanied by violent nausea. She rushed to move the gelignite to Mark's room and to wipe any fingerprints off with a cloth. After hesitating for a while she telephoned the number of Donny's lodgings in Aberdeen. He was not there. She jumped up and looked in a haphazard way around the flat to see if there was anything else that the police might find that could link Donny to the robberies or the gelignite. In a fit of panic she tore up their wedding photographs. Then she decided to move the gelignite again and took it downstairs to the communal kitchen and put it in a carrier bag under the table. She would have to wait until dark to dispose of it. Every now and then her heart beat erratically and seemed to drop right down to her womb. She made herself a cup of tea and went back upstairs to the flat. She remembered Jerry Haynes's persistent questions about Donny. Now she understood that he must have been digging for information.

It was five o'clock and she was lying flat on the bed when the distant buzz of the doorbell sounded from downstairs. Ella flew down, in the unrealistic hope that Donny was making one of his unexpected returns.

She opened the door. Jerry Haynes stood there in jeans and a cotton denim jacket, with the wind blowing strands of hair across his mouth. He grinned and stepped forward to come into the house:

'I heard about the raid and thought I'd keep my head down for a few days. Then I thought I must come and see if you and Donny are OK.'

Ella blocked his way.

'It's not safe,' she blurted out. 'You can't come in. Mark's not here.'

'What's happened?' Jerry looked taken aback. He shifted from foot to foot on the doorstep. 'Where's Donny? Is he around?'

'Have you got your car here?' she asked, frantic for a diversion. He nodded.

'Can you help? Can we go straight away? Donny is at Fort Halstead in Kent. I've just spoken to him on the phone. He needs a car. They're planning to do something with explosives at the government installations there. He wanted me to find you. He needs someone to drive ... maybe the getaway car or something. I don't know.' Her imagination failed her. 'I don't know why. He said to try and get there before dark. We must leave straight away. He just telephoned. He's waiting. Please, can we go? I need to get there before dark. Don't come in the house. There's not time.' She was gasping for breath as she spoke. There was a feeling that her throat had been scraped dry of moisture with a knife. 'Can we go?' she croaked. 'Can we go straight away? Is that OK?'

Jerry looked hesitant. There was a puzzled expression in his brown eyes.

'I suppose so. Who else is down there?'

'Several of the others, I think. I don't know. Everyone that's involved. All of them.'

She snatched up her bag from the hall table and followed him out to the green Simca parked in the road. All Ella wanted to do was to get him as far away from the house as possible. She would think of something else to do while they were on their way.

*

In the car Ella remained silent.

'Can you look in the glove compartment for the road atlas?' said Jerry. 'It will have Fort Halstead marked on it. I'm not sure of the route.'

Ella kept the road map on her lap. She was in a sickened daze. They drove through Bromley. Saturday afternoon shoppers milled around on the pavement and traffic choked the air with grey fumes. On Monday, she remembered, she would have to dance in *Les Noces*. She misread the map, confusing Catford with Bromley and then missed the signpost to the A224. Jerry retraced the route. She could hear an odd zinging in her ears and her heart thumped.

Then suddenly London was behind them and they were driving through open countryside. On her left the hillside seemed abnormally close. Ella could see every tussock, hump of earth and blade of grass. Jerry was saying something about 'the bastards deserving whatever they get'.

'Yes. The bastards.' She mumbled but her mouth was dry and it came out in a whisper. She looked sideways at him, then out of the window. A hawk hovered in empty sky ahead of them. Woodland closed in and the winding road forced Jerry to slow down. Thin tree trunks flickered past like the barred gateway to some enchanted region of sunlit green and gold. Part of Ella became detached and flew through the trees, dipping and dancing over the tree-tops.

Jerry was laughing a triumphant laugh. He seemed to be brimful of enthusiasm for what lay ahead.

'It's a brilliant idea to target Fort Halstead. A government defence institution. Whe-hey. That will get them really rattled. They never know who's going to be hit next: judges, the military, politicians, big business. Don't you know the names of the others? That worries me a bit. You have to know who to trust. Who are they? Donny will definitely be there, will he?'

'Yes. He's there,' she said, the lies crawling on her lips like bees.

He put his foot on the accelerator. He asked her whether Donny ever used another name; whether he had a passport in another name; whether he would try and leave the country after this.

'I always thought Donny was probably the leader in all this.'

When Ella turned to look at him her vision fractured into a double astigmatism and asymmetry of vision. Suddenly the inside of the car pulled itself sideways into an elongated trapezoidal shape. She could see Jerry a long distance away, very small, as if he were at the end of a tunnel, but he was something else, a fox maybe. Then his face loomed back into normality next to her and she could see a fleck of spit in the corner of his mouth as he chatted.

'I always wanted to be more involved. Can you check the road map for me? We're somewhere near Rushmore Hill.'

They saw a sign to Fort Halstead.

'Where exactly are we to meet Donny and the others?' asked Jerry.

There was a band of pain across her chest. She thought her ribs would burst. Outside birds shrieked like a flock of schoolgirls. In front of her eyes the print on the road map swarmed off the page to become a thousand miniature bees circling her head. There was a deep humming in her ears and the sensation of tiny drummers beating under her skin. The right side of her vision billowed out like a ship's sail. She blinked several times to correct it. When she dared look round again at Jerry's face she noted with curiosity that he seemed to have several eyes all different shades of brown, two or three in his head and three or four others circling around his face. One eye was the colour of a Highland peat burn and another the colour of a stag's eye.

'Turn left here. Right here. Fort Halstead is up here.'

'Could you open your window,' she heard a voice saying. 'It's a bit hot in here.'

He wound down his window as they raced along.

'You are a good driver.' It was her voice again from far away. 'Where did you learn to drive like that?'

Ella's passenger seat was overshadowed by the trees on her side of the road. As he cornered a bend she was suddenly plunged into the dark. He was saying something. The head that turned towards her was the head of a calf with a quizzical look in its liquid brown eyes.

The image of the Japanese swordsman waiting to strike floated in front of her. Out of nowhere she was lunging at Jerry from the dark side of the car. Instinct made him put up his hands to defend himself. He lost control of the wheel. He tried to regain purchase on the wheel and found other powerful hands wrenching it from his grasp, turning it this way and that. The surrounding hedgerow, bushes and trees came loose from their moorings and rotated in a circle around the car. The white markings on the road leaped upwards towards him. Ella saw Jerry's head flip back, then jerk violently forward. The crown of his head impacted the windscreen and went through it just as the screech of the car bonnet on the road and the explosion of buckling metal shattered her ear-drums. Everything went black.

It was a beautiful summer day. The car lay at an angle on its roof near a ditch with its back wheels still spinning. Steam seeped from under the edges of the mangled bonnet. Ella did not know how long she had been hanging upside down before she managed to disentangle herself and clamber out through the window of the crushed door on her side. Tiny cubes of opaque glass from the shattered windscreen lay on the ground like apple blossom. Some of the glass had sprayed on to her clothes. She brushed it off and walked round to the other side of the car. Her legs were shaking. Jerry's side of the car was so crushed that she did not see how he could be in there.

She sat on the grass verge next to the ditch letting the soft breeze caress her face. A dry retch brought the taste of vomit to the back of her throat. Her left temple throbbed with a nagging pain. Twenty feet away a dog was sniffing at a round object on the other side of the road. At first she could not discern what it was. There was blood on the ground beneath it and one or two flies buzzing around. She thought they must have hit a dog or some other animal. Then she recognised the strands of long brown hair and averted her eyes from the sight. Emptied of all strength, she remained seated on the muddy grass four yards away from the wreckage. Nothing happened. Nobody passed.

After a while Ella realised that fate was offering her another chance. She hauled herself to her feet and started to walk away from the car. To her left stood a peaceful row of detached country houses with gardens set back from the road. On the other side fields of barley and rye grew, protected by hedgerows. The tremendous strength that her body had gained from years of physical training now stood her in good stead. She walked for twenty minutes without seeing anyone.

She came to a bus stop and sat in an unfamiliar bus shelter that smelled of urine and was covered in graffiti. A single-decker country bus came along with 'Westerham' written on the front. She boarded it. They came to a crossroads and the driver took a right turn. When two police cars, sirens blaring, raced past them in the opposite direction, Ella turned her face from the window and leaned back in her seat to remain out of sight.

Chapter Forty-One

'I wasn't expecting you again so soon.' Alice wiped her hands on her apron.

'I thought I'd come back. Donny's working in Scotland.'

Ella exchanged pleasantries with her mother. She felt hollow inside and her legs ached. She wandered into the kitchen and helped herself to some biscuits, then went back into the front room and lay curled up on the sofa in front of the television. Alice brought her daughter a cup of tea. Ella stared at the over-bright figures on the screen. They made her head hurt. Her mother always had the colour contrast too bright. After about twenty minutes she fell into a heavy sleep. When she opened her eyes again it was eleven o'clock at night.

'You must be tired, sleeping like that.'

'I am. Think I'll go to bed now.'

In the middle of the night she woke with a huge gasp as if she had breathed in all the air in the world.

In the morning she saw that her left temple was swollen and bruised. She brushed her hair in such a way as to cover it. When she came down to breakfast she said:

'I'm leaving the Royal Ballet. I might go to Surinam for a bit and then join another company.'

'What do you want to go there for?' Alice looked up puzzled from the brass toasting fork she was polishing.

'I thought I'd like to see some of Dad's family again.'

Alice stopped her work and stood with the rag in one hand.

'I suppose you know what you're doing. What does Donny say?'

'He wants to work on the fishing boats for a while. He won't mind.'

'I washed your tights out last night. There was blood on them and a big hole in one leg. How did you do that?'

'I must have caught them on something.'

The next day Ella took the train from Dover back to London. That night she found a brick in the garden, wrapped the gelignite and the brick in a tea-towel and zipped the package into an old leather shoulder bag. She felt terminally weary. She took the underground to Blackfriars, stood in the middle of Blackfriars Bridge, leaned over the parapet and let the bag drop into the seething tarry waters of the Thames.

*

The next time Donny telephoned from Aberdeen he seemed a very long way away. She could feel them floating apart on a sea of withheld information. She told him that she had got rid of the gelignite.

'Good,' said Donny. 'That's the end of all that shit.'

She told him nothing about what had happened with Jerry.

'And I'm leaving the Royal Ballet. I've found myself an agent. He might be able to find me work with the Ballet Rio in Brazil. He's a good agent.'

'Look. An agent is only a thing that sits on your shoulder like a parrot shouting "Pieces of Eight". Just dance. That's all. It doesn't matter where. Go to Brazil. That'll be good. That's how we must always be. Able to go where we want. I can always find you through your mother.'

She had hoped he would dissuade her from going. She wanted him to ask her to join him. He was laughing, buoyant and gay:

'We'll meet up somewhere and tell each other our stories. What about going to Paraguay? I always fancied Paraguay.'

'Maybe.' She sounded doubtful. She looked out of the window. On the pavement below a boy cycled round and round in circles.

*

Donny stepped out of the phone box. His optimistic tone had been a front. He, too, was suffering some sort of paralysis of the spirit. A bus was leaving for Culloden. He boarded it. When he got there he leaned against one of the tombstones with his eyes wide open. There was a heat wave that August. The grass seemed to be burning around him. In the end he felt as if the blazing sun had caught his whole head of hair and set it afire. After that he began a long wandering. As the sun faded, he went back to the docks and decided to head for the trawler bound for Norway. The frozen wastes would be enough to break his arms. Everywhere he went the world seemed to be in a state of decay. In the end he left the land and took to the sea.

*

The director of the company did her utmost to persuade Ella to stay. Ella sat in the office wearing a blue suit. She looked demure, her hair plaited into a gleaming French knot at the back, as her future opportunities with the company were explained. She was smiling as she listened but her shining dark eyes were impenetrable. Everyone was shocked that she had taken the decision to leave. Nobody could make her change her mind. Ella was polite but unmovable. There had already been interest shown by the Danish Royal Ballet and a Los Angeles dance company. The most attractive offer came from the Ballet Rio in Brazil. That contract would start in six months' time.

Chapter Forty-Two

Ella's first major success with the Ballet Rio was in *The Firebird*. The ballet opened at the opera house in Manaus near the wide silver blade of the Amazon River. The first performance took place on a night muggy with heat, but Ella danced best in the heat, which relaxed her muscles. She wore a plumed spiky black-and-red coxcomb headdress and a bristling scarlet tutu made to resemble macaw feathers. There was a new quality to her dancing. She had become a creature that hated the touch of a human. A wild bird. Full of hate. She beat her arms in a frenzy, attacked, fought and whirled. In South American folklore firebirds eat men. For a human to lay a hand on the firebird's body would be a terrible thing. Ella transformed herself into the most savage of heroines. Her firebird was a primitive, bestial creature; proud and bursting with hatred; predatory and arrogant. It was a dazzling performance, danced with such ferocity that even her partner became nervous. She danced out the pleasures of extremism and the love of danger. 'Beauty allied to terror', wrote one of the critics. Overnight she became an enormous success in Latin America.

At first she missed Donny, mourned him and on those tours of Argentina, Chile and Peru felt an urge to wander around street markets calling out his name. Gradually she understood that he was already with her, a necessary condition of her being, the pure gravitational force of her existence.

Some years later another dancing role added to her notoriety.

The role was Salome. By the time she danced Salome some depth charge had been released into her performance giving it a new tragic consciousness. The set for the show consisted of enormous rust-coloured iron walls dripping with painted blood. Around these walls were inscribed in words the story of Salome. At the beginning she danced with her back to the audience wearing a series of multicoloured veils. Later in the ballet she spun round and round letting the veils drop to reveal a crimson costume as if she herself were drenched in blood. There was a slow erotic fire at the core of her body. At the point where she danced in the blood of the man she had killed, Ella's magic-hipped, erotic Salome performed alone in the spotlight's circle. Her black hair was loose like a maenad as she held up the severed head of John the Baptist. It caused uproar when she first danced the part. She danced it in Caracas, Bogotá and Quito.

Once, in the eighties, the company went on tour to Peru and spent a season in Lima. During the day she worked out in a studio run by an accomplished dancer called Juliana Gabo in a smart part of town where the houses had bougainvillaea climbing white-washed walls. She liked Juliana who chatted to her as she washed out leotards in the sink. Juliana always spoke in a conspiratorial whisper:

'When we went to teach dance in the countryside we discovered that the children of the *indígenas* were half the size of the children in town. The sight shocked us all. I will show you.'

Juliana drove an old car. They bumped along dirt tracks to a village on the wide plains of the Altiplano where snow glinted on top of the distant Andes. The two women stood on the outskirts of the village. It was true. The barefoot ragged children who scuffed up the sandy ground playing football were stunted compared with the city children.

'You see,' said Juliana on the way back. 'Dancing was not enough. Now I am a member of Sendero Luminoso. We are a revolutionary organisation.'

'I understand.' A wave of darkness came over Ella as she remembered the car crash in England.

That night the two dancers held on to each other's hands in the studio after everyone had left. They embraced. They whispered and exchanged confidences and caresses. Later in bed in Juliana's apartment Ella told her about the shame of being told she was too dark to dance in *Swan Lake*. Juliana was indignant and held her and kissed her all over her body making tiny buds tingle and blossom under Ella's skin. She looked hard into Ella's eyes:

'Yes. I can see you have the eyes of an *indígena*.'

When Juliana was arrested some years later and sentenced to twenty years in jail Ella experienced a spurt of fury. She read in the papers that Juliana spent her time in prison teaching the other inmates – whores, petty thieves and crack-dealers – the benefits of regular exercise to their health as well as the secret ecstasies of dance. Ella sent her cards of love and support.

Ella and Donny communicated sporadically across continents on crackling and unreliable telephone lines. She asked him if he would like to come and live with her in South America. He said:

'No.' His voice sounded far away over the phone. 'It's too hot. I prefer the snow. I am going to Finland. Anyway, I hate the feeling that I'm going to be somewhere for the rest of my life. It makes me want to get walking down the road. Even when I stay somewhere for a while I am always secretly planning to leave the next day. Don't worry. I will always be in touch.'

She had taken his telephone call at the stage door after a performance of *La Bayadère*. The venue for the ballet that evening was a shallow-domed circular concert hall not far from the Plaza de Armas in Lima. Ella was standing by the stage door. She replaced the telephone on the hook and puzzled over what it was that bound her to this man despite other relationships she enjoyed with both men and women. If it had just been an ordinary marriage that flourished or failed, how much simpler that would have been. She hung the phone up and stepped outside. The audience was streaming down the steps into the cold night air of the city. She shivered as a wind blew in from the Andes. Someone was playing an accordion. Two old men danced in the square. They held on to each other's arms and rotated in a gentle waltz like elderly satyrs.

*

That year the company had a season in New York. Two balletomanes stopped her in the foyer of the Lincoln Center. They were charming young American sisters with soft hair pinned in coils. Each of them sported a delicate gold watch on a slender wrist and they both wore chic silk jackets that ballooned as they walked making them seem fluid and graceful, although Ella sensed some rigid inner puritanism which controlled their interior mechanisms.

'It's wonderful that you are having such a great success here in New York.'

'Thank you very much,' replied Ella as the two women glided on their way. She watched them go. It's not the dancing they like here, she thought. It's the smiling.

'May I congratulate you? Let me introduce myself. My name is Johnny Caspers. I think we met once a few years ago at a "Friends of the Ballet" do.' A bearded man eagerly shook her hand. 'I organised my New York business trip especially to coincide with your tour.' His eyes were shining with emotion. 'We have something in common. A Surinamese background. My family were Surinamese Jews. I've admired your dancing for years.'

'Thank you.'

'Next time you come back to England please get in touch. I organise some of the galas at Covent Garden.' He gave Ella his card. After he left she felt a sudden quite unexpected urge to return to the rough tropical vegetation of Surinam.

As the years passed, Ella kept to her strict routine of training. There was a succession of lovers, both men and women, but the stable elements in her household were her dance classes, three tortoiseshell cats and Marijke from Surinam whom she had known as a child and who worked as her maid. The company gave her fewer leading roles and now she taught and gave master classes to the next generation.

One day, in her apartment behind the Rua Ouvida, Marijke prepared a *banho de cheiro*, a 'blue bath', with steaming aromas of rosemary, rue, rose-mallow and basil. While Ella was bathing and massaging her feet, Marijke stomped into the bathroom with a letter from England. Ella's Aunt Doris had written to say her mother's health was failing. She must return if she wanted to see her alive. Ella weighed up the risk of return. It was over thirty years ago. Nothing more had ever been heard about the death of the police driver. It was an event that hardly even ruffled her consciousness. She suffered no guilt, only occasional unease at the thought of discovery.

'Marijke. I am going back to England to look after my mother. First we will go to Surinam and find somewhere to live. I have decided to settle there when I retire. You can stay there and get the place ready. When the time comes I will join you.'

Narrator's Intervention

I must put salt on the story there for a minute. There I was in the Head in the Sand café, not working very hard I must say – life itself being so savage, so hilarious and unpredictable that not much invention is required – when real life intervened. I looked up and saw my wife, Ma Brigitte, belting down the road towards me. She had thrown a red scarf over her head and I could see from the expression on her face that some enormous stick had stirred up the shit. She came in and flung herself beside me trembling so much that the gold bangles rattled on her wrist and I could smell the sweat from under her flabby arms. She grabbed hold of me. Her eyes rolled back until only the whites showed and her pupils turned inwards to look at her brain.

'Terrible news.' She gasped and her eyes swivelled forward to look at me. 'Your grandfather Papa Bones is dead. You must go back to Surinam immediately. You know how quickly they does bury the dead there. Mind you, at least they bury. Over here they cremate.' Ma Brigitte shuddered. My wife has a dread of fire. I took her to a nearby restaurant and fed her with kebabs and hot chilli sauce until she recovered. Then I hurried home to pack.

*

Saying goodbye to my grandfather was sad. A soft white mist shrouded the giant Royal palms in the burial ground. When the last of the mourners had gone I fired a salute from my Heckler & Koch rifle. Boom. Boom. The noise echoed through the graveyard.

It was not till I left the cemetery that I saw Ella de Vries standing there, fresh and demure as ever. She came over to shake my hand: 'I only met your grandfather once or twice but he was such a well-known character in Paramaribo. I came to pay my respects.'

'Thank you. What are you doing here? I believe you are a big star now in Brazil. In fact, I keep a photo of you.' I was shifting from foot to foot and my heart was ricocheting under my ribs. She smiled in the face of my sheepishness and suggested we go for a coffee.

We went to a small coffee shop situated between two historic buildings, the Jewish synagogue and the Mughal style mosque near to where Papa Bones used to hold court.

'I've decided to base myself here in Surinam when I retire from dancing altogether. I came to look for a place. There's a village in the interior where I spent time as a child. My friend Marijke who works for me is already there. But first I'm going to England to look after my mother.'

'Come and visit me in Mambo Racine's when you are in England. You can dance in a different way there.'

'I most certainly will. I shall be in England in two weeks' time.'

What a gorgeous creature. That black hair. The mango-coloured dress. Those elongated black Carib eyes. I dribbled a bit as I watched her leave the café and brave the heat of the afternoon.

*

It was the eighth day of Papa Bones's wake and in Surinam that is the day when the spirit of the deceased likes to be entertained by stories. Naturally he likes the stories to be about himself. Tongues loosened with rum, friends and neighbours stood up in turn and regaled each other with stories of Papa Bones, his love of gourmet food, his eroticism, his obscenity and his ability to dance. Not to be outdone, I told the story of when he was walking in the bush after a furious row with my grandmother and he saw the shimmering colours of a female anaconda in a hole in the ground. Immediately he began to feel there was a woman near him, walking close by, who wanted to seduce him. When he came home he wouldn't have anything to do with my grandmother. In the next room she could hear him laughing and giggling like he was in love. He could see a beautiful girl with him. But there was nobody there. Only he could see this girl. He refused to make love to my grandmother. She realised that the spirit of the anaconda was seducing him away from ordinary life. Some people stop eating altogether when this happens. My grandmother knew that snakes don't like hot pepper. She took some bricks out of the wall near the pan where the farine is parched. She made Papa Bones pass through the hole in the wall, bricking it up behind him while she burned peppers in the farine pan so that the snake spirit would not follow him. After that he was all right again. The audience at the wake burst into applause.

It was altogether a good send-off for Papa Bones and I returned to England with the sense of a job well done.

Chapter Forty-Three

Ella did not attend the wake. She went back to Wieni by boat to sort out her future living arrangements. Marijke met her at the landing-stage. To Ella's astonishment there was nothing left of the village except the collapsed wooden and palm-thatch structures of abandoned houses.

'Come,' said Marijke. 'I've taken over what used to be the president's house. We can stay there. It was his fishing retreat and it's been deserted for years. It's one of the few houses left standing.'

'What happened?' asked Ella as she went in and put her bags down in the empty dusty front room.

'There was a massacre.' Marijke slung up a hammock for Ella from the house beams as she spoke. 'The government tried to cover it up but there is still evidence.' She gave a sour grimace. 'As we say in the village, "You can hide your grandmother but you cannot stop her coughing." Come with me.'

For an hour Ella followed Marijke along the trail. As they penetrated further into the bush, skeletons started to appear as if refusing to be excluded from the riotous uproar of a party. One laughing skeleton stretched out in front of them. It had partly emerged from a mound of red earth. Vine flowers wove through the ribs and snaked up the legs in mimicry of a Hollywood film star from the thirties. A black beetle sat motionless on the brow of the skull decorating it in a startling way; the delicate symmetry of its body sharply outlined against the white bone. The skull-head was laughing, bone-arms thrown back in hilarity and legs wide open in sexual invitation. Another skeleton was propped up against a tree where it had fallen with its head drooping as if recovering from a hangover.

The shrubs rustled and cracked. Ella jumped with fright. Out of nowhere a skinny Trio Indian man appeared with a look of horror on his face. He had no teeth. The folds of skin around his mouth made him look permanently aghast. He was short and only reached her shoulder. He held up his hand and gestured for the two women to follow him. Two fingers on his hand were missing. The fingers ended half-way in bulbous stumps.

He guided them to the bank of a small creek. On the opposite side of the creek some fifty barefoot people were approaching through the trees. It was like staring into the face of a mass suicide, as if they belonged to a former life, as if they were waving from across the River Styx. Some women carried children. As the ghostly crew came towards them down to the bank of the creek they started weeping. They were shaking. No-one spoke. There was only the sound of wailing and gasping sobs. It was not just tearfulness. They stood beneath the trees in the throes of a collective grief that enveloped and contained them like a cloud as if they were bewitched. Unreachable. Some buried their faces in their hands, their bodies quivering with misery. One or two came limping forward and showed wounds, mutilated stumps. One man pulled back his trouser-leg to reveal a hugely swollen broken knee joint. They were clearly starving. They had fled after the massacre. There was not enough food. They had forgotten their nomadic history and no longer knew how to survive.

'There is nothing you can do,' said Marijke. 'They run away from everyone who tries to go near them.'

'What happened?' Ella asked again.

'There was a dictator here. They say investors with the Dutch HCB bank funded him. We never knew the whole story. One day his soldiers came and shot up the whole village. People said they did it to get rid of their spare bullets and equipment rather than carry it all back to the camp. Others said that villagers had got wind of his drug-dealings and gun-runnings. Whatever the reason, the soldiers came and burnt out the houses and slaughtered the villagers. A few survivors ran off into the bush. They run away from everyone.'

'We can't live here,' said Ella.

'Of course we can.' Marijke was looking around the ex-president's house. 'This is still in good condition. I can make it nice. One or two people have come back to settle. There are other people living nearby. More will come back eventually. But we must arm ourselves this time.' She lowered her voice even though there was no-one else there but the two of them. 'There is a consignment of arms coming in to Paramaribo.'

Back in Paramaribo Ella agreed to do interviews for the local papers. She was now well-known in Surinam and recognised in public. The weather was humid and muggy when a group of journalists and photographers took her to the Waterkant for a photo-shoot. To everyone's surprise there was a huge police presence there just where the ferries leave to cross the pink-brown river to Meerzorg. Marijke pulled at Ella's sleeve:

'The police are searching the boats for illegal weapons. Look.' She pointed to a boat. On the deck was one wooden container marked 'Wieni'. 'Those would be for us.'

Ella turned quickly to the photographer with an engaging smile:

'Why don't you take photos of me sitting on the boat?'

She climbed on board and sat firmly on the chest containing the guns. The police, deferring to the power of celebrity, stopped searching the containers around her. Some even asked for her autograph. The cameras clicked. She sat looking relaxed with her legs dangling over the edge of the container and her long feet tapping against the side of the box.

'Do you mind if I stay sitting here for a while,' she said, taking in a deep breath of the warm air. 'I haven't been on the Surinam River for a long time.'

Chapter Forty-Four

When I returned to London Ma Brigitte attacked me for not paying the rent and before I could pick up the threads of my novel she strong-armed me into caressing the ivories again at Mambo Racine's.

I should explain the layout there. On the ground floor are the casino's gaming-tables where the atmosphere of quiet concentration is ideal for those who have chosen to hand responsibility over to chance. The croupiers move smoothly around in dark green waistcoats, crisp white shirts and spotted bow ties.

On the second floor there is a private club for corporate entertaining which caters for any rich odd-ball who drops by. The girls who work there are known as the Gaslight Angels. They mainly come from Surinam, Guyana and the Caribbean. Kickster Rose is my favourite. She's harsh and thin as a wire coat-hanger. At work she wears a tight short black dress. Bollinger champagne costs up to five hundred pounds a glass. House champagne is one hundred pounds a glass. The glasses are like huge bowls. I first spotted Rose throwing hers away under the table. The girls pay ten pounds a night to work there. They're fined if they turn up late and once they've arrived their bags are taken and they cannot leave again until 2 AM. The tips are huge.

On the third floor is the dance venue with its blue underfloor lighting where the DJs work the turntables all week and there is a chill-out room for the drug casualties. The barmen, seemingly trained at the Academy of Derision, wear their hair greased and tufted in the latest fashion and treat the clientele with a slight sneer. On Tuesdays it is Gay Night and on Thursdays it's Tranny Tropicana when the place is overrun with stunning transvestites who have spent the whole day getting ready.

The bar with my upright piano is at the very top in a room designed in the eighties with black and white chequered flooring and chrome railings dividing the space into drinking booths, each of which holds a square aluminium-topped table and four metal chairs. There are clusters of lights shaped like chemical laboratory pipettes full of toxic-looking pink fluid at various points on the walls.

Who should come in on my first night back but Michael Feynite the retired Situationist architect? He was drunk.

In the eighties and nineties Feynite used to drink regularly at Mambo's, spending hours by my piano weeping and maudlin telling me about his wild crush on Felix Caspers. The crush faded but they remained good friends. I hadn't seen him for a while. His flat, classically Grecian face was a little puffier now and it was difficult to tell in the pink light whether his hair was blond or grey. He stood swaying, his shoulders drooping in a despairing slouch:

'What are we to do? Spectacle is king. We are in the age of celebrity. The idea of revolt has been abandoned. The curse has fallen on the sleeping beauty. England is in a coma and the dream of reason brings forth monsters.'

I continued playing an old Motown medley. He shuffled towards the bar and ordered a double Baileys – a habit from the time when he hung around with cheap south London gangsters in a pub near the Elephant and Castle. Then he returned and sat next to me.

Feynite's prime obsession as an architect had been to design cities. He thought that architecture should be a summons to revolution. But gradually he lost hope and in his disillusion he took to designing enormous cities that were already in ruins.

'I've cut out the middle stage where buildings and monuments are fine upstanding examples of a particular civilisation,' he explained. 'I've cut straight to the downfall.'

His drafts, drawn up in great detail, showed cities that had already been reduced to catastrophic wreckage: magnificent towered buildings tottering sideways; bomb sites; destroyed offices; adventure playgrounds of chaos where streets of stone had escaped from the architects' restrictions into a free-form poetry of their own; anarchy's Disney World; a Legoland for grown-ups where all the metal twisted unexpectedly into new forms of installation art and all the glass had exploded joyously to form its own crystallography.

He had come across some old newspaper clippings from the seventies which had prompted a fit of melancholy nostalgia. He pulled them out to show me:

'Look at these.'

In the first photograph Feynite himself had long blond hair that hung in a Veronica Lake curve obscuring half his face. His arms folded and wearing a cravat, he stood at the back of the group. Hector Rossi was holding a frying-pan and pointing to it with a disarming grin. Mark Scobie sat in a chair looking serious and Byronic in front of two girls in long skirts and cotton blouses whose hands were covered in ink from an old Gestetner machine. They all appeared to be young, intense and glowing with a sort of ardour. The yellowing newsprint made it seem as if those previous lives had been preserved in the supernatural light before a storm. The newspaper headlines screamed: 'Utopian criminals! Barbarians at the gates! British terrorist captured in Italy! Libertarian monsters.'

'And look at this one when I was even prettier.' Feynite waved a second clipping at me.

The second photo had been taken when he was the boy lover of a famous ballet critic. It showed him with the critic and Picasso in a restaurant in Antibes when they were all on holiday together.

'Picasso did a line sketch of me in that restaurant but I sold it to raise money for the cause. Hey ho.'

Feynite put the clippings back into a bulky folder of notes. His speech was slightly slurred:

'Felix was going to drop in for a drink and say hello but I just had a text saying his flight was delayed. He's flying out of Gatwick this week.'

Then in the way that drunks can be cautious about what really matters to them he placed his folder of notes, designs and clippings on top of my piano and told me to hang on to them:

'Keep these safe for me. I'm pissed and I might lose them. They're my prophetic designs. I'm going downstairs to check out the dance floor,' he explained, before making his way unsteadily towards the exit.

*

One week later there was another surprise visitor at Mambo's. My heart gave a jump when Ella de Vries poked her head around the door. She was wearing a Cossack fur hat and had just arrived back from Surinam. She surveyed the room with mischievous curiosity.

'Your grandmother was clearing out and asked me to bring you some of Papa Bones's stuff. I brought it straight away as I'm leaving tomorrow for Kent to look after my mother.'

I nodded towards her and continued playing:

'Unpack them for me please and let me see. I'm not supposed to stop playing while there are customers still here.' (There was only one other person there but I wanted to impress her with my professionalism.)

The first object she unpacked was a black silk opera hat, the sort where the crown can be flattened down and will spring up to its full height when you need it. Underneath the hat was a box of cigarillos, a pair of dark glasses and a bottle of Black Cat rum. Then she pulled out a shabby black tuxedo that smelled of mothballs and a long fold-up ebony cane carved in the shape of a rifle. On closer examination I discovered that it was, in fact, a real Hechler & Koch sniper's rifle which I taped to the inside of my piano lid.

'Oh look. How lovely.' She showed me a silver chain with a tiny silver spade hanging from it.

She placed everything carefully on the piano top. I was inhaling that intoxicating scent of fresh lemons that always seemed to surround her.

'I will come and see you properly when I am back in London again,' she said.

'Yes. Please. Come and have a dance with us. A different sort of dance.' I winked my thanks at her and she made her way to the lift leaving me short of breath and in need of a heart defibrillator.

Luckily Kickster Rose came up shortly afterwards. She flashed the grin of an attractive rodent at me and flung herself down in one of the chairs. The last drinker had left the bar. I opened the bottle of Black Cat rum.

'Oh my god, I've got Whore's Elbow,' shrieked Rose, examining the carpet burns on her elbows and knees.

I lit a cigarillo and opened up my new top hat with a flourish. I put it on at a rakish angle. My voice often drops an octave at the thought of sex:

'Show me how you get those carpet stains again,' I said.

It was dawn before I left Mambo's with a crucifying hangover. I hurried to the Head in the Sand café to continue work on this novel.

I sat there fingering my new silver chain and the little silver spade. As a narrator I have a responsibility to my story and my characters. I must push on. If I don't dig the grave, they don't die.

Part Three

Once admit that life can be guided by reason
and all possibility of life is annihilated.
Tolstoy

Chapter Forty-Five

When Ella stepped off the plane at Heathrow she came back to an England she barely recognised. Like a phoenix London had regenerated itself. On her second evening Ella walked from her hotel to Blackfriars Bridge where, as a young girl, she had thrown the sticks of gelignite into the black waters of the river. She looked downriver towards Tower Bridge, Canary Wharf and the tall twinkling buildings all along the riverbank; a glittering, postmodern, global space, which contained a million offices geared to the production of wealth; the ultimate pleasure dome where there were no great ideals left to fight for. London displayed herself like a spangled pantomime dame.

She was pleased to leave it all behind and return to the unchanging quiet of the Kent countryside. The sight of Hector Rossi approaching her some weeks later on the cliff-top with that enquiring expression on his face and the unexpected development of an affair intrigued her. It seemed to signify the past re-enacting itself in a different form, rewriting itself as it might have been. She did not know whereabouts in the world Donny was. He had said he would come when her mother died. The bond between herself and Donny was of another order. It disobeyed the laws of time and space and belonged to a different dimension altogether. Hector was very present. She felt earthed by him.

*

Hector was standing by the curtained window before undressing. Ella sensed a degree of wistfulness as if he wished he could tell her whatever was on his mind. Sometimes there was a floating feeling about him as though he might be capable of taking enormous decisions easily and in a sort of dream. She wanted to put a protective arm around his shoulders but thought he might resist. He always reacted with a determined buoyancy and airiness. Like a light ball bouncing on water, nothing ever seemed to pull him under. She was naked and towelling her shoulder-length black hair dry after a shower when he asked suddenly:

'Did you say that Donny was coming back soon?'

'Yes. He knows my mother is dying. He will turn up in his own time. There's no knowing where he is.' She sounded evasive.

Hector came over and helped rub her shoulders with the towel:

'By the way, I've seen Mark Scobie recently. Do you remember him?' Hector was frowning a little as if his vision was out of focus.

Ella hugged the towel around her:

'Yes. Of course I remember him. Vera Scobie's son. Don't have anything to do with him. I never liked him. Donny hated him. He's a cold fish. Stay away from him.'

'Oh don't worry. Everything will be all right. I can handle it.'

'So you say.'

'It's nice that I don't have to rush back for once. Barbara has taken Dawn to Bluewater. There's a weekend dolls' house convention at a hotel there. I'll get back by nine so that I can say goodnight to Dawn on the phone. They'll expect me to be on the landline.'

Ella could hear in his voice the affection for his wife and child. She threw the towel on a chair and slid into bed. She was smiling at him and turned to rest her head on her hand while holding up the covers for him to get into bed.

'Are you having doubts about us? Getting cold feet?'

'No. Not really. In fact, when I'm with you all my worries disappear.'

How easily he warded off fears, she thought, and any approaching darkness.

'Are you ever depressed by the way things have turned out?
England, I mean? Politics?'

'I am an optimist to the point of euphoria.' He took hold of her
warm hand under the bedclothes and squeezed it.

*

When Hector reached home later that night after seeing Ella all the
lights were on in the house.

'Where have you been? Dawn's not well. I've been desperately
trying to get hold of you.' Barbara had that familiar look of stony
fury on her face.

'I didn't think you were coming back till tomorrow. You said you
were going for the whole weekend,' Hector blustered.

'There was an explosion in the Bluewater shopping centre. The
police evacuated everyone from our hotel. Good thing really. That's
how I noticed Dawn was overheating. She had a fit. I had to take
her to the William Harvey Hospital in Ashford.'

Barbara's voice was raised:

'I tried to get you on your mobile but it was switched off. You
shouldn't do that.'

'What happened to Dawn?'

'The hotel central heating was too hot. It made her sick.'

Hector was surprised to hear himself shouting:

'You know that something's wrong with Dawn's internal
thermostat. Why the hell did you let her overheat? You know it's
dangerous.'

'She's all right now. Go upstairs and check.'

Hector switched on the light and looked at his sleeping daughter.
Her face was flushed red in patches. When he examined her more
closely he could see a rash with tiny white pimples under the skin.
He felt her forehead. It was warm. A wound grated in his chest. He
should have been with her when she fell ill. He felt under the duvet
and found her hand. It was warm but not burning. He came back
downstairs. Barbara was putting washing in the machine. She looked
up at him with tired anxious eyes.

'What explosion are you talking about?'

'I don't know. Someone tried to blow up the Bluewater shopping mall or something.'

He went upstairs again to sit by Dawn's bed. The blue light on his mobile was flashing. The text message read:

'Need to know. Are you with us? Mark.'

Chapter Forty-Six

Victor Skynnard sat on the train to Kent with the finished manuscript of his play in a satchel over his shoulder. He settled back into his comfortable seat. Vera Scobie had paid for his first class ticket. Victor was pleased to be escaping from London, from his debts, final demand notices and threats from creditors. A theatrical success now would solve everything. It was a matter of persuading Vera to play the part of Kundrie in his new play.

Something odd had happened to Victor the week before. He had paid a visit to the National Theatre and become unexpectedly tearful. Around him in the foyer, shiny-haired young girls wearing Alice bands behaved well; elderly white-haired women with soft features talked quietly to each other. One wizened old man with a Paisley cravat round his neck carried cups of coffee on a tray to his friends. Instead of scorn for their comfortable, middle-class life Victor felt an overwhelming affection for these people who loved theatre and the arts.

But now, seated on the train and confronted with the day's newspaper headlines, Victor fell back into his usual state of impotent rage. He put the paper down on the seat beside him and decided he must stop fuming out of consideration for his kidneys.

Victor thought again about his play. He was anxious for it to be put on as soon as possible. He had been reading on the internet about right-wing conspiracy groups who were trying to co-opt the Holy Grail stories into their own political philosophy. One particular group troubled him: the Revolutionary Knights of the Temple of Set based in Muswell Hill. For a while he had been intrigued by their literature. They made a convincing argument that publishing and journalism were now the main cover for British secret agents. According to them all Britain's top assassins were writers of international reputation. Victor studied one of their print-outs from Google: 'The star system within literary fiction is carefully stage-managed and used to reward agents of the Knights of Set for their work.' Victor began to think about the current stars of the literary firmament. Was it possible that Martin Amis, Tom Stoppard and Julian Barnes were all government spies and trained assassins? The cream of literary London? Why hadn't he spotted it before? What chance did he, Victor Skynnard, have against that sort of opposition? No wonder my work is not well received, he thought bitterly.

As the train continued Victor's enlightenment spectacles of reason and optimism suddenly fell off and for a minute he saw the world as a seething panorama of terrifying ogres, potential murderers, random violence, pagan coincidences and meaningless events. He shut his eyes until reality had passed and his normal illusions were back in place.

*

Victor dozed off and missed his stop. He had to call Vera and ask her to pick him up at the next station.

Over coffee at the kitchen table Victor explained the political purpose of his play. Vera, wearing a brightly coloured kimono, sat opposite him in her spectacles, her elbows on the table. She listened with an oppressive intensity that gave the impression that her listening was more important than what Victor was saying. He forgot what he was talking about for a minute and then plunged on:

'The curtain goes up and the play starts with a massive storm and forks of black lightning. Parzival is sheltering in a launderette. You see Parzival is the only non-believer who seeks the grail. It's a theme that has resonance for the current tensions between Islam and the West.'

'But does this play tell us what people are really like?' enquired Vera.

'No. Of course not. This is political theatre. It tells people what they're supposed to be like.'

'What part do you have in mind for me?'

'Kundrie the Monstrous,' Victor announced with enthusiasm. He grabbed the script from his satchel to read aloud the description of the character. 'She is fashionably dressed in gold brocade and peacock feathers. Talented. Speaks many languages. She travels on a Hungarian mule. Seductress and sorceress. She is a hailstorm, destructive of happiness. She always brings grief. She has coarse black hair, a dog's nose, tusked jaws and dirty fingernails.'

Vera looked doubtful:

'Shouldn't we be doing a play about asylum seekers?'

'No. This is the fault line of the day. The Parzival legend came out of the Crusades and the conflict with Islam. Its roots go back to Cuchulain, Adonis and Dionysus. They are all various aspects of Dionysus. The title of the play is *Dionysus Revisited*. You look worried but listen to this. Kundrie also doubles as Venus, goddess of beauty. Really she's a symbol of American capitalism always re-inventing itself.'

'American capitalism is not doing too well at the moment.' Vera sounded unconvinced.

'But the play ends with Venus making a long solo speech to the audience explaining the world situation and suggesting a solution to the Palestinian/Israeli conflict.'

Vera looked at the script with renewed interest.

'You're probably right, Victor. These are the issues we should be addressing.'

Victor jumped to his feet and gave the air a feeble punch. He executed a dance of triumph like a stick insect attempting to tango. Vera stood up:

'Now Victor. Why don't you take the dog for a walk in the grounds and let me have a quick read of the script then we can talk some more. You go off for a wander. You know we might even get

Mark to direct it if he manages to stay over here. He's been running a touring improvisation theatre in Australia for years.'

Victor's heart sank. He had other directors in mind with good commercial track records. Besides, he wanted as little to do with Mark as possible. Vera whistled for the Borzoi which came bounding down the stairs and jumped all over Victor, knocking his coffee cup over with her tail.

'Poor darling.' Vera ruffled the dog's ears. 'She's got fox-mange. Fox-mange is hugely expensive.'

Victor walked out on to the wet grass of the garden and tried to shoo the dog away from him in case he contracted some variety of fox-mange himself. He let the animal loose and it bounced off and disappeared through a hedge to dash round in circles in a field. Victor made his way to the barn, went in and shut the door to make sure the dog couldn't join him. He sat there for a while wondering what had happened to Mark Scobie. There was no sign of him in the house and he hadn't liked to ask Vera. Now he particularly didn't want to bring up his name in case Vera pressed the case for Mark to direct the play.

After half an hour he slipped out of the barn and called the dog who was sniffing at the trunk of a nearby tree. The creature came lolloping over and shook itself, spattering Victor with drops of water. Together they made their way back to Vera in the kitchen.

Vera got up from the cluttered table and waved the script at him as he came in. She beamed:

'I like it very much. The Royal Court Theatre has been begging me to do something there for a long time. I shall ring them and see if they're interested.'

Victor aqua-planed over his anxieties about the play's director:

'That's wonderful,' he said. 'By the way, I forgot to ask. How's Alex? Where is he these days?'

'He's in Sri Lanka with the remnants of the Tamil Tigers. He wanted to do an interview with Hector Rossi – do you remember him? – but I persuaded him against it. Frankly, I thought the Tamil Tigers would be a safer bet.'

With much embracing and mutual congratulations the two said goodbye. Victor waited for the train back to London in a state of hopeful perturbation.

On the train Victor studied the man sitting opposite him and envied him for not being, as Victor himself was, burdened with the worries of state. There was nothing distinctive about him. He looked to Victor like any average man from some office somewhere. Victor stared at his red tie and white poplin shirt. Here was a man, eating a sandwich, reading the paper, wiping his mouth; a man who was doubtless kind; a man preoccupied with family life who was not gnawed to the bone like Victor by political ideology. Victor felt the tears come into his eyes. The ease with which he was becoming tearful these days was a bit of a problem. Could he be wrong? Was he, Victor, so completely out of step with the rest of the nation?

When the train drew in to Victoria the two men got off and John Buckley took a taxi to the MI5 offices for his meeting with the head of the Secret Intelligence Service, leaving Victor to make his way home by tube to Camden Town.

Chapter Forty-Seven

Buckley sat across the desk from Sir Peter Gray, head of the Secret Intelligence Service. Gray was speaking. As he listened, Buckley tried a little experiment. Every now and then he looked away and tried to recall Gray's features. They always escaped him. It was a forgettable face; an indoor face unmarked by any strongly held belief or crisis of conscience. It was a face that had slid through school and into the prefecture; a face that had bent over university examination papers and then glided effortlessly into the civil service.

'We've lost credibility,' Gray was saying. 'You only have to read the newspapers and join the dots to see that. Nobody's forgiven us for the intelligence fiasco on Iraq. The tube bombings didn't help and we had no prior intelligence on the Glasgow airport incident. I'm worried too that there's going to be a change of direction with the new Obama administration. Just when things were going our way with ID cards, secret police cooperation throughout Europe and so on. We want to get all that legislation through without there being an uproar over civil liberties and that's always easier to do after an event of some sort. It helps push the government in a certain direction. There are votes in anxiety. In some ways an attack would be useful as long as we could either pre-empt it or immediately pick up the perpetrators.'

'What are you suggesting?'

'We need to create an enemy and then defeat it. Something on a reasonably big scale.'

'Haven't we got enough enemies without needing to invent them?'

'Sure. I'm not underestimating those threats. We wouldn't take our eye off the ball. But we're not in control of their timing. What we need is a propaganda event. Propaganda of the deed as they used to call it.'

'Are you talking about a few minor explosions somewhere?'

'Something bigger.'

Buckley frowned:

'The trouble is that anything big would need experienced operatives from Special Operations or the military. You'd need someone from the Royal Engineers. They know how to blow up bridges and roads and so on. That's the problem. Too many people knowing about it. It would be better to persuade one of the already active groups of jihadis or militants to do something but that requires infiltration and that takes time. The whole department is rushing to recruit and train Arabic speakers and young Muslims but we're nowhere near ready to place agents provocateurs yet.'

Gray could tell that the idea interested Buckley by the way he was starting to mull over possibilities. He pushed further:

'An attack need not necessarily be here on home turf. It would be useful if something could be proved to have been organised from here – with immediate arrests and so forth. Rather like Hamburg in relation to the Twin Towers. Something would have to happen. Nipping a plot in the bud before anything has taken place doesn't have the same impact. Perhaps Special Branch might help.'

'Special Branch hate us. They look on us as over-educated pen-pushers. They despise us because we don't have powers of arrest. The most effective thing would be to "turn" someone already active within a group. Someone who needs money or needs something that we can give them. Someone who is beginning to have doubts about the cause. Or someone that has a secret.'

'Any ideas?'

'I'd have to think about it. There have always been secret agents who turn into revolutionaries and revolutionaries who turn into secret agents. We've been keeping an eye on Hector Rossi. He's been in contact with another old Palestinian activist. They might be planning something – which I rather doubt but you never know. We can have them picked up. Special Branch are quite skilful at making arrests which alarm the public and then quietly letting people go later when there's no evidence.'

'Well look into the whole thing, would you? And let me know.'

The two men stood up. The afternoon had grown grey and overcast. Through the plate-glass window a small squat tugboat could be seen emerging from between the rust-red iron stanchions of Vauxhall Bridge. It was the only movement. Otherwise, in the dull light the view of the Houses of Parliament took on the lifeless lines of an austere Victorian engraving.

Chapter Forty-Eight

'I'm dying Ella.' Alice de Vries looked up at her daughter from the bed. 'Go and get a bottle of champagne. I've had a lovely life. We'll have a drink.'

Ella had made a bed up in the small dining room next to the kitchen when her mother could no longer manage the stairs. Alice's sister Doris came on some nights to keep vigil at the bedside. Death like birth is not a precise art. It was five days since the doctor had said that Alice would not last much longer. Ella brought down a mattress and slept on the floor by her mother's side.

The next morning Alice looked at Ella and pulled an ominous face:

'I've never been too tired to get up before. Why did I have to go and get old? You're a good girl to come back.'

Her hair against the pillow was ragged like white flames around her head. In the kitchen next door the kettle whistled on the gas stove and the frying of sausages and tomatoes made a spluttering noise as Doris poked them round in the pan. Alice grumbled:

'I haven't got the strength of a louse. Look at me.' She flicked back the eiderdown to reveal two spindly legs poking out from her winceyette nightie. 'My shanks have gone to nothing. I'm wasting away. My legs used to be like beer barrels. I'm not going to last much longer, I can feel it. I'm up the creek without a paddle. I'm going tomorrow.'

But she did not go the next day or the day after. Neighbours came in to say goodbye:

'They haven't called you yet, then,' said the woman from next door who dropped in on her way to work.

'Yes they have. But I haven't gone, that's what,' Alice said, lifting her head from the pillow and waving her fingers over the sheet.

'How are you, Alice?' The postman put his head round the door.

'Just hovering, thank you.'

It is rare for a woman to flirt on her deathbed but Alice de Vries was an exception. One of her admirers, an old man of eighty-five, arrived carrying a battery-run cassette player. He sat by the bed and fiddled around until he fixed the cassette in the slot. Then he switched it on and played 'Plaisir d'amour'. She fluttered her eyelashes and smiled at him coyly. Later the old man was seen in tears walking away from the house with the cassette player under his arm.

Alice managed to swallow a mouthful of tinned salmon which Ella fed to her in bed:

'That's luxury. I haven't had tinned salmon since your father died. That tea was lovely. Well, that's the last tea I'll ever have. And another thing. Never take any notice of deathbed promises. They're all a load of rubbish.'

But it was not her last tea. Several days later she was still there. Ella recognised the look of exasperated impatience that came over her mother's face.

'I'm a long time dying, aren't I? Oh come on. Let's get it over with.'

Only when the visiting nurse took out Alice's teeth to moisten her mouth with damp cotton wool did Ella realise that her mother was ancient. Curlicues of old flesh swirled like the curved indented lines on a seashell. Alice's face seemed made entirely of dizzying whorls, like an ever-moving weather chart with isobars of frowns and smiles and troughs of high pressure or low pressure whenever she raised her eyebrows. The doctor had left Ella a bottle of Oromorph in case Alice was in any distress or pain. The chart of Alice's face changed abruptly to forecast suspicion as she examined the bottle that Ella held up for her to see:

'The doctor left this for you.'

'That doctor's trying to poison me,' she said.

The next day when Ella bathed her mother's face there was a movement under the blanket at the other end of the bed.

'I'm woggling my foot to see if I'm still alive,' she said. 'Yes. I am.'

When Hector phoned Ella whispered down the phone in the front room:

'No. I can't leave. Sorry. Can't really talk now. I'll be in touch.'

'There's a lot of troubles in the world,' said Alice. 'I'm finished. Ooh what a shame. And there's so much to do in the world. I don't want to leave all this, you know.'

'All what?'

'All this washing up and wiping down.'

Sometimes Ella held the bowl while she vomited. The vomit was dark cherry-red. While she was still able to get out of bed Ella and Doris helped her on to the commode. The days passed. Alice became progressively weaker but continued to examine her own death.

'Why is this taking so long? What time is it? Nine o'clock? Silly doctor. He said I hadn't got long. I thought I'd be dead by five.' Then her mind wandered and she asked: 'How do you spell artichoke?'

Once when Ella bent over the pillow to hear what she was saying a small wizened fist came from below the sheet to give her a playful punch on the nose. Alice's younger sister Iris came down from London to say goodbye.

'I wish I wasn't going,' said Alice.

'Going where?' asked Iris.

'Berserk,' answered Alice. And then later she touched the wallpaper beside her with her work-worn hands and fingered the yellow and gold bedspread. 'I don't want to leave all this.' She examined her hands. 'Look at these hands. More wear and tear than a pig's nose.'

One night at two o'clock Ella called the local nursing team

because she could no longer tell whether or not her mother was breathing. A nurse arrived with a doctor. The doctor lifted Alice's nightie and gave her a final injection:

'Your daughter is here with you,' he said.

'Wonderful. Lovely. You should see her dance,' murmured Alice.

Ella was left on her own. She held her mother's hand. Alice was still warm but not moving. After a few hours Ella called the medical team again:

'I think she's dead. I can't tell.' She whispered in case her mother could still hear.

When the nurse came back she closed Alice's eyes. In death Alice looked slightly windswept and hoydenish as if she were resting after a struggle or as if she were on a boat at sea, never looking back, setting off on some new journey having left everything else behind.

It was four o'clock in the morning. Ella was on her own. Her mother's death had seemed so natural that she did not shed any tears. Two hours later and before daylight a black windowless van pulled up outside the house.

'We're going to put mother in a black plastic bag now. Perhaps you'd like to wait upstairs.' The lugubrious man from the funeral parlour clasped his hands together and waited for her to leave. Ella climbed the narrow stairs. When she came down again the rumpled bed was empty with only an indentation where her mother had lain.

Ella watched the windowless van draw away.

Minutes after the van left there was a knock on the door and Donny stood there. He was wearing a tweed suit and a black raincoat. His hair and moustache were silver. His face was set in its own folds of tragedy. His embrace was strong and reassuring. They sat together drinking teas as if they had never been parted.

'Thanks for coming,' Ella said. Donny looked surprised.

'Of course I would come.'

Chapter Forty-Nine

On the day of her mother's funeral Ella helped her aunts to make sandwiches for the guests. Ella could hear Donny's voice in the kitchen, his voice so much deeper than the others. At eleven o'clock the hearse arrived like a shocking and unwanted guest that everyone had secretly hoped would never turn up. Ella sat in the first car with Donny. Their car followed her mother's hearse through the lanes of Kent. It was as if Alice was leading them on one last adventure through the pale misty fields sown with blue-green cabbages. In the church at the crematorium Donny stood next to Ella holding the funeral programme. For the first time she realised what a tuneful voice he had.

When all the guests had left after the funeral tea Ella slipped out of her black dress and walked about in the flame-coloured petticoat she had brought back with her from Brazil. She and Donny cleared everything away. After they had finished Donny opened a bottle of wine. He sat in Alice's old armchair and Ella sat on the floor beside him and leaned her head against his knee.

'You can take anything of mum's that you think you might need.'

Donny looked around the room and shook his head:

'I don't need anything,' he mused. 'All these material things that float past you during your life, the houses, the rooms that pass over you, the paintings on the wall that fly by – it's like walking through a train. I don't need anything. To love nobody and to be loved by nobody, that's my freedom.'

Donny had spent some years working on the fishing trawlers off the Portuguese coast before going back to the Norwegian fjords and then over to Iceland. Something about one of the cartoon posters on the wall reminded him of Rabelais. He started to talk about Gargantua and Pantagruel.

Ella twisted around on the floor to look up at him:

'I'm always surprised at what you know.'

'I read on board ship when I get the chance. What was that piece you read at the funeral?'

'It was from *The Tempest*. Mum saw me dance the part of Ariel once. I thought that bit was right for her funeral:

> ... We are such stuff
> As dreams are made on, and our little life
> Is rounded with a sleep.

'How did the piece begin again?' asked Donny.

'It started with "Our revels now are ended."' Ella jumped up and fetched the volume of Shakespeare. She found the passage. Donny took the book and read it out loud slowly and with panache, savouring each word. Then he flicked through and came across another passage and read that:

> ... But this rough magic
> I here abjure, and, when I have required
> Some heavenly music, which even now I do,
> To work mine end upon their senses that
> This airy charm is for, I'll break my staff,
> Bury it certain fathoms in the earth,
> And deeper than did ever plummet sound
> I'll drown my book.

Donny leaned back in the chair fingering his silver moustache:

'That word "plummet" – did you know that the same ways of measuring depth with a plumb-line are still used today? The word comes from the Latin. That's where we get the word plumber.'

He looked through the book again and chose one of Shylock's speeches to read out loud. He read slowly with great gusto and relish – like a pirate. Then he put the book down:

'Well, now my revels are just beginning. Where's her record player?' He looked through some of the records that Alice had collected over the years and picked out an old Beatles album.

'Don't put it on too loud. What will the neighbours think? After a funeral?'

He turned it down a little. But after a short while Ella could not resist the music and suddenly jumped up and danced a few steps. The room was small and crowded with furniture. She loosened her hair, let it tumble to her shoulders and raised her arms over her head. She wore a lacy black vest and the orange petticoat flared out with the movement of her hips as she wove her way around the chairs and side-tables and the sofa.

'Mum would love us doing this,' she said. 'But there's not enough room.'

Donny's green hazel eyes gleamed with appreciation:

'I love you dancing.'

For a moment a shadow came over her heart as she thought of Hector. She stopped and went over to lie in Donny's arms:

'Why did you never come and see me performing then?'

'I can't bear to be trapped in the middle of a row of seats.'

'I've been asked to be part of a gala charity performance at Covent Garden. They want me to do a short piece which I danced in Brazil. It's just a matinee. I'd like you to come. There might be drinks at someone's house afterwards.'

'Well I might come there then, not to the show, just for the wine. Unless it's at one of those middle-class places where you get cut off at the knees by a glass fucking coffee table.'

Ella giggled as she lay in his arms and stroked his forehead. There was that odd compulsion to tell him about Hector. After a pause she said:

'Do you remember somebody called Hector from when we lived in Bethnal Green?'

Donny anticipated her next words:

'Stop. I don't want to know.'

She was unable to resist:

'He lives in Kent now. Not far away.'

'So what?'

After a while she said:

'What makes you so wild and impossible?'

'I'm not wild. I'm just honest.'

'You are wild. Mr Undecidable – neither one thing nor the other. You're always contrary.'

'No I'm not.' Donny became thoughtful. 'It's when you give people up that you become wild. Family and so on. You're not living then. You're out of it. When the responsibility goes – you're free to do anything you want. You're free from sadness and happiness. It's then that you become really dangerous.'

It was half past four in the morning by the time they finished talking and went to bed.

*

A week later they were watching television when Donny leaned forward to look more carefully at the screen:

'Isn't that what's-her-face?'

The screen showed the crowd at a film premiere waiting outside a London cinema to see the celebrities walk down the red carpet. Paparazzi and press cameras formed a host of poke-bonneted old women, black-clad gossips huddling together alongside the red carpet, their non-stop tongues clicking and flashing ferociously as they shrieked towards each newly arrived victim. Klieg lighting drained the scene of life.

Vera Scobie stood next to Alex on the red carpet giving a practised smile to the cameras. She had aged considerably.

'Vera Scobie, you mean.'

'No.' Donny was pointing to the woman standing behind Vera Scobie. The woman with blonde curls, wearing a low-cut dress, who stood in front of the cameras, looked charmingly rueful. She tossed her head back in a way that showed off, with seeming innocence, her cheekbones.

'My god. You're right. I think it's Hetty Moran.' Ella peered more closely at the television and stared at the image of Hetty who, after all these years, still managed to gain magical access to any apparently sealed world. The camera moved on. Ella laughed:

'Goodness. That's a surprise. It looks like her. I wonder what she's doing these days.'

Donny switched off the television, stood up and stretched.

'I'm going to bed. I don't want any more of the past catching up with me. Never did like the past. It leaps at your throat like a mad dog.'

Ella stayed curled up on the sofa until she began to grow cold. She had never spoken to anyone about the car crash and the police driver's death. It remained a buried secret. She looked at Donny's shoes thrown down by the sofa. After a while she switched the lights off and went upstairs.

Chapter Fifty

On the night of the funeral Hector had driven on impulse over to Ella's mother's cottage to offer his condolences. Through the window he saw Donny's silver hair gleam in the lamplight. Donny was tapping the arm of the chair with his hand in time to the music as Ella spun around the room. Hector watched them from outside for ten minutes and then drove home. He was surprised at how the sight affected him with a mixture of anger and confused pride. The bond between Donny and Ella looked unbreakable, as if it had its roots in another world.

At home his resolve stiffened. There was no point in continuing to see Ella. The relationship could go nowhere. Affairs of the heart were enfeebling. That great spreading weakness called love had thrown him off track. It was a distraction from the serious political activity he had been missing. He took a decision. He telephoned Mark:

'Can we meet? I don't want to speak on the phone.'

The two men met in a pub in Folkestone. Mark ordered the drinks and waited by the bar. Hector noticed that the pale waxen complexion of Mark's younger days had been replaced by a coarser pastiness, pockmarked by an adult bout of chickenpox. From habit Hector checked that they were out of range of the CCTV camera.

'What exactly do you need me to do? I might not be able to do much. My daughter is still a priority. I can't leave her.'

Mark seemed centred and relaxed:

'We're not asking much. We need your Dungeness fisherman to take us across the Channel. That's all. I have a false passport so I'm fine but the others don't want to use their passports.'

'I can organise the fisherman if you give me the money. If you want to avoid standard surveillance I suggest you travel to Dungeness on the children's light railway. No-one would be expecting you to use that.'

'Good idea. Thanks.' Mark sipped a beer. 'What decided you? I really thought you'd given up.'

Hector frowned:

'I don't know. Conscience. The bankers make me sick. Governments worldwide rush to save them. I can't wait for a mass movement. I'll be dead before one coalesces in this country. Seeing Khaled recently too – that's reminded me of Lebanon, Gaza and this country's complicity in everything – torture and so on. The political parties are all full of tossers. I'm forced back to tiny individual direct actions. Crazy maybe but what else is there to do? Who is this banker you're targeting?'

'A man called Butterfield. The bank has been a major player in Holland's colonial past. It was founded on the proceeds of slavery. It's a symbolic act really. On the other hand if the banking system is wobbling we might as well give it a push.'

'Let me know when the time comes and I'll meet you in Dungeness.'

The two men grasped hands in affirmation of something they thought had been lost.

Hector drove home with a sense of renewed empowerment. There was that old excitement of the hunt. The outlines of houses and the cars on the road around him seemed preternaturally bright and clear as he put his foot down on the accelerator and sped along the M20.

*

That night he phoned Khaled in Preston. Khaled sounded tired and disappointed:

'I've come to a dead end. I don't think I'm going to find this half-brother of mine.'

He'd traced his brother's mother to a small terraced house with a storm porch. An elderly man wearing a raffish orange waistcoat let him in. Khaled's first glimpse through the open door was of a pair of feet in slippers, a lap covered in a rug and then there she was, sitting in a wheelchair under the window, an old shy Highland woman with a magnificent coif of white hair swept back from a long haunted face. Khaled went over to shake her hand. She was humble but dignified and slightly overawed by her visitor.

'What shall I say to him?' Khaled heard the anxiety in her voice as she turned to her husband.

'He's very nice. You'll find something to say.'

She gestured towards the bed:

'You want to know about my first husband – your father. Sit down there on the bed.'

Khaled sat down as she continued:

'Well he was tall and he was arrogant. He was older than me and he never told us about you. We never knew he had another son.' She leaned over to hand Khaled some photographs. 'He's deid the noo and I'm married to Eric here so I don't suppose it all matters. There's a lot of your people in Preston now, Pakistanis. We're on the way out and you're on the way in.'

'I'm Palestinian.'

'Oh well. It all begins with "p", I suppose.'

Khaled studied the photographs of his father taken in North Africa, a European stranger in military uniform:

'I believe I have a half-brother.'

'Och aye. I gave birth to ma own grave-digger there. Dinnae ask me where he is. I dinnae ken.'

'Can you tell me anything about him? Perhaps I could track him down.'

'We called him Donny to distinguish him from his dad. I had him in Edinburgh.'

Khaled listened carefully as Mrs McLeod told the story of his half-brother.

*

His birth had been marked by a fall of snow.

The maternity hospital in Edinburgh was a draughty chilly place. The soup they gave her was grey like a bowl of clouds. They had put her in a side room on her own after he was born because of the amount of blood she lost. She lay high on the hospital bed under starched white sheets. For the first two days she felt dangerously well and excited as if she were flying or the bed were airborne. Gradually she came down to earth.

On the third morning she woke and noticed a bright diffuse light all around her. It was so noticeable that she pulled the sheet over her head to see if it was still visible. It was. Even with her head under the bedclothes there was a luminosity in the room. For a few moments she thought she was phosphorescent.

When she finally pulled down the sheet and looked towards the window she realised that it was snowing outside. A bone of frost lay in the bottom right-hand corner of each window pane. The room was freezing. Her body was warm beneath the covers but her face was exposed to the icy chill of the unheated room. The baby lay in his cot in the corner. Outside, only a few hundred yards away, a blizzard of snow had settled over the green mounds of Arthur's Seat. Now the snow was falling in earnest, mummifying everything in huge clumsy bandages. She raised herself up on her elbow and looked out of the window. As she looked something odd happened. The whole of Arthur's Seat appeared to break up, the outline became ragged as if the hill had exploded and then settled back to its old shape. She looked away and blinked but when she looked up it happened again. Gingerly, she lowered her feet onto the cold linoleum and shuffled over to the window. She pushed back her auburn hair and put her hands up to feel her tender milky breasts.

When a nurse came in she asked her about it.

'That's just the white gannets blown off course from the Bass

Rock,' said the nurse. 'The flock takes off and settles back down again. It looks like it's an explosion.'

Pale light from the snow threw the shadow of the cot rails onto the wall making a huge cage around the baby, which was squalling like a bagpipe gone berserk in its cot.

'Oh, shut up, shut up,' she said, lifting the infant now rigid with fury into her arms and trying to soothe him. But his body arched back as though from the very first he was trying to launch himself out of her arms.

Khaled listened carefully to the white-haired old lady who spoke now in tones of accusatory grief.

'I blame his grandmother. Filling his head with all those stories about the army. We were staying with her in Lochinver. Donny was eight. He was playing outside. Then in the silence of the mountains came this buzzing noise like an invasion of bees. The noise grew louder until it filled the whole sky. Around the curve of the mountain came this platoon of Seaforth Highlanders marching to that snarling sound of the bagpipes. I'd always tried to keep him away from the army. Ma two brothers were killed in the war. So was ma father. But as soon as he saw them Donny said, "I don't want to be a civilian. I want to be a soldier." And he never changed his mind. He joined up as a boy soldier. I saw him once after he left the army and I never saw him again. He just disappeared. We looked everywhere for him but it was nae use.'

Khaled did not know how to comfort the old woman:

'I'll do my best to find him.'

'Och. It's nae use. We've been trying for thirty years.'

Khaled sounded tired and defeated as he relayed all this to Hector. He'd tried various registers of births and deaths without any luck.

'I'm coming back. It was worth a try. I'll come and say goodbye to you and then I'll go back to Hamburg. I need to go home now. I've been watching the news ... the news about Gaza ... It's sickening.'

Hector could hear the distress in Khaled's throat that prevented him from finishing the sentence.

*

The next morning while Donny was still in bed Ella telephoned to book a rehearsal room in a Folkestone dance studio where she could take up her ballet exercises again. She was looking forward to it. The gala was a benefit performance to raise money for retired dancers. Ella joked that she was one of them and was dancing to raise money for herself. She resumed a regular routine of barre work and exercise which physically refreshed her.

Donny stayed at home in front of the television with a firm grip on the remote control, flicking backwards and forwards between programmes every few minutes. Ella could tell he was growing restless. One day she came home to find him packing his bags upstairs:

'Are you going away then? Aren't you going to stay and see me dance?'

'I might come and see you dance but I'm going for a wander first. Give me the theatre ticket anyway. I'll head towards London. I might walk.'

'Walk to London?' Ella looked at him in astonishment.

'Yes.' Then he added with irritation, 'Don't keep asking me things. I don't know. Maybe I'll walk. Maybe I'll take a bus.'

'I'll drop you at the bus station if you like.'

'Don't bother. I feel like walking. I want to be on foot for a while.'

She felt her usual confusion when he left. She watched him walk briskly away wheeling his bag. He looked each way as he crossed the road then he turned the corner out of sight without looking back.

Ella tried to occupy herself by putting some of her mother's clothes into black plastic bags to take to a charity. Then she made herself a cup of coffee and phoned Hector on his mobile.

'Hi Hector.'

'Hello Ella. I'm sorry about your mum. How are you doing?' He sounded more formal than usual.

'I'm OK, thanks. I'm just sorting through mum's things. Donny was here but he's left.'

There was a silence.

'Was that nice?'

'Yes. It was fine.'

There was another pause before Hector spoke:

'Look Ella. I'm really sorry but I don't think we can go on seeing each other any more.'

His tone was stiff and brusque.

Eventually she said:

'That's OK. If that's what you want.' Then: 'Are you sure? Is it your family or what is it?'

'Yes. Partly. I can't explain right now. But I think it's better if we leave it.'

'OK, Hector. If that's how you feel. Don't do anything dangerous. I'm sad.'

'I'm sorry.'

'I still love you.'

There was silence.

'Phone again if you change your mind.'

'OK. I will. Bye for now then.'

Ella stood amongst the black plastic bags bulging with her mother's old clothes. She felt as though her marrow had turned to ice.

Chapter Fifty-One

Mark Scobie, accompanied by Shahid and Massoud, climbed into one of the train's red carriages and hunched up in the child-sized compartment of the Hythe and Dymchurch Light Railway.

The plans were that they would make their way to a small flat in Javastraat, a dull working-class district of Amsterdam. Mark was assigned to tail Butterfield. After the kidnap Butterfield would be taken to the flat in Javastraat and held there. Money would be raised from the kidnap, backed up by an attack on the HCB bank, one of the major banks in Amsterdam. Shahid's dreams of a suicide attack and martyrdom were to be postponed for the time being. The assault on the bank would be a straightforward car-bombing.

Massoud wrote the number of the house in Javastraat on his wrist in biro. Shahid stared straight ahead looking relaxed and beatific. It was half-term. There was a holiday atmosphere on board the train as it trundled through Romney marshes. The whistle hooted. Excited children hung out of the windows. The smell of manure from the fields wafted into the open carriages mixing with the faint smell of coal smoke from the engine. When they reached Dungeness the three men got off the train with their bags and made their way to where the fisherman and his boat waited for them a mile down the coast.

*

Hector was already there holding Mark's motorbike. They lifted the motorbike on to the boat then together the men pushed the boat down the metal runners to the sea and all jumped on board except Hector. The engine started and the boat chugged slowly away.

Hector watched the boat leave. Then he turned and made his way back up the shingle beach. The sun came out as he passed the fisherman's cottage. Yellow broom and sea kale grew in the garden. A rusted rake leaned against the fence of the empty house. A huge weight lifted off his shoulders. He dialled Khaled's number:

'Khaled? We can meet tomorrow if you want to say goodbye. Do you mind meeting in Ashford? It's still a bit awkward for you to come to the house. I'm thinking of taking Dawn out somewhere in the morning. We could meet in the afternoon.'

*

Mark Scobie was familiar with Amsterdam. Shahid and Massoud relied on Mark to ferry them around when they arrived. He showed them where to wait for a tram to Javastraat while he went ahead on his motorbike and waited for them outside the house. When the three men went in together they were greeted by Adi Lukman, a short, buttoned-up Indonesian man in a white prayer hat who ran a small publishing company from the downstairs part of his home. He showed them upstairs to where they would be staying. The smell of dhal cooking drifted in from somewhere at the back.

Shahid and Massoud went out to look for a kebab shop. Mark stayed behind. He had been assured that Lukman was trustworthy but an unsettling wave of paranoia prompted him to go downstairs and talk to the man so that he could make up his own mind.

Lukman did not engage much in conversation. He nodded at Mark and continued with his stock-taking in the front room amid piles of old cardboard boxes filled with cheap paperback editions. Mark looked around at some of the books and tried to indulge in small talk. It was clear that Lukman was a publisher who at some level hated books. Dusty piles of unsold volumes were stacked in his uncarpeted front room. Small, shabbily produced booklets in Dutch and English with the pages stapled together sat on the shelves. Mark flicked through one of them. It contained fuzzy photographs and printing that reproduced itself in blurry double vision. Most of the publications concerned Indonesian history and politics. There were titles such as *The Non-Capitalist Path of Development in East Timor*; *Indonesian migrant life in north-eastern Holland*. The pamphlets included reports of the Moluccan train siege near Amsterdam in the seventies and an account of the *coup d'état* in Surinam.

After a brief conversation Mark ascertained that Lukman's parents had spent years in Indonesian jails under Dutch rule in the forties leaving him in an orphanage. These publications were his form of belated and dusty revenge. Mark listened as Lukman stopped what he was doing and quietly explained that lately the written word had not been enough to assuage his hibernating anger. He was committed to further action before he grew too old to do anything.

'Yes.' Lukman, his face, yellow as a slab of toffee, gave a mild nod. 'I know. You are going to bring someone here. Someone from one of the Dutch banks.' He broke into a slight smile. 'I am pleased to help you in that respect.'

Reassured, Mark went back upstairs to inspect the premises and work out where Butterfield might be most securely imprisoned. He had just decided that Butterfield should be chained to a radiator when the jitters propelled him into the tiny toilet. There was hardly enough space to turn around. As he sat there he checked to make sure there was no escape route. Then he recalled Butterfield's size. He was a big man, overweight. He might not even be able to get in through the door of the toilet. They would have to provide him with a pot. He finished, pulled the ancient chain on the cistern and rinsed his hands in cold water. It was a relief when Shahid and Massoud bounded up the stairs bringing back the kebabs and soft drinks. He would have preferred a stiff whisky but did not want to offend them.

That evening the two men responsible for providing the explosives arrived at Javastraat. Both men were postgraduates at the University of Leiden. Sadiq was a second-generation Yemeni and Abukar originated from Somalia. They all shook hands. Shahid, his face wreathed in embarrassment, apologised for the presence of Mark, an infidel. The

Yemeni, a relaxed man in his forties, whose cracked lips barely covered his protruding teeth, smiled:

'These days it's easier to plan stuff if we cooperate and plan beyond national or even religious borders. At the university we've also been obliged to make strategic alliances. We have mutual interests. You wouldn't have been able to get to Holland without your friend Mark's contacts. And it's better to have someone like Mark tracking your target. He's white. Either of you would be too conspicuous.'

Shahid nodded doubtfully. The Somali man, who chewed khat leaves as he spoke, added:

'The bank is our prime target. Dutch colonial history has been anti-Islamic – you only have to ask Lukman downstairs about that. The bank has been complicit in all of it. Right now the brothers in Holland are being subjected to increasing anti-Islamic and anti-immigrant legislation. They're under surveillance all the time by the Dutch secret service. That's why we wanted you lot to come over – you're not known here. There's talk of banning the burkha and being forced to speak only Dutch in the streets of Holland.' He sucked his teeth.

Mark was unwrapping the packages of explosives. He looked at the brick orange explosive rolled in a spool between layers of plastic and raised his eyebrows in appreciation:

'Semtex. That wasn't available in my day. We relied on good old gelignite.'

'There is enough there to bring the whole bank down. I'm a science graduate,' said the Yemeni with a grin.

Shahid's eyes shone with commitment:

'But it's got to be coordinated with the kidnap. It's the kidnap which will raise funds for us to continue. We're all set, *inshallah*. For the next couple of weeks Mark is going to keep track of Butterfield's movements. When we know the pattern, we'll fix a date and choose the place and time. It will take four of us. He's a big man.'

Sadiq laughed and teased Shahid:

'Is that enough? People aren't so easy to kidnap. They have untidy legs. They don't go in the sack so easy.'

Shahid rose to the bait:

'There won't be any sacks. Don't worry. No sacks. Guns and a car.'

Chapter Fifty-Two

Hector woke the next morning with the sunshine streaming into his eyes. Dawn was still sleeping. Barbara was already dressed and downstairs. He was amazed to find how light-hearted and well-disposed towards the world he felt now that certain decisions had been taken.

Downstairs in the kitchen he clapped his hands together and rubbed them as he looked out of the window:

'It's a gorgeous day. I was thinking of taking Dawn out somewhere in the car this morning. What do you think?'

'I think she'd love it.' Barbara was smiling.

Hector looked at his watch. He had time to take Dawn for an outing and come back before going to meet Khaled in Ashford.

*

As Hector drove through the woods near Aldington he felt an unexpected burst of joy. The first coolness of autumn was in the air and the leaves were a blaze of tangerine and brown. Ladlefuls of sunlight dripped through the trees and on to the road. Dawn sat next to him. She was wearing a bright stripy woollen cap from Peru with long earflaps that her mother had bought from Oxfam. For a while, when they had been driving down Stone Street, Hector thought that a red Rover car was following him. He decided to turn into a muddy narrow side lane and pull up just in case he was being tailed. There was some woodland there which Dawn would enjoy.

It would be very obvious if the other car turned in with him. The Rover slowed down but then continued on its way and his uneasiness was dispelled.

'We'll stop in a minute and you can pick some flowers for mum. There are loads of foxgloves in these birch woods.'

Hector parked the car on a muddy incline and they crossed the small road to the woods opposite. There was something endearing about his daughter's flat-footed walk as she went ahead of him. He caught up with her and took her hand. To enter the wood he had to lift up the wire latch of a gate and manoeuvre them both through it. The light was mellow and there was a smell of woody decay in the air. The ground throughout the wood was carpeted with fragile white wind-flowers. Hector was puzzled. Wind-flowers were usually out in spring. It crossed his mind that it might be something to do with global warming. They followed the path through a copse of silver birch trees with Dawn stopping to trace the parallel black slashes around the trunks with her hand. The narrow footpath was covered in layers of dead brown leaves.

'There are the foxgloves, Dawn.' Hector pointed to some clumps of mauve speckled flowers.

Hector sat on the fallen trunk of an oak tree. It was damp and there were rotting hollows in the trunk. Dawn trudged up and down seeking out foxgloves. Wood pigeons cooed in the distance. Deeper in the woods there were thickets of bracken, pale silver and deep green. A greed took hold of Dawn and she tore at the flowers, dropping most of them. She came stomping up to Hector with tears in her eyes.

'What's the matter?'

'My hands won't hold them.' Her face crumpled in distress. 'I can't pick as many flowers as mum deserves. I want her to have them all.' The spotted flowers were crushed and dropping from her hands.

'No. That's plenty. She'll love those. You don't need any more.' He wiped her nose with a handkerchief.

'What's that noise?' asked Dawn.

In the distance there was a grunting and then a distinct clacking sound like a game of dominoes being played by giants. After a moment's pause there was a snorting sound and then a harrumphing whinny and a sigh.

Hector stood up. Trotting directly towards them down the path at a brisk pace with the light through the trees behind him was a solitary black and grey boar. The brown amber eyes were close-set. Its long narrow snout widened in the middle. There were two pairs of short tusks, upper and lower. A mane of spiky bristles stood up along its back. The powerful muscular body was more than five feet long. Hector saw it with outstanding clarity. It was so large and clear that for a minute he thought it was something else that had escaped from some other unknown dimension. As it approached and sniffed the air Hector could see on top of its forehead a patch of lighter brown hair, stiff and dry as hay. Hector pulled Dawn behind him for safety. The creature stopped about fifty feet from them and pawed the ground, lifting the hoof slowly as if from a great depth below the ground.

The beast gave no sign or indication that it was upset until it began to charge. It lowered its head and started running. Now it began to zig-zag as it ran towards them so that Hector became paralysed not knowing which way to flee. The charge was fast and unpredictable. He had time to think only that the creature must be guarding its piglets before the mighty muscular body collided with him knocking all the wind from him. The wild boar's tusks were razor sharp. The tusks lowered, jerked up sideways and ploughed through his jeans and groin flinging him to the ground. With the violent impact he was thrown backwards on top of Dawn. The animal turned and trotted back the way it had come.

When he opened his eyes Dawn was looking down on him. He went to get up but his leg gave way under him and he became flooded with weakness. The white wood anemones beneath him turned purple and scarlet with blood. The top of his jeans had become bloated pouches filled with blood. When he applied pressure the blood overflowed onto the belt. He knew an artery was severed. The wound was too high in the groin for him to tie a tourniquet.

'Dawn. See if you can go and get some help. Can you find your way back to the car?' He pointed in the opposite direction from where the boar had retreated into the woods.

Dawn nodded.

'Here are the car keys.' His fingers were wet with blood. 'Can you go and bring my jacket from the car? My mobile phone is in the pocket. Can you do that?'

He watched her receding figure, walking with that determined gait, until she disappeared from sight.

Fifty yards away from where Hector lay stood a copper beech tree. As he looked up the sunlight on the leaves made them glow as if they were on fire and turn a golden bronze the colour of his copper engraving plate. The branches and leaves seemed to spread over his head as a sort of shelter although he knew this must be some sort of hallucination because the tree was too far away for the leaves to reach him. He managed to undo the belt of his jeans and undo the zip. He looked down in puzzlement at the satiny pink entrails that spilled from the gash in his groin. A paralysing pain gripped him from so deep inside that it seemed to replace his entire body.

A little while later Hector felt something. Dawn was patting his face. She was squatting beside him. Tears rolled down her cheeks:

'I can't find the road,' she said.

'Never mind.' He was surprised to find he no longer had the strength to hold her hand. Black specks and blotches began to appear in front of his eyes. A huge grip seemed to squeeze the air out of his lungs. A slowly gathering blackness grew from the outer edges of his vision coming in towards the centre and threatening extinction.

Chapter Fifty-Three

All afternoon Khaled sat in the Hot Chocolate café in Ashford trying to reach Hector on his mobile. There was no reply. He left numerous messages. He hesitated over whether to phone him on his landline but decided against it in case his wife answered. It was unlike Hector to be unreliable. Even if his mobile was out of order Khaled would have expected Hector to call him from a phone box. Maybe something had come up. There was a small travel agent on the opposite side of the road with a red Rover parked outside. Khaled went in and arranged to fly to Hamburg the next day. He hung around reading a newspaper for another hour before deciding to go for a curry. From the restaurant he phoned his wife and told her that he would be coming home tomorrow. In the end it was too late to get back to London, and feeling irritated he booked into a small bed and breakfast on the outskirts of Ashford for the night.

There was a slight disturbance around midnight when another guest booked in. Khaled was woken by the man's deep voice coming up the stairs. The owner of the voice sounded slightly drunk and Khaled could hear the annoyance in the landlady's tone as she showed him to his room.

At six in the morning Khaled woke in confusion to the sound of the front door being broken down and multiple footsteps running up the stairs. There were yells of: 'Police. Armed police.' Two policemen in full riot gear burst into his room and yelled at him to get dressed. Minutes late Khaled was hustled, half-asleep, shaken and protesting down the stairs and into a waiting police van. A second police car waited nearby.

Donny, having arrived at midnight after a night of drinking, had slipped out early leaving forty pounds on the dresser in the hall to pay for the night's lodging. He was wondering why there were police vehicles and policemen milling about in the street outside. They ushered him roughly out of the way. As he walked away from the house he saw a handcuffed man being dragged out and secured in the back of the police van. The van screeched off at speed. A second police car followed accelerating away. Donny jumped back on to the pavement to avoid the speeding car. The police driver glanced back over his shoulder and caught Donny's glare. It was like looking at lightning; too terrible, too sudden and too different even to be understood.

*

The sun burned morbid and pale over the Kent landscape until gathering rain clouds blotted it out. Donny continued to walk. Seeing the police bundle the man into the back of their van had angered him and gave an extra pace to his walking. By ten o'clock he was on the A20 near Charing. To his right cars hissed by on the road. He reached the top of a hill. In that setting, with the view laid out in front of him, it was possible to believe that the land might roll back revealing the old animals and the old way of life. Clouds closed overhead. The air darkened around him. A long low clap of thunder sounded like a train rumbling through the sky. Donny stopped to undo his bag and take out a dark green waterproof cape. This he put on. Lightning blinked and the wind made a mad tree on the horizon dance as if it were being electrocuted. He watched it for a minute and then put his head down and continued through the storm.

*

Some kind of icy feeling spread through Ella's sinews and ligaments and tendons as she watched Hector's death reported on local television. She stared at the screen in disbelief. There was no-one whom she could tell. With a shock she realised that it would not even be possible for her to attend his funeral. She flinched away from thinking about the way he had died. Dawn had been discovered sitting with him by a couple walking their dog.

For a long time Ella stood looking out of the window. The rainstorm had subsided into misty drizzle. Two horses remained motionless in the field opposite. She remembered something Marijke had once told her when a similar soft rain fell in Surinam:

'It's the sort of rain that falls when a good man dies.'

The floorboards creaked underfoot as she wandered around the cottage. For a while she lay down on the bed. Her whole body felt thin and unnecessarily angular, like a heap of collapsed triangles. She got up and went to the kitchen to make tea. The rain had stopped and the sky cleared. It was dusk. Fiery crimson and pink snapdragons blazed under the wall forming disorderly blurred rivers of colour. Everything made her think that Hector was the man with whom she could have been happy. Donny was a constant in her life but too distant and unreliable – even if he was a fount of excitement. Hector was steady, affectionate and courageous. Or had been.

That night she lay in bed unable to sleep. She thought of Juliana Gabo still in jail in Peru. Then she wondered what Marijke was doing and recalled the crowd of near phantom Amerindians who had gathered on the bank of the creek. It was shocking that someone should die after being attacked by a wild animal in England; in Kent with its cosy patchwork of fields and hedgerows and its tamed woodland. The thought made her sit bolt upright in bed. After a few minutes she forced herself to lie down again and tried to sleep.

It was dawn before she drifted into a doze and dreamed that she was standing outside her mother's cottage when a vast swarm of angry white bees, like locusts or flakes of snow, swirled past her blotting out the view of the horses and surrounding fields. She could hear the noise growing louder as the blizzard of bees wheeled around and flew back to settle all over her until her limbs and her face looked as if they were made of tiny white blossoms seething with movement. Then, bizarrely, her first dance teacher appeared saying: 'You are very heroic to carry on. Very professional. That's what I was always taught to do if anything went amiss. Just keep going. I trained under Biddy Pinchard you know.'

In the morning Ella drove to the Folkestone studio hoping that the workout would ground her and stop her thoughts from flying all over the place. Although her body responded to the old habit of disciplined movements she felt that something in her had been displaced or was out of kilter and her balance was less secure than it might have been. It's my age, she thought, as she lay on her back on the floor and worked her legs. She lay still for a while and was surrounded by the aloe-smell of her own sex. After a while she gave a big stretch and her whole body yawned. She just lay there. Her eyes felt dry with exhaustion.

Donny rang, out of the blue, and told her he would definitely come to the benefit gala at Drury Lane. She was surprised and pleased.

'When is it again?' he asked.

'Two weeks' time. I gave you a ticket. The date's on the ticket,' she said. 'That's great. I'll look forward to that.'

The sound of his voice cheered her.

Two days later Ella answered the phone to Johnny Caspers who was speaking from his office at the HCB bank in London.

'Hello my dear. I just want to reassure you that your costume has been shipped over from Brazil. I had it couriered to me personally at home. It's arrived safely. Will you be in London at all before the performance?'

'I hadn't planned to but I could.'

'We'd like you to have a look at the set of *Così Fan Tutte* which is the set that will be on stage at the Royal Opera House when we do the gala. It's a matter of knowing whether you can perform on it or whether we need to take some of the scenery down and make some alterations. The set will be up from Tuesday.'

'Yes. I'll certainly come and check it out. I can come on Tuesday if you like.'

'That would be perfect. I'll make arrangements. If I can't bring the costume myself I'll see if my son Felix is free. He's a pilot and I think he is off work this week. We are so thrilled that you're doing this benefit gala. It's sold out. That means we've already raised over two hundred thousand pounds.'

Chapter Fifty-Four

Michael Feynite's doorbell rang at four in the morning. He went downstairs bleary-eyed to answer it. Felix Caspers stood there, his legs tightly encased in blue jeans. He had discarded the respectable groomed look of an airline pilot for the dissolute look of an omega male who went in for petty thievery and rent-boy work. He wore pale red lipstick. Feynite yawned:

'You look as if you've just come from a Berlin nightclub.'

They went up to the bedroom and Feynite climbed back into bed. Felix perched on the edge of the bed and started to gabble:

'I was at Sprite's.'

'What was it like?'

'All right. I danced till I passed out. Came round in the chill-out room. Feet like ice. Frankly, the only time I feel happy is when I'm in women's clothes. It's then that I feel I can do anything. I know I can pass. On Saturday I went to a gig and nobody knew I wasn't a woman. I can swear to it. My friend Larry finally told his mother he's a tranny and she was so freaked out she slipped and broke her arm.'

Felix could not keep still. It was either rouge or there was a hectic flush on his cheeks. He sat on the edge of Feynite's bed and fidgeted with the edge of the thin cherry satin coverlet. Feynite yawned and enquired:

'What are you doing here?'

'Can you take a look at these marks?' In the dim light from the bedside lamp Felix rolled up his sleeve and pointed to a purple raised welt with a lump under the skin on his forearm. Then he proffered his cheekbone. There was a similar lesion there but smaller and less pronounced. A look of tension and fear passed across his face.

'Do you recognise them?'

Feynite examined the marks. He paused before saying:

'Are you asking me if it's Kaposi's sarcoma?'

Felix nodded and bit his lips, spreading the lipstick around his mouth. The lights from a passing car swirled around the walls of the room. To Feynite he suddenly looked like a pretty thirties flapper.

'You must have seen it often enough in the eighties.'

'For fuck's sake, Felix. I don't know. You must go to a doctor.'

'But what do you think?'

'It looks like it, yes. It could be.'

Felix's cheeks blazed red. He put his head in his hands.

'Thirty years of gay liberation and I can't even tell my parents I'm gay. I don't know why but I can't. Do you think I could tell them I've got the virus as well? You don't know what a Jewish family is like.'

'You can't be sure. Go to the doctor. The medication is good now. It's survivable.'

'I don't want to survive on pills for the rest of my life.' Felix was moaning. He lay on the bed with his head in Feynite's lap while Feynite patted his back. Felix rolled over and pulled back his top lip. Feynite could see a series of solid purple-red lesions encrusting his upper gums:

'How long has this been going on?'

'Ten months.'

'You idiot. You need treatment. Go to a hospital. Tell your GP.'

'I can't. He's a friend of my parents. He'll tell them. I know he will. And I'm worried about my annual pilot's medical in two months' time. I'm working for El Al now. At least that's something that pleases my father.'

Feynite wanted to go to sleep. He switched the light off. Felix was lying with his head buried in the duvet:

'I'm going to cut my wrists.'

'Well, that's one way of annoying your mother. Ruin the carpet and get out of paying the bill.'

'Have you ever felt like suicide?' Felix asked.

'Suicide no. Murder yes.'

Felix giggled and kicked his shoes off. The two men lay in the dark:

'Who did you want to murder?'

'Sursok the banker,' Feynite replied without hesitation. 'When I was a young architect Sursok asked me to renovate his house. I spent months on the draft sketches. He took one look at them, swept them off the table onto the floor and said: "Boring. Think outside the frame. Try being original." I was sick as a pig. I got my revenge though. Do you remember me telling you I was locked up once on remand in Brixton prison? Without revealing the source of my inspiration I gutted and renovated Sursok's house so that the interior was more or less a replica of F Wing. Sursok liked my new plans. He was impressed. He'd never seen anything like it. I knocked out all the flooring of the four-storey house and reproduced the painted brick and stone walls, the high arched window at one end, the wire-netted galleries and metal stairways of the prison. To connect with other parts of the building I constructed iron gantries and walkways which made all the echoes and clanging sounds you get in nick. I had everything painted in the standard issue institutional cream and dark green you get in Victorian prisons. All in all, his house is a dwelling fit to house a corpse. Every time he pads around the house he is following the footsteps of a thousand felons without realising it. What makes me laugh is that the elite of London society flock there to admire the unusual design. He paid me a fortune. That's why I don't work. I live off the rent from tenants. Idleness is my new rebellion.'

Felix gave an excited shout of admiration:

'I must tell my father. He works with Eddie Sursok at the HCB bank. What a riot. By the way my father has organised tickets for his gala at Covent Garden. Do you fancy coming? I could do with some support. I'm falling apart.'

Feynite's eyes were shutting:

'Well, I'm falling asleep here. Yes. Tell me the date.'

'Can I stay here tonight? I have a short-haul flight to Brussels early in the morning.'

Feynite reluctantly rolled over and made room in the bed. After ten minutes Felix asked:

'Do you know anyone with a gun?'

But Feynite was already asleep.

Chapter Fifty-Five

Victor Skynnard had been reluctant to attend Eddie Sursok's party. It had been his father-in-law's idea. He skulked in the background hoping that nobody would notice him and accuse him of selling-out. Now that his play was being produced he felt that it was unnecessary to ingratiate himself with Sursok. But his father-in-law had insisted and arranged to introduce them so that Victor might have something to fall back on should his play not succeed.

Sursok's parties were no longer ostentatious. Even he had understood that the conspicuous consumption of bankers was not tolerated during this period of economic collapse. He now held his parties at home. His guests included cabinet ministers and fine arts experts as well as business magnates.

Victor made his way over to the long buffet table laid with silverware and crystal while his wife Mavis networked around the guests on behalf of one of her charities. Victor watched her gloomily. A slight curvature of the spine made her drift weightlessly across the room like a seahorse. Mavis's apparent diffidence hid an iron resolve. Victor had always suspected that she did good deeds out of spite, to make others appear wanting. He blamed her sister for encouraging this charity work. Her sister had been deserted by an atheist husband and in an inspired act of revenge brought up her daughters to be devout Christians. The two sisters conspired together in the malicious commission of charitable acts. Mavis, however, supported him financially and so did her father. Caught thus between a cushion and a soft place, Victor was reluctant to change his circumstances.

Just then he caught a glimpse of the profile of the man on his left. After a fraction of a second he recognised with a frisson the familiar face of the minister of defence. Victor was just about to approach him and say something ironic and dissenting when the man turned away. His evening-jacketed back annoyed Victor, as did the single babyish curl of white hair that sat in the nape of the man's neck. After his first feeling of involuntary awe at finding himself next to such a well-known and important person Victor became excited by the idea of how easy it would be to kill him. There were plenty of knives on the table – albeit rather blunt and folded with forks into linen napkins. While having no intention of actually doing it, Victor hugged the possibility of murder to himself as he helped himself to food. The politician had no idea that a potential assassin was standing next to him munching his way steadily through asparagus and Roquefort cheese wrapped in Parma ham.

'I've received these extraordinary anonymous letters,' said the minister.

Victor backed off a little way in case the letter had been one of his own. He went and stood on his own near the huge window at the end of the hall and remained concealed behind an iron pillar.

*

Upstairs Eddie Sursok stood next to a one-way window in a tiny room no bigger than a prison cell. He surveyed the scene below. Next to him stood a short fussy man with a pointed beard who frequently fell on his knees to fiddle with a muddle of cameras and sound equipment. The man was a sociometrist hired by Sursok to analyse the party. The little technician explained his work to Sursok:

'What I'm doing is measuring all the social encounters that take place. I track the energy vectors of groups and undertake the mathematical mapping of social encounters. I've set up one camera with a fish-eye lens that covers most of the room. That one shoots every two minutes. The other two cameras close in and focus on the sociometric action. Over a thousand digital shots will be recorded during the evening. Then I analyse them. I study all the social contacts and networks – who spoke to whom, etcetera. And I report it all back to you.'

He pointed to one of the monitors. It showed guests giving furtive glances around the room trying to work out who to talk to, who was the most important person in the room and whom to avoid.

'Ha. I've spotted the sociometric isolate,' said the technician with glee. The camera focused on Victor Skynnard lurking behind a potted palm and taking the opportunity to pour his unwanted cocktail into the plant pot.

Sursok's attention was caught by an attractive woman who had stopped to talk to a cabinet minister:

'Can you zoom in on that group?'

Hetty Moran wore a low-cut black dress with the tiny straps pinched in a few inches down from her shoulders. The few lines on her face were as fine as cobwebs. She was the star of her own production, creating her own movie around her as she moved along. All milk-white arms and soft blonde curls she drifted around the room with an amiable smile on her eager-to-please face, exuding an aura of careless seduction. Over the years Hetty had mastered the insouciant shrug. Even on the monitor there was something shimmering and ungraspable about her. Quick-glancing and coquettish she moved from group to group:

'Hi. I'm Hetty.'

It was possible to read her lips.

'The sound is recorded too but I don't have the playback equipment working yet,' said the technician.

Now the screen showed a fair, heavily-built man with an innocent face and small piggy-eyes who was following Hetty Moran's movements with undisguised admiration. Sursok watched as Stephen Butterfield made his way over to her, kissed her hand and took her arm in a proprietorial way, leading her away to talk to her on his own.

*

Victor was bored. For once he was grateful when his father-in-law came over.

'This all seems a bit of a waste of time.' Lord Pankton looked around the room. 'I wanted to introduce you to Sursok but he doesn't appear to be here.'

'That's all right. I'm not much of a social climber,' said Victor.

Lord Pankton nodded in agreement. In his opinion his son-in-law was more of a social descender:

'We might as well go. I've called the car.'

As he did not want to pay his own and Mavis's fare home Victor agreed to leave, which rather left his murder plans in the deep end of the swimming pool without their water-wings.

From upstairs Sursok watched Hetty Moran talking to Stephen Butterfield. Even on the monitor it was possible to imagine that she was putting up a bright parasol of lies and truth strangely entwined and twirling it in front of the bedazzled man. Behind the radiant appearance, the bright fake smile, the wide-eyed pretence of interest, there lay a dark cavernous hollow as empty and dangerous as an underground car park at night. Hetty was enjoying herself. The performance was not only for others. It was also put on for some hidden part of herself, that very secret audience which observes and approves in the darkness. Stephen Butterfield could not take his eyes off her.

*

A week after the party Sursok's titanic sleeplessness had reached a pitch where he did not even attempt to go to bed. Insomnia drove him to the kitchen. He raided the fridge and ate crystallized ginger in ice cream.

Something which the sociometrist revealed had appalled him and kept his eyes from shutting all night long. When the soundtrack was added to the visual recordings Sursok suffered two destabilising shocks. Firstly, he heard several people laughing about an email they had received from Caspers pointing out the similarity of Sursok's house to parts of Brixton prison. Sursok had padded in his slippers through his empty house that night and looked up aghast at the high window set in the wall and the wire netting between the stone galleries as he gradually understood what he was seeing. Secondly, he heard Butterfield telling Hetty how he was so much in love with her that he couldn't concentrate on work and that Johnny Caspers had promised to keep an eye on the Sursok shipping deals while he showed her Amsterdam and Paris.

By the next night, after listening to the audio tapes again, Sursok's mood had swollen to one of grim hatred. The following morning he made a thorough check on the state of his business affairs. He was horrified by what he found. He had undertaken enormous acquisitions in the ship-building industry. This involved acquiring companies at a good price from both private concerns and national governments. Contracts and loans had been negotiated from Japan to Holland. He had reckoned on owning twelve per cent of the industry worldwide. His new company was registered in Holland for tax reasons. Butterfield had been in charge but it was Caspers who was ultimately responsible for the operation. On checking, Sursok discovered that contracts had not been properly negotiated. Had the contracts been completed before the global financial crash his fortune would be intact but shares in shipping had plummeted with fears of reduced trading capacity during the recession. The bank was heavily involved at every level. Interest on the loans had soared and there were clear implications of fraud and malpractice. His financial empire was in jeopardy.

Sursok wandered around the kitchen. There was a choice to be made. He could report the whole matter to the Financial Services Authority. The fraud squad would then become involved. That would almost certainly mean that Caspers would be investigated and charged with negligence or fraud. It would be the end of Caspers. He spooned some ice cream into his mouth and chewed on the fragments of ginger. But if he did that the fragility of his shipping deals would be exposed. Shares in the bank would be in free-fall and it was one of the few banking concerns that had so far escaped nationalisation. Most of his enormous fortune was invested there. Sursok brooded. He could not sell his shares too suddenly. It would look like insider dealing. He sank down in a kitchen chair under the weight of his thoughts.

Chapter Fifty-Six

Butterfield was euphoric and oblivious to the drizzling rain as he shepherded Hetty Moran along the Prinzengracht in Amsterdam. He pointed out his favourite buildings. His eagerness and enthusiasm irritated her. She found Amsterdam dreary and dirty. In the afternoon he hailed a taxi and showed her his official flat, a five-bedroom luxury apartment near to the HCB bank complex where he worked. After she had looked around the flat he took her to the bank itself. Hetty stood in the vast lobby:

'Wow.' She rolled her eyes in surprise.

The bank was designed to channel 'forward-thinking energy for the future'. It was a feng-shui bank. Opposite each lift was a marble mosaic. Butterfield showed Hetty the water statue carved in Carrara marble. He took her for lunch at the Salvador Dali Restaurant on the second floor. The building consisted of ten multi-storey towers each one connected by a three-hundred-and-fifty-foot walkway. Every tower boasted a glass-roofed stairwell. At the back there were streams and rills, gardens with red-bricked paths and pergola-covered walkways where the staff could relax in their lunch hour. The bank was a city in itself.

That evening Butterfield took Hetty first class by train to Paris. They went to Montparnasse for a light meal. Hetty sat on the crimson velvet banquette under one of the hanging lamps with a gold-fringed shade. Her curls gleamed in the lamplight. A slim white-jacketed African waiter took their order. While Hetty was ordering her meal Butterfield reached into his briefcase and took out a scroll of papers.

Once the waiter had gone he raised his eyebrows in anticipation of her happiness and handed her the documents across the table:

'I'm giving you the flat in Amsterdam. I had it made out by the bank's legal department. I will be there with you most of the time when I'm not travelling.' He leaned across the table. His face was coated with a fine film of sweat.

'You have transformed my life. I thought I would never be happy again. Do you want champagne?' His lip was trembling.

Hetty stared at the document in her hands:

'I don't know what to say. I can't.' She handed the documents back. 'Honey this is not what we're about.'

Butterfield gave a delighted laugh without taking his eyes off hers:

'I knew you'd say that. It's the sort of person you are. But I want to be generous to my Aphrodite – she of the beautiful buttocks.' He laughed again and an expression of lascivious and gleeful expectation passed over his face.

Later on she picked up the scroll again:

'It's so cute the way they do all that legal stuff, don't you think? The red ribbon and the seals and everything.'

Butterfield's happiness was such that he felt as if he were filled with helium and might float off the ground altogether.

*

At six o'clock the next morning Hetty Moran awoke from a deep sleep. She lifted the alpine drift of white linen sheets and slid silently out of bed leaving Stephen Butterfield asleep. He had chosen the Hotel les Citronniers in Rue Jacob because he thought it the most romantic place in the world. The hotel kept to its old-fashioned style, the walls lined with faded damask patterns of red and yellow; a wooden galleon of a bed; black oak beams jutting from the yellow plastered ceiling. A single lift with a rattling iron lattice gate lumbered from floor to floor. There were no electronic cards to open the rooms, just a solid metal key on a brass tag.

She looked at the humped figure lying under the sheet. Butterfield's flabby cheek was squashed against the square white pillow, pulling his mouth open in a harmless snarl. With each exhalation there was a whistling sound from his nostrils and an accompanying tremor of his upper lip.

Hetty experienced a flash of incandescent fury. Her pattern was always the same. After each seduction she would fall into the sleep of the dead then wake and want to escape in order to be reborn all over again as a seductress. She did not want to be the object of Butterfield's enjoyment. She wanted to be the object of his desire and the best way to remain desired was to postpone his satisfaction. The memory of Butterfield's epileptic thrusting and humping on top of her the night before filled her with rage. She determined to snatch back the joyfulness he had stolen from her.

She trod carefully towards the bathroom lest the floorboards creaked. The door clicked lightly behind her as it shut. The bright light on the white tiles made her wince. She examined herself in the mirror – the pretty, featureless face, the blonde curls, the round eyes. She raked a hand through her hair and then smoothed the frown lines on her forehead with the tips of her fingers. The only way to recreate herself as a figure of allure, both in her own mind and his, was to put as much distance between them as quickly as possible. She threw some water over her face, dried herself and dressed. Then she sat on the edge of the bath for a few minutes.

Back in the bedroom she tiptoed towards the dresser. Scattered on the glass top were an elegant leather wallet which contained his credit cards; his asthma inhaler, spectacles and her pearl stud earrings. She took her earrings and left everything behind except the legal documents stating she was owner of the flat. These she put in her handbag. Then she gathered her overnight bag, stepped out into the cramped corridor and closed the door quietly behind her.

The front door of the hotel opened onto a small paved courtyard lined with lemon trees which led through a stone arch onto the Rue Jacob. As soon as she walked out into the yard Hetty's spirits lifted. The first *tabac* had already opened. A man with malicious black eyes and a wine-drinker's crimson cheeks swept the pavement in front of his shop. His black hair sat on his head like a dead spider, dense in the middle with crooked strands affixed to his forehead.

'*Bonjour, monsieur,*' she said cheerfully, throwing him a bright smile as she passed.

He straightened up from his broom and wiped his hand on his long white apron as he watched her heading towards the taxi rank. As if knowing she was being observed she suddenly turned and gave him a flirtatious wave.

*

Four hours later Stephen Butterfield left the hotel puzzled and distressed. He walked past the *tabac* which still smelled of disinfectant from the freshly mopped floor. There was little morning traffic in the secluded Place de Furstemberg. He tried Hetty's mobile number again. It was switched off. Could she have been taken ill? He sat down on one of the wooden benches. They were supposed to be returning to Amsterdam by train. Perhaps she had slipped off early to buy something. Perhaps she had gone on ahead to prepare some sort of treat for him. His plump fingers trembled a little as he lit a cigar. Perhaps he should alert the police.

Opposite him he noticed a motorcyclist in a leather jacket leaning his bike against one of the trees. Butterfield watched the motorcyclist take a bag of crumbs from his pocket and begin to feed the pigeons. The pigeons fanned out elegantly, heads down, like police looking for a murder weapon.

A thin elderly woman walking with a cane came into the square leading an excited brown and black whippet on a leash. While the dog rushed around the small square from tree to tree, the woman sat erect on a bench near Stephen, her hands immobile in her lap like a dead bird's claws.

A shadow of pain passed over Stephen's face as he remembered Margaret, his wife. She had gone off on a sailing holiday to Portugal with friends who were besotted with boats. A squall blew up. The boat overturned. He thought of her death in the rolling blue waters of the Atlantic. It would have suited her, a leisurely athletic death with her limbs executing their own dance in the waves, her body continuing its play-acting at life in the billows.

For a moment he stared down at the patterned perforations on the toes of his black shoes. Something caught his attention. At first he thought it was a brown leaf. He bent to look more closely and saw that it was like one of those dried brown pods of a Chinese lantern plant. There was something odd about it. The thing was rocking steadily from side to side as if it had a life of its own. Gradually the rocking built up speed and as Butterfield watched, the muddy dragonish larva split wide open and a shimmering nuptial insect arose and staggered from it. The gleaming wet creature dragged itself off towards some bush to dry out in safety.

Butterfield stood up and took a last puff on his cigar before throwing the stub into some bushes. He remained unaware that the man in the red and black helmet pushing his motorbike was following him. When Butterfield finally hailed a taxi to the station Mark Scobie followed behind on his motorbike.

*

Hetty leaned back in her seat on the Eurostar train to London. Opposite her sat a young student. He had laid out sheaves of handwritten notes on the table and was studying them. She pushed them aside a little to make room for her coffee carton. In response he raised his head and flung his arms in an extravagant stretching yawn and gave her a warm smile:

'My thesis.' He slapped his hand down on his notes. 'Finished! I've been at the Sorbonne doing the last bit of research. I had to do it by hand 'cos I had my laptop stolen. It's taken five years but it's over.' He gave a loud whoop of delight which made her laugh.

'Is it about Nietzsche?' she asked. He was wearing a T-shirt with 'God is dead. Nietzsche' written on it.

'No. It's about a French philosopher Jean Bodin. Are you American?'

'Sure am.' A look of sadness crossed her face as she briefly considered launching into the story of her narrow escape from the Twin Towers, but then couldn't be bothered.

He gathered the notes together and put them in a folder. They fell into conversation about his travel plans. After a while the conversation petered out and the student fell asleep. The train passed through brown raked fields. Hetty shut her eyes. By the time she opened them again the train was pulling in to St Pancras station in London and the student was wrestling his backpack down from the overhead rack.

'Bye then,' he said. She watched him push his way down the aisle towards the doors. Only when she stood up did she see the folder of notes he had left behind on the seat. She waved and shouted after him but he had already disappeared into the crowd. She put the bulky folder in her shoulder-bag and manoeuvred herself out into the aisle. A minute or so later she saw him pushing his way back along the platform through the disembarking passengers in a panic. He waved his arms and shouted across at her:

'I've left my thesis on the train.'

'Oh no.' She pulled a face of commiseration as he darted past through the throng of people.

She took the escalator to the main part of the station. On the concourse she walked quickly over to a large litter bin, took out the folder of notes and thrust it down amid the rubbish, covering it with some used cartons. Without looking round she walked towards the entrance to the underground station.

*

Back in the Javastraat flat Mark ran his hands through his hair in exasperation as he reported to the others the unpredictability of the target and his liaison with a blonde woman. The pattern of his movements was erratic. When Mark phoned Butterfield's office in Amsterdam the next day on some pretext or other he learned that Butterfield had unexpectedly gone back to England and would be away for two or three days. After heated discussions it was decided that Mark should follow Butterfield to England in case his irregular comings and goings were to affect their plans.

Chapter Fifty-Seven

The next Tuesday Ella made her way to Covent Garden. Caspers had made arrangements for Felix to meet her at the stage door and give her the costume but she deliberately arrived early to have a look round on her own. It was over thirty years since she had set foot in the building.

When she arrived the scene dock was wide open for the stagehands to change sets and so it was possible to glimpse right through to the stage from the street. Two long trucks were parked outside with their back doors gaping open. Ella decided to slip in that way rather than go through the stage door. She stepped inside, tiptoed over the tangle of wiring and cables gaffer-taped to the floor and made her way through to the darkness of the wings. Behind her the open scene dock let in the bleak light of day, making the painted scenic flats look garish. Men were shouting and calling out to each other. Up in the flies other stagehands carefully lowered sections of a painted house down to the ground.

She crossed the stage and looked out at the familiar horseshoe shape of the dimly lit auditorium, now refurbished with gilt paint and plush velvet. The pass-door with its intimidating signs demanding silence allowed her through to the corridors and dressing rooms at the back. Immediately she was lost. The whole building had been redesigned and renovated. She could not recognise the backstage corridor where dancers had rushed headlong to examine the cast lists for the new ballets and where the offices used to be. Eventually she located the dressing rooms. She tried a few doors out of curiosity but they were all locked. A female wardrobe assistant scurried past carrying an enormous pile of white petticoats. She decided that the rehearsal room at the top of the building must still be the same. It was a vast room constructed to be exactly the same size and proportions as the main stage below. Ella made her way up three flights of stairs to the top floor.

She pushed open the door. Standing on his own in the middle of the empty rehearsal room was a beautiful young man in an expensive camel-hair coat. He stood facing her, completely composed, doing nothing. The coat collar was turned up at the back framing his head. Ella was struck by the smooth peach bloom of his complexion. It must be make-up, she thought. His gaze was steady but he seemed to be both aware of her and in some sort of self-absorbed dream. There were traces of eye-liner on his eyes and some smudged violet eye-shadow on the lids. He held a dog-lead in his hand.

'I'm sorry,' she said. 'Are you working?'

'No. I'm not.'

Suddenly, she noticed a small Yorkshire terrier at the side of the room sniffing at her Brazilian costume which lay over the side of a trunk.

The man snapped a command at the dog which came to heel.

'Oh that's my costume.' She turned to look at him. 'You're not the pilot, by any chance?' she enquired.

'I am the pilot. I'm Felix Caspers. How do you do?'

'I'm Ella de Vries.' She held out her hand. 'I thought we were going to meet at the stage door.'

'I just wanted to have a little look around.'

With calm assurance he assumed control of the situation. Ella was reminded of a schoolmistress showing a new girl the ropes.

'Now then could you check that everything is here and correct?'

They walked over to the chest. Ella took out the costume. She handed each item to him as she brought it out. He took each one like an experienced assistant in a ladies haberdashery shop waiting on a customer.

'There should be a white shawl,' said Ella.

'It's over here. I was looking at it.' He went over and collected the shawl. He gave it to her. Then he picked up the little dog in his arms.

It irritated her to realise that he had been going through the clothes before she arrived:

'That's nice. Well thank you so much for bringing my costume. Are you coming to the show?'

'I think so. It depends on my flight schedule.' He hesitated. 'As a matter of fact I've always longed to be able to dance myself. My fantasy would be to dance with you but here I am, a qualified airline pilot.' He chuckled. 'Perhaps I could come to a rehearsal?'

'I think we only have one dress rehearsal on the set.'

'You have my father's number. Johnny Caspers. Maybe you could let me know. My father is a banker with HCB. He's made all his money out of deals with Surinam. He told me you have connections there.'

'Yes. I've just come back.'

'He loves to do all this charity stuff. I suppose I have Surinam to thank for my private education and upbringing and my pilot's training. I have to thank potty little Surinam for that.'

Anger rose up in her like a tree. There was an odd buzzing in her ears. Tinnitus. She shook her head to try and get rid of it:

'Would you thank him again from me for doing all this. I must go and find someone from wardrobe and see if it's all right to leave my costume here.'

She left him standing where she had found him in the middle of the room, quite still with the dog in his arms.

Chapter Fifty-Eight

All during the encounter with John Buckley, Mark Scobie stared straight ahead of him. Buckley had intercepted him quietly in Green Park near Butterfield's Mayfair flat and presented him with his MI5 ID:

'It's all right. I just want a brief chat. Not to worry. I don't have powers of arrest.'

The two men sat on a bench on the south side of the park. Buckley came straight to the point:

'In return for your help we guarantee your being able to return and live in England permanently with no police on your tail and all the past forgotten. The thing is you have a secret. And we know about it. We are keen to restore our credibility with the public and with the government. The best and quickest thing for us to do was to "turn" someone.'

Mark continued to stare in front of him. High overhead a plane's vapour trail drew a white keloid scar across the blue sky. Buckley sounded apologetic:

'You don't have much choice I'm afraid. DNA techniques are very advanced now. The Italian police let our forensics examine the knife used on Agnelli in Milan. Your DNA is all over it. We have concrete evidence against you for his murder.'

Buckley gave Mark a sympathetic glance:

'Don't worry. It's not the first time this has happened. You don't need to say anything. Unless you voice some objection here and now I will take it that you have agreed to work with us.'

Buckley waited for several minutes. The drone of a plane overhead had that melancholy note which heralds autumn. Mark continued to stare ahead.

The fall from grace is a silent event. Mark Scobie said nothing.

A new tone of geniality entered Buckley's voice:

'Good. That's settled then. What we want you to do is simply continue with everything you have been doing. We are not working with the Dutch secret service and so we need you to report back to us to ensure that everything is going ahead smoothly. We will find and rescue Butterfield after the kidnap. We want the attack on the bank to go ahead. We will arrest Shahid and Massoud immediately afterwards.'

Mark took a few moments to absorb this information. Then he turned to Buckley:

'How did you know about me?'

'We were keeping tabs on Hector Rossi. The house in Littlestone was bugged. When you popped up on the scene it was an unexpected bonus.'

'Does Hector know about any of this?' Mark's face registered sudden suspicion.

'Oh didn't you know?' Buckley sounded concerned. 'Hector Rossi is dead. Some kind of accident in Kent.' Buckley allowed the shock to sink in and deliberately left the implications vague. 'We have picked up Khaled.'

'Khaled didn't have anything to do with anything.'

'Well. He's useful to us in terms of the conspiracy laws. Phone calls etcetera. Which reminds me.' Buckley's voice was crisp and clear as he handed Mark a mobile phone: 'Use this telephone to contact us. Everything is scrambled, encoded and screened.'

Mark weighed the phone in his hand. It was heavier than most mobile phones. Buckley flicked him a sidelong look:

'I'd better be off now. Thank you for your help. All you need to do is carry on as you have been doing – but keep in touch. It's the best way forward for you, I think.'

Mark looked emasculated as he watched Buckley make his way towards Piccadilly and hail a taxi.

Chapter Fifty-Nine

'Ellaaaaaaa.'

Two weeks later Ella was walking towards her dressing room when a matronly woman she did not recognise, raincoat flapping and clutching several bags, started to run down the corridor towards her.

'It's Manuela. Don't you remember me?'

Ella reconfigured the chubby features until she could discern in them the face of the young dancer she used to know. She shrieked in recognition and they fell into each other's arms. Ella unlocked the door of her dressing room:

'Come in. I've been given a room to myself.'

The dressing room was decorated in pastel colours. There was a rack for costumes; a table for refreshments and drinks; two armchairs upholstered in pink and blue and the usual counter and mirrors surrounded by bare light-bulbs for make-up. From the room next door came the sound of a tenor practising his scales.

'Oh my god.' Manuela flung her bags on a chair. 'I've been following your progress in Latin America. Look at me. I've gone to seed. I've got three grown-up daughters now and one of them is in the corps de ballet here. They're doing the opening of *Les Sylphides* for this benefit and she's in that. I'll introduce you.'

'Do you remember the rat?' Ella's eyes were sparkling with laughter.

Manuela screamed:

'Of course I remember the rat. It was *The Sleeping Beauty* wasn't it? I certainly remember that bloody set. There was this terrible creaking noise when the flats were flown in and out. All the trees wobbled and we used to catch our tulle skirts on the cut-out branches. What happened again?'

'It was the garlands. There was this pile of horseshoe shaped garlands for the Garland Waltz. They were made of dried flowers and miniature sheaves of wheat, rye and barley all woven round this wire frame. They were stacked in a pile on the floor and the assistant stage manager stood in the wings and handed us each one as we went on stage. Just as I was given mine this huge brown rat that had made its nest in one of the sheaves shot out and ran into the wings. And then I looked down and saw that it had either given birth or miscarried or something. There were four tiny bald pink rats the shape of haricot beans curled round each other on the floor.'

'Oh my god. I remember. And then the music started and we all went on in that long chain, smiling, dipping and winding with the garlands held over our heads. And you and I didn't dare look at each other because we were laughing so much. I was waiting to see what would happen if another rat fell out of the garlands and into somebody's hair. I nearly died.'

The two women sat there with tears of laughter rolling down their faces. Ella wiped her eyes with a tissue. She undressed and pulled on her black woollen leg-warmers and a leotard:

'I'm going to the studio to limber up a bit. Are you coming? We only get this one dress rehearsal.'

They went upstairs. There was a buzz of excitement in the studio which was full of dancers warming up. The clip-clopping of so many pairs of pointe shoes on the floor made it sound as if a troop of horses had assembled. Ella joined them. People introduced themselves. She relaxed into feeling part of a group again. The rim of gloom that had been around her stomach since Hector's death dissolved. Her spirits rose and she began to enjoy the physical pleasure of the workout which the other young dancers conducted in turn.

Chapter Sixty

The Covent Garden Theatre was full for the gala matinee. Johannes Caspers and his wife Lillian sat in the plush red front row seats of the dress circle. Caspers smiled and gave little waves of acknowledgement to other friends in the audience. Felix sat in the row behind with two white-haired acquaintances of his father, a writer and an actor who looked indistinguishable from one another. Felix was in a sulk. Michael Feynite had let him down by not coming and using a hangover as an excuse. Downstairs in the stalls Donny kept his black coat on and looked uncomfortable seated at the end of a row where he could stretch his legs and make a quick getaway if necessary.

Ella's piece was third in the running order after the corps de ballet had performed some excerpts from *Les Sylphides* and two of the opera singers had sung a duet from *The Pearl Fishers*.

'Casa Azul', the short piece that she was to dance, had been specially choreographed for her in Brazil. The steps were not too athletic for a dancer of her age and allowed her to show off the qualities of simplicity and passion for which she was best known. The ballet was commissioned after the company director visited the graves of those murdered during the military regime in Brazil. This was its first showing in England.

The lights went down and the curtain went up on Ella's performance. The piece was set in a graveyard. It was only ten minutes long. She danced the part of a stunning ghost, all whitened, of a woman whose husband was murdered by the secret police. Her costume consisted of a simple white skirt and white blouse both edged with white brocade. She wore a huge black Brazilian hat with a red rose fastened to one side. Her face and arms were streaked with water-based white make-up. The ghost of this woman lived in the graveyard and lamented being exiled from the ordinary human world. She danced with an urn containing her husband's ashes which magically turned into flower petals as she scattered them over the stage. The ghost then returned to sit outside and watch a family through the window of their house which bordered on the graveyard and which had vines and strands of ivy swarming down its walls. The family were watching a Brazilian soap opera shown on a huge silent television screen. As she sat there another window opened over the screen and the sound of singing poured out over her head.

As soon as the lights went down before the next piece Donny slipped out of the auditorium.

*

'Well done. Well done.'

Johnny Caspers and his wife Lillian made their way into Ella's dressing room. Ella had been in the shower taking off the body make-up when they knocked. She quickly threw on an old pink and green cotton dressing-gown and pinned up her hair. Felix, accompanied by the elderly writer and actor, along with Manuela and her daughter crowded into the room with them.

Ella did not recognise Felix, who wore a sober grey suit and had slicked his hair back, until he congratulated her:

'The costume was all in order then.'

'Yes. Thank you.' She pointed to where the costume had been thrown higgledy-piggledy over the rack. He went over to straighten it and hang it up properly.

Johnny poured out the champagne he had brought and served everybody in the room:

'Ella, I've brought you a special bottle of wine from my cellar. I'll put it on this table. I've been round saying thank you to all the performers.'

'Great. Has anyone seen Donny, my husband?' asked Ella. 'He was supposed to be coming.'

No-one had. Manuela, in a mist of Jo Malone scent, bustled over to Ella and embraced her:

'That was great. Listen, we've all arranged to go to that place you suggested. Mambo Racine's. We've made a private booking for a Ladies' Night in two weeks' time. In the dance-hall venue. It'll start late, after that night's show. Everybody's coming – all the corps de ballet, some of the other girls, dancers and singers from the English National Opera. It's going to be fun – a leggings, lust and leotard night. You have to wear mad dance gear.'

'Wonderful,' said Ella. 'I'll be there.'

'I know Mambo Racine's,' said Felix.

'Sorry. This is ladies only,' said Manuela.

About twenty minutes later voices were heard coming down the corridor. One of the voices had an unmistakably rough timbre, different from the well-modulated tones of the people in the dressing room. Conversation faltered as Donny McLeod came into the room. He was saying something to someone who remained outside. He glanced around as he came in. His silver snow hair and black coat swinging open created a theatrical presence which imposed itself on the rest of the room. Ella noticed that he was a little unsteady on his feet.

'Very good. Very good.' He addressed Ella ignoring everybody else. Then he headed straight for the drinks table. Ella jumped up and gave him a kiss. Conversation in the room regained its momentum. A minute later a man's voice, high and garbled like a record played fast and at the wrong speed, was calling Donny's name from the corridor outside. Donny went to the door:

'Did you find the toilets OK?'

An ancient wizened man with wispy hair and the unmistakable air of a thief stood in the doorway. He stepped inside bringing with him the boiled cabbage smell of the penal system into the powder-scented room.

'Do you remember Sil, Ella? I found him sitting in exactly the same spot in the same pub where I left him thirty years ago. Go and help yourself to a drink, Sil.'

Donny made an expansive gesture towards the table. Within seconds Sil had located the bottle of expensive wine and handed it to Donny. Ella was smiling with sheer delight. She introduced Donny to Felix:

'Donny, this is Felix Caspers. He's a pilot.' Donny opened the bottle and waved it at Felix, offering him a drink. Felix sounded prim:

'No thanks, I'm flying in the morning. I'd lose my licence.'

'Christ. A pilot, eh?' Donny narrowed his eyes. 'That's something I'd never do. Get in a plane.'

'You're phobic are you?' Felix's expression had a trace of condescension.

'It's not fear,' shot back Donny. 'It's logic. Why should I get into anything that's not attached to the ground? Without wheels or anything. If a plane had very tall wheels I'd get in it. Besides I know that if I get into a plane it will fall down. I reckon I save several hundred people a day by not flying.'

Felix frowned:

'As a matter of fact there are other things that are dangerous for us pilots. I've been getting terribly swollen ankles recently on long-haul flights. I should really wear some of those elasticated stockings that stop you getting deep vein thrombosis. I've already got high blood pressure. I get headaches too.'

'High blood pressure? Puffy ankles? Well that's the end of the high heels then,' mocked Donny.

Felix cast an anxious look in the direction of his mother.

'And while you're at it,' said Donny, 'why don't you cut out the middle bit? Death is the next step. Don't bother with all that intermediary stuff – the limping and groaning and moaning "Oh my puffy ankles".'

Conversation in the rest of the room ground to a halt. Ella was looking on with amused anticipation. To cover the strained silence one of Johnny Caspers' white-haired friends came over:

'Hello. I'm a friend of Johnny's. I'm a writer.'

Donny swayed as he studied the man who had a sweet face and a benign smile:

'You're a writer, are you?' He turned away looking for a glass. 'I love being alive. Write that down somewhere.'

'Here, Sil. Some cunt here is calling himself a writer.' The people in the room had retreated to leave an empty space around Sil who blinked his watery eyes and emitted a high silly giggle.

Felix stepped forward, his lips tight with disapproval, and confronted Donny:

'I don't think you should use that sort of language in front of my mother. It's boorish and objectionable. I think you should apologise.'

'What language?' Donny asked, gleefully. 'Cunt? But I thought this was the age of equality. We've had Moby Dick. Now it's time for Moby Cunt. CUNT.'

Felix looked at Donny with scorn.

'I don't even begin to find you funny.'

'Oh dear. Have I made you glum?' said Donny with a hint of menace.

To Felix's irritation his father shouldered him out of the way and intervened:

'How do you do? You're Ella's husband. I'm Johnny Caspers. I'm the banker who helped fund this event, for my sins. At least there's one banker who can be said to have done something good. We're not popular at the moment, I know. I think it all went very well, don't you?'

Donny looked at him with humour, sizing him up:

'You're a banker, are you? Oh well. You might need some of this.' Donny pulled some five-pound notes out of his pocket and let them flutter to the ground. Then he added in a conspiratorial whisper: 'If you must know, my friend Sil here and I are boracic. We're going to have to get a donkey and paint it black and ride it to the poor-house at night so that no-one will see us.'

Felix turned on his heel and left the room.

Donny grasped Ella by the waist and lifted her high into the air so that her head nearly knocked the shade of the overhanging light and the other people in the room staggered back to get out of the way. Ella gave a gasp of laughter as he lowered her to the ground.

Johnny Caspers was indicating to his wife with his eyes and a slight gesture of his head that they should leave:

'We must be going. The people here will be wanting to get ready for the evening show. And Lillian and I are just off to see *Antony and Cleopatra.*'

'Oh, really,' said Donny. 'Say hello to them from me.'

'Donny. You're terrible.' Ella said after they'd left. Donny gave a theatrical sigh and poured himself an enormous helping of wine.

'I know, I can't help it. What we want is war, isn't it Sil? War is great. People sing. Peacetime is boring. In wartime everyone is saying, "Let's go down the tube and play the accordion."'

Manuela winked and kissed Ella goodbye as she left with her daughter:

'See you on Ladies Night at Mambo Racine's.'

The elderly writer and his actor friend said their goodbyes and could be heard talking as they made their way along the corridor to the stage door.

'What a ghastly man. Must be from the Highlands. Got all their touchiness. They can sniff out an offence anywhere, even if it's well concealed.'

'Yes. Wonderful projection though,' said the actor who sounded regretful, as if he had recognised in Donny some divine release from the constrictions of normal civilisation. 'Wish I could have a voice like that next week when I open at the Alhambra.'

When everyone except Donny and Sil had left the dressing room, Ella gave a yell of laughter and danced around the room before throwing herself down on the floor flat on her back with her arms above her head:

'You never change. Pandemonium. Pure pandemonium. I love it. I'm middle-aged and I still love it.'

*

As soon as Felix left the theatre he headed towards Piccadilly looking for a taxi to the airport. He intended to stay at the airport hotel before the next morning's flight. The encounter with Donny had infuriated him. He had wanted to stay and chat with Ella after everyone had gone. He was curious about the Ladies Night at Mambo's which he heard Manuela mention. A progression of clouds raced towards him over Eros and the roofs of Piccadilly. They seemed to be moving very fast, the fastest he had ever seen clouds move. Wisps of the edge of the turbulent darkness were forming and re-forming around the main body of cloud. He stopped and stared. He thought he saw a face in the clouds, eyebrows pinned together in a frown. The face loomed over him. A giant fear took hold of him and he turned to make his way back to Leicester Square, rushing in headlong flight towards the underground station where he took a train to Heathrow.

Chapter Sixty-One

The emergency meeting of the Schifting took place at the HCB bank's London headquarters overlooking Berkeley Square. The Schifting is a group peculiar to the Dutch banking system. Dutch banking rules are different from most of the rest of Europe and allow for such a group to exist. It consists of influential controlling tycoons who operate through contacts as friends of the supervisory board.

Eddie Sursok stood by the window. His brooding presence affected everyone in the room. The eleven other men were already seated around one end of an enormous oval polished table. The chairman spoke first:

'I think we should try and avoid the involvement of the Financial Services Authority just now. They are smarting from their very public failures as regulators and are trying to exercise tighter controls on everything.'

All those sitting agreed it would affect the bank's shares if the affair was made public.

'I don't agree. In fact, I'm certain of the opposite.' Eddie Sursok was staring moodily out of the mullion window. 'Unless we involved the police immediately it will look as if we have been covering something up. Bankers are attracting enough odium as it is.'

The other men all looked up in surprise. Sursok was well-known for a pathological preference for secrecy at all times. It was an obsession with him.

'Someone must be held to account.' Sursok turned around

to face them and continued: 'The sums of money are enormous. The losses could affect the whole banking system. Caspers bears responsibility for that. It's going to become public anyway. If the press gets to it before we do it makes the bank look bad. We should control the agenda. It would be better to contact the Fraud Squad immediately.'

'Shouldn't we support Caspers – at least give him a chance to explain?'

'It's too late,' said Sursok.

'What about Stephen Butterfield?'

Sursok mulled over the question of Butterfield:

'He's certainly been negligent. At the moment he's in Amsterdam. He must take part responsibility for this mess. But I hold Caspers ultimately responsible.'

Sursok had the sort of gravitational pull that seemed to suck his colleagues into the black hole of his will. The chairman turned on his swivel chair to check that everyone was in agreement. There was a heated discussion. At the end there was a vote and the chairman announced:

'I shall undertake to inform the Financial Services Authority with the full understanding that they will inform the police, gentlemen. We will try and ride out the bad press and placate the shareholders.'

Chapter Sixty-Two

Johnny Caspers had barely finished organising the gala before it was
necessary to make the final arrangements for another occasion – the
alfresco meal at his Wiltshire country house to celebrate his friend
Arnold Thorpe's Nobel laureate. He always worried about the mix
of guests. The unknown quantity this time was Butterfield's new
partner. Nothing he could do about that. He would just have to
wait and see. The caterers were booked. He looked up the weather
forecast on his laptop. The weather should be fine.

*

The long buffet table stood next to the wall and the guests helped
themselves from big dishes of potato and apple salad, fried aubergine
slices, chicken drumsticks, cheeses, avocado salads, a joint of rare
beef and a salmon in white sauce. Silver ice buckets containing the
white wine were placed at intervals along the table.

Felix arrived straight from a flight still wearing his captain's
uniform. He came over to say hello to Feynite who was already
seated at the table.

'Where are you just back from?' enquired Feynite.

'New York.'

'Lucky you with all those lovely stewards.'

Felix flushed and laughed:

'I have to keep at least one eye on the instrument panel.'

'Have you seen a doctor?' Feynite asked in a low voice but Felix flashed him a furious look and turned away.

Other guests started to arrive. Uniformed maids served the wine. Lady Barm, a thin-faced old lady who wore glasses with one huge fish-eye lens, hobbled towards them across the grass clutching a book. Her brother, a small elderly man, author of several books on the English butterfly, followed close behind with his wife. They were the Caspers' nearest neighbours in Wiltshire.

'I hear revolutions are forbidden in the new Europe.' The speaker was an irascible man in his forties with a face as red as if he'd recently been scalded and fine grey corkscrew curls on either side of a balding pate. His lower lip glistened with indignation.

'Revolutions are always forbidden, Jumbo,' said Lillian Caspers soothingly. 'Where did you see that, anyway?'

'Here. I read it right here.' He took a copy of the *Independent* from under his arm and jabbed one of the columns with his forefinger. 'Listen. "The interior ministers of Europe have agreed on a definition of terrorism. It includes people who hope to alter the political, economic or social structure of the European Union."' He slapped the paper down on the table. 'Me, for example.'

'But Jumbo you hate revolutionaries. You're a Conservative MP. You belong to the Tory Party, the party of the buzzing loins.' She glanced towards the house and called to her husband:

'Darling, here's Arnold.' Lillian rose from her seat with pleasure at the sight of the approaching guest.

Across the lawn came the poet. He was in his seventies and walked with two sticks. Johnny went over to greet him and took his arm. He regarded Johnny from rheumy eyes. There were patches of dry scurfy skin on his face:

'My feet are not what they were.'

Lillian clapped her hands:

'Arnold is here. Lunch everybody.' She helped Arnold sit down and instructed one of the waitresses to bring him a plate of food.

'How did you come to be a poet?' asked Jumbo with the gruff politeness of someone not in the least interested.

363

'I come from Whitley Bay. I wanted to be a tugboat captain,' Arnold looked around for a knife and fork, 'but unfortunately fate made me into a poet.'

'I've often thought I might turn my hand to writing when my political career is over,' said the politician.

The poet tucked into his food:

'Why don't you politicians stick to murder and leave art to us.'

Every now and then when the poet spoke it was like the flash of colour in a kingfisher's wing as it flies along the riverbank.

'I take it you have never thought of using your gift for words in the realm of politics,' continued the politician, unabashed.

'I have a puritan streak. It comes from my nonconformist background. I was brought up at school to believe that plain direct English was the best. Milton, Blake, Wordsworth. The truth-givers. That makes a political career out of the question. Besides I have lost interest in all forms of government. I distrust both the whims of kings and the passions of crowds. Words are my sails. I have to set them right to catch the wind.'

Notwithstanding his claim to a streak of puritanism, Arnold Thorpe golloped his food sloppily with the eagerness of a glutton. He tore at the baguette with his hands as he spoke and a shower of crumbs fell from his hands and mouth onto the table. He belatedly tried to catch them. Johnny chose that moment to intervene:

'I was wondering if you ever take commissions, Arnold. We at the HCB bank would pay you a fortune to have a piece written specially for us. We have a wall of Carrara marble in Holland. It could be inscribed there.'

'Never,' said the poet, looking around for the mustard.

'Do you have to suffer to be an artist?' Felix asked, toying with his wine glass. 'I mean to have an unhappy life.'

The poet spoke with his mouth full:

'I know we writers are supposed to thrive on tragedy and I've looked for storms and upheavals in my private life but actually I've had a disgustingly happy marriage and I've had a disgustingly happy life.' He shrugged at the hopelessness of his case. 'I'm still married to the same woman I fell in love with at the age of nineteen.' He picked at his teeth. 'I'm the artistic victim of married bliss.'

Bottles of chilled wine were passed up and down the table.

'Where's Butterfield?' Caspers asked Lillian. 'I've just noticed he isn't here. Did he contact you?' Lillian shrugged and shook her head.

Margot, the butterfly man's wife, excused herself and whispered to the woman next to her:

'I have a weak bladder. I must find the toilet.'

In the middle of everything, Lady Barm suddenly pushed back her chair, started to wave her arms about and lift her knees up and down as though marching on the spot. Her book lay open next to her plate:

'I usually do my exercises every day but today I forgot so I shall do them now.' She cocked her head sideways continuing to stare at her book through her enormous magnifying eye-glass while lifting her legs up and down: 'My sister Lucia taught me these exercises before she went loopy. She was always a bit odd. Tried to hang herself on her wedding day with her bridal belt of flowers. Her daughter has a vegan Rasta boyfriend which means she has to gobble her lamb chops secretly at the end of the garden.'

Suddenly, the poet spat out an exclamation of annoyance. He had accidentally taken a bite of sliced cold potato mistaking it somehow or other for a biscuit.

'It's the Americans I don't like,' said the butterfly man. 'Did you know that Shirley Temple was, in reality, a middle-aged dwarf? The Americans can fingerprint us, photograph us and make records of our eyeballs from outer space. The Americans are everywhere.' He leaned forward and growled. 'We must shake them out of the trees.'

A waitress poured out more wine for Johnny Caspers who was regarding his guests with affection.

'Would you recite something for us?' asked a young musician who had been trying all through the meal to pluck up enough courage to address the poet.

'No.' The poet pointed at his full mouth.

Arnold Thorpe kept to a strict routine. He liked to write from nine o'clock until midday and then eat lunch before having a nap in the afternoon.

'Is there anywhere I can lie down for my nap, Lillian?' His forehead puckered slightly with concern for his own well-being.

'Where's Margot?' said the butterfly man noticing that his wife was missing. 'She's been gone for ages.'

Margot returned looking flustered. Looking for the toilet she had made her way through a lumber room of old statues wrapped in sheets and white plaster death-heads staring down at her from the top of cupboards. Finally, she had found the lavatory:

'I locked the door and when I tried to leave the handle came off and I was locked in. I've been stuck there for ages.'

'Only common people lock the lavatory door,' said Lady Barm. 'Who are these people?'

It was assumed that Lady Barm was referring to the other guests until people realised that she was looking at three men in mackintoshes walking purposefully down the slope from the house towards those seated at the table. The mackintosh of the one ahead of the others flapped slightly as he walked. The Caspers' housekeeper was running in front of them. She came straight up to Johnny:

'Mr Caspers.' She was breathless. 'It's the police.'

Caspers wiped his mouth with a linen napkin and rose to his feet.

'Mr Caspers?' The dark-eyed, reserved officer from the Serious Crime Division addressed Johnny. The table had gone silent.

'Yes. What's happened? Has there been an accident?'

'Is there anywhere we could speak in private?'

'If it's nothing urgent, can't it wait? As you can see I have guests.' In his confusion Johnny sounded arrogant. 'I certainly can't speak to you right now.'

The police officer looked around at the assembled guests:

'We're from the Serious Fraud Office. I am sorry sir but we do need to question you right away with regard to matters at the bank.'

'Is this something to do with Butterfield?' Johnny asked the officer.

'It's something to do with you, actually, sir.'

The party watched as Johnny excused himself and walked away with the police, his napkin still in his hand. Lillian hurried behind. Felix snatched up his airline captain's hat from the table and followed.

Arnold Thorpe pulled a grim face:

'That's why you should always have lawyers. Lawyers – I'd like them around me all the time. Lawyers in my pocket, under my lapel, in my cuffs, hatband. Dripping with lawyers, that's what I want to be. I often conduct my own defence in my head over the smallest misdemeanours as well as on counts of murder. Oh dear. Poor Johnny.'

*

Felix waited outside the room where his father was being questioned. After about twenty-five minutes Caspers came out. Felix watched his father's face go grey as he was ushered into the back of the police car.

'Phone Larry,' said Johnny from the back seat of the car. Larry was the family lawyer.

Felix nodded. He suddenly felt protective towards his father. The sense of estrangement between them over his decision to become a pilot waned. He was aware of his heart beating fast as he watched his father being driven away.

'Fraud?' Caspers was asking the police with concern.

Chapter Sixty-Three

Felix waited with his mother to collect Johnny from the police station after he had been bailed. The family solicitor was with Caspers when he came out. There was a blizzard of press flashlight bulbs. Caspers' face was like a shattered windscreen before it falls. He tried to give Lillian and Felix a reassuring smile but when his mouth opened he exhaled a faint gasp and clung to his wife's hand in the street. Felix looked at the diminished figure of his father. The solicitor advised them that there would now be a delay before committal proceedings to the Crown Court.

The next day the arrest was all over the newspapers. Overnight Caspers' life capsized.

For the next two weeks when he was not away working Felix watched his father spend hours conferring with lawyers. His father had been forbidden entry into the HCB bank. Felix saw his father's humiliation as the calls to Sursok were not returned. Johnny's familiar bearded face seemed to have contracted all over by half an inch. Lillian stood by Johnny's side as he telephoned. Felix observed his father's body crumple as time and time again Sursok refused to speak to him.

'I can't believe that Eddie Sursok would do this to me. Why would he do this? Why did he go straight to the FSA? Why didn't he give me the chance to sort things out ... the benefit of the doubt? It couldn't be because I'm Jewish, could it? Where is Butterfield? He will back me up.'

'We'll go and find him,' said Felix.

*

Three days later they traced him. On his return to England Butterfield had been able to find no sign of Hetty. He went back to Amsterdam only to discover that the locks on the Amsterdam flat had been changed and he could no longer gain entry. He was forced to book into a hotel near the bank. At night he sat in his hotel room either staring at the wall or with his head in his hands. In a state of confusion he went back to London.

Two days after he returned to England to look for Hetty he had been found on the concourse of Euston station wearing extraordinary yellow Rupert Bear checked trousers, a bright blue jacket and bow tie. He was wandering about handing out eggs to people. Eventually, the station police approached to ask him what he was doing.

'Have you heard what's happened to Hetty?' He looked up at the policeman, anxious and miserable. 'She's been abducted by her dog.' Then he gave a quivering smile and waited obediently while the police called an ambulance.

When Lillian and Felix found him he was in a private hospital off the Cromwell Road. They walked through the blue-carpeted corridors until they came to the ward. Butterfield was in his own room on a locked ward. Hunks of his hair had fallen out.

'How are you, Stephen?' asked Lillian.

He still had the same bright expectant smile:

'Hello Lillian. Hello Felix. Nice of you to come. I won't be here long. Look, there's a cat in here somewhere. It's a very hot day and I need to help the poor thing out of its fur coat. Can you help? I want to get him into his pyjamas. I can't think much beyond that, I'm afraid.'

'Do you remember anything about work? About the bank? Have you heard what's happened to Johnny?' Lillian asked in desperation as she held his hand. Butterfield did not reply. He just stared into space.

'Have you seen the cat?' he said after a while. 'It's a tabby. Lovely little thing.'

The next time Felix visited him he had been moved to a long-stay hospital. He wore a plaid and corded dressing-gown. His eyes were dull with medication and he remained glued to the TV set in his room. He waved an arm for Felix to pull up a chair next to him:

'Sit down. Do sit down. The four horsemen of the apocalypse have all come to tea in my television set.'

'It's hopeless,' Felix told Johnny when he reached home. 'He can't remember anything. He's barking.'

Johnny made an effort to continue his life as usual. But when he tried to organise his house parties many of the invitations remained unacknowledged and unanswered.

Felix observed his father carefully. His life as a banker had seemed safe and watertight. Now it was as if his father had launched himself on a river which was in reality a tomb he secretly desired. He discussed his plans for the future but he talked of life as if all the time wishing for death. His business acquaintances mostly deserted him. He smiled at those one or two who still came to see him. He never stopped smiling and his eyes shone constantly so that everything – all worried glances – rolled off them. In the evenings Felix found Caspers upstairs listening to his beloved Mahler. His father would put his finger to his lips, shutting his eyes to indicate that he did not wish to be disturbed.

Chapter Sixty-Four

Mark Scobie chose to telephone Buckley from the red light district in Amsterdam. Shahid or Massoud would never go there. Shahid had walked once down Damstraat and along Beursstraat and returned to Javastraat with his revulsion and hatred of the decadent West confirmed. Massoud had not even bothered.

Mark could hear the cold annoyance in Buckley's voice.

'You say that your abduction target, Butterfield, has disappeared?'

'He seems to have had some sort of breakdown. We're thinking of postponing everything. The others are not keen to go ahead. They wanted to raise money with the kidnap and encourage them to pay up with the attack on the bank.'

'You personally have a lot riding on this, Mark. The whole venture seems to be breaking down. We made an agreement. If you don't fulfil your part we won't be fulfilling ours.'

Mark pulled his leather jacket closer around him against the cold wind. He moved into the shelter of a strip club doorway. The neon lights danced and blinked over his head:

'Buckley, you told me yourself that when you keep people under surveillance you need between fourteen and twenty people just to tail one suspect. How did you expect me to do it on my own?'

'You managed in Italy all right.' Buckley's tone was sharp. 'Look, we need you to push ahead with the attack on the bank. A home-grown conspiracy is what we need. Try and persuade them it's necessary. We don't want Special Branch sneering at us even more than they do already. We told them to pick up Khaled. We'll look idiots unless there's some sort of substantial outrage to back us up. After the event we will liaise with the Dutch secret service and we will be there for the arrest of Shahid and Massoud. The Dutch can arrest their own citizens. Sort it, please.'

Buckley hung up. Mark walked around the city, along canal banks, over bridges and down alleyways. He took deep breaths to control his emotions. Every now and then his feelings rose, agitated, like a flock of birds and settled down again. Eventually he caught a tram back to Javastraat.

*

When Mark returned to the cramped flat Shahid was sitting cross-legged on the floor, disconsolate and downcast. He had packed his bag. Massoud was smoking a cigarette and looking out of the window. Neither of them spoke when he came in. Mark ran his hands through his hair and took off his jacket:

'Look. We need to have a serious meeting about what to do next.'

Shahid looked at him with suspicion:

'What is there to do next? We don't know now whether we should ever have trusted you in the first place, grey-boy. It was a crap plan.'

Mark's mouth became a little dry with apprehension lest some instinct had led Shahid to guess what he had been doing. He spoke calmly:

'We shouldn't give up yet. We owe it to all those people who are in jail or who have suffered under Dutch colonialism. You don't need to pack your bags. When you see Sadiq and Abukar at Friday prayers tomorrow ask them if they could come here for a meeting.'

*

The next night it was raining. Sadiq arrived, an imposing figure in his white *dishdasha*. Abukar, similarly attired, tramped up the stairs behind him. Five minutes later Lukman abandoned his publishing activities downstairs and slipped quietly into the room. He then went out again and returned with some wooden chairs that he used for a children's educational group that met on Sundays. He also brought an electric fire. The men sat in a circle under the unshaded electric light bulb hanging from the ceiling. Sadiq blew his nose on an enormous handkerchief and spoke first:

'I'm not sure it's worth going on with this. We should postpone everything – then work out an alternative plan with a new kidnap target. There are other bankers working for HCB.'

Massoud sounded worried:

'But we can't afford to keep coming and going. I have to provide for my family. Besides the more often people like us travel the more likely the police are to pick us up. And you wanted to involve people from another country so that the Dutch police were not alerted.'

Mark leaned resolutely forward in his chair and looked round at everybody:

'Let me be quite candid. I know I'm not one of you but in my experience you Muslim guys are the only really radicalised force around. Coming back from Australia I've found the same feeling in Bradford and Brick Lane and now in Amsterdam. An energy. An optimism. A sense of fellow-feeling and courage. I can't tell you how much I admire that and miss it. I'm certain we should continue with the plan and I'll tell you why. People are beginning to see that Western democracy is a sham. They are beginning to see through it. It's been rumbled. Democracy is a fig-leaf. It covers up that big prick that tries to fuck everything in sight. Capitalism. The banking system is at the heart of it. Politicians are subservient to it. Torture, state and military power are at the bottom of it.'

Shahid was frowning and making patterns with his foot on the floor. Mark stood up and began to walk round the room. Then he came back and stood by the group, his speech gathering momentum:

'We have a chance to do something. Terrorism, like revolution, has an illustrious history, doesn't it? We should continue that tradition of resistance. I think we should go ahead and attack the bank. There might not be another opportunity for all of us to act together. I'm sorry that the Butterfield kidnap didn't work but we can, at least, do something. It's a wonderful thing that we'd be doing. Striking a blow for a billion oppressed people.'

There was silence. From outside they could hear the pneumatic wail of a tram in the night air.

Abukar removed the green wad of khat from the side of his cheek:

'I just want to be practical. Would it work? That's all I want to know.'

Mark put his foot up on the seat of his chair:

'We should do it now. Who knows when there will be another time? There's a banking crisis. Most people in Europe loathe the bankers and their bonuses. It would be a popular gesture. A beacon for others.'

Shahid flicked a half-smile at Mark. He played with his long hair as he spoke:

'We don't tolerate usury. Maybe you'll come round to the idea of a caliphate after all.' He got up slowly from his chair and spoke, staring at the floor: 'I agree with you in so far as I hate these corrupt democracies.' He looked up. 'Why is it that anything done in their name is made to sound acceptable? Just because the voting cattle are too apathetic to stop them they carry on with their wars, mass killings, torture. They've caused destruction and misery worldwide.'

'Who's for going ahead?' asked Mark. Sadiq rocked back on his chair, put his hands behind his head, rolled his eyes back and looked up at the ceiling. Then he rocked his chair forward again:

'Let's do it.'

A sort of electricity went around the room.

'I think so too,' said Lukman in his soft voice.

Shahid kicked his packed bag away:

'I've changed my mind. I can't wait. We'll go ahead. Some other time I'll go to my own clouds of glory with Allah.' His eyes suddenly glistened with tears.

Sadiq laughed and put his hands on Shahid's shoulder. 'Come on. Come on. Let me show you the sword-dance. It's an old Bedouin tradition. Abukar drum out the rhythm for us.' Abukar pulled up a chair and began to drum with his flat hands on the wooden seat of his chair. Massoud put out his cigarette and joined them. They put their hands on each other's shoulders and began to move around in a circle, stamping their feet. They went faster and faster. Mark stood next to them clapping his hands. In the end the circle broke apart as they stumbled over the chairs and stopped.

Lukman's wife could be heard calling him down to eat.

'Let's go now and check out the bank,' suggested Mark, capitalising on the excitement that had seized everyone in the room. 'We can just drive past. We need to remind ourselves of the layout. Decide on timing and so on.'

Half an hour later five of them were in Sadiq's old car. Lukman stayed behind to eat. They drove slowly through the rain relishing the power of what they were about to do. They passed the illuminated towers and front lobby of the bank and pulled up opposite the complex of buildings. Through the glass doors could be seen the gigantic atrium constructed of quartz and steel and glass illuminated by halogen lamps. A steel rainbow arched across this entrance lobby and extended over the whole of the ground floor. Shahid became both grave and euphoric at the sight:

'This is what I came to do, *inshallah*. It makes me feel that I've finally become an adult, as if I am doing something serious for my own people. As if I'm being tested by Allah. I feel proud of myself.'

'We will do it on Monday night. Midnight,' said Sadiq. 'We'll bring the car and park it further down the road at about eight o'clock. The truck will be ready nearby. We'll wait and then after midnight we can rig the truck with the explosives and put a paving stone on the accelerator.'

That night Mark lay in his sleeping bag on the floor. Despite the changed circumstances there were the same gut-churning nerves that he had felt in the seventies as well as that overwhelming adrenalin rush of excitement. He could hear Shahid in the next room listening to a CD of one of Abu Qatada's fiery sermons. A faint feeling of hilarity came over him. He had believed every word of what he said at the meeting. Now he would be able to bomb a bank and get away with it.

Chapter Sixty-Five

The Ladies Night at Mambo Racine's started late to accommodate all those dancers who were appearing in shows. Before the dance floor became crowded Ella sat with Manuela having a drink at one of the tables.

'This will be fun. I don't like the blue underfloor lighting though, do you? It makes us all look dead. Apparently there's going to be a DJ,' said Ella.

'That girl in the sound box,' said Manuela.

They looked up at a girl in the sound box. Behind the glass window she could be seen with her headphones on. She wore black lipstick and a black satin dress and her permafrosted blonde hair fell into a neat bob as she bent over to inspect the decks. Next to her stood a black girl with a fibreglass helmet of straightened and lacquered hair surveying the scene below. Behind them was a red plastic crate of records and CDs.

Just then the swing doors opened and about twenty girls came in shrieking and sliding over the polished floor. Some brandished bottles of Vodka and cans of Red Bull. A few of them had tied their hair up in great bows with ribbons or scarves. They wore every possible combination of dance gear: tights, leg-warmers, frilly cotton knickers, leotards and short chiffon overskirts.

'I mustn't go too mad,' continued Manuela. 'I'll embarrass my daughter. She's coming with the others as soon as the show is finished.

These girls must be from one of the musicals. There are some coming from *Carousel* and *Mamma Mia*, I think.'

Ella and Manuela also wore a mixture of mad dance attire. Ella wore a yellow ochre and black striped lace camisole with black tights and black woollen leggings. Her hair was pulled back and lifted into a tight knot. As a joke she had six inch oval gauze wings perched on her head. Manuela was bursting out of a lizard green leotard. Manuela sighed as she examined her bulky legs and thighs:

'I'm so fat. Look at my cleavage. It looks as though someone has stuffed an arse down my blouse. We'll all look like idiots at our age.'

Ella laughed:

'No we won't. Dance doesn't bother with age. You should see the ninety-year-olds winding their waists at Carnival in Brazil.'

As if to prove her point an elegant old lady in her eighties with a sprightly gait came towards them.

'Oh goodness. It's Madame Sourikova.' Ella jumped up to embrace her old Russian dance teacher. As the teacher smiled, deep cracks – the crazy-paving of age – opened up all over her face but her eyes burned with life. The hum of the sound system being turned on and the crackle of a microphone stopped further conversation as the night started with an announcement:

'I am Cream-Tease, your DJ for tonight working the decks alongside Lady Krylon. A big range for ladies only. Some dance-hall stylee. Mash-up and Re-Mix. I'll have mixes by Terra Diva and others. Reggae. Soul. Hardcore. Garage. Jungle and Hard House. The sizzle has gone underground, girls. Rock is stale. Pop is dead. It's soul-sizzle all the way so join us in the underground. But I'm kicking off with something cool and icy – Subliminal Session 2 from Cookie Dough Dynamite.'

Trance-Master music swept through the venue and a hypnotic bass drum pumped out like blood from a stab victim. Manuela's daughter turned up with the ballet crew and waved to her mother as they moved straight to the dance floor under the strobe lighting.

One girl with a body like a swan's neck, long, sinuous, bendy and seductive started the dancing. Any observer could see that this was not going to be a normal dance-club evening with people jigging on the spot. Groups of dancers from their various shows entered into physical dialogue with each other. One set would do a sequence of movements with leaping twists and outrageous high-kicks, half improvised and half taken from the choreography they knew. Another set copied them. Then dancers from the ballet replied by executing a series of flying turns across the floor, ending with provocative wiggles of the hips and backbends over each other's arms. The DJ watching from above orchestrated tunes that moved the crowd from one mood to another. The dancers responded, flooded with an inextinguishable energy that surged up from their feet.

Amongst those quick limbs of youth one awkward girl stood out. She had long blonde hair and a fringe. She wore a short black dress and attracted attention by hurling her uncoordinated arms and legs around the dance floor, caught up in some fantasy that had not been translated to her body. People assumed that a friend must have brought her. They sniggered and exchanged glances and then had to move out of the way as she spun ecstatically around the room, unaware of the spectacle she made, bumping into other dancers.

Ella, Manuela and Madame Sourikova were soon up and dancing with the crowd. Even Ella had forgotten the excitement of dance liberated from the constraints of choreography. Below the level of reason the angels and ogres normally kept in the cellar came out to dance, to rove and roar, growling and singing. One girl did a solo turn with spinning, can-can kicks, her torso arched back like a bow before she jumped into a back-flip. It was as if she had burst out of some two-dimensional region into a third dimension, her body scrawling its own message on the air in explosive hieroglyphics. Everyone started to scream and clap in time to the music.

Ella let go of Manuela's hand and went over to their table to catch her breath. Then she glimpsed a figure in the doorway. The figure stepped back out of sight behind the doorpost in order not to be seen. It was Donny. Ella ran over to see him. Her eyes took a minute to adjust to the dark outside the strobe lights of the dance floor. He looked grim and serious.

'I'm away,' he said.

'Where to?' she gripped his elbows.

'I don't know. I'm just away. That's all.'

He disentangled himself. His features were set and grave. She saw him clearly set against a ragged fire of darkness, a radiant blackness. Eventually he spoke:

'Get back to your dancing.' Then he was gone.

Ella went back to the dance floor. The coloured strobe lights flashed around her and she felt as though she were balancing on top of a plain of sadness. Manuela was fanning herself by their table and moving gently from side to side with the music.

The music began to pump out a ferocious beat. The body has its own language. Ella crouched half-way to the ground with bent knees and started stamping her feet. It was the Djuka dance she remembered from her childhood in Surinam. The movements were grotesque and required tremendous physical stamina. She looked like some giant insect. Others copied her. Soon the floor was filled with a seething mass, a swarm of crouching insect creatures drumming their feet. The whole room became intoxicated with a raw and rowdy sort of violence.

A fight broke out. A group of women locked together ricocheted backwards and forwards across the room. Punches were being exchanged. Some women tried to hold others back. Someone screamed:

'It's a bloke.' There were shouts of outrage.

Ella moved towards the mass of writhing bodies that had fallen to the floor. She could see Felix Caspers with his hands clutched to his head as he desperately tried to hold on to his blond wig. Someone kicked him in the face. The wig was ripped away from him. One woman put her foot on his chest and seized his arm as though to wrench it off. Then people started to claw at his clothes. He had on women's underwear. His penis lolled insolently against his left thigh poking out from under the lace crotch of his panties. Someone tore at it but he managed to cross his legs and roll away.

Ella pushed her way through to him, grabbed him by the forearms and hoiked him up.

'Aaah. I know him. He only wants to dance. You said you wanted to dance with me once didn't you? Well, come on.' And she took hold of his hands, crossed his wrists, dragged him to the centre of the floor and started to swing him round. People gathered round and started to take photos on their mobiles. Felix was half naked. He was no weakling but her strength was immense. He was gasping, swallowing lungfuls of air. She leaned back to get a purchase on the ground and swung him around. His body made ugly shapes, all knees and elbows as he tried to keep his balance. His false breasts fell out of his skimpy brassiere. He was losing his footing and when he fell she jerked him to his feet again. She whirled round faster and faster until he was unable to keep his feet on the ground. Then she let go.

There was a crack as his head hit the doorpost. No-one moved towards him. They watched him crawl away down the stairs on his hands and knees holding his head where the blood seeped through his fingers.

The shaken DJ had enough sense to put on some hypnotic techno, Terra Diva, hoping the wash of monotonous humming sounds would introduce some calm back into the situation. Everyone danced separately now. The desire to make whole again was enormous. The dancers moved alone in their orbits, each one trying to get back to a centre which no longer existed. Not one of them knew where the centre was. Everything spun further and further apart.

At the end of the night a calm, lazy stupor overtook everyone. Nothing was said. Ella put on her coat and helped Manuela, who was slumped in her chair at the table, to go and look for her daughter.

Then Manuela half woke up and said:

'How did he get home without his clothes?'

Ella shrugged:

'No idea,' she said.

Chapter Sixty-Six

Two nights later Felix Caspers arrived at my flat with an Elastoplast on his forehead. I mention this in order to exonerate myself from any blame for what was about to happen and to let you see how peripheral my involvement was. I'm only the narrator. I can't be held responsible.

He was wearing his airline uniform and looking nervous and agitated. Those were the days when Johnny Caspers' imminent trial was all over the newspapers. His blue eyes had a feverish glint.

'Good to see you again.' He shook my hand with a prim handshake. Weight loss had made his Adam's apple even more prominent. I thought how slightly built he was for a pilot in charge of such a huge machine. He shook his head and refused my offer of a coffee:

'No. Sorry. I don't have much time. I'm flying to New York tomorrow on a cargo flight and then back to Amsterdam and on to Tel Aviv. I hope you don't mind my coming but Michael Feynite said that you had all his architectural notes and writings. I'm desperate to get hold of them. Do you think I could have them?'

I wondered whether to hand the notes over to Felix or not. I knew the effect they would have on him. In the end I decided I would. I'd have to suspend my moral judgement but then it was only hanging by a thread anyway. I went over to the dresser and took them out.

'You want Michael Feynite's notes? Here they are.'

Felix started to pore over the files straight away. There were several volumes filled with Feynite's neat obsessive handwriting.

In tune with his opinion of himself he had entitled his work: *My Brilliant Notebooks.*

Felix gave a little snort of laughter at the title and then read out from the first notebook:

'*The times are such that we have to take individual action – an idea which I understand perfectly well is both noble and pathetic.*'

Felix looked at me:

'I don't think suicide is wrong or immoral, do you?' He sounded defensive. 'Some people find family life suffocating. I do. The trouble is I don't really belong anywhere else either – or anywhere I'd like to be.' He hesitated and then carried on:

'Feynite said you might have a gun. He always suspected that you were some sort of hit man on the quiet. It's a fantasy of his. I could do with a gunman.'

Oddly enough, I had nursed that sort of fantasy myself.

'Or you could be my driver,' said Felix.

'I'm getting confused here. I thought you needed a gun.'

'I did, at first. I wanted a gun to shoot myself. Then I thought I'd better get somebody else to do it in case I couldn't go through with it.'

I was offended:

'Oh no. I couldn't do that. I fancy myself as an assassin. Shooting someone who wants to be shot is not the same thing at all. That's not an assassination. That's more of an assisted suicide. What's all this about a driver, then?'

'I thought I'd like someone to drive me to a secluded spot and then do it.'

'Is driving all you would need me to do – if you're now having to shoot yourself?'

'I think so.' He was smiling. It was all a joke.

'Why don't you just get a taxi?'

'Moral support. In case I chicken out.'

'Look. I'm not a hit man. I'm a novelist. It's not my job to provide moral support. It's my job to set the moral compass spinning.'

'Anyway,' Felix looked serious, 'for a suicide to make any impact there needs to be something bigger ...'

He took off his hat and sat down on the sofa. His blond hair was greased down and crinkled in tight waves. He picked out more fragments of Feynite's notes to read out loud, stifling a laugh:

'Listen to this. *"Violence has stayed in the cupboard for a long time. Time it began to push open the door."* And listen to this bit. *"I am not interested in organising mass movements to overthrow the bourgeois order, but interested in killing representatives of that order to bring about a better world or in attacking physically those institutions which do people harm. The arrogance of the strong must be met by the violence of the weak."'*

Felix shook his head:

'I must take these away with me and read them properly. I haven't time. Have I got all the notes here?'

'Yes. That's the lot. There are loads of his draft sketches here as well.' I passed him the large portfolio and he opened it. The folder was entitled:

'*My passionate celebration of destruction and despair, joy and terror.*'

There was sketch after sketch of the magnificently designed ruined cities which were Feynite's most recent obsession. Felix appeared to be enthralled as he flicked through them. For a moment he looked at me directly. His eyes widened then narrowed with shrewd assessment. He got up suddenly and walked over to the window holding his captain's hat in his hand. His white shirt with a blue stripe and the narrow blue tie made him look like a young American chief executive officer. There was an odd compression to his lips. He continued to stare out of the window gently fingering the contours of the raised welt on his cheekbone:

'Have you heard what Sursok has done? Sursok has destroyed my father. "God of the rubbish-heap. Bringer of smallpox." That's how my grandmother describes Sursok.'

'Why did he treat your father like that?'

Felix turned to face me:

'Nobody knows. None of us has any idea.' Felix stared out of the window again for a moment then walked back into the centre of the room. 'I hope the HCB bank crashes to hell and all the shareholders with it.'

The vehemence of his hatred was startling. There was a silence. After a while he spoke:

'I want to bring Sursok and the whole of HCB to its knees.'

'Wouldn't that affect your father too?'

'No. It's too late for that. My father is not going to escape jail.'

The mention of his father affected him. Quite unexpectedly his chin wobbled and his eyes filled with tears that overflowed from the bottom rim. He nodded and his Adam's apple bobbed up and down again. He was in a fluster as he gathered up the notes. I had the impression that he wanted to rush away somewhere in private to read them. He picked up his captain's hat. I saw him to the door.

'Thank you for these,' he managed to say as he left.

*

The following morning Felix drove to the airport. It was October. The sky was bright blue. On either side of the road blazing orange fingers of chestnut leaves drooped from the trees. Further down the road other trees were turning yellow as if sunlight were dripping through them. He was due to fly to New York to pick up some cargo and then return to Schiphol airport in Amsterdam for refuelling and fly from there to Tel Aviv. He felt a sense of calm exaltation. He picked up Feynite's notes from the passenger seat and kissed them. He had spent the whole night reading them. Then he opened the car window so that the cool breeze would help him stay awake. He put on a CD of Missa Lumba sung by a Congolese choir and hummed along to it.

Chapter Sixty-Seven

The same sense of calm exaltation was experienced by Shahid as he waited in the flat in Javastraat. This was to be the night. He felt noble, spiritual and generous. He had prayed. He offered to cook for the others while they waited for evening but in the end Lukman brought them up some food. It was decided that they must try and eat despite nervous flutters in their stomachs. At three o'clock in the afternoon Sadiq and Abukar arrived. There was a tangible feeling of love and trust between all the men although at different times each one of them experienced a racing heart and terrible doubts. Mark joined in the attempt at cool-headed practicality. They smoked and told jokes. The day before there had been a trial run and Abukar in his nervousness had driven the wrong way round a roundabout. Shahid switched on the television and they watched the build up to the Feyenoord versus Ajax match to be played that night.

*

The Boeing 747 cargo plane which Felix was to pilot to Tel Aviv weighed eight hundred thousand pounds. It was early evening and the plane was on the ground at Schiphol airport. Other planes like giant white pessaries were parked in their designated spaces. Two mechanics in green overalls signalled to Felix that everything was in order. Before he taxied down the runway Felix took off his jacket. Eventually, the white nose of the aircraft lifted like a weightless erection and the plane left the airport. On the ground below the city lights of Amsterdam glittered like a spread of cheap jewellery.

Immediately after take-off the quartermaster went to the back of the plane to check that the cargo was secure. On the manifest it said that the cargo was perfume and flowers. In fact, the cargo also contained fifty gallons of DMMP, a component of sarin nerve gas which the Israelis had ordered. While the quartermaster was in the back of the plane Felix Caspers quietly secured the lock on the cabin door. All flights had recently been fitted with these security locks. They prevented anyone from entering the pilot's cabin. He had brought some make-up, a red lip-liner and a little rouge which he took out of his airline bag. Then he changed his mind and decided he did not need to put it on.

*

The towers of the HCB bank were clearly visible from the air. The flight path overflew the south-eastern outskirts of Amsterdam, the sort of wasteland that accrues round every major metropolis in Europe. Not far from the bank was a dreary estate of nondescript tower blocks called the Zuidermeer. That estate too was a landmark visible from the cabins of overflying aircraft. It boasted two run-down supermarkets and an overhead railway which gave out an electric moan as it rumbled along, weaving its way through the blocks at second-storey height. Local people called the estate 'Sranen-tonga', Surinamese for 'bush-language' because so many of the occupants were immigrants from Surinam, Ghana or the Dominican Republic.

From the air the outline of the estate looked similar to the structure of the HCB bank nearby. The flats had a sort of bleak brightness. They tried hard. They did their best. Pa and Ma Tem had migrated there some years before and decorated their walls with paintings and carved wooden pieces from Surinam.

A few hundred yards away in the Groningen block opposite, early evening lights were already being switched on and off in the flats. As families settled down to watch the Feyenoord versus Ajax football match, different square windows lit up or went out turning the block into a giant arcade pinball machine. Outside, a certain steeliness had already entered the autumn wind.

*

Just after seven in the evening with dusk approaching, three men were sailing their boat on nearby Lake IJsselmeer as many of their ancestors had done before them, indulging in that Dutch love affair with water. The colour of the grey sky was one degree lighter than the waters. Each of the sailors wore a waterproof puffa jacket against the wind. They were all looking up at the sky to where the Boeing 747 plane slowly headed east. One of the men leaned forward to switch off the boat engine. The droning whine of the plane engines receded allowing them to hear the sound of the wavelets slapping at the side of the boat and the irregular snapping noise of the sail in the wind. Planes in that area were often low-flying because of the proximity of the airport but something about this plane worried them.

Their boat passed under a low stone bridge. The men ducked momentarily into the gloom. As they emerged into the early evening light they saw the plane tilt to one side and make an unusual three hundred and sixty degree turn back in the direction of Schiphol. The plane was flying low enough for the men to identify the El Al markings on the body and tail. It was flying far too low.

The plane climbed a little again before levelling off. Now it was flying horizontally in the direction of the HCB bank and the Zuidermeer. The sailors could see that the plane lacked the rows of lozenge-shaped windows found on passenger planes and knew it must be a cargo plane. One of the sailors used the marine telephone to report what they were seeing. He looked at his watch. It was a quarter past seven.

*

Groningen block stood directly opposite Kampen block on the estate. Marthi Brandt, a blonde woman with over-treated dried hair sat in her front room drinking Hoegaarden beer. She was angry with her teenage son Hans who had stormed out of the flat earlier. What worried her was that he would go down to the basement where the crack-sellers hung out. She took a swig of beer and went over to the window. From there she could see Pa Tem's flat and the mad spiders of black and red graffiti that ran along their balcony. Ma and Pa Tem had been good friends to her when she was deserted by her husband. She envied their home life. Domestic accord was what she wanted more than anything. She felt that she was the only woman on the estate whose life was deformed by loneliness. The low growl of an approaching plane hardly registered on her.

*

The airport controller radioed through:

'El Al 1917, just to be sure, you say that engines number three and four are malfunctioning?'

'Number three and four are out and we have ... er ... problems with our flaps.'

'Problems with the flaps? 1917, your speed is?'

'Say again.'

'Your speed?'

'Our speed is ... er ... two hundred and sixty.'

'OK. If you need to return you have about thirteen miles to go. Speed is all yours. You are cleared to land on Runway 27. Continue descent to one thousand five hundred feet.'

The sailors on the lake watched in silence as the plane descended in a shallow gradient towards the level high-rise tops of the Zuidermeer. There was something wrong. The plane was too low.

*

Far below in the Javastraat flat, Mark waited while Shahid and Abukar took it in turns to use the toilet, yanking impatiently at the chain when the cistern didn't fill quickly enough. Sadiq, Abukar, Shahid and Massoud performed their ablutions, washing their hands and feet. When they had finished it was seven fifteen. They checked their watches. The plan was that they should go and park near the bank at eight o'clock which would give them time to make sure the truck was ready and the explosives properly primed. They embraced each other. Sadiq was grinning. Shahid slipped his copy of the Koran into his pocket.

'We'll set off at half past seven,' said Mark. 'It doesn't take nearly that long to get to the bank but we want to make sure that there are no unexpected hold-ups on the road.'

After a quick glance round to check that nothing had been left behind the men trotted down the stairs. They said goodbye to Lukman at the door and made their way past the kebab shop to the car.

*

When the towers of the HCB bank came into sight Felix Caspers lined up the plane manually and aimed the aircraft in the direction of the bank. Then he spoke to the control tower:

'OK. We are at one thousand five hundred feet now but we have a controlling problem.'

'You have a controlling problem as well? Roger.' The control tower's operator sounded slightly disbelieving. He could hear something in the background, a banging and someone's voice muffled and indistinct saying: 'What are you doing? Raise all the flaps. Lower the gear.'

Then came the terse sharp voice of Felix Caspers:

'Going down. 1917. Going down.'

The controller heard a sound he could not identify until much later when the tape was replayed and he understood it to be the intermittent buzzing signal of the ground-proximity warning system.

*

Ma Tem was the first to respond to the approaching growl of the plane as it drowned out the sound of the TV:

'My god. This thing is falling.' She let the plate shoot off her lap, grabbed her husband and ran with him into the bedroom. They flung themselves on the floor but were too big to fit under the bed and lay next to it with their hands over their heads.

In her bedroom in the neighbouring block a young girl recently arrived with her mother from Ghana sprawled on her bunk-bed listening to Snoop Dogg's rap on her iPod. She could hear a sort of vibrating hum over and above the music. She took off her earphones and sat up. The noise grew unbearably loud. The whole room juddered.

Her mother, standing in the front room, felt that her ears were splitting open and peeling outwards from her head. The room suddenly darkened. She could not understand what she was seeing. The light from the window was blocked by the outline of the enormous Boeing 747 which filled the entire space between the Groningen block opposite and their own. She saw the laminated white nose of the aircraft slanting downwards and tilting to the right. She even had time to register the over-painted studs of the aircraft's door. For two or three seconds the great body of the plane seemed to hang immobile in the air at a downward angle outside the woman's window. Then the enormous blade-shaped wing of the plane sliced down towards the apartment like a giant executioner's scimitar.

*

Only when Felix saw the children's playground below him did he realise his mistake. Paralysed with horror and disbelief he made a weak and futile attempt to guide the roaring uncontrollable monster through the small gap between apartment blocks.

*

Standing at her window in Groningen block opposite, Marthi Brandt was immobilised by the deafening roar of the descending plane. Way over her head the great belly of the plane, landing gear hanging uselessly out, slid down over the roof of her own block. It plunged downwards at the same angle as the children's slide in the playground below. The evening light caught the underbelly which gleamed grey as it lunged towards Groningen and Kampen blocks. And all the time, the engines revved at higher and higher speeds giving the impression that at the last second it could defy gravity if it chose and climb upwards again.

At the moment of impact she blinked. When she opened her eyes there was sky where there had previously been buildings. Across the way there was now a gap in the shape of a broken outline of India. The sight was almost instantly obliterated by billowing mushrooms of black smoke. The bang when it reached her was deafening. It blew all the glass out of her windows and reduced her apartment to darkness. Still she stood there with fragments of glass on her clothes and in her hair, aware of the cold breeze on her face.

At the crash site a gigantic unstable flaming outline of the plane's nose reared up over the top of the apartment blocks. A blazing ragged figure of dark orange fire like some raging phantom of the plane itself hung in the sky before disintegrating into a myriad of separate fires. There were more minor explosions. Showers of sparks flew through the air like tiny brilliant hyphens only to be swallowed up by the smoke. Then beneath the billows of black smoke which erupted continually into the sky she saw the mountain of rubble that had been the halves of Kampen and Kasteel estates glowing like lava from a volcano. The cold breeze was replaced by heat on her face through the broken window.

She had no idea how much time elapsed before the sound of approaching sirens wailed through the night: ambulance sirens, police sirens and fire engines all rushing to the scene. The estate had been built in a curve. What greeted them was a vast and blackened theatre that was both stage-set and auditorium. The balconies and front walls of the surviving apartments on either side of the epicentre of the crash had been ripped off leaving the charred interiors of people's homes exposed like tiers of boxes at a theatre, several with curtains on fire, some with wallpaper torn off the walls. The explosion had left the adjacent buildings looking as though they were made of fluttering rags. In a few minutes, Kampen and Kasteel had been transformed into an infernal coliseum.

For the first ten minutes even the emergency services did not know what to do. Fires burst from windows like so many divas leaning out to perform an aria. Little flames fluttered coquettishly against the dark background before being extinguished by smoke. The flames became a dancing chorus appearing gaily everywhere as in the opening scene of a light opera. There was a fuzz of pinkish fireballs visible in what was left of some apartments and in the rubble at ground level she saw row upon row of rippling flounces, flurries of white gaseous flames, frills, ruches, the swirling petticoats of a fiery can-can.

Marthi Brandt turned away from the window. Her own room was unrecognisable, bizarrely lit by this new light source. Her limbs moved slowly as if she could not wake from a deep sleep. She knew she had to find her son. She snatched his photograph from the mantelpiece. When she opened her front door residents were hurrying silently down the stairs as if they no longer trusted lifts or any mechanised form of transport.

On the ground outside people gathered and stood in informal groups. People held on to each other. There was not a lot of talking, just a sense of disbelief.

*

One mile away in the cold night air Shahid and Mark Scobie stood arguing desperately with the policeman at the roadblock close to the HCB bank. The Dutch policeman insisted that access to the whole area was now restricted to keep routes clear for the emergency services and to see that the fire did not spread. The roads would not be opened until the crash investigation was completed. The men had tried other routes to the HCB bank but it was the same everywhere.

They walked back to their vehicle. Shahid was nearly crying. Massoud looked grim. In a fit of temper and frustration Shahid threw his backpack over the fence of a construction site as they passed. He walked ahead of the others with his head bowed. When they reached the car Sadiq leaned out of the window with a worried expression to ask them what had happened.

'We could try again in a few days,' suggested Massoud. Sadiq shook his head:

'We've been seen by too many Dutch police. We'll have to abort it until we can plan something else.' He started the car and they drove back to Javastraat. They stopped in an area of forested wasteland and buried the explosives.

As soon as he was able Mark made a phone call to Buckley in England and told him about the debacle.

Chapter Sixty-Eight

At the site of the crash one of the crowd of onlookers pointed to one of the stricken flats in what remained of Kampen block. From the ruin of her apartment a woman, in flames, threw her child who was also in flames from the fifth storey and then jumped herself. She fell like an expended Roman Candle, loose yellow flames from her clothes twisting vertically upwards as she plummeted to the ground.

Firemen aimed their hoses at the centre point of the crash. Grass and plants were on fire in front of them and so was the pond where some of the fuel from the aircraft had fallen. Marthi Brandt pushed through the crowd clutching her son's photograph:

'Have you seen this boy?'

Fifty yards away ambulance men led survivors to safety. People whose homes were destroyed were shepherded to transport that would take them to a nearby sports hall for the night. Marthi turned around the corner of Groningen block. As soon as the glare and heat of the fire were cut off she could feel the cold wind blowing. She hurried towards the underground car park, night-time haunt of crack-sellers and addicts. It was empty. The click of her heels echoed as she walked through calling Hans's name. She walked up the ramp and out into the open again.

This side of the estate was largely deserted. It was some distance from the source of heat. Two hundred yards away flames wrestled with strong winds. The flames which had, at first, been crimson and pink turned yellow and orange under the powerful hoses of the fire brigade. The end flats of each block were not too badly damaged. The plane had struck in the middle. Marthi looked around in vain for a sign of Hans. She noticed the silhouette of a woman standing next to a concrete bollard facing towards the fire. Marthi stumbled towards the woman.

'Excuse me, but have you seen my boy anywhere?' She held out the picture.

The woman turned. She had pretty blonde curls. Her mouth was soft and innocent but with some of those merciless cracks around it that come with age.

'I'm so sorry, I don't speak Dutch.' The accent was American.

Marthi repeated her request in English. The woman studied the photograph and then looked directly at Marthi:

'I'm sorry. I haven't seen him. Isn't this just awful?' She put her hand up to the side of her face in bewildered horror. 'I asked the police if I could help but they just told me to stay away.'

Marthi Brandt thanked her and hurried away. A moment later, she felt an arm link into hers. It was Hans, tears streaming down his face. They clung to each other for a while. Then mother and son made their way back to what was left of their home.

*

Hetty Moran continued to gaze towards the fire. She had seen Hans running from the flats in panic but could not resist the opportunity to let the woman remain in torment for a little longer. She shivered and pulled her jacket closer round her shoulders. She had been in the apartment purloined from Stephen Butterfield when the noise of the crash reached her. Almost immediately the news appeared on television.

Hetty walked towards the relatively undamaged end of Kampen block. She ducked under the red and white ribbon that police used to keep people out and let herself quickly through the heavy swing doors of the apartment block. Residents had been evacuated. It was dark inside. Water from the fireman's hoses and from burst water pipes ran everywhere. The lift door was jammed open and the rank smell of urine filled the lobby. Hetty found the stairs next to the lift. She started to climb, feeling her way slowly with her hand on the wall. Suddenly from above there came the sound of descending feet. A beam from a torch came round the corner and dazzled her. A family was running down the stairs towards her, all wearing anoraks shining with damp.

'We're looking for Jaap,' they said, hardly pausing to wait for a response. Hetty stood back and let them pass. The family had disobeyed police instructions and run back to look for their son. They ran out into the night.

Hetty slipped quietly up the stairs. On the third floor she hesitated, wondering how dangerous it was. Then she decided to risk it and went on up to the fourth floor. She stood in the corridor. There was a warm mist in the air which she mistook for fire smoke and then realised it was steam where water from the firemen's hoses had encountered the heat of the building. The floor was slippery. Light from arc lamps outside penetrated unexpected cracks and fissures in the walls. She tried the front door of one of the flats but it was stuck at an angle and impossible to open. She moved cautiously on. Further along she found a front door that was open. Plaster fell down as she pushed her way in.

Once inside she could just make out the wreckage of an apartment. The front wall was entirely blown off so that the place was open to the skies. There was no sign of the inhabitants. The firemen's hoses had been trained on the flats for nearly five hours and everything was drenched, charred and unrecognisable under piles of wet plaster rubble. The side wall had partially collapsed giving a direct view into the kitchen where the ribbed plastic interior of a dish-washer lay exposed. Even the most everyday object seemed strange. Everything was transformed. What she assumed to be a clothes horse turned out to be a shattered chair.

Keeping well in the shadows so that she would not be visible in the floodlights on the ground, Hetty clambered over debris to sit down against the back wall of the wrecked home. The night breeze felt fresh and sharp on her face. She was reasonably sure that she could not be seen from the ground. A certain amount of danger was necessary. It gave a sort of moral balance to what she was doing. Where she sat bits of jagged plaster stuck into her back. She tried to make herself more comfortable as she looked out onto the scene below. The enormous curve of the coliseum surrounded her and an extraordinary feeling of power crept over her as if she were centre stage and in control of the world. For a while she looked out from her eyrie. Below, the small figures of the emergency workers moved ceaselessly to and fro around the pond in the floodlights. Ambulances waited, rotating lights flashing. Vehicles moved off taking the homeless to a sports hall. It was now half past three in the morning. The initial gigantic pall of smoke overhead had cleared. Above she could see the purple sky over the city and stars between the clouds.

She inspected her surroundings. A splintered chair leg caught her eye. That would do. She tore her skirt with it. She tried to cut her legs and thighs and the back of her neck with a rough piece of plaster. Some blood came but not enough. For the next ten minutes she tried banging her head against the wall as violently as she could bear, stopping for a bit and then doing it again, trying to take herself by surprise. Suddenly it occurred to her that the whole edifice might collapse and she had an urge to scrabble out of it. The panic passed and she lay down and pulled some of the wet rubble and plaster on top of her. The plaster retained some heat from the fire. A feeling of great peace and contentment came over her.

After a while she became uncomfortable. She changed her position. This she did several times during the night. Eventually, just before dawn, she moved nearer the front so that someone would be able to see her. She pulled more rubble over her body and arranged herself in the position in which she intended to be found. The rubble was damp and warm and smelled of lime. She lay staring at the stars. She felt remarkably alert. Truly alive. It was as if this great shattered arena was a stage-set especially constructed for her performance. She shut her eyes and tried to doze.

It was nine in the morning, in the grey light of day, when the youngest member of the fire crew spotted her. He was with his colleagues in a huge yellow crane that had been brought up to the front of the building with a clench claw to take away some of the wreckage. His eyes were alight with triumph as he pointed to where some rubble lay half covering a woman's body. They could see that her eyes were shut.

Hetty heard the excited shouts. She allowed her eyes to open the merest crack and saw the men shouting and gesticulating to other emergency workers. She began to hyperventilate so that her pulse would be irregular when help arrived. She drew deep breaths until she felt dizzy.

It was not more than a few minutes before she heard the scrunch of boots in the rubble and reassuring voices. She lay absolutely still making her breathing as shallow as possible. Solicitous hands quickly removed the pieces of debris and plaster that covered her. This was it. The wonderful moment of recovery. Someone was feeling for her pulse. She felt her left eyelid being raised as a paramedic tried to determine her level of consciousness. The voices around her spoke earnestly in Dutch. She was lifted with the utmost care onto a stretcher. Someone was stroking her head.

Hetty Moran was carried down the four flights of stairs. The stretcher felt as if it were floating on its own. She was a princess on a palanquin. The stretcher-men made their way to the ambulance with their precious burden. Seated inside the vehicle were Pa and Ma Tem. Someone had placed a jacket around Pa Tem's shoulders.

Every disaster has its heroes. After the crash Pa Tem had gone looking in their part of the building, which was relatively undamaged, for neighbours or children who might be trapped. His face and hands were badly burned. The brown skin of his face had come off in strips showing pink flesh below. The palms of his hands too were bright pink with third degree burns. He had stayed all night with people watching outside, helping where he could. In the morning his pain was so acute that Ma Tem insisted on bringing him over to the ambulance. The ambulance men explained that there was a serious stretcher case coming in. He would have to wait. They would come back for him.

Pa Tem, half-blinded by the effects of the fire, raised his hand in acknowledgement. They climbed down from the ambulance. Pa Tem settled on a bench to wait patiently with his wife's arm around his shoulders.

In the ambulance a transparent oxygen mask was quickly fitted over Hetty's face. She was wrapped in tin foil in case of hypothermia and tucked cosily under one of the red ambulance blankets. The oxygen began to make her high. It was hard not to giggle. A wave of exhilaration swept through her. Voices spoke Dutch over her head. The ambulance siren wailed. Someone took hold of her hand. After ten minutes or so she felt the ambulance slow down. The doors were opened and once more she felt herself being lifted. A chill morning breeze brushed her face as she was carried to the hospital entrance. She opened her eyes a fraction. An arm was holding open the transparent swing doors of the casualty department. The stretcher was lifted onto a trolley and there was the hollow echo of rubberised wheels as she was pushed through draughty corridors. She suppressed the urge to laugh.

After a preliminary examination which revealed no major injuries the hospital staff, overstretched with the sudden influx of patients, hurried off to deal with more serious cases. An auxiliary nurse was appointed to clean her up and she was taken to one of the private rooms that had been requisitioned for the emergency. As her trolley was pushed into the room the raised square white pillow on the bed beckoned to her like an empty canvas on which she could paint a new portrait of her own choosing. She had not spoken. When the nurse tried to take her details she just shut her eyes. Three doctors stood in the doorway.

'Generalised shock,' said one of them.

When they had left Hetty Moran snuggled down in the warm bedclothes delighted by the feeling of being absolutely safe.

Chapter Sixty-Nine

Mark Scobie took the call at his mother's house in Tenterden. Vera had been delighted to know that he would be staying in England for good and there would be no repercussions from the past. On the phone Buckley sounded more sanguine than Mark had expected:

'Well no-one could have foreseen that. I think we'll have to put that one down to experience. You've made some useful contacts which will be helpful to us in the future. We'll let Khaled go quietly. We won't pick up Shahid and Massoud. Keep in touch with them and see what transpires. They won't stop there.'

Mark switched off his mobile and watched the Borzoi dash round in circles in the garden. Vera came into the living room.

'Darling. Can you run through this last scene with me? I'm not a hundred per cent sure of my lines and it's the important end section about the Palestinian/Israeli conflict. We're opening for previews on Thursday.'

*

Standing in the foyer of the Royal Court Theatre on the first night of his play Victor Skynnard felt himself to be a man of distinction in the arts. He put aside his worries about debt, the state of the economy and his part in the overthrow of the system as he settled into his seat and waited for the house lights to go down.

The opening night of the play, however, was a disaster. A scenic flat fell down from the flies in the middle of the first scene and at one point, towards the interval, Victor looked round in fury as he thought he heard the slow resounding toll of a bell. It was a critic groaning.

I met him in the Head in the Sand café a few days later. He was clutching a sheaf of creditors' bills and was very down in the dumps. He pointed at my notebook:

'You're writing a novel. Do you think art can make any difference to the world?'

'Probably not,' I said. 'But it might upset things a little. It's one way of having a quarrel with the world. Art is what those of us do who are too frightened to be terrorists.'

*

Two days later Victor Skynnard hanged himself from the flies of the Royal Court Theatre. Nobody was ever quite sure whether or not he had clambered up there to check on the piece of loose scenery that wrecked his first night or whether he was overcome by failure, debt and the loss of political direction. The play was performed beneath him twice before he was noticed. The actors never looked up to see the body swinging gently over their heads. Vera glanced up once but her short-sightedness made her assume that some bit of the set had come loose again.

*

His memorial, held in the theatre, turned out to be a stunning occasion that only someone with his bad timing would have missed. Left-wing notables turned up. People cracked jokes, told anecdotes, wept and applauded Victor's radical life. It was agreed that, in general, these days funerals and memorials are more exciting than weddings. Someone remarked that Victor's great gift had been to understand that there was no such thing as too much flattery and noted how skilful he had been at buttering his way everywhere.

Vera spoke as if Victor had been too good for this world and might at any minute rise up and hover above them like some sort of political reproach incarnate. Her son Mark was present in the auditorium but did not speak.

The director of the play did speak. He was a man who suffered from megalomania – not that surface megalomania that hides deep insecurities but a megalomania that was confident and enduring, written right the way through him like a stick of seaside rock. His tribute to Victor consisted mainly in talking about himself, his own successes and achievements. He failed to mention Victor until the very end when he suddenly remembered why he was there and announced hastily:

'Three cheers for Victor Skynnard.'

As people drifted out of the theatre and into the autumn sunshine they realised that Victor was indeed dead and the world seemed a poorer place.

Chapter Seventy

Ella had packed up her mother's house. She made a quick dash to Amsterdam to visit Pa and Ma Tem and reassure herself that they were recovering well. They were surprised to learn that she was going back to Surinam but wished her luck. Before leaving England for good she decided to visit the place where Hector's ashes had been scattered. She had found out from his workplace that the ashes had been taken to Norfolk, to a place where he and Barbara and Dawn spent many of their summer holidays. They used to stay in a house since destroyed by fire.

A farmer gave Ella directions to where the house had stood. Flat bare fields stretched to the horizon. There were no trees. The landscape was vast, grey and ashen, ploughed with furrows in the orange clay soil that led the eye to where the distant horizon met leaden skies. To Ella it felt apocalyptic and wonderful. She understood why Hector would have loved it there. The wind was sharp and carried the smell of the earth. Where the house had been she saw the large square patch of burnt ground.

She stood there for a while imagining that she could hear the crackle of burning again. Fire was Ella's favourite element, a purifying Dionysiac fire that could sweep through everything rotten and corrupt and carry dust and ashes into the air. From the blackened earth where she stood burst new grass, full and vital, an immeasurable natural life. At the edge of the burnt area a few brilliant green shoots had sprung up. But she could see no sign of where Hector's ashes might be. It was October and there was a chill in the air. After walking about for a while she grew cold and decided to leave. She traced her way back to the lane and the open fields.

At the side of a field opposite the house site she came across a raised rectangular patch of rich black earth. To her surprise she found that the earth had recently been turned and planted with crimson and purple fuchsia, sweet william and anemones. The turned earth was blacker and richer than the surrounding fields. She could see the tip of the urn where they had buried it. Stuck in the ground was a sign hacked crudely into a piece of wood:

'Hector. Dawn. Barbara.'

It was as if his ashes had turned into a blaze of flowers that burst through the earth.

'Thank you,' she said to the farmer as she passed him on the way back.

*

When Ella de Vries returned to the interior of Surinam she and Marijke took over the ramshackle country retreat that once belonged to the ex-president. Marijke served her with devotion. Ella looked elegant and out of place swinging in her hammock. She had brought with her a few books and a supply of her favourite Paloma Picasso perfume. At night she slept with two dogs on her bed. Goats wandered in and out of the house. She still carried out her daily routine of ballet exercises on the bare boards of the main room.

Very occasionally, not more than once or twice a year, a card from Donny found its way there as he made his way further and further north. She pinned these up on the wooden plank wall.

In later years her legs would become thinner and her shoulders crabbed but Ella continued with her ballet exercises, holding on to a long wooden shelf to do the barre work. She still danced and despite her age there was the ghost of something beautiful in her movements.

A Goodbye from Your Narrator

I rather miss Victor Skynnard coming into the Head in the Sand café. But it's as well that I have no distractions. I am in a hurry to finish. This book is the way I can admit to an association with crimes and misdemeanours but avoid prosecution. I hope I have done justice to Hector's earlier heroic acts of terrorism. This new offence of 'indirect incitement to violence or terrorism' is aimed at those who while not directly inciting it, glorify and condone terrorist acts knowing full well that the effect on their listeners will be to encourage them to turn to terrorism. What can I say? Does giving Felix Caspers those notebooks count? What about this book? But I think I can enjoy writing the details of the events, knowing that there will be no redress or comeback. A work of fiction is a way of committing a crime, getting away with it and then boasting about it afterwards. Confession is sweet. Public confession, doubly so. Public confession without retribution is exquisite.

When I finished the last sentence I lifted my head and took a final look around the café. Its bentwood chairs are uncomfortable. I shan't be sorry to see the last of them. I indicated to the proprietor that I wanted the bill. I have finished. The End. I got up and stretched, feeling that I too had been released from a spell. Isn't that how all good stories end – with the breaking of a spell and the release of the spellbound from enchantment? Now I can look around me in the bright light of day. Here in front of me is the café, the muddy olive decor, the plants in their terracotta pots, the polished wooden tables and the gurgle of the coffee machine. There is a 'Soon to Close' notice up, of course. No-one escapes the recession.

I tidied up my notebooks. Enough of these pale escapades in the head. Fiction is only the tame cousin of reality and Felix Caspers had given me an idea. Novel-writing has proved to be time-consuming compared with assassination – that underestimated tool of political reform. When I go to work at Mambo Racine's tonight I will check that my Heckler & Koch sniper rifle is still waiting for me, taped under the lid of my piano.

Better cover myself, I suppose. Any resemblance between the living and the dead is entirely accidental. Sorry. Any resemblance between the characters and any person living or dead is entirely accidental. Sorry about that.

Baron S.

Acknowledgements

If Euripides were around I hope he would excuse my loose re-working of themes from *The Bacchae*. I also acknowledge standing on the shoulders of many other authors who have given us versions of Venus and Adonis.

For some of the feeling and atmosphere of the Palestinian camps in Jordan in the 1970s I am indebted to Jean Genet's *Prisoner of Love*.

Thanks to Liz Calder – always an inspiring critic.

There is one image, stolen from Lorca, that has remained in my head but I'm afraid I cannot remember which play or poem was the source of my theft.